DECEMBER REIGN

Book One of The Lore of Man

ANTHONY HARY

9Ravens LLC

5115 Excelsior Blvd 421, St Louis Park, MN 55416

Visit our website at www.9Ravensllc.com

First Edition: October 2019

The characters and events portrayed in this book are fictitious. Any similarity to real persons, living or dead, is coincidental and not intended by the authors. To the extent any real names of individuals, locations, or organizations are included in the book, they are used fictitiously and not intended to be taken otherwise.

December Reign – Book One of The Lore of Man

Cover Illustration, Book Design, and Internal Illustrations by: Anthony Hary

Editor: Tracie Savvy, from Savvy Geek Designs

ISBN: 978-1-7333972-2-3

To my Moon, my Queen, my Always. Thank you for introducing me to a world where magic is real, and anything is possible.

DECEMBER REIGN

BOOK ONE OF THE LORE OF MAN

ACKNOWLEDGMENTS

Projects like this are no small effort, often taking years to complete. I would like to say "Than you!" to everyone who supported me through this process. My wife, Tracie, I am so grateful for your deep support and faith in my dreams and ambitions. My brothers Levi, Jason, Willis, Austin, and Cory, you guys motivate and inspire me. I look forward to you figuring out the mysteries of Winston's journey. To my beta readers Cory, Nicholas, Esteban, Nichole, Gerald, Josette, and Dustin, I cannot thank you each enough for your willingness to read this novel, and provide me with real feedback. Hope you all return for Book Two of The Lore of Man. Finally, I need to thank all the support from the backers on Kickstarter, for their enthusiasm, and financially supporting the production of this book! Alyssa, Iloy0037, Jason, Eric, Jennifer, Alex, Mike, Dustin, Michael, Rob, Austin, Duane, Crystal, Rod, Justin, Sophia, Levi, Matt, Michael, Svenbo, Rora, Michael, Megan, Jason, Dexter, Cory, Eric, Shelly, Christina, Eric, Tristan, Hal, Terry, Candice, Chance, Blaisdell, Phil, Tiffani, Sean, Hunter, Almos7, James, Bob, John, Tony, Paul, Mason, Keith, Jesse, Daniel, Michael, Douglas, and James.

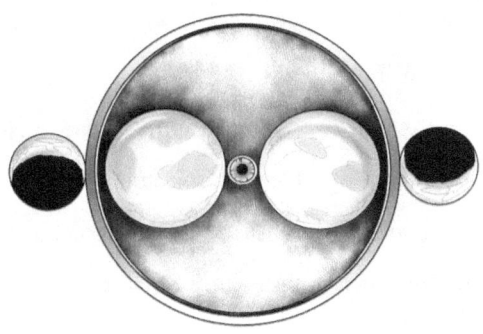

1 – DOORS BETTER LEFT CLOSED

"Be careful as you drive home tonight. The weather is changing out there, folks." Came the over enthusiastic voice of the classic rock station personality. "To help keep you warm, in this winter wonderland, we've got Foreigner's - Hot Blooded, and Hot Night in a Cold Town from John Mellencamp lined up. Kicking us off is the man in black himself, Johnny Cash, with Ring of Fire." The opening horns and upbeat tempo of the song came in as the radio personality read off the perfunctory identification call signs for the station. Winston turned the radio down as he pulled up to the front gate of Boltex Electronix.

"Good evening Winston." Came the warm greeting from the guard on duty.

"Good evening John. How have things been going tonight?" Winston asked.

"Slow and steady, like most nights." John replied as Winston scanned his badge. "Still have some of the researchers working late, but most of the staff have gone home for the holiday weekend."

"Lucky them." Winston said.

"Yeah. Lucky them." John agreed with humorous appreciation in his voice. "You visiting family for the holidays?"

"No. Not me. I picked up shifts to cover for Pablo and Juan so they could get out of town for the weekend. Guess they are visiting family in Texas."

"Not good to always be alone, Winston." John said, a fatherly concern coming out in his voice.

"I know. I appreciate you looking out for me. Thanks." Winston said, shaking John's hand. "Hear we have a storm coming tonight. Guess we get our white Christmas after all."

"I guess so. Don't matter to me. I'm Jewish."

"That's right. I'm sorry man, you've mentioned that before." Winston said.

"Not to worry. Here. Hold on; I've got something for you from Margie and the kids." John retreated back into the gate station a moment, and returned carrying a sealed plastic bag. "Here you go. They wanted me to share some of our cookies with you."

Winston accepted the cookies and gave the bag an examining look. "Did you eat some of these?" Winston asked accusingly.

A subtle smirk teased at his lips. "I may have quality tested a couple." John said. "Hey, I'm just looking out for you and your young figure. Besides, those spritz cookies are my favorite." Both men laughed.

"Tell them thank you from me, John." Winston said. "I should get inside and get to work. Stay warm tonight."

"Thanks Winston. Don't get lost patrolling those sub-levels now. We don't need another incident."

"Hey, that was Pablo's fault. I know how to read the floor maps." Winston chuckled. "Have a good night." He said as he drove forward toward the main complex.

The weather report wasn't kidding. Five hours into his shift, Winston looked out on the Boltex parking lot to see a field of snow. He could only guess which mound of white happened to be his car.

"Roamer One to Control, upper level 2 is clear in all sectors except G. Members of the Oscar research group are still up here crunching numbers. Over." Winston said into his radio.

"Roger that, Roamer One. Staff still in sector 2-G. Will monitor. Please proceed to sub-levels. Control out."

"Yeah, great." Winston mumbled to himself. It's not like this was a tough gig. It's all routine, and protocol, which he was plenty used to. He supposed that was one good thing to come out of his time in the Army. That, and a whole lot of doing what you're told. He wasn't the only ex-military member of the team either. John at the gate said he was Navy, and Winston knew of Jarheads that worked the day shift. He only saw them at corporate recognition events. Which was fine by him.

The sub-levels were easy to do at night. They were all a series of sealed doors, and one way rooms. The halls were a bit maze-like in areas, and Pablo had gotten lost during his first month on the job. Literally had to sit down and wait for someone to come find him. Winston knew these hallways, and he could tell if there were others down here by the air pressure. As he stepped off the elevator on to sub-level six he could feel something was off.

"Roamer One to Control, please advise. Do we have scheduled activity on sub-level six? Over." Winston radioed in.

"Negative, Roamer one. We have no record. Over." Control

said.

"Control, be advised, I have a feeling something is wrong, down here. Over."

"Come again, Roamer One, did you say a 'feeling'? Over."

"Copy, Control. Be advised. I will investigate and report. Roamer One out."

The hallways on the sublevels ran on standby power at night, leaving one in every three lights on. It was enough to see by, especially after your eyes adjusted. Winston worked his way through the halls passing office doors, and activity rooms where tests and experiments took place. Every door he checked Winston knew he'd find nothing. His gut was telling him if he was going to find anything it would be when he reached the priority level rooms. Seemed to be that kind of night. He continued onward. Gradually working his way past each room, until there was one room remaining. If the halls were a maze, this was the room the maze led to. Positioned at the end of its own short hall, twisted into the center of the levels arrangement. Winston took a deep breath and started walking. Hoping with all he was that this was just some spooky, middle of the night, mind trick that his body was playing on him because he was tired. Everything else was looking normal. Surely this last room, in the center of everything, would turn out to be a formality check, and nothing would be amiss.

The door was open. Which in general terms is not usually a situation to cause alarm. Doors are left open all the time. That's true for most doors. Not for this door, however. It was the door, with a capital "THE". The kind of door that opens to a vast wealth of information, power, or truth. It's a door that protects the things held within from prying eyes, and dirty fingers. Or in some cases may protect us from it.

Winston approached the door slowly, his hand upon his holster. Light flickered from within the room beyond the door. In all his years on patrol he had never seen anyone enter this room, let alone leave the door open. As he approached the doorway he smoothly removed his gun from the holster, holding it against his chest, the barrel angled slightly down toward the ground.

"Control to Roamer One, report." Came the voice through Winston's earpiece. He started, taking an inadvertent step back. "Report in, Roamer One. What have you found?"

Those fools in Control always know the worst times to communicate. Winston cursed them to himself, and turned the volume down on his radio, not wanting it to spook whomever he was sure to find somewhere they do not need to be. He continued on, moving smoothly into the room beyond the door.

Stepping through the threshold of the room was like stepping into another world. The sleek, clean lined modern architecture of the Boltex complex disappeared, and was replaced with what appeared to Winston to be a subterranean corridor. Damp stone lined the walls, and floor, with the whole thing looking to have been carved directly out of the rock. The flickering light he'd seen in the hallway proved to be coming from a series of lanterns lighting the passage. The place was damp, and he could feel the pressure change in his ears as he fully stepped into the space.

The corridor extended for about twenty feet, and then seemed to split, or bend in different directions. Winston continued forward, his gun still at the ready. Entrances to rooms were on either side of the corridor, the first on his left looked to be a reading room, the walls were lined with books. The next room, on his right, had scrolls, and what looked like partially eaten loaves of bread. He didn't stop. He wanted to see what was at the junction point ahead.

Reaching the end of the initial part of the corridor he could see it did indeed split in two directions. To his left was a door, and to his right, a window. *Wait. A window? That isn't possible.* He was on sublevel 6 of the complex and it was 2am, there is no way there should be a window. Certainly not one with sunlight shining through.

Stepping up to the window Winston saw an open green pasture, the sun was indeed shining, and not far off was a cliff that seemed to drop off into… *No. That isn't possible.* The Boltex complex was located in Farmington, Minnesota. He was in Farmington, Minnesota. Yet here he was looking out an upper level window, of a stone building, near the edge of the cliff that dropped out into the ocean. That was the ocean wasn't it. Certainly a sea of some sort, because beyond the spread of grass and rock all that could be seen was water. Churning, violent water.

Winston stepped back from the window. "Shit." He said quietly. "What is this place?" He asked himself as he turned towards the door behind him. He walked up to it, testing the handle. There was no clasp, or lock, the door opened gently upon his touch. Winston pushed it the rest of the way open and stepped inside.

On the opposite wall from the door was a large curtain, hanging heavily over what was likely a window. There were no lanterns, in here, and Winston was unable to make out much detail. He moved to the curtain, gripping it to move it aside, and opened it. The same bright sunlight he saw in the other window spilled through. This window was large, and opened out upon a grand landscape.

"You would, wouldn't you?" said a voice behind him. Winston turned towards the sound to find a man in chains, bound to the wall.

His face turned in shock as their eyes met. "You're not him." Called the man, who now turned his eyes to the area of the wall near Winston.

Next to Winston were a pair of empty shackles, similar to what the other man was wearing. Chains meant to bind a soul. Winston looked sharply at the restrained man. "What is this place?"

The man's eyes were wild, spit flew from his mouth as he continued. "Where is he? He was not to be let loose. What have you done?"

Winston, acting upon instinct, turned from the man, running out of the room, towards the door he initially came through. As he moved he turned on his radio, and heard static. He engaged the radio's call button.

"Control! Come in, Control. I have an UFP, and possible insurgence on sublevel 6. Repeat. UFP, and insurgence on sublevel 6. Over." He finished his call as he neared the door, and a figure moved to stand in the opening.

It was another man, tall, thin, and looking as disheveled as the other man still chained in the other room. He looked up through his brows towards Winston. He looked like the man time forgot, and he was just staring.

Winston trained his gun on the man. "Don't move! Get on your knees, and put your hands behind your head." He instructed the man.

In his ear Control replied "Roamer One, Please repeat."

"On the ground, now!" Winston repeated as he reached for his radio. "Control, I have a UFP, and an insurgence on sublevel 6. Send a containment team."

The man stood, still, staring, examining Winston with his dark eyes.

Jutting his gun towards the man, Winston repeated "Down on your knees, hands behind your head, do it now!"

Their eyes met in the unmistakable way where one soul sees another. The man's lips moved, stretching into a smirk.

"I've knelt quite long enough, young man." He said, as he reached his hand up to the side of the door, and closed it.

"No!" Winston yelled, running to the door. He grasped the handle and with everything he had he prepared to shove it open. To his relief it gave way, and flew open. His jubilation was short lived as he felt the floor move out from under him, and the world spun, as Winston began falling down the stairs.

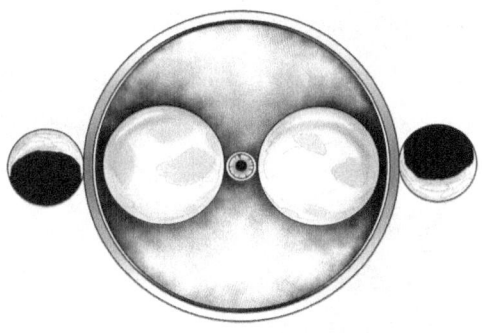

2 – CHAINS THAT BIND

The taste of blood and dirt is no substitute for coffee. It also does little for aided alertness; however, it can promote a person to strive to wake up with haste. Winston stirred from his place on the stairs. Hitting his head in his fall caused him to blackout, and wake up wedged in the bend of the stairs. His left leg extended awkwardly, his head throbbing, and blood came from the collection of scrapes and cuts from his fall.

He looked around, located his gun a few stairs down, and retrieved it. Climbing to his feet Winston headed back up the stairs. At the top he closed the door behind him, pausing to look at it. Where was he?

More importantly what happened? How does someone walk through a door, in a hallway 120 feet below ground, and find themselves on the upper level of what appears to be a stone structure near the sea? Is that even possible?

That's a silly question, considering it obviously had happened. Winston was here, in a stone structure perceivably far from Minnesota, the sun shining, the sea on the horizon, and no perceivable way back to where he was. There was one option, one possibility for Winston to get home. The man in the room.

Winston resolved himself to get answers. He'd have to ask the man, perhaps by force, but Winston would ask nonetheless. The man was chained up, but would that make him more or less likely to want to talk? He certainly wasn't pleased to find Winston standing there, instead of the other man, the one who trapped Winston here.

Winston shuddered at the thought of him, and the look in his eyes as he registered Winston. The sight of the man's hand upon the door. How he smiled as he shut the door, it was as if he knew precisely what he was doing. Shutting that door and locking Winston away in this unknown place. Also, what did the man mean when he said "I've knelt long enough"?

There would be time enough for all that later. At least Winston hoped there would be. He walked down the corridor, and into the room. The other man was on his feet now, and had moved as close to the door as he could. Winston walked in firm and fast, and the man stepped back from the abruptness of his stride.

Winston realized he was still holding his gun. He holstered the weapon, and held his hand up to the man. "I need to talk to you. Can we.."

"You let him get away!" the man yelled. "You fool! You let him get away."

"I had no idea you were even here. Either of you." Winston said. "Hell, I don't even know where here is. Do you?"

The man seethed, hard breath and spit confronting his clenched teeth. He turned away from Winston, as if to retreat to the darkest part of the shadows. The room went quiet, with the exception of the man's breathing. He was clearly working to contain himself, his rage. Certainly becoming angry would not do him much good while being chained to a wall.

"What is your name?" asked Winston.

Nothing. No response at all from the chained man, only more taut breathing. Frustration rose in Winston and he turned his back to the man, and looked out the window. Not looking out, per say, more looking through, and not taking in the details of what was beyond. He was too caught up in his mind. What was happening? Where was he? He needed to evaluate what he knew.

He was clearly on an upper level to a building that looked to have been constructed in the middle ages. Stone everything. Walls, floors, ceilings, all of them were some kind of stone, or slate. The window glass held a subtle distortion common to older or aged glass. Though he knew he was in the upper level, he had no idea what this small, castle-like structure was, or what else was held within. For all he knew there were armed men below them, as clearly this was meant as a holding cell of some kind. If Winston casually walked out and down the stairs, who's to say that whomever was waiting below wouldn't refrain from attacking him, thinking he was attempting to escape.

Speaking of escaping, who was that man who trapped him here? And how in all that physicists hold dear was this scenario even possible? How did Winston go from being 120 feet below the frozen earth of Farmington, Minnesota, to being here? Furthermore, assuming that part could even be explained, how did the portal change when that man shut

11

the door? In one moment it was a passage from the hallway on sublevel 6 of the Boltex building, and then POOF! It's a curved stairwell of pain and bruises. So frustrating.

Winston slapped his hands down on the window ledge, leaning his weight onto his hands, and hung his head, trying to control his own breathing. The sun was falling in the sky, and on top of everything else he was hungry. Hungry? How long had he been here? This was not good. Surely these men didn't simply exist in this room without sustenance, and the ability to care for bodily functions.

Looking around the room, the light was limited, Winston went to the window and opened the curtains fully to allow as much light as he could inside. The man in the corner turned from the light. Winston looked about. There was no food, nor a place to store food. He remembered the bread down the hall. The partially eaten loaf in the other room. As he left the room to find it he noticed a bucket to the inside left of the entry, just within arms reach of the chained man at his furthest extension. He could guess what that was for and felt no need to verify.

Winston found the bread. He knew he should have been more restrained, been paying more attention to the space around him, yet in that moment he was consumed with hunger and ravenously engaged the loaf of bread. His mouth almost too full to chew successfully, he leaned his head back and savored the taste and feeling of the bread in his mouth. It wasn't fresh, and yet not old either. The edges were slightly hardened from exposure to air, but that did little to dampen his enjoyment of it.

As he lifted a second bite he began to take in the room around him. Scrolls were stacked along the walls, sorted, and some left at differing phases of openness around the room. They looked old and fragile. Yet not so old they couldn't be touched. Did people still use scrolls these days to record data? He supposed it was possible. I mean, anything is possible until it's not. Right?

The writing on the scrolls was not familiar to Winston, though he was unsure if it was due to the script being in a different language, or simply being difficult to discern. Not desiring to stir up more potential trouble than he was already in, he refrained from digging through them to find ones he could easily read.

Next to the scrolls on the table where he found the bread was a platter, with a serving pitcher, and small cups, all of metal. *Was that silver?* Winston checked the pitcher and there was liquid inside. He poured himself a small amount and smelled it. It was familiar to him as the mix of dry fruit and wood danced upon the air to meet his nose. He sipped it. *Nice.* He thought to himself. It was wine, a simple, rich, red wine. He finished the glass. As he lowered the cup to pour some more he thought of the man in the other room. There was only going to be so much time before someone came up those stairs to either find this bread and wine, or check on their captives, and there was nowhere for Winston to hide. He would need to secure answers before that happened.

Returning to the holding room Winston found the man still huddled on the floor, turned toward the corner. His breathing seemed to have become more regular, though Winston doubted this would leave the man more inclined to communicate. Which is why Winston had returned with options.

He set the platter on the floor, between himself and the chained man. The sound of metal hitting stone captured the man's attention and he turned to look toward Winston. Beyond his head and eyes he didn't move, he only watched.

On the platter was the serving pitcher, two cups, and as much bread as Winston could fit. He poured the man a cup of wine, leaned forward over the platter, and set the cup as close to the man as he dared. He wasn't about to be grabbed by this man. He then poured himself a cup, and took a sip right away as the man was watching him, signalling that the drink was safe for them both. Winston then set the pitcher on the floor, retrieved a piece of bread from the tray, and then left the tray with the remaining larger portion of bread near the man.

Taking his cup and bread, Winston backed toward the wall behind him, near the vacant chains of the escaped man. He decided not to look at the other man. Instead he looked about the room. It clearly was not originally meant for its current use. This looked to have been a bedroom of some kind. Or at least a room meant for living, and not keeping prisoners. Evidence of wall tapestries lingered, though hard to see in detail due to the only light coming in through the window, and some through the hall outside. Winston couldn't believe people lived like this once. In that moment he was struck by a deep appreciation for electricity, running water, and the ability to regularly wash his hands. He was going to need to get out of this mess one way or another, and soon.

"My name is Michael Scot." The man said. His voice ought to have been a gunshot with how it cut the silence of the room. Winston started. He had resigned himself to the idea that this man may never speak to him with any purpose. Yet here he was. Michael Scot.

"Nice to meet you, Michael. I'm Winston." The man grunted in response, his mouth currently full of bread. Winston figured that was indication enough to continue. "Can you tell me where we are?"

"Scotland." Said Michael. Winston couldn't believe it.

"Say what? Scotland?"

"Aye. Can you nay tell by the smell in the air?" Michael said, bringing a faint chuckle to his voice. "Sorry." He continued, composing himself. "Surely you already knew you were in Scotland. I'm not meaning to be an ass. If'n I could tell you anything more specific, I would. Hell, as far as I know we could be anywhere. Been in these bonds for far too bloody long to know for sure."

The man's, Michael's voice didn't sound very Scottish. In as much as Winston knew a Scotsman to sound. It was there though, the burr, and cadence one would expect. Only this one was smoothed down, like a man who had traveled the world, and spoken with people of many dialects. This was not of high importance at the moment however. Information was needed.

Winston knew he needed to redirect, as this man clearly only knew about his own circumstances. "Why are you in chains?" he asked.

"Don't you know? That's how one deals with the likes of me." Michael said with mild contempt in his voice.

"What do you mean by 'the likes of me'?"

Michael smiled, chewing another mouthful of bread. He didn't reply right away. Instead he allowed his eyes to linger on Winston. After finishing, he took a deep drink of the wine. This was his third cup.

Winston asked again, "What are you?"

Michael leaned his head back against his wall. The watery reflection of his eyes pierced through the shadows in an almost haunting way, as he considered his response. He leaned forward, and set his cup on the floor. Light fell upon his face, and he made clear, penetrating eye contact with Winston. "I'm a wizard, boy. A wizard." Michael said.

3 – GET THE KEYS

Anything is possible, until it isn't. Right? Sometimes, it goes the other way. Sometimes things are impossible, until they're possible. Human flight, communicating to space and back and around the world in real time, fitting countless books worth of data on a piece of plastic and metal no bigger than a fingernail. Impossible. Right?

Winston had lived a life; he'd seen the impossible become possible. Yet now he was looking at a man, who for all intents and purposes was locked in a castle, and he was claiming to be a wizard. Clearly this revelation can be only one thing.

"Bullshit." Winston replied after a moment to process. "That's utter bullshit. Wizard." he scoffed.

Michael smirked as he retrieved the pitcher for more wine. "Perhaps next time you will be certain you ask questions you are prepared to receive the answers to, before ye ask them." the last of the wine dripped into his cup. "Bullocks." He said in response, raising his glass to Winston. "Cheers!"

Winston rose to his feet, shaking his head dismissively, not entertained or convinced by Michael's statements. If anything he was now more frustrated than ever to have lost time to such nonsense, when he knew his time frame for smoothly escaping this mess, were rapidly closing.

"I am a wizard." Michael reiterated. "There is no reason to lie about that."

Winston turned to Michael. "Prove it."

"Prove what?"

"Prove you're a wizard." Winston demanded. "Wizards do magic right? Show me something to prove you're what you claim to be."

"Are you a man?" Michael asks.

"Of course. What does that…"

"Prove it." Michael interrupted.

"What? No! I'm not doing that."

"Why not? Ye claim yer a man. Say I only prove my wizardry to men. Prove to me that yer a man."

"I don't need to do that." Winston said.

"Because ye don't need to prove what you are?"

"Well… Yeah." Winston said, feeling a pang having been outwitted in the admission.

"Neither do I. You asked, and I told ye. I am a wizard." Michael said, emphasizing the final words.

Winston stood in place. He knew he couldn't really argue the logic, but there was a part of him that wanted to know. Is he really a wizard? All the mess that this moment was, could be pushed aside for a brief interlude if this was true. How many people would ever be able to say they met a real wizard? Winston looked at Michael who had rested his head back and looked to be savoring the last mouthful of wine from his cup. Winston reached down to unclasp his pants.

"No. No. Stop, boy!" Michael exclaimed upon realizing what he was doing. "I was ribbing you to prove a point."

"Wait." Winston said, clasping his trousers. "You're not a wizard? I knew it!"

"Oh no. I am a wizard. I also happen to have my own wand. With no interest in seeing yers. Thank ye." Michael said. "Truth is, I couldn't prove it to ye even if I meant to."

"Why?" Winston asked. "If you are what you are, even if I agree that you shouldn't have to prove it, what keeps you from being able to?"

Michael held up his wrists. "These. It's the iron. Magic isn't so grand a thing that it can't be thwarted." His wrists made a loud clang as he dropped them to the floor between his legs. "So long as these encircle my wrists, I'll be doing no magic of any kind. It's a damned travesty if you ask me."

"And if they were removed?"

"That'd be a fine thing. It's been quite some time, and I'm not sure what I would be able to do."

"That's convenient." Winston said with an amused tone.

"It's the truth, boy."

"Stop calling me boy."

"Settle now, Winston. Near all souls be youth to me." Michael said. "It isn't any disrespect."

"Sure." Winston acquiesced, gesturing toward Michael. "You look all of forty five." Whatever words Michael may have said in reply came out as a snicker and a smirk. "Alright." Winston continued. "Who was the other guy?" he asked, fingering the empty chains hanging from the wall near him.

"His name is John Nottingham. At least that's the name I knew him by."

"Why are you guys here? Or were here, before he escaped."

"Yes. Grand fine job with that." Michael playfully rebuked.

"That wasn't, at all, my fault. I was on patrol and had no idea I'd find myself here." Winston said. "I found a door open that was not meant to be left open. All I was trying to do was my job." That last bit cascaded out of Winston with a hint of fire and anger.

"John is a crafty one. I'm sure not much blame rests on you in the end." Michael said. "Now ye know to keep yer eyes open with him for next time."

"Yeah. Next time."

"We're in... Scotland, boy. I'm not sure where to be exact. They occasionally would move John and I and the others, together or separately, throughout the year." Michael explained. "Leaves me unable to say for certain regarding our location. I can tell you who would know, who is responsible for holding us."

"Who?" Winston asked, regretting immediately how urgent and eager his voice came out.

"You need to get me free from here first."

"How the hell am I to do that?" Winston asked. "I can't even go back home the way I came, and you expect me to get you out of here?"

"That door isn't going to magically get you home again. I know what he did. Not sure how he got free of the bonds, but I know what he did to connect that door you came through, to the one from whence you came." Michael looked firmly at Winston. "You need me to get ye

19

home."

"Suppose you're right, and I believe you. I looked through those other rooms. I didn't see a key." Winston said. "I also have zero idea of who, or what, is downstairs. Though I doubt I can just walk down and ask to take you with me."

"Aye, I doubt that would get either of us very far."

"At least tell me who is down there?"

"Shouldn't be more than a couple of guards. One of them, should have the key."

"What are you suggesting?" Winston reached for his gun. "Do I walk in and pop 'em both. Then search their bodies for the keys?"

"Would if only it were that easy." Michael smiled.

A few moments later Winston found himself walking down the stairs. As he passed the spot where he had woken from his fall he couldn't help but ask himself, what the hell are you doing? He was following the advice of a potential madman, definitely a man chained to a wall. Should he trust him? He couldn't say. What Winston was certain of, was that he had no intention of ending up like Michael. With the doorway that got him here only leading to these stairs, it was these stairs that would lead him to his way out.

Sounds began welcoming him as he descended the stairs. Not loud or robust, but it was definitely the sound of conversation, and familiarity.

"Should we feed 'em?" came a voice, deep and rough sounding.

"So long as they eat once a day, they'll live." Replied a high voice, still as rough, only an octave or two higher in tone than the first. As if both their vocal cords were being rolled with stones when they spoke. "And 'sides, the master won't be returning for at least another day or three. Why worry?"

These two were clearly a sharp pair, and it only sounded like a pair. Just as Michael had said he suspected. Winston continued easing himself down the stairs. Thankfully slab stairs don't creak, or moan when you walk on them. Though you do need to be careful for loose rock bits, and how your footfalls resonated off the solid surfaces as you move about.

Reaching the edge of the stairs Winston peered around the corner. Again it was just as Michael had predicted. Though if he was telling the truth, for as long as he had possibly been in confinement, this had all become routine. For the guards, and for him. At this point they were comfortable, and it was nothing for them to leave the keys, and their weapons lay about, rather than upon their person.

Their backs were to the stairs. It was definitely only two of them. Winston was able to move from the stairs, to an adjacent spot across from the entry to the stairwell, that allowed him to hide while maintaining a limited line of sight on the guards. In position he allowed himself a moment to assess the scene. Were they playing cards? Eating? He simply couldn't tell beyond the fact that they appeared to be big men, seated, and Winston believed he caught a glimpse of the keys upon the table.

Right on cue the gun fired upstairs. Winston agreed to leave Michael the gun, partially because removing his security officer gear would help him move more smoothly, and his focus was to gain purchase of the keys. Beyond that, Michael was going to use the gun to further weaken a portion of chain, ideally splitting the link, and allowing him to pull the chain from the wall. They'd still need the keys to remove the manacles from his wrists however. So the plan was to have Michael allow a span of time for Winston to get into place, as Michael had recommended. After the time had passed, Michael would use the gun on the chain, freeing himself, and also calling the guards up stairs in the process.

Thus far the plan was working. Winston was securely in place, and the gunshot keenly captured the guard's attention. They turned from their positions and rose. Perhaps rose is a bit of an understatement. They stood to a stature, often reserved for trees and birds in flight. As they turned Winston worked to get a better view of them.

"Get your weapon." Said the closest guard.

"Keys?" The other asked.

"No." The first guard replied, pausing in his speech, as he secured his own weapon. "There will be no need for them."

That is when Winston saw him. At least he assumed it was a him by the voice and stature. It was a bit difficult after factoring the large nostril snout, fur covered figure, and aggressively curved horns extending from the guard's head, just behind the eyes, near the ears. Winston froze.

"Shit."

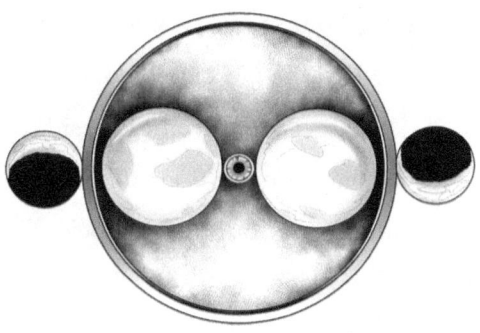

4 – A LEAP OF FAITH

Surely as wonder and fear filled the minds of those who first witnessed the moon eclipse the sun, it was the experience for Winston as the two huge creatures stepped into clear view. Their hooved feet clopped upon the slab floor, and a low grunting sound accompanied their exhaulations. The guards looked like giant bulls walking upon two legs, layered chain weaved armor hung over portions of their bodies. Wait, was that metal? No. The chain armor looked to be made of wood. Why wood? Winston did not have time to speculate further, as the creatures moved to head up the stairs. Their footfalls were like small pockets of thunder, parading past him. Mere strides quickly moved them up the stairs and around the curve of the passageway. Winston looked about, collecting himself; he had to find the keys. He could do this. This wasn't too different than what he had to endured in the war was it? Sure it was. Still he had no time for thought. He needed to act.

Rising to his feet, he left the protection of his seclusion, and looked about for the keys. They were just there on the table, weren't they? Where did they go? Did the creatures take them with as they headed upstairs? No. The larger one specifically said to leave them. Where…? Ah, there they were, on the floor. Winston must have missed the sound of the keys hitting the floor in the shock of watching the creatures rise and ascend the stairs.

Winston collected the keys. As he stood he quickly looked about the room for anything he could use, either as a weapon, or a clue as to what to do next. There were certainly weapons. He was not to sure how well he would be able to use a sword, or mace however. He did find a nice looking knife. Near the table where the guards had been eating was a spread of food. Without thinking he grabbed a towel from the counter, laid it out, using the knife he cut away portions of what looked like cooked ham. He wrapped bread, cheese, and dried meat inside the cloth as well. To his left he found a bag with a strap on it. Winston retrieved it and placed the wrap of food inside.

"Time for us to leave!" Michael's voice came sharply from behind Winston. Turning toward the voice Winston saw Michael, slightly hunched over, clutching the loose chains of his bonds to his chest. "Run boy!" Michael said, his tone more insistent this time. It was an odd tone that did not match the mischievous shine reflecting in his eyes.

Michael showed no sign of slowing as he reached the room, and passed by. Winston in turn expelled himself from the room, following Michael as he raced away. Winston had no idea where they were going, or how this frail looking man could so suddenly move so quickly. Those chains had to be heavy to carry, and it couldn't be comfortable to run with Winston's gun tucked into his waist belt the way Michael had it.

That is when the thunder returned. Thunder, and a roar. The guards had realized both their prisoners were gone.

"Run, lad. Much. Faster." Michael called out. Somehow increasing his own speed as they reached a door.

The light that ripped through the open entryway attacked Winston's eyes. He ran, simply ran. No thinking, and barely able to see for a time as his eyes adjusted to the change. His hand clutched tightly to the strap of the bag holding his food and knife. The ground became soft beneath his feet, and as his eyes focused he saw they were now fully outside. The grass was so green.

"Where are we going?" he asked Michael. Another roar. Closer. Louder now. It came trumpeting out from the entry to the would be prison building. It resonated at such a level that it was almost physical, and collided against Winston's back as he ran. He stumbled slightly but maintained his footing. "They're coming!" Winston yelled, knowing his observation was as unneeded as mosquitoes in summer.

"Is that what that was?"

"I just..." Winston began to reply, and cut off, upon hearing the cacophony behind him as the beastly guards were colliding with the tables and furniture of the eating room in their haste for the door. More thunder and roaring, they were not going to be happy. Winston pressed forward, looking toward Michael, and gauged his trajectory. Surely he knew where they needed to go. As Winston looked in the direction they were headed, having put a fair distance between themselves and the stone building, it appeared Michael was leading them into nothingness. As in the actual nothingness of the cliff's edge.

"Where are we going? Michael!" he called out, working to control the panic in his voice.

Michael didn't reply right away, instead looking back over his shoulder, showing a slight smirk on his face. "Do keep up, boy. I'd hate to lose that sack of food you carry."

At the close of his words, a surreal sight unfolded before Winston. He watched as Michael, thin and frail looking in the sunlight, his clothing in an ongoing debate on whether to stay clothes or turn to dust, his arm muscles tight, strained, as he clutched the chains tightly to his chest, and launched himself off the edge of the cliff. Michael twisted at the hips, thrusting down through his legs, to his feet, and propelling himself unreservedly into the open air beyond.

Michael turned in the air, looking back toward Winston, and called out. "Don't lose those keys, boy!" Came his words, in an increasingly fading manner as he fell below the lip of the cliff edge, and out of Winston's view.

Winston stopped in his tracks. Was he really about to follow this mad man off a cliff? Wasn't this a question his mother had asked him throughout his youth? Something about, if your friends did, would you? Winston reached in his pocket, pulled the keys out, and placed them into the sack with the food. Behind him came a clear and resounding roar. *When did they get outside?* His eyes shook in their sockets, as if struck by the sight they were beholding. These huge bull-like creatures charging toward him, majestic and powerful in their glory under the shining sun. The ground trembled with increasing violence as they closed the distance between themselves and Winston.

Winston shook his head, knowing a lose-lose situation when he saw one. At least in this moment one option came with a great view, and he'd sooner take that over being trampled, and gods know what else from these creatures.

Clenching his jaw in resolve, he secured the strap cross body, over his shoulder, and turned back towards the cliff that had consumed his mysterious new friend. With all that he could muster Winston ran. Dirt flew up behind each demanding step, his utility boots biting deep with each thrust down into the soil. *Can a guy swim in utility boots?* Sure they could, he had to do that in basic training didn't he? He could do it now. I mean, that's assuming he would even reach water below. He could see the sea filled horizon, however he had no idea how close the waves came to the base of the cliff. For all he knew it was rocks and a broken spine waiting for him beyond the grass.

The ground shook, almost dancing out from under his feet. *How close were the guards?* No way he could turn to look. Not without slowing and worse, getting caught. It was then he felt the ground hardening, rock sounding beneath his feet.

This was it.

Remembering Michael's leap, he twisted at the hips as he thrust down hard off the cliff's edge. Winston mimicked the maneuver. Everything spun in shades of blue, green, and white. The water, the sky, the clouds. He turned in the air, eventually looking back from whence he came, just in time to see the beastly guards stop at the edge of the cliff. *Were they going to jump?* No. No they were just watching. *That can't be good can it? Did he push out far enough? Was there water below?* He hadn't looked down when he jumped, and had no idea what lay beneath him.

Winston tried to turn again, to pull away from looking up. He couldn't. He looked back toward the guards, they were standing upon the cliff, weapons clenched in angry fists, as they watched him fall. Even as they shrunk with the distance, their huge size was undeniable. *What were they?* Winston had no idea, and wished he'd had paid better attention in mythology class.

The impact was sharp and sudden, like a single clap performed with two tanks. The pressure and sound came all at once. Winston's mind was able to acknowledge the sensation before the world went black.

5 – HUMANS DIE HERE

Before.

"Swim you pukes!"

The yelling voice of Winston's Commanding Officer was enough to make a soldier consider drowning. It was harsh, abrupt, and sharp enough to be confused with the grinding of metal, or the songs of dying cats. You'd think a CO requirement would be to at least have some bass in their voice. Sergeant Foster clearly was left out of that part of the evaluation process.

"Swim, soldiers! Don't flail like sloppy children. Swim!" The Sergeant called out again. "You crying over there, Connors? I'm doing the tough work today." Sergeant Foster taunted from the boat. "You got this easy. It's a short swim today. Only 8 more miles to go!" the Sergeant said, an evil, vindictive smile turning the words. "Latrine duty this afternoon for you sorry saps. Welcome to the best day of your whole fucking week!" What a prick.

***

Now.

"He'll wake when he wakes." Came a voice, subtle and unclear. Winston's head was spinning, heavy, and pained with pressure.

"How did he get here?"

"John. The bloody scoundrel found a way out of his bonds." The man chuckled. "Shite. The fool went so far as to make a doorway to where the boy is from, and in doing so they switched places. The poor boy never knew what he was in for."

Winston knew one of the voices was Michael's. Who was the other? Is that, a woman? Everything sounded like his head was in a bucket. By the moon and tides he needed to get his senses in check. What was that she just said?

"My point is that he has seen much, and isn't rightly supposed to be here. What's more, he isn't to know of what we do, or what we are."

"And these grand insights lead you to wanting to kill the boy?"

"It is an option worth considering." The unknown woman replied in the kind of tone one uses, when deciding on whether to have wine with dinner. Utterly casual, and disconnected in her possible enjoyment of what was to come. "You know well, what binds me here. Whatever must be done, I'll not sink for the sake of a human."

Winston knew he needed to get up. He rolled onto his side. Lord that hurt. What specifically was causing the pain was unclear. It all just hurt. All of him. The pain flushed his system, he swayed, and shook like a young fawn, as he rose to his feet. Thank the builders, for having a wall close by. It would need to work as his aide while his body remembered how to survive this dance with gravity.

With one hand navigating his balance against the wall, he looked over his shoulder at the two figures nearby. One was Michael, the other was definitely a woman. She was tall, and powerful. Impressively so.

"Now, let's not do anything crazy, boy." Michael said. "Acting like that, a person could think you're prone to making ludicrous choices." He smiled wide and fully. "Ye know, like jumping off cliffs blindly." Michael gave way to chuckling, followed shortly by the woman.

Winston found himself subject to the pull of Michael's infectious chuckling. Soon the three of them were wrapped up in rich laughter. For all the pain in his body, this felt good. Winston was alive, and he was laughing.

The guffawing settled down, and Michael helped Winston to a bathing room. He encouraged Winston to wash, and dress. As odd as it may sound to take a bath, so soon after almost drowning, Winston found himself looking forward to soaking in the hot water. Michael left him to it and he was pleased to find the bath was full, and waiting for him.

Alone in the room, Winston leaned against the wall, the tub, whatever he could to maintain his balance as he removed his clothes. They smelled of the sea. That unique aroma that only a true sea can give, of salt and sun, that somehow seems clean and fresh.

He must have been unconscious for a while. Winston's clothes were stiff in places where they had dried against his body. It felt like removing the carapace from a crustacean as he stripped his shirt and pants from his flesh. He was relieved to be free of the clothing, and eager to slip into the warm, welcoming bath.

The water came up to Winston's neck. He was struck by how well he fit within the tub. Winston was no small man at six feet, three inches tall; and being just over 200 pounds. Most tubs did not come with the space allowed for such consuming relaxation. He looked towards his feet, worried this experience would be short lived by losing the water to the overflow drain. There was no drain. For that matter, there was no faucet. Nor was there any drain at the bottom of the tub itself.

Winston's efforts to examine the tub, and the room around it, churned the water. A basin this full was sure to spill over, and yet it did not. Winston stopped moving, watching the water settle. The tub seemed as full as when he had entered the tub. Not simply as full as when he initially immersed himself into the water, rather it was always full. Thinking back to when he entered the tub, he couldn't recall the water rising in relation to the edge of the tub itself. Now as he churned about, it remained just as full. He gave into curiosity, splashing the water towards the edge of the tub deliberately with his hand. The water splashed up from the tub, through the air, and down toward the floor. Yet there was no splash of impact. The water never hit the floor, and no matter how hard Winston splashed the water level never changed.

"What the hell is this?" Winston asked.

"Magic."

Winston started, jumping half clear from the tub. It was the woman Michael had been talking to. How long had she been watching him? Did she not realize he was nude? Certainly she knew now. Winston's concern was not because he had any insecurity in being naked, and certainly not in front of a woman. You were what you were.

Still, this was commonly, the kind of experience, people entered into mutually.

"Hi. Ummm... What?"

"It's magic. The water. The whole tub is magic."

"Say what?" This was not helping Winston feel any more comfortable with the situation.

She smiled at his naiveté; at knowing his mind struggled to keep up. "You could be in there all day." She said smoothly. "The water will never cool, your skin will never prune, and no matter how you splash, or who joins you, the water level adjusts accordingly."

"That's amazing." Winston found himself saying. "I need to get a double sized one for company."

"Do you find this bath too small?" she asked.

"What? No. No." He said. "You just mentioned having someone join me. There's no way, with as large as I am, that another person could fit."

The woman didn't reply. Instead Winston noticed her eyebrow raise, and the inquisitively mischievous look that spread across her face. His muddled mind disrupted his perception of what happened next. Winston was lost in questions of what she could want? What was she doing here? Did she plan to kill him? He did hear her mention killing him, didn't he? With all these questions, he watched without realizing that as she stood before him, she removed her clothing and walked toward the tub.

"Oh my..." he said, not intending to speak.

The woman smiled, and climbed into the tub with Winston. The smooth warmth of her legs brushed against his own, the water moved against his chest, and Winston watched as her own chest persisted in their argument for buoyancy as she sunk into the water. Breathing in deeply, Winston strived to correlate what had occurred and found himself eye to eye with a gorgeous specimen of a woman, who was in a tub with him, water up to both of their shoulders.

"That is amazing." He said.

"The tub will expand to fit as many as needed. It will even increase in size for you alone should you will it."

"That is impressive, only I wasn't talking about the tub." Winston said.

The woman's eyes squinted, examining him. "Do you know who I am?" She asked.

"No."

"Do you know where we are?"

"I just woke up. I have no idea how I survived."

"You don't seem surprised by the magic." She observed.

"That's likely due to the concussion, and your boobs." She splashed the water at him. Surprising him as it hit his face, though the over spray never reached the floor. He raised his hands in surrender. "I'm just saying that I am still recovering. I'm sure the weight of all of this will hit me soon enough." Winston said. "Honestly, just say what you need to say. This has long since passed my scope of understanding."

The woman looked at Winston, her eyes keen and focused. She breathed out, leaning back, and assumed a lounging position in the tub. Their bodies moved against each other beneath the water in a manner most pleasing to Winston. He didn't react however, at least no voluntary reactions as he could help it. He simply looked at her. A smirk moved across the woman's lips, her eyes moving away, and then back to Winston.

"I think I like you, for a human." She said. "But you will need to prepare yourself to survive what's to come."

"What do you mean?"

"Sweet child, you are in Faerie." The beautiful woman said with a smile. "Humans die here."

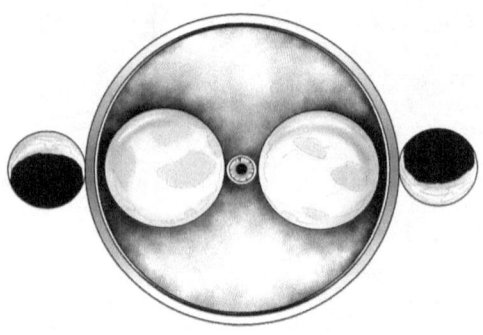

6 – STORIES AND COMPANIONS

"Are you going to kill me?" Winston asked between bites of his meal. Goodness, this was delicious. What was it again? Some kind of meat, fruit, and gravy dish. Man, he did enjoy gravy. Winston had never tasted anything like this meal, and even with this being eighth plate… wait, was that right? Yes. This was his eighth plate, and he still had no idea what he was eating.

Imagine for a moment the most delicious meal you've ever enjoyed. The tantalizing aroma, the way it pulled upon your senses, tempting you back for seconds or even thirds. Remember the taste, and how it didn't simply stimulate your taste buds, rather it seemed to dance with your tongue, and send sensations of fulfillment and pleasure through your whole body. See again its presentation, and how the colors were a spectacle for your eyes. A call for your mouth to water, and your hands to act, bringing the food quickly to your mouth. Imagine this fine meal, being able to enjoy bite after bite, plate after plate, never feeling full, nor gaining weight. It is just you and the food. Eating and enjoying every pleasure filled moment.

Michael straddled the seat across from Winston. "Ye know, I've heard it is not wise to eat Faerie food." He said, taking a bite from a bright colored fruit. "I'm thinking yer unwise not to." He chuckled.

Winston finished his food, and set the plate to the side. "I'm serious, Michael. First you tell me I've jumped from Minnesota to Scotland, next we launch ourselves off a cliff, and when I wake I'm joined in a magical bath by a powerfully striking woman who tells me I'm in Faerie, and humans die here! How am I supposed to respond to that."

Michael sighed, and set down his fruit. "How was yer bath, boy?" He asked in a dry tone, lacking any feeling of sincere interest. A stark contrast to Winston's memory of that experience.

Winston had to swallow at the memory. Clearing his throat. She was more than magical. The bath was magical, to be sure. But she, she was something beyond what his vocabulary could accurately convey. How could his throat get so dry so quickly? Winston reached for his drink, and Michael watched him as he took a long, deep pull on the delicious beverage.

"Listen, boy." Michael continued. "I'll only be telling ye this once. Or at least I hope I only need tell it once. Listen nonetheless." He leaned forward, looking straight at Winston. "We ain't friends. Sure, I'm fond of ye. Especially seeing as ye helped me free. But we ain't friends. That'll be a distinction needing to be earned. Being what it is, I also have no desire to see ye die. Nor will I be killing you. Now, I cannot speak for Mhara."

"Mhara? Is that her name?" Winston asked.

"Aye. Did ye two share all that time naked in a tub of water, and ye did not learn her name?" Michael bit of his fruit, shaking his head. "She is a tricky thing, that woman."

Winston found himself nodding, but why? Did Michael really know everything that happened in the bath? More importantly, what exactly did he think happened? "Michael, I…" He began.

"Damn it boy. You be careful with Mhara, do you hear me?"

"Yes. But I."

"Oh, I'm sure ye did. Ye wouldn't be the first. All that woman needs is a man's attention, and a wee bit of water." Michael said. A troubled expression took over his face. "Swear she'd mount an ape if it came close enough to the sea."

"Mount an ape?" Winston repeated, perplexed. A sense of urgency pulled at him as he realised the assumptions Michael was making. Hoping to quickly alleviate the misunderstanding he stated quickly, "Michael, we only spoke."

"Aye. Of course ye did." Michael said, thick with sarcasm. "Best to stay the gentleman."

"We only spoke. There was no mounting. Believe me, I'd have welcomed it." Winston said. "We talked as we soaked in the bath."

Michael stopped, looking plainly at Winston. "Truly?"

"Yes."

"Damn, boy. Yer something special." Michael said as shook his head and ate more fruit.

"What is she?" Winston ventured after a time.

"We're not having that conversation here, lad." Michael said. Taking the last bite of his fruit, and tossing the remaining core into the corner where a small group of pigs were curled up sleeping. "Know this.

38

You are better off having just spoken. Being mounted by her is not a ride you'll soon find yourself off of." He concluded with a smirk.

"If you say so." Winston said, leaning back in the chair and looking at the pigs as the smallest one stirred. Enticed by the smell of the ripe fruit the small pudgy thing began to feast upon the forsaken fruit, working to eat it all before the others awoke, lest trouble be found. "Is this really Faerie? Like, really, really."

"Aye. Really."

"I must have hit that water harder than I thought. This can't be real. I'm dreaming, aren't I?"

"Nah, though you may soon wish you were."

"Why do you say that?"

"We're in Faerie, boy, and though I have no intent to kill ye, do not become mistaken." Michael said. "Mhara is dangerous, and beyond her, there are many, many things here that would love to kill a human. Some, thankfully, will do it quickly. Others will just play with you. Painfully."

"I need to get home." Winston said, almost as much to himself as it was a part of the conversation.

"Aye, it's not as simple as that, unfortunately."

"What do you mean? I got you out. You're free of your bonds." Winston stood, his stress growing. "Get me home."

"Now, keep your facts straight, boy. Jonathan brought you into this."

"Yes, and he's gone."

"That he is. His absence doesn't change the fact that I am a fugitive, and you aren't supposed to be here." Michael said, standing to join Winston. "Come with me."

Michael led them out of the meal room, and up some stairs to a small platform atop the cottage they were within. With each step up, Winston's view of the expanse grew, and the splendor of the scene collided with Winston's established understanding of reality. Radiant colors, more rich and vibrant than any he had ever seen, filled contours and details of the forest about them. To their left Winston could identify the sea, and in that moment also felt the closed off nature of their current location. Though the cottage was in the middle of a forest, it was also for lack of a better word, hidden.

"Is this a safe house?" Winston asked.

"That's a way to see it." Michael said. "This is Mhara's place. Where she brings… guests."

"Where is she?" Winston asked, realizing for the first time he and Michael were alone.

"She'll be back. She is currently swimming. She'll return in the evening."

Swimming? All day? What a peculiar woman. Winston dismissed his growing questions, and got back to what he needed to know. "Why can you not get me home? That, Jonathan, was able to get me to Scotland easy enough."

"You should have never walked through that door."

"We agree on that point!" Winston assured. "What I am having difficulty with is what exactly happened, when Jonathan closed that door, and trapped me here."

Movement in the foliage grabbed Winston's attention. Turning he saw a medium sized creature bound away, toward the opening to the sea. The sun shined onto its bounding form, making a silhouette of the creature. Winston thought he could make out antlers, and a fluffy tail. A stag? Surely of some sort, wasn't it? He felt increasingly sure of what he was witnessing up and to the point, where the stag extended its wings and flew out through the canopy of trees.

"I tried to explain this when ye were eating, but you'd not gathered yer senses." Michael began. "Humans aren't supposed to be here. Granted you're only here because I brought ye. Felt wrong leaving ye to drown with all ye done for me."

"Thanks for that." Winston said. His hand involuntarily rubbed at his neck as he struggled to maintain eye contact with Michael.

"Aye. You're welcome. Now listen." Michael said, stepping alongside Winston. "The last humans to come to Faerie uninvited were, viewed by many, as vile enemies of the realm. Before then, much of Faerie lived free, and after the humans time here, things changed. A mandate was initiated by the King of Faerie himself, and there were certain things that were adopted without explanation. One of those changes were that no one from Faerie caused trouble in yer world, and no one from yer world came here uninvited."

"Couldn't you just, invite me?"

"No. I cannot. Due to my circumstances there are certain limitations to what I can do, or where I am supposed to go." Michael's voice hardened. "Damn, boy, I'm supposed to be chained up against a wall in a keep, for Merlin's sake. Yet, thanks to ye, I'm home. As it were. Yet I shouldn't be. There's no way I could invite you to be someplace I am not supposed to be myself."

"Heh. Merlin. That was funny."

"Well." Michael shrugged. "He prefers Myrddin, but it's best not to overuse his name, lest we desire his attention." He whispered.

"Wait! Merrrrrlin, as in the Sorcerer Merlin... You're saying he's real?"

"Of course he's real, boy. Humans are a clever lot. Yet, ye often think yer far cleverer, than ye actually are. One doesn't simply think up a personality the likes of his from nothing. Also, be clear. He is King in this realm. Not that I can blame you for the confusion." Michael said. "Arturus and his knights were a yappy bunch."

"You mean Arthur? As in, King Arthur?"

"Aye. Boy, yer lot painted him a pretty picture, didn't ye?" The disenchantment in Michael's tone was clear. "It can wonder the mind how shiny shite can look from a distance."

Winston looked at Michael in shock. Did he just say Merlin, and King Arthur for that matter, were real? "Are you saying Arthur was real." He asked Michael.

"Ha! No. Silly boy."

"Oh, heh. Good." Winston said. Feeling relieved he wasn't being asked to accept even more in this surreal experience.

"I'm saying Arturus is real."

"What!" Winston exclaimed. "What do you mean, *is* real?"

"Old Arturus, and some of his knights for that matter, are still alive. Arturus still lives in Old Britannia for that matter. Silly old fool." Michael said nonchalantly. "Ye need to focus now, boy. Do not get distracted by tales and legends."

"But. He lives in Britain?"

"Aye. Aye. With his knights manning posts throughout your world." Michael shook his head. "Ye need to listen, now. Jonathan is of the group not pleased with what the Arthurian Mandate did to our realm. He blames Arturus, the King, and holds the whole of humans in contempt for what happened to him. For what he lost. What he thinks he's lost at least."

Winston turned to look at Michael, to see his face. Winston needed to know if this was real. He looked more than serious. A sense of resolve and purpose had entered Michael's features, and his eyes seemed to burn. Not simply of intent, but of actual fire. As if behind his words, and within his body itself, lay a flame that ached to come out.

"If he is loose, he'll desire a return to his prior ways. I need to find him. Simply returning ye home will mean your death. I'm certain. Even now Faerie looks for ye. Each soul in the kingdom felt it the moment a human, entered the realm. They don't know where ye are, but they know you are here. They will know when ye leave, and if ye leave suddenly, I know of at least one of Faerie who will hunt ye down, and slay ye."

"That's comforting."

"Isn't it?" Michael snickered. "Not to fret too much. You'll be fine. Hopefully."

"Hopefully?"

"Aye. I won't leave ye to wither on the vine, as it were." Michael said with a smile and a gentle squeeze to Winston's shoulder. "There may be great uncertainty ahead, yet if we can find Jonathan, we may be able to sort this all out."

"Thanks. I think." Winston said.

"Think nothing of it, boy. When you've been around as long as I have, ye learn to see if a man is one of honor or not, and ye my boy are disgustingly honorable."

"How do we fix this then?" Winston asked.

"We need help, clearly. I'm only one wizard, and though I'm recovering from my imprisonment, I'm but one against an unknown force." Michael said, while turning towards the stairs.

"Wait." Winston called. "Where are you going?"

"Mhara is back. Didn't you hear her return?" Michael said.

"Return? No." Winston hadn't heard a thing. Not a rustle, shuffle, or stirring. He also hadn't seen anything, and they were on the roof weren't they? This place is so odd. He followed after Michael, heading back inside. This time the stairs didn't lead back to the meal room. When they reached the bottom of the stairs, at the only exit from the stairwell, Winston and Michael found themselves standing at the end of a great hall. One far larger than any room the cottage had any right to contain.

Chairs, and benches lined the walls. Weathered glass windows ushered in warm sunlight. There was a small dais at the far end of the room, though nothing was upon it. It was as if they thought to use this as a great gathering hall and changed their mind. No house banners, or ornamentation upon the walls. Only a few hanging plants, and large drawn curtains for the windows, could be seen. As Winston's eyes followed the curtains up he was struck by how high the ceiling was. Had they really walked down that many stairs to get here? For that matter, were they even in the same cottage? Certainly they couldn't be. This had to be another trick, like the door that got him into this mess. It was that. A mess.

"Hello my friend." Winston heard said. Looking toward the voice he realized Michael had reached the group at the other end of the grand room. Standing with him and Mhara were three other figures, all of which were towering in stature, and varying in their levels of girth. Two of the figures wore helms, armor, and flanked the central figure who was a sturdy looking man with white blond hair, and a flowing beard. This man looked powerful. Not simply of muscle. He looked to possess power at a level that would move hordes of listeners to act, and here he was clasping hands with Michael, of all people.

"Mhara gave us word, and we are here." The powerful figure said. His voice was deep and resonated with a commanding tone that matched his stature.

"Did she tell you everything?" Michael asked.

"I told him." Mhara asserted.

"Of course." Said Michael. "What I meant to ask was.."

"We have it all in place, my friend." The powerful man said. "Is this the human?" he asked, his pale eyes turning to Winston.

Winston waved as he walked up, feeling unsettled as those powerful, light blue-green eyes examined him. The accompanying soldiers turned their heads toward him as he joined the group, in unison. That wasn't creepy at all. A small shiver collected in Winston's spine and goose bumps cascaded over his body.

"Calm yourself, child." The powerful man said. "We're all friends here."

"Hi, I'm Winston."

The powerful man extended his large, gloved hand toward Winston. He clasped hands with the man almost instinctively. The man smiled, looking toward Michael, while maintaining his firm grip on Winston's hand. "Does he know what he is?" The man asked.

"No, I don't believe so." Michael said.

"Mmmmm… Yes." The man said, turning his commanding gaze back toward Winston. "Yes, I believe he'll do splendidly."

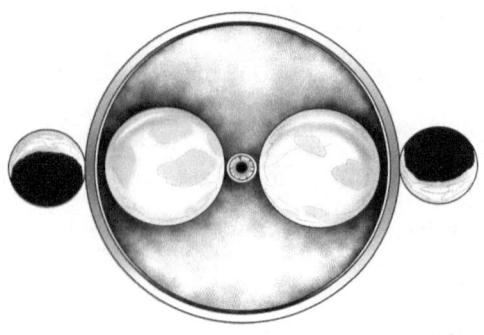

7 – NOT EVERYONE CAN BE SPECIAL

Before.

"Do you think we'll ever be anything?" Sam asked in the spontaneous way he did.

"What do you mean? We're soldiers. That is something."

"Right, I know. Do you ever think it'll mean anything though? Do you think we'll ever do anything special?"

Winston didn't know what to say to that. He'd only ever thought this far. Become a soldier. That was what he was supposed to do wasn't it? His father was a soldier, and his father before him. Not the most glamorous choice as he sat there, in the middle of the night, on some empty exercise in futility. Standing watch over a base full of allies, in the heart of the Midwest United States, where the populace often wondered why it still lived here due to the weather. Surely an enemy would never attack here. Nonetheless, Winston was here, with Sam, freezing their butts off in unison. "I don't know." He said. "Maybe we will, maybe we won't."

Sam nodded.

"Not everyone can be special, right? Otherwise, no one would be."

"Yeah." Said Sam. "Never thought of it like that. Don't you want to be special?"

"I just hope that whatever we do, it has value." Wiston said.

"Me too, man. Me too."

They sat there for the rest of that night, entertaining each other with silly stories, and mild conversation. Little did they realize that all they knew would soon change. Within days their battalion was shipped off to war. Every member of their unit was either injured or killed, except Winston. Reports claimed he was miraculously able to survive an open firefight, to retrieve Sam, and pull him back behind the line.

Winston held Sam as he bled out from wounds to his abdomen and legs. His eyes were wide and unfocused as he looked up toward Winston. Sam's eyes looked, yet seemed to not ever be able to actually see him. Sam's voice was panicked, hopeful, and fleeting. "Winston? Win... We need to get out of here."

"Shh. Shh... I've got you, Sam. I've got. Hang in there buddy." Winston assured, as he looked for help. Another unit was moving in from the west. "We're getting out of here."

"Win?" Sam said. Sounding like he wasn't sure he was there.

"Yeah man. I'm here."

"It was worth something, right?" Same asked, coughing. "Everything we've done. It had value, didn't it?"

Winston's stomach fell, and panic danced with pain inside his mind. He needed to save his friend. He needed to get him home.

"You know it, brother." Winston lied. "It was damn near special." He said, forcing a smile into his voice.

Sam's lips stretched into a soft smile. "I told you we'd be something. I told you we'd be special."

"You sure did, man. You sure did!" Winston said, clinging to his friend, his brother. Willing Sam's life to continue. Wanting so badly to be sitting watch, in the middle of a freezing Midwest winter night. He wanted, and willed, and hoped it, all for nothing, and he knew it.

Sam's body fell still, the shuddering need for life and air that it had once fought for, now gone. Winston clung to him as the support unit arrived. He didn't hear them as they spoke to him, checking on his own condition. Even as they took Sam away, he clung to him. He clung to his life, their friendship, and vowed to never stop pursuing a life of value. He may never have it. Not like Sam did. Winston had been the only member of his unit to survive the incident unharmed. Not a wound or scratch on him. No matter how the doctors, investigators, or his Commanding Officers responded to his good fortune, Winston was numb. That didn't matter. Nothing else of his time with the Army mattered without Sam. Sam was special. And now, Sam was dead.

***

Now.

Winston's feet hung, freely swinging off the edge of the viewing platform atop the roof of the cottage. For as long as he had been sitting up here, days could have elapsed. The others were downstairs eating, commiserating, or planning for all he knew. As delicious as their meal was, Winston held himself to only one plate this time, and politely excused himself from the meal. He had little interest in incessantly vague conversation that seemed to say everything about nothing, and nothing about everything for an obnoxious span of time. These Faerie folk seemed to only speak that way. Instead of suffering that further, Winston figured he would sit up here and enjoy the view, until they had something for him to actually do. To his relief the stairs seemed to always lead up to the platform, no matter which room you started in at the bottom. Winston found that he liked the view from up here, and was thankful Michael had shown it to him. Sitting alone brought back fond memories of watch duty with Sam.

Fionn and his warriors, the Fianna, seemed to have much to convey to Michael and regale. After their ominous introduction in the great hall, Winston was happy to leave them to it. Not to mention how Fionn's pale eyes unsettled Winston. Fionn also seemed to lack any interest in expounding upon his comment about Winston, nor was he allowed a clear opportunity. Not in the least due to Michael quickly interjecting and changing the topic as soon as he said what he did. Evidently there were opinions and topics that were not for Winston to know, so Winston excused himself and retired up here in solitude.

Leaning back on the palms of his hands, Winston looked out toward the opening to the sea from the forest, tracking the light and waiting for the sun to set. The sun hadn't seemed to move; at all. Nice as a sunny day is, this was getting ridiculous. Winston couldn't help feeling like he should sleep, yet without the sun setting he couldn't get mentally settled on the idea. He wasn't even tired. To that end, how did they even know when to eat food?

The thought struck him. The sun doesn't seem to move,

meaning it may never set or rise. No morning, no night. When they've eaten they aren't eating based on a time of the day, they simply eat as desired. When they ate, Winston never felt sated. For that matter, how do they even tell time? The longer he is here, the more disconnected he felt. The more disconnected he felt, the most concerned he became for his sanity. Saying this place was insane was like saying a hurricane was mild picnic weather.

More than anything else, Winston was anxious to do something. Waiting, and being subject to the whims of individuals he didn't know, or understand, unsettled him. It was these kind of circumstances that got friends killed.

"You should run laps."

One would think at this point Winston would have been prepared for anything, with how spontaneous this place was. He wasn't, and the voice gave him a start.

"Surely you can do something more than sit on this roof all day."

Winston looked around carefully. There was no one on the platform with him, and he began working his way through the surrounding trees, and foliage, looking for the source of the unidentified voice.

"He seeks us out." Said a voice.

"Both of us?" replied another voice. Or was it? It sounded exactly like the initial voice.

"Look at his eyes. He looks! He looks! He'll not find us." The voice said, taking on an excited, and vigorous eagerness. "He looks!"

"Leave me alone." Winston muttered, lowering his eyes. "Whoever you are."

"Aww, he hurts."

"Such pain. Such sorrow. Tender hearted soul."

"Tender is good. Do we eat him now?"

This got Winston's attention. He had no interest in being food for anyone. Rising to his feet, he looked around feverishly. "Enough of this." He called out.

"Why are you yelling?" Asked Mhara. When did she get there? Mhara was standing within arm's reach of Winston. Her clothing different, she now wore leather weaved armor, a pteruges wrapped around her hips, the leather straps accentuating her curves. Goodness man, focus.

Collecting himself, Winston asked. "Did you hear that?"

"Hear what?"

"Voices. Well, actually they sounded like the same voice, talking to themselves, about me." He said, pausing. "About whether or not to eat me." Inside himself Winston hoped his facial expression and body language didn't match the feeling he had saying those words.

"Ah. Yes. Those would be pixies." Mhara said in a tone, one commonly uses on children. "They are harmless, more or less, but they see everything. We need to go."

"Because they saw me?" Winston asked.

"No." Mhara said as she headed toward the stairs. "Because I said so. Though, them seeing you, doesn't help matters. Let's go now. Follow along." She led them down the stairs, and true to form they exited into a different room entirely, from the one Winston had left when he first ascended the stairs.

"How do those work?" Winston asked regarding the stairs. Yet Mhara was not listening.

They were in the stables. Stalls lined the left wall, brushing and cleaning stations were on the right. Mhara had Winston wait where he was while she retrieved something. Everyone was there, each conducting different tasks. The Fianna brushed and saddled the horses, while Fionn and Michael looked to have gathered supplies and were now bent over a map of sorts debating how they planned their route.

Mhara returned with a bundle in her arms and dropped it at Winston's feet. "Put this on, and give me your clothes." She instructed.

He complied, finding himself surprised by how comfortable he was stripping down to nothing in this room of relative strangers. As he removed his pants he realized Mhara was watching him. He thought of the bathing room. She noticed his recognition and smiled.

"Fionn should not have said what he did. That was spoken carelessly." She said.

"I know I'd like to know what the hell he thinks he sees in me with those creepy eyes of his." Winston confessed.

"He's a warrior, from time immemorial. He knows warriors when he sees them. He saw that in you, Winston." She said, using his name. Winston couldn't remember if she had ever said his name before, and he liked how it sounded from her lips.

"I was a soldier," Winston said, emphasizing the 'was'. "Is that what he means?"

"In part." She said, coming around to help him with part of his equipment. "There is more to it than that, I'm afraid."

Winston turned, eye to eye with Mhara. Gods she was beautiful. Cursed impulses, he had to focus. Locking eyes with her he said sternly "Tell me everything."

"Death has looked upon you, and you it. You have looked into the eyes of the great collector, and lived. More than that, Death never touched you." The words came from Mhara as dryly and matter of factly, as someone reading a shopping list.

Winston shuddered, a dark and painful memory returning to him. His eyes slipped from hers. He felt her hand touch his arm.

"Death is known here. He is of the few beings that traverse both our realm and your own." She said, using her other hand to lift his head and bringing his eyes back to her own. "Some of us in Faerie can sense, you could say, Death's presence. We can also tell those who have felt, and escaped his touch."

"I was the only member of my unit to not die or become injured, I lost a friend." Winston said, fighting emotions as he spoke reflexively. "I don't understand why this matters."

Mhara took a controlled breath. "Where we are going is dangerous. Some of us may die, however you will not. Death's touch is too fresh. We need you, Winston."

"Where are we going?"

"We're going deeper into Faerie. To a place even Death only visits if he must."

"And you think I will be beneficial in this?" Winston asked, fastening the last belt in his equipment. He stood before Mhara feeling oddly sure. His new clothes hung soundly on his frame, as if tailored just for him. The tunic and trousers were secured down by belts and straps. Leather pauldrons rested on his shoulders, rerebrace on his upper arm, and vambraces on his forearms. He was also wearing new boots, that secured via weaved straps midway up his calves. Those felt like it may take an army to pull off without untying first. Quite comfortable. Winston had trouble keeping the smile from his face.

"You will be beneficial, Winston. You're special." Mhara said.

Special. The word threatened to pull Winston from this moment. Sam had wanted to be special. He deserved to be special. Special was not a mantle he was comfortable wearing.

Their conversation came to a welcomed closure for Winston, as Fionn and Michael walked over to join them. Winston could see the Fianna were waiting outside with their horses. At least from what he could tell, Winston thought those massive things were horses. They sure sounded like them.

"Is he ready?" Fionn asked.

"Winston, I am going to need another favor from ye." Michael interjected.

"Mhara may have hinted at that, when she had me dress in this." Winston said, gesturing at his new attire.

"Good." Michael said, cheerfully sidestepping any acknowledgment of Winston's sarcasm. "It was important for you to change into more regionally acceptable garments, to help you blend in. Remember, all of Faerie likely knows you are here. Where we are headed it is all the more important to maintain our subterfuge."

"We ought go before night fall." Fionn said.

"Nightfall?" Winston asked. "The sun never moves here."

"Ignore him." said Michael.

"Come, Fionn. Let us prepare to go." Mhara said, Ushering the large warrior away, and retrieving an impressive fur-lined cloak for herself.

Winston looked at Michael once they were alone. "You're going to get me killed."

"Aye, it's possible some of us may die. This yet must be done."

"What exactly are we doing." Winston asked with a complete lack of patience in his tone.

"We believe we know what Jonathan is up to, and who he is aligned with. Because of this we need to retrieve an object of great power before he does."

"What is it?"

"The Sword of Darkfyre." Michael said, his expression as serious as a stone.

"Okay, and where do we find this sword."

"Above the throne of Winter, in the heart of the Unseelie court."

Winston didn't say another word. What would it have accomplished if he had. He knew he was here, in Faerie, and for all he knew, his only means home was to go along with whatever Michael and his companions had planned. Their eyes met, and Winston nodded in silent acquiescence. Michael handed him a cloak. It was lighter than expected, and Winston liked the color. He put it on and they joined the others outside, and mounted their horses to leave.

Winston took it all in. He was riding with a wizard, a mysterious and beautiful fey woman, and an eternal warrior, into one of the darkest depths of Faerie to retrieve a sword of all things. All in the hopes that this would help them stop a mad wizard, who Michael had been chained up with in a stone keep for some reason, from doing something truly vile. Even with all that Winston knew, this entire effort could be in support of Jonathan and his plans, whatever they may be.

The sun did indeed set as they left that magical cottage, whatever it was. As the day went to rest, other areas of the world awakened, to welcome the night. Winston wrapped his cloak about him, as if he could already feel the chill of the throne of Winter pressing upon his bones. All he could think of were Mhara's words to him in the bath, "humans die here."

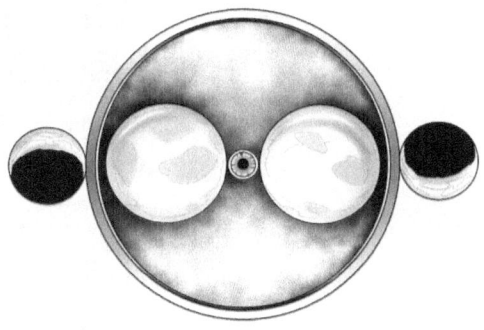

8 – STEPS TOWARDS WINTER

Falling feels a lot like floating in place with the rest of the world racing to catch you. When it caught Winston it was much like the way a semi-truck catches a drop of rain. Sharp, sudden, and lacking any level of cushion whatsoever, but it caught him, whole and true.

Winston thought to take in a deep breath before hitting the surface of the sea, and whether he was successful made no difference. The impact pressed out of him any air, feeling, or sense of place that he had in his possession. Winston went limp, and after a brief moment of buoyancy his body began to sink into the sea. A wave rolled over him as if old Poseidon was tucking him in for a night's rest. His eyes caught momentary flashes of color and light as the sea took him down further and further.

His lungs began to burn with need for air. Was it instinct that kept him from breathing this whole time? Whatever wall was holding back that basic need for life, was slowly deteriorating, as his body regained awareness from the stun of hitting the water. His arm and leg muscles began to stir. Every use of his muscles added to his devastating need for air. His eyes wouldn't focus in the sea water. How deep was he? Could he make it back to the surface for air in time?

A pressure, firm and guiding, pressed against his body pushing him forward. It moved like a creature of the sea, its body thrusting to the motion of the waves. Winston could feel a smooth, slick hide like texture. His hands found a fin and he held tight. His speed increased beyond what his body was able to accomplish on its own. His lungs burned with a treacherous need. The water at his nostrils and mouth threatened to invade his body. It was more than his mind could control. The need overpowered him, pulling open his clenched jaw, and pulling the water inside him.

In the shock of his body's betrayal, his grip on the creature loosed. As the hide began to slip away beneath his fingertips it seemed to warm, and move. The whole sea around him warmed, and felt thicker. Fingers, a hand, they clasped around his wrist. The grip was strong, the touch soft and comforting. Winston's mind was fading, the water pushing his consciousness into submission.

He could feel the coolness of the air affront his skin as his body broke the surface of the waves. The hand released him, and Winston began crawling. Yes, he found sand was under him. As if to share its own opinion on things, his stomach churned in protest. Winston lurched. His lungs and stomach enlisting his entire body to tighten and convulse, as the sea water was expelled from within him. A reprieve. Winston looked about for something to aid in his relief. Still his eyes wouldn't focus, as they burned from the seawater. One more surge of expulsion ripped its way through, and out of his body. A wave crashed against him, and he knew he had had enough. Winston pulled himself as far as he could manage from the water, finding dry sand. He collapsed, his face pressing hard into the sand.

As Winston gave into unconsciousness his eyes finally pulled closer to focus and he saw what he could only assume was his savior of the sea. It had two side fins, large, and flat. With a strong tail, and a head like a small puppy with tiny ears. Is it a seal? A seal was saving him? That wasn't too strange, was it? Seals are always getting along well with humans. Yes, that was perfectly acceptable. He watched the seal as it remained at the water's edge. Watched as the seal turned over, removed its own head like a cowl, and slide out of its skin to stand in the silhouette of a full, curved, powerful woman. A woman?

"Mhara? Mhara!" Winston called out in a start as he awoke. The cool, blue haze of the night around him in was a perfect contrast to the warm, golden sand of the seashore.

What was that? Was that a dream? No, that felt too real. Winston could almost taste the sea upon his lips. He looked over the group, no one else had stirred. He breathed a sigh of relief, pleased he had not disturbed them. Perhaps it was nothing.

Curling up the corner his bedroll Winston prepared to settle back down to sleep. Which would have worked out well if he hadn't seen those eyes looking directly at him. They seemed to glow in the dim light of the night moon. Had he been there this whole time? Silly, of course he had. They had all agreed to take turns standing watch, though Winston doubted any in the party needed sleep the way his body required it. With all the other things he'd seen thus far, it wouldn't be a stretch. Nevertheless, they set up camp to sleep.

Fionn sat; just beyond the foot of Winston's bedroll. Legs crossed, arms resting on his thighs. He had relieved himself of the armor he had been wearing. Something about how nothing they'd meet in this area of Faerie calls for such a heightened level of protection. For his part, Winston figured the eternal warrior was just this side of institution level crazy.

"Um. Hey." Winston said, sitting up straighter.

"Ho, good friend Winston."

"Did I, umm. Was it loud in my sleep?"

"Yes." Fionn said plainly.

"Oh." Winston said. Not expecting such a firm affirmation. "Is that why you are sitting there?"

"No, child. I am here waiting for Death." Fionn said, a cool and comfortable tone to his voice.

"Death? Like you are waiting for Death, the being, or waiting to die?" The warrior slightly tilted his head. It felt like an acknowledgement to Winston. A sign of respect. Maybe. "That was silly of me. I'm sorry." Winston said. "I don't follow what you mean."

"Not at all, young one. It is unique for me to meet another soul, which Death has allowed to pass. He may eventually come for you." Fionn said, straightening his back. "For my part, I wait. To face him, may well prove to be my greatest adventure."

"Him? Do you know Death is a man?"

"I'm sure Death is neither male nor female. He could be both. Who of us can be sure?"

"Yet you call Death, him. Why?"

"Between the genders, none is more historically devastating than man. Few forces in any realm can contest with the effect of Death and his power." A serious look spread across Fionn's face as he continued. "If our life is a game, in the end it is Death who wins the day. As a warrior, I must respect that."

"I see." Winston said, finding he could truly understand Fionn's perspective. Having seen the wages of war, and witnessing the loss of lives, in the end it is Death who is ultimately victorious.

"You may be the only one here who does." Fionn acknowledged.

Unsure how he should conclude the conversation, and not particularly wishing it to continue, Winston sorted his bedding again. "Well, then. Good night." Winston said, lying back down. Silence fell around them. As time passed, Winston was able to make out the sounds of the night, the stirring animals, the breathing of those around him. The night was vast, and ominous. He closed his eyes ready for sleep.

"Why do you call her name?" Fionn asked.

Winston rolled on to his back. Fionn had clearly heard, and Winston felt an apprehension in acknowledging the answer to his question, let alone actually discuss it with Fionn.

"Selkie's are glorious. They are powerful, regal, lovely, and truly dangerous warriors. Yet you call to her as if you know her. Not simply as you know of her, but with familiarity and intimacy. Why?" Fionn pressed.

Winston leaned up on his elbows, looking at Fionn. "We did share a bath." He said, grasping for levity in the situation.

Fionn smiled.

Curses, it's like his eyes can see the blood as it courses through your veins. Winston had never seen eyes like his before, in their iridescent pale blue green. Maybe someone in Faerie hasd sunglasses in this perpetually medieval feeling world. At the very least Winston wanted to get this man a blindfold. "I just." Winston started to say. "I don't know, okay. I feel like I can trust her."

"Perhaps on land."

"What does that mean?"

"Do you know what she is, child?" Fionn asked.

"So far, she's a friend." Winston said, feeling a stirring of defense, and sitting up fully to look at the warrior. "Do you even know how I got here? One minute I was working my job, doing the night rounds on sublevel six. I found a secured door left ajar. Upon inspecting the situation I found myself in a castle like structure, during the day, on the other side of the ocean. Or so Michael claims. I found him to be chained to a wall, and because of him I saw this guy Jonathan as he closed the door I had walked through, unceremoniously locking me in Scotland. I helped Michael escape his bonds, and run away from two huge, bull faced, guards..."

"Minotaur?" Fionn interjected.

"Is that what they're called."

"Yes."

"I didn't know."

"Michael hadn't mentioned that it was they who held him. Interesting." Fionn said.

"I bet. Michael seems to relish his secrets." Winston said. "Never seen anything like them before myself. When Michael came down those stairs saying we needed to go, I followed." He paused, appreciating again how insane the entire scene was before continuing. "Well, Michael's genius plan was to run us clean off a cliff, and I must have hit the water hard. The next thing I know I'm waking up in that cottage where we met. Mhara is there, she helps Michael see to my healing, we talked in a bath, and then you and your men showed up."

Fionn sat listening. His eyes focused as if Winston's words were the most important words he'd ever heard.

Winston continued. "In all of this, she's the only one who has seemed to care about me, for me, and not due to what she may be able to get from me. Does that make sense?" He asked, pausing and looking firmly at Fionn. "She is a friend."

"Anything is possible, I suppose." Fionn said, his eyes taking on a fatherly concern. "You are a trusting soul, young Winston. This quest of ours will challenge you. Do not let your need to trust, skew your objectivity."

What the hell was that supposed to mean? Winston didn't know, and didn't at present have the energy, or interest to ask. Sharing the account of recent events left him worked up. His breathing was sharp, his muscles tense. Though he was convinced his efforts were futile, Winston knew he really should try to sleep more.

"How long will it take to reach the Unseelie territory?" he found himself asking instead.

"Like your world, Faerie is vast. There is no shortcut to where we are going. Sure we can move from this realm to your human realm, yet within realms, we are bound to the laws of that world."

"How long will it take?"

"Days."

"That's not bad." Winston said.

"To get to the Port of Hollows." Fionn continued. "That is the first stop on our journey. We need supplies, and I will collect more of my men. From there, it will take us the better part of two weeks, to reach the edge of Unseelie territory."

"Well, shit." Winston said. "You sure we can't just ride a giant eagle to the mountain?"

"A what, to where?" Fionn asked, confusion clear on his face.

Winston chuckled to himself as he moved to lay back down. "Never mind. I should really sleep."

"We don't have large eagles." Fionn said, clearly not ready to move on. Winston looked at him as he continued. "We do have dragons."

Winston shot back up, more erect than before. "You have what? Seriously?"

"Dragons. Many species, of many sizes and temperaments."

"Can we ride one of those to the throne of Winter?" Winston asked.

Winston couldn't believe what he was hearing. Dragons? All the stars of heaven couldn't amount to the excitement he would feel if he actually got to see a real dragon. He couldn't help himself and had to ask if they could ride one.

"No." Fionn said, bursting Winston's hopes. "Our path does not lead us to the Elvin kingdom, and there is the only place you would find ride-able dragons. Lest you caught and raised one yourself."

Winston's eyebrows felt as if they were in the hasty journey to the back of his neck. "So you're saying there are Dragons we could ride?"

"Not where we are going."

"But they exist."

"Yes of course."

"So awesome! I need to ride one." Winston said, his voice like a young boy.

"You have the soul of an adventurer!" Exclaimed Fionn with a guffaw. "Ha! And the heart of a warrior. This is a good day." He said, clearly amused with Winston.

"Hey!" it was Michael's voice. Where was he?

Winston looked about, finding his bedroll. It was vacant. When had he left.

Michael came in from the side of camp, sword drawn. He looked like he had been running for a time. Was Fionn even standing watch at all? No, clearly. Winston knew this need for sleep was a sham. He must have simply been here to talk to Winston. What was happening?

"Up! Up!" Michael's voice was urgent and hard. "Get the bridles off the horses, and douse the embers of the fire. Then get everyone in close."

"What is it?" Mhara asked as she rose from her slumber.

Winston looked over seeing her complying. The other warriors were as well, quietly obedient as always. Winston moved to gathered his bedroll, and put it into his pack, moving to place it by his saddle. Which had been removed from his horse when they set up camp.

"My brother." Came Fionn's commanding voice. "What pursues you?"

"No me, my friend. Us." Michael said. "It's the knights of winter."

Fionn pulled his sword, turning toward where Michael had come. "Ho, the Fianna will fight." He proclaimed. At his words his men stopped what they were doing and drew their swords to stand with him.

"No!" Michael said.

"We do not run?"

"We don't have time to run. Don't be a fool. You confront them here, and we will all die." Michael said, pulling Fionn to him by the arm. "We will die."

This seemed to pull Fionn back in. "You have a plan?"

"Yes. I always have a plan." Michael said, sounding almost relieved. "They are too close for us to successfully run. Strip the horses bare, and gather all of our gear together." He said, as he started walking in a backwards circle, dragging his heal into the frosted, snow speckled dirt. "Send the horses away in every direction, and then get inside the circle."

Everyone complied. The horses were shooed off, and the supplies were gathered within the circle. Michael picked up a single log with embers from the remnants of the fire before snuffing it out, and threw the log as far as he could to the side. It landed on the wet ground and immediately began smoking.

"Everyone kneel down." Michael instructed as he led by example. "Stay quiet. Don't move. Ye move, and they may see us."

Fionn and his men positioned themselves in a triangle shape, each of them facing out in a different direction from the circle. Mhara knelt next to Winston, near the center of the circle, by the supplies. She had drawn her sword and laid it across her bent leg. Michael was near the edge of the circle.

"What is he doing?" Winston whispered to Mhara.

"Hush." She rebuked. "He is setting a veil."

Winston watched on as Michael pulled a knife from his boot, placed the blade to his skin and cut into his forearm creating a flow of blood, that he then directed down upon the circle in the dirt. Michael's lips seemed to move, but Winston heard no sound. Starting from where the blood met the circle, rose a wave of power that discolored the night. Like a golden crescent stream, it expanded out, following the circle's line, until a dome covered the six of them. Winston could feel the power hanging around them. His eyes passed along the walls of the dome, and along the line of the circle, watching as the flow of power shifted back and forth like liquid.

He could have spent the rest of the night lost in watching the manifestation of Michael's magic in this dome ebb and flow. All that stopped when he felt Mhara's hand clasped his wrist. Winston's presence retreated back within himself, and he looked at Mhara's hand. Her grip was strong; her touch was soft and comforting. Winston looked down at her hand upon him, then up at her. Her face was wrought, her eyes drawn hard into the distance. He followed her gaze toward the crest of the hill. The scene was awash with golden hues, and yet beyond the trees and shapes of the forest he could see it.

The lone figure rode upon a beast that looked to be one-part horse, one-part beast of burden, and 100 percent dangerous. From the haze; other riders joined the figure, thicker, and somehow less demanding than the first. They were saying something to the first, and there was a nod of approval. Then like the rumblings of the moving earth came the sound of the riders moving toward where the log from the fire lay.

They examined it, and there was undecipherable yelling as they saw the hoof prints of the horses. The first figure, the leader, looked about for a time, then reigned in their beast, and rode back below the crest of the hill. The other riders followed her and as they rode away the sounds of their departure wasn't so much heard, as it was felt in the declining vibrations of the ground beneath them.

Michael turned to Fionn, who gave Michael a nod with a fist to his chest, as if to acknowledge the wisdom of this choice. Michael looked toward Mhara who also nodded. Her grip loosening from Winston's wrist.

"Who was that?" Winston whispered to Mhara.

"They are the Knights of Winter, and they are clearly looking for something." She said.

"Was that their leader upon the hill?"

"Aye." Came Michael's voice. "Bheur, herself."

"Who?"

Mhara looked to Winston. "Bheur. The Queen of Winter."

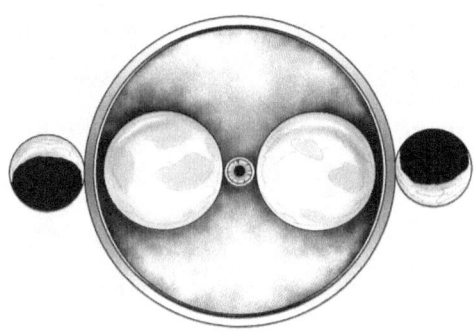

9 – CAMPFIRE STORIES

The cool night air passed easily through the camp. Michael looked up from checking supplies to see Mhara returning. "Oi! How many have we been able to retrieve?"

"All, but two. Fionn and his men haven't given up in their efforts."

"They are a persistent lot, those lads."

"Michael?"

"Aye. I know."

"He should be allowed to know. He should be told."

"Aye." Michael paused, looking toward Winston as he continued working on the night's fire. "He deserves a lot more than I can give him currently."

Mhara said nothing more, instead moving to aid with caring for the recovered horses. Michael didn't move. Their progress had been slow going the last couple days. Much slower than Michael would have preferred, and he made no secret of it. There was little that could be done about it, however. They had needed to recover their horses, while not drawing upon them, the attention of the Knights of Winter. To have the Knights this far from the throne of Winter, something significant must be taking place. The kind of significant thing that Winston and his companions would not do well to be associated with. Certainly not with the Queen leading her Knights personally.

They searched as best as they could after the Knights had left. Fionn and his men had been able to retrieve most of the horses after a day or two of searching. They may need to make due with less mounts than they started with. They'll still have enough for each member of the party to ride; they'll simply need to adjust how their supply storage.

It was no simple thing when the Knights had vacated the area. Michael stayed up all night maintaining their veil, doing his best to keep any creature of Faerie from detecting them as it passed them by. He said something about how the only way to be sure it worked as a true veil is if it was connected to the sight of the wizard who created it. Without that connection the veil would distort whatever was inside, working as a camouflage, but it would not have as complete of an effect.

The following morning Fionn, and the Fianna began working to collect the horses. Something was said about how the horses were trained for this kind of thing and would know to return. Winston thought that sounded a bit fantastical, but all things considered, he couldn't claim to be necessarily surprised.

Winston and Mhara slowly moved the groups gear on to a sled of tied tree branches. They would then take turns among them pulling the sled along. During the initial stretch of their walk Winston was pulling the gear, and asked Michael if there wasn't a spell to help make moving the gear without the horses easier. Michael shook his head and made a quip about how cell phones have ruined the minds of today's young.

As the sun was setting they found a spot near a thicket of trees. Much denser cover than the previous night, and Michael suggested they set up camp there. His logic being that the denser coverage would allow him to use a different kind of veil, with a mirroring effect, one that wouldn't require him to stay awake for however long they may need to stay put. Using an opening to the grove, they set up camp within the trees, and Michael's veil worked so well that Winston couldn't see the entrance to their camp the first time he came back from relieving his bladder.

This was their second night in the thicket. Winston was thankful for the ample supply of dry wood and kindling. He learned the hard way their first night traveling that the wood here in Faerie is more temperamental than he was used to. With the group being stationary for a while, he made a point to gather plenty of wood for the night, and enough to take with when they go. Tonight's fire would be a good one. Winston struck the flint and smiled as it came to life.

"Yer pretty skilled at that, lad." Michael said.

"A childhood of boy scouts, and serving in the army can teach a guy a thing or two." Winston replied, warmth and appreciation in his voice. "Never know when the knowledge of tying knots, eating roots, and starting fires may come in handy."

"How're ye holdin' up?"

"I'm still working to get settled on all of this." Winston said with a gesture towards the world around them. "It's been days, and at this point when I get home, I mean…" Winston took a breath. "Will I have anything to go home to? I'm sure my job is gone. Hell, they may think I'm dead."

"Aye. I can't say fer sure how this it'll play out. I'm sorry for that."

"Shouldn't have gone through that door." Winston stated plainly. "That was stupid, a careless rookie move, and I know it. I should have waited for backup. Still, even then, some or all of us would be stuck here. Ya know?"

"Hmmm…" Michael murmured. Clearly thinking.

"What is it?" Winston asked.

"Why'd you go through that door?" Michael finally asked.

Winston knew the answer, he'd known it when he did it, but he wasn't sure he wanted to say it out loud. Some things sound obnoxious when given voice. Really, what difference would it make now? He was stuck here, and as far as he knew there was no getting back without Michael's help.

"Winston?" Michael asked. "Ye alright?"

"I felt drawn to it." The words came out of Winston as smoothly as a breath.

"Aye." Michael's voice sounded resolved in its tone.

"It was as if I knew the door would be open before I even saw it. Once I did, there was no stopping me from entering." Winston recalled. "Damn. I even shut off my radio and ignored Control's calls, because I needed to see for myself."

The still of the night filled in between them. Silent, except for the crackling of the growing fire. Michael set another log on the flames, not looking at Winston.

"Were we ever in Scotland?" Winston asked, a thought coming

to him.

"No, lad. At least not your Scotland."

"Shit. That's how he did it, isn't it? Jonathan. He opened a passage from Faerie, to my world, using the door as a threshold. Meaning I've been stuck in Faerie the whole time."

"Aye, that is a fair way to explain what happened."

"Do you have any idea what he is doing?" Winston asked sharply. "Why did he even want to go to my world?"

"Jonathan, like me, is unique. Every so often a creature of Faerie will mate with a human, the result is us. Wizards, as it were. No wizard is fully human. Similarly, no wizard exists free of a connection to Faerie. Some are more Fae than others. Merlyn is pure Fae, as far as we know." Michael stoked the fire. "Jonathan and I, we are at least half and half."

"Okay, but what does he want?" Winston asked again.

"Patience, boy, this isn't as easy as telling you the time, or that supper is ready."

"I'm sorry."

"Nah, don't be sorry. Just listen. Alright?" Michael looked at Winston, their eyes sharing an acknowledgement. He continued. "Because our magic is from Faerie, that strength is rejuvenated here. The longer we are away from that connection, the lower our resources become. There are ways for wizards to exist for years without returning to Faerie, but they age differently when not here, and an imbalance can be created."

"An imbalance?"

"Aye. You see, our realms are separate, and connected. We draw from each other, and yet never take more from one without replacing with something of equal value from the other."

"That makes sense. Like a scale."

"Close enough."

"Is that the same reason you said that all of Faerie knows I'm here?"

"Aye, it's connected. There was a shift in the balance. That same shift is part of why Jonathan was able to make the passage from the tower, to your world."

"But what is he after?" Winston asked impatiently.

"Freedom, boy! Damnit." Michael snapped. "Sure he loosed himself from our bonds, but he wants more. More than to be free of his chains. More than to be out of that tower. He wants to be a wizard, free of Faerie."

"Can he do that?" Winston asked, now unsure he wanted the answer.

"He believes he can. Which is all that matters." Michael said matter-of-factly. "That's why we need to get the sword of Darkfyre before he does. He believes he can use the sword to sever the part of him that binds him to Faerie."

Winston couldn't fathom how a person could get to the point Jonathan was at. How does someone convince themselves that the intangible can be severed from the tangible, like cutting the soul, from the life and body, it is bound to? In the face of that daunting question, there was yet one more that pressed in Winston's mind even more. A question he needed Michael to answer. "How do you know?"

There was a pause. A look of recognition settled upon Michael's face. He knew Winston was asking this to be assured that Michael was not a part of Jonathan's plot. "I was there when he learned of it." Michael said, sounding remorseful. "There were concerns about

Jonathan, and what he was mixed up in. I was tasked with finding out what these may be."

"Is that why you were locked up together?"

"Aye, we were caught with our hands in the cookie jar, as it were, and I couldn't give away the ruse just yet. They locked us in our bonds, and had been moving us about while they waited for word from Merlin."

"Wait." Winston interrupted. "Were they using you as a bargaining chip?"

"Exactly right. Bloody fools thought that just because we were wizards, they could use us in some political maneuver to gain more power in the realm."

"Who had you locked up?"

"May, The Queen of Summer." Michael said plainly. Ignoring the look on Winston's face he continued. "Jonathan had his heart set on retrieving a scepter which rests in her possession. He believes with it, and the sword of Darkfyre, he can be a wizard free of Faerie. Free of any external restrictions. Jonathan believes he will be god-like."

"Are you insane?" Winston exclaimed.

"I may be a tad mad, but what is it you are asking?"

"You followed a suspected criminal, participated in his effort to rob the Queen of Summer, got apprehended, and now your plan to stop him is to steal from the Queen of Winter? Are you insane?"

"Aye, well, you put it that way and it does sound a bit daft." Michael chuckled.

"You are crazy." Winston asserted. "This place is crazy. Am I ever going to get home?"

His heart was pounding between his ears, and he needed to

collect himself. Winston looked away from the conversation with Michael, and searched the camp around them. The horses were tied to a nearby set of smaller trees. Fionn and his men were gone, presumably off hunting game to eat for the evening meal. Mhara leaned against a thicker tree near the horses. She must have noticed them talking and kept her distance, but why? It's not like they should be talking about anything overly sensitive is it? Yet there she sat, fiddling with her blade.

"She saved me, didn't she?" Winston asked. He took a breath, calming further. "When I hit the water, after jumping off the cliff, it was Mhara that saved me after I blacked out wasn't it?"

"Aye. She pulled me to shore, and went back for you."

"What is she?"

"She's been your friend. That is all ye need worry about."

"She is something though, isn't she? Something of Faerie?" Winston asked, looking directly at Michael. "From what you said, all the residents of Faerie are in some kind of group, or kind."

"True, and knowing this kind of truth about one of Faerie, knowing what she is, would give you power. Power of knowledge, and in some cases, access to power over them." Michael said soberly. "To some of Faerie this would make them more vulnerable than they may be comfortable with. As for Mhara, when the time comes, she'll tell you what she is ready for you to know."

"I only ask because I remember something from my fall." Winston assured. "In my memory, whatever saved me changed shape while doing so. One moment it was a sea creature, a seal, and in the next it took the shape of a woman."

"The mind can imagine silly things in such moments, boy." Michael said.

"Perhaps." Winston said. "I'll let it go either way. Like you said. It's her information to share."

"Wise lad." Michael said with a nod.

"But you're really a wizard?" Winston asked, a childlike curiosity in his voice.

"Clearly." Michael replied with an, isn't it obvious, tone.

"And Fionn and his men?"

"The Fianna? They are warriors. Straight forward lot really. What you see is what you get with those blokes. Be thankful they are on our side."

"The plan is to make it to the port, and connect with more of his men?"

"Aye, we'll need 'em the further we go into Winter."

"How many does he have?"

"No one knows." Michael said. "Some tell they seen him with hundreds at a time, some say thousands. I know he always travels with two, and he claims he can call upon his men for as many as the situation needs." Michael leaned back. "Suppose we'll see, won't we?"

"I suppose so." Winston agreed.

"Forgive me for saying so, but with all your talk of getting home, do you have anything to go home to?" Michael asked.

Winston started, unsure how to respond to the probing question.

"Not making a judgment, lad. Truly, I find myself wondering if'n you weren't meant to be here." Michael said.

It seemed as if Michael had more to say, and likely would have, had it not been for the disembodied foot, that slammed into the back of his head. It launched him forward, over the fire, and out of the thicket of trees.

Winston scurried after him, catching up to where Michael had slid to a stop in the lightly snowed grass outside. Mhara was there in an instant, blade still in her hand.

"What happened?" she asked.

"I don't know." Winston said. "We were talking and he suddenly flew forward out of camp, as if something kicked him in the head and booted him out here."

A laugh, low, thick, and heavy rolled out of the thicket from behind the veil. Winston watched as a large silhouette began to walk through the illusion. The ground trembled as the thick-legged figure's hoofed feet hit the ground just beyond the veil. The rest of the silhouette's figure smoothly followed the hoofed foot into view. Winston knew what was coming. The thick legs led to sturdy hips, a wide barrel chest, muscled shoulders, and a head like a bull. Mist plumed out of his nostrils as he looked down at his handy work.

Winston couldn't believe it. How did they not hear him coming? For that matter, was he alone?

"Clean work, cousin." Came a voice from behind them, clearly the beast was not alone. A deep and full laugh percolated out of the second Minotaur. "The Queen will be pleased we retrieved one of them."

"Perhaps she will be equally pleased, if we bring back his head." The first Minotaur said. "Accidents do happen while one tries to escape."

The two Minotaur laughed, seemingly oblivious to the three of them on the ground. Mhara wrapped her arms under Michael's and lifted him with ease. They didn't have time to evaluate which way was their best path; they ran.

The forest seemed to vibrate at the roar of the beastly guards as they turned in pursuit. Each hoof fall shook the ground under their feet, threatening to toss them off balance.

"Run, Winston!"

"I am running!" he called back.

It was a fruitless effort. In less than five strides the first of the minotaur were upon them. It hit Winston like an automobile to the ribs, lifting him off his feet and sending him through the air, as if gravity were of little consequence here.

He hit the ground hard. Harder than the impact that sent him flying. Dirt and snow filled Winston's mouth. The world spun, and he desperately tried to catch his breath. With each heaving effort he tried to crawl away, as if it would do better than running. Winston hoped he was simply brushed away as an obstacle of no interest, and that they continued to pursue Mhara, and Michael. Which would give him a chance to catch his breath. He knew his hopes were for naught as he felt the subtle trembles of the ground as one of the beasts came close to him. Was it stopping? The footfalls halted, and a deep chuckle started. It was laughing at him.

"Silly human. Only one of you creatures would believe jumping off a cliff would actually keep us from finding you and the wizard." The massive beast said.

"That..." Winston coughed. "... wasn't my idea."

"It's of no matter. Soon my cousin will have the wizard and the Selkie pup, and this game will be concluded."

Winston continued to try to back away, worming back as he watched the minotaur loom over him. What had he called Mhara, a

Selkie? Winston didn't get far, scurrying himself up against a tree.

"You, however, are no one." The beast said, looking down at a pinned Winston. "No more value than mud on my hoof."

Dazed, dizzy, and backed against the tree, Winston watched as the giant bull raised its hoof to crush him beneath it. Reality flooded in on him. This beast was about to stomp the life out of him, and there was nothing he could do. Winston strived to move, his eyes darting around looking for purchase. Once again he heard the roar, a familiar sound now, only louder as the creature was right over him. The hoof was going to kill him. The world trembled and shook in the wake of the roar. Hot breath shot from the beast's mouth and nose. Winston closed his eyes and wait for the hoof to drop, almost welcoming it. The hoof came down, hitting the root of the tree to Winston's left.

Winston opened his eyes. The beast continued to roar, only now its roar was mixed with pain. A thick, blue, luminescent blade, covered in cold indigo flames that seemed to give off no light, jetted from the creature's chest. The minotaur had clasped it's hands around the blade in reflex, trying to remove the sword. Winston watched as the blade ripped back into the beast, and out from the giant bull's body. Winston's eyes followed the flowing swoop of fire from the blade as it swung back around to come down upon the minotaur, connecting to the left of the bulls massive head, between the neck and shoulder. The blow was powerful, and vicious, severing through the beast and cleaving off its head and right arm from its body.

The creature's carcass collapsed to the ground, steam and blood flowing out from it. Instinctively Winston tried to move away from the body as it fell. He worked his way around the side of the tree, and through the steam rising from the body. In the chaos of the scene

Winston saw a figure standing behind the fallen beast. A figure in black plate armor, holding what Winston could only assume was the sword of Darkfyre.

The figure stepped forward, removing their helm. The helm gave way to a powerful, beautiful woman who looked down at Winston. Her eyes were as ice, and her skin a pale, smooth glow. She pushed her raven hair back from her face behind her ear, and looked at him.

"I am Bheur, the Queen of Winter. Rise. Now. That you might live."

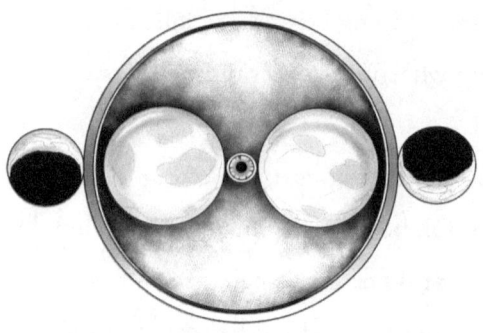

10 – OLD FRIENDS

Before

"It's good you found work, Winston. How are you liking it?"
She asked.

"It's fine." Winston said, holding a cup of coffee between his
knees. His eyes were down, looking toward his feet on the grey-green
carpet. "Pays the bills, ya know."

"That is always good." Her voice was warm, soothing. Winston
figured all therapists and counselors probably sounded this way. Like
they were the audio sensory equivalent of a tender hug. Something in
their schooling he supposed. "What I'm wondering is how you're
feeling about the job. Are you fitting in? Is the staff structure conducive
for you?" She asked.

"Yeah. Yeah. Boss is cool. Every day has a schedule. Stuffs
pretty easy to follow." Winston sipped his coffee. He'd held it so long

the steam was gone. "No one's shooting at me there. That has its benefits." He concluded, a halfhearted chuckle added to his delivery.

The counselor didn't respond right away. Her head was down as she scribbled notes on her pad. Winston sipped his coffee and again considered the oddly neutral-cool palette of the office. Even in its blandness it stood in stark contrast to the rest of the VA facility.

He'd been coming to therapy for weeks at this point. Part of a program designed for veterans, with prescribed care for PTSD. Winston didn't know if it was helping. He wasn't comfortable admitting he had PTSD, but the evidence outweighed his prideful opinion. He knew he couldn't feel bad about it. A person doesn't live through what he did, seeing what he saw, and watch his friends die while he lived, then simply walk away unaffected.

"Have you been keeping a journal, like we discussed?" The counselor asked.

"Ah, no." Winston admitted sheepishly. "I'm sorry, Counselor White. Haven't gotten around to starting that."

"That's alright. You can start it any time. Do you think you could work on the journal before our next appointment?"

"Yeah. I think I can do that."

"You're working nights, correct?"

"Yes, mam. Works out well for me. Less people and everything."

"Are they giving you time off for the holidays? Do you plan to visit family?"

"No." Winston said.

"No, they're not, or no, you don't plan to visit family?"

"Both. Kinda." Winston took another sip. "I don't really have any family to see. So I volunteered to work."

She flipped through some papers in her lap, and didn't seem to find what she was looking for. The councilor made a note in her pad. "I didn't know that." She said. "I was unaware you were without family."

"That's ok. Can't expect you to know everything, Counselor." Winston said, showing a half smile. "Grew up in foster care. Never knew who my parents were."

"Did that contribute to your choice to enlist in the Army?"

"I guess so. I wanted to do something better with my life. Figured I'd use the GI loan for college when I got out." He said.

"Is that still your plan, Winston? Do you plan to go to college?" Counselor White asked.

"Maybe." He said. "Not right now though. Think I'm just gonna work a while and see where that goes. Ya know?"

"I understand. You can start college at any time after all."

"Yeah, and who knows what the future holds?"

"Anything is possible." Counselor White said in her warm, soothing way.

***

Now

Winston woke up screaming.

The world was blue around him. Cold, frozen, and powerful, the room seemed to be there, and not there at the same time. There was a scurrying sound coming from behind him. No. From below him. Winston was laying on a hard table, stone perhaps, it was remarkably warm for the perceivably cold environment. Winston couldn't move.

Listening to the chattering sounds he noted they sounded like voices in a language he didn't know, that now joined in with the skittering noises of what seemed like tiny footfalls around him. There was one distinct voice, and it seemed to be issuing commands by its tone. After it finished, Winston could hear another set of tiny feet flee from the room, and away from them.

"Hello?" Winston called. "Hello, who is there?"

"Quiet. Quiet." Came a voice again from below him, now in Winston's language. "You're not in any danger. No Danger. No Danger for you. Not currently."

"Where am I?" He asked. "And who are you?"

"No. No. That shan't be. You'll be staying quiet now, whilst Shoma works." Came back the seemingly feminine voice. Not feminine like a human, more pitchy, and rough around the edges. As if each word were fighting its way out of the creatures mouth. "Yep. Yep. You'll be staying quiet. Tender work before me. Much to do. Much to do. Quiet, Quiet whilst Shoma works." Shoma concluded, and they started to hum.

Winston needed to get out of wherever he was, but he couldn't move. It was more than a matter of bonds keeping him in place. He couldn't even move his toes. Was his back broken? What happened in the woods? How did he get here, wherever here was?

Next came the twinkling sounds of chains, and a slight whistle from the spinning of a wheel. A pulley system? Rising to his left Winston could see the top of a figure. It was blurry and difficult to make out details, but it was definitely the top of the creature's head. It was pulling on something. *Was that skin?*

Panic flooded Winston's brain, that looked like skin and tissue the creature was pulling at. *Was it from his legs?* He couldn't feel anything beyond the pressure of the hard stone table below him, and his body's inability to move.

"What the hell are you doing?" Winston yelled.

"Now. Now. Shush, child. Yes. Shush, shush while Shoma works."

"Fuck that shit. You tell me right…"

"Not good. Not good!" Shoma exclaimed slamming something against a hard surface. "Such language is vile and mean to Shoma. Mean. Mean. I work to help you." Shoma assured. "Patience now. Patience. Your kind may heal quickly, but you still need help. Yes. Yes. You need Shoma. Shoma is here. Hush now."

Panic turned to frustration, followed by rage, and fear. Winston couldn't move, he couldn't feel, and perhaps that was a blessing considering what Shoma appeared to be doing.

Winston breathed meditatively, forcing himself to relax. Though his body was already numb, it was yet a challenge to release the tension coursing through him. He controlled his breathing pattern, and worked to moderate his mind by counting to himself with each breath. Inhaling through the nose, and exhaling through the mouth.

In. Out. In. Out.

Whether or not, and to whatever extent Shoma continued to work Winston didn't know. Instead, in his efforts to calm himself he lost consciousness. An unknown span of time later Winston's eyes opened again. No screaming accompanied them this time. No dreams either. Though by the dry filmy feeling in his mouth he was sure he had dozed off. The light was noticeably different in the room, while continuing to still give off a cold tone of blue. There was no chattering, nor shuffling, and no sounds of moving parts nearby to welcome Winston as he awoke. He was alone then? Had Shoma finished their work?

Winston tried valiantly to will himself into movement to no avail. Stationary, and trapped to the hard, oddly not cold table, his eyes able to move, and yet only see the upper portion of what looked to be a lofty room. So he stared. He looked at each crack, contour, and detail. He focused his ears like he learned in the Army, controlling the sensory information coming in, and allowing his ears to tell him what was around him in the room, and the hallway outside. He continued this effort, losing himself in the untold minutes or hours he invested towards his efforts, his mind grew ever more consumed by the pattern of the surfaces of the upper walls and ceiling. Using his mind's eye, he started connecting the details into shapes, faces, and elements of memory.

He began picturing them move within the surface of the ceiling. Seeing them move, jump, run, dance, and sway he started attributing characteristics to the figures. Winston created stories for them, imagining what gave them purpose, names, hope. He recalled how he used to do this in his barracks some nights while on deployment. Looking up at the canvas walls of the barracks, the ambient light of the base around them shining in through polycarbonate windows. For a moment it was as if he was there again, with his unit, with Sam. That's when he heard it.

Winston let go of everything he was thinking, and listened. He knew he heard it. A sharp exhale. Like one would give when mildly amused by the silly frolics of a child. He strained, past the sound of his own breathing, through the pounding of his heart, he listened, and he could hear it. Calm, controlled breathing, neither deep, or shallow, but definitely breathing.

"Impressive display." She said.

The words filled the room the way lighting fills the sky in its focused, powerful way; affecting all the world around it. He knew that voice. A shivering waving passed over his body, causing bumps to rise upon his skin.

"I've not seen such a display of genuine playfulness in quite some time."

What did she mean? Could she see what he was imagining? The moving picture show he imagined all in his mind, was she seeing it too? Winston looked toward the ceiling. Nothing was out of place. Nothing had moved. Surely there was no way she could have perceived what he had only imagined.

There was a click, with the slow movement of chains as the tabled dropped. Not far. An inch, maybe two. It bobbed for a moment and then started to pivot, raising his head up, while simultaneously lowering his feet, leaving his pelvis in roughly the same spot. Winston still couldn't move. Yet as he was adjusted he saw her.

She leaned casually against the wall, almost as if nothing were happening. She rested in a casual comfort and security, like she was waiting on an old friend. She didn't have her armor on, or the sword. Winston discerned this meant that they must be back in Winter, in her home. Rather than the armor he had seen her in previously, she wore a long dark tunic that split at the hips, and hung to her calves at the front and back. Her raven hair was pulled back to the sides, flowing open and loose in the back, and a small lacey crown of faint jewels ornamented her head.

She smiled at him. Her eyes holding a gaze of familiarity. "We have much to discuss."

"Let me go." Winston demanded, feeling the least bit of interest in speaking to her.

"You're not a prisoner here. Your current bonds are in place to aid in your healing." She stepped toward him as the platform came to a stop. "I am only working to help you."

It was her, just as he had seen her previously, the Queen of Winter. Even without the armor, or the beast she rode, she stood powerful and lovely. Her voice was soothing, and almost warm. Winston struggled to be comfortable as she approached from her place against the wall. Her form, now better illuminated by the few lanterns hanging upon the walls, was both beautiful and intimidating. Winston's breath caught in his throat. It fought him as if not knowing whether to flow in or out. The air pressed forward from his lungs in exhalation. She looked at him. Her cold eyes meeting his. No glasses. No writing pad to hide behind. Winston grasped for the words.

"Hello, Winston." She said smiling.

"Hello. Counselor White." Winston replied.

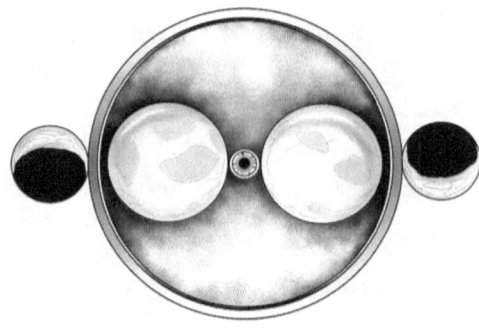

11 – DINNER AND THE WIZARD KING

Feeling your body return to functionality is not a process easily explained. On the outside we may assume it is a lot like feeling our blood work its way back into an extremity which has been pinned awkwardly for a time. As the muscles, and nerves are rejuvenated through the return of blood flow within the body it is accompanied by a unique mixture of pain, tingling, and the rush of hot and cold sensations. Yet when it is our whole body that has been affected, the experience, though similar, is also the difference between headphones, and a live rock concert.

Winston wasn't sure how long he had been lying on the slab in this room. He was certain it had to have been days. Servants had brought him food, drink. They'd even washed him. Which was the first indicator that he was naked. Shoma had been by a few times, and it was through her, he supposed it was a her, that he learned she was tending his injuries. In the moment Winston hadn't connected the fact that being hit by minotaur as he was, had resulted in many broken bones.

"Good. Good." Shoma had said. "You are healing well, you are. Yes. Yes, you are." She patted him kindly on his head, as if he had accomplished something special. "So many broken bones. So many bones. You heal fast don't you. You do, you do. It was believed, and Shoma knows it to be true. Shoma has seen it. Special you are. Special indeed."

What had been broken? With his eyes active he had been able to discern Shoma performing work on both of his legs, his left arm, and his chest. The more she worked, the more Winston found himself thankful he was limited to the use of his eyes and mouth. Though he couldn't help worrying that his injuries had been more severe than broken bones.

Bheur hadn't returned. Her presence lingered with Winston. He had questions. Questions that need answering. Yet in the moment they shared, where even in his restrained state he could have asked those questions, he blacked out. Winston was frustrated and embarrassed that it had happened. Not much he could have done. With his reported injuries, perhaps the better perspective was to be impressed he had been conscious at all.

It was she though, he was sure of it, Counselor White. As she had came close all he could see was the neutral-cool palette of the office, her eyes behind her glasses, her hand scribbling in her notepad, it was his counselor from the VA. She could be no one else. He even saw it in her face when he addressed her. The truth of it. Recognition and appreciation, while also conveying a kind warning for him to be careful.

Perhaps it was good he blacked out. Giving him time to

consider this revelation, even if it only left him with more questions. He was no longer asleep, and moment by moment the rest of his body was returning to him. And boy did it hurt. Pain. The kind that a person only has when sleeping for far too long, unmoving, on a hard surface.

Waves of fire, and ice flowed throughout Winston's body, as feeling returned to him. There didn't seem to be an order to this process of reanimation. Feeling, and movement came to his left hand at the same time he was able to move and feel his right toes. His stomach came to life quickly. Winston, and anyone within his vicinity knew this by the sudden rumble of protest that rolled out from his core as his body advocated for sustenance. Next, Winston's head, and neck didn't fully engage together, his head dropped forward with the pull of gravity, completely unrestrained by his neck muscles, as his platform was positioned in an upright state. As his chin met his chest Winston could see the scars on his body from Shoma's work, the aftermath of the damage done to him, and in that terrible moment of clarity he realized his semi functional body was no longer securely affixed to the platform.

Winston struggled to proficiently use any limb he could to try to stop what was coming, to no avail. Following the momentum of his head falling forward, his primarily limp form began to follow suit, and fall forward off of the platform. As the weight of Winston's body moved, his knees gave way. Winston tumbled to the floor. His body didn't protest, or react much at all, until his skin came into contact with the bitter cold floor.

"Ahhh! Shit, that's cold!" he cried out. The sharp sensation of the icy floor ripping his limbs to life as he scrambled to his feet. *Where were his clothes?*

Now on his feet, Winston looked about the room. He couldn't

make heads or tails of what most of this stuff was, and worst of all, he didn't see his clothing. What he did perceive was the familiar shuffle of little feet. He moved against the wall. As if proximity to a larger form would somehow camouflage him.

Shoma entered the room. She was definitely a she, let's just leave it at that. Not to say she was a treat to look upon, only that her form made it clear she was herself. She entered the room and began moving about her business. No reaction whatsoever was given by her to Winston not being in bed any longer, or his naked form against the wall. She entered the room, walked over to her table, and began making notes in her book.

Winston moved to peer out the doorway into the hall. It was empty and the path to the left seemed to go on forever.

"Not wise. Not wise." Shoma said behind him. "You should get dressed you should. Dressed is good. You are yet naked. Dressed is good."

Winston turned to look at her. She was still writing in her book. She didn't appear at all concerned that he was awake, mobile, or nude. "I'd get dressed if I had clothes." He said. Instantly feeling poorly about being so short with her. No pun intended.

"Ah yes. Ah yes. I have them here." She said. Shoma reached under her table and removed a parcel. Shoma set the item on the edge of the table she was working on, and went back to her journaling.

The parcel was more like how a gift would look. It was wrapped in shimmering purple linen, with accenting embroidery, and silvery looking ornamentation on the end. The wrap was tied closed with a silk ribbon that crossed both ways over the parcel. The ribbon was also a silvery color, with an iridescent sheen reflecting off as the light hit it.

"You open gifts. You open gifts, you know." Shoma said, still not looking up from her work.

Winston didn't know what to say to that, so he opened the gift. Untying the knot on the ribbon was all it took. As soon as it was loosed, the parcel unfolded itself on its own. From inside the wrapping came multiple pieces of clothing, and two pixies. Winston was startled by their appearance.

"Suppose we can't eat him now." He heard one say.

"Maybe later we shall feast, but not now. Not now." Came the reply. He had heard those voices before. Atop the cottage. These were the same pixies that were plotting against him when he was resting on the platform. *Oh joy, they found him.*

Winston chuckled to himself. He could see clearly now why he hadn't noticed them previously. They couldn't be more than a few inches tall. The two pixies flew up and around him, assessing his condition.

"These clothes are not for him." One said.

"Surely not. Look at him." Replied the other.

"He is stiff looking."

"And also pudgy." The other said, poking his side.

"Hey!" Winston said. "What do you want with me."

The pixies rose, floating in a spinning rotation around his head and shoulders.

"Get dressed." One said.

"Yes. Dressed. Get dressed. You have guests waiting." The other said.

"Guests?" He replied.

"Enough of that. Enough of that. Pot, Kettle, do as told." Came

Shoma's voice from the turning of her pages.

Before Winston could voice his concern, the pixies were on the move. The room was a wisp of energy as the pixies pulled out garments, and dressed Winston in each article of clothing. A process Winston found himself appreciating as he used to struggle with his dress uniform, and there was no way he would do this costume any justice without instruction, or at least help. Minimal effort was needed by Winston, this was all a flow for him. They lifted, moved, adjusted, and positioned him together and separately, while sliding on, and fastening down his apparel. The entire experience seemed to happen in a breath. As soon as they started, they were done.

"Thank... Thank you." Winston said, looking down at himself.

"Now we eat?" Said one pixie.

"Yes. We eat."

"Wait." Winston said in protest. "I thought you said..."

"The dinner. The dinner. They must take you to dinner." Shoma said, looking up from the book she had been writing in. "Very nice. Very nice. You'll blend right in. Now go."

The pixies led the way, murmuring to themselves the whole time. The hallways were broad, ceilings rose to staggering heights, and yet there seemed to be very little echo from their noise. Various paintings and mirrors adorned the walls. Lots of mirrors. Which seemed odd to Winston. Why have so many mirrors in a corridor, and not small mirrors either, some were easily eight feet tall.

"Which of you is Pot, and which is Kettle?" Winston asked as they walked.

The pixies turned to look at him.

"He's Pot, I'm Kettle." Said the one on the right.

"No. I'm Pot, and he's Kettle." Contested the other.

Winston thought to clarify and decided to drop the matter. The one who claimed to be Pot wore a vest of some kind, while Kettle had a tunic and arm bracers. That was all the more Winston could make out, they were simply too small to study while moving. He figured they likely always went in a pair and he'd be wise to address them simultaneously. That is if he ever had to. As far as he knew, where they were going could be the last place Winston would ever go.

"Where are you taking me?" He asked, not expecting a clear answer.

"To eat." Kettle said.

"To eat." Repeated Pot almost at the same time.

"I know that, but you said something about guests?"

"Guests, true."

"They wait for you."

"But who?" Winston paused, wincing at the rhyme.

"The Queen and court."

"Though not all attend."

"She prepares a night for you."

"Before all things end."

"What?" Winston said. "What is ending?"

"This way." Came one voice, Kettle again, Winston thought.

"This way." Came the other.

Wide double doors slowly opened in front of Winston. He hadn't been paying attention to their environment as they moved along, and hadn't seen where they were or how they got there. Vibrant cold lights shimmered and danced through the air as the doors opened. *Were those more pixies, or tricks of the eyes?* Shades of blue, purple, green, and white swayed to and fro, back and forth, like a wildly timed synchronized performance. Winston stood there, staring at the ceiling, mesmerized.

Someone's hand gently touched his arm. "Good to see ye up and moving about." Said the smooth, familiar voice.

Michael stood next to him, also in a new outfit. Not the same as Winston's. They were similar in cut, but different in color, and pattern.

"Michael? What the hell is going on here, man?" Winston asked.

"I know. I know. It will all be explained." Michael assured him. "First we need to get through dinner."

"I've been a prisoner here for I don't know how long. Now they have me in this fancy suit, or whatever it is, and you expect me to simply sit for dinner? Are you out of your mind?"

"Aye, I know. I know. But ye weren't no prisoner. They were tending ye. Healing you up for what's to come."

"What's to come?"

"Presently? Food." Michael smiled, wrapping his arm about Winston. "I'll be telling ye now. Don't eat anything that changes color, or smells of mint."

"Mint?"

"Aye, trust me. You'd live, but you'd wish ye hadn't."

Michael led them out from the end of the room and into a sea of laughing and smiling faces. Though that's using the term 'faces' in its most general sense. All around them was a cacophony of appearances. Some faces were like that of animals; dogs, cats, wolves, and bears. Winston even saw one he would have sworn was a bat. There were guests who looked like they stepped directly out of a Hollywood produced fairy tale, and others out of a nightmare.

Winston took it all in; the sights, the smells, the sounds, and stayed close to Michael. They traversed the floor and made their way to an area of the room that was raised like an island apart from the main floor. Upon it were tables for sitting and eating. It was then that Winston heard the music playing. It was soft, orchestral, and familiar. Like a song you'd play for a baby, he thought.

"Have a seat, Winston." Michael said, pulling out a chair for him.

They sat, both at the same table, Michael to Winston's right. Others began to join them. The table filled up smoothly, seating what appeared to be upwards of 40 people. They were all in their own form of dress attire. Formal, clean, and ornamented. With what he'd seen so far, Winston found himself guessing at who these characters may profess to be. Surely not characters though. No, this was real. He was here, and this was happening to him. Nonetheless he gave way to speculation. In his mind he ran through every legend, fairytale, and myth he knew; looking for details that would connect a character of legend, to a guest at this table.

"Trying to figure it out, aren't you?" Michael asked.

Michael was right, he was trying to figure it out. How could you not? Growing up Winston was surrounded by characters mythological tales or lore. From Disney to the Grimm brothers, there was no shortage of tales to stir and fantasize a young mind. Here Winston was sitting among these figures of Faerie that were the living personification, and likely the inspiration for those tales, he knew.

Across from him, seated a man dressed all in white. Not a flat tone, as differing shades of white fabrics, with hints of light grey, made up his attire. His robust beard moved with his jaw as he spoke. Winston couldn't hear the conversation he was in, yet occasionally he picked up on the man's laugh. It was a warm, jovial tone. Winston couldn't stop watching him.

"Staring isn't polite." She said as she sat in the chair to his left. Mhara looked radiant in her weaved dress of deep blues, greens, and purple.

"Your dress looks like the ocean." Winston said, trying to suppress his surprise in seeing her.

"Thank you; I think." Mhara replied with a coy smirk.

"Is everyone here?" Winston asked.

"Aye, though you'll not be seeing Fionn and his men in the great hall." Michael said.

"What the hell is going on?" Winston asked. "The last thing I remember we were getting attacked by your old guards. One of them almost killed me."

"Almost." Mhara said in a matter of fact tone.

"I don't know how ye lived." Michael added. "He broke you up pretty good."

"I hadn't noticed." Winston quipped. "Seriously guys. I've trusted you this far. Now we're in the middle of what looks to be a banquet dinner, with all manner of creatures and things. I feel like all I keep getting is more questions, and no answers."

"Perhaps I can help." Came a voice so smooth, calm, and deep that you'd think it could calm a storm. Winston looked back toward Michael, the direction which the voice originated. Standing behind him was the man in white. Winston could see now that he was wearing a style of robes, layered, and wrapped over and within themselves.

"Here, your majesty, allow me to move." Michael offered.

Your majesty? Winston thought. It was only then that he noticed the staff, as the great man leaned the staff against the table as he accepted Michael's seat.

"I'm sorry." Winston began.

"For what, dear boy? You've done so well, thus far. Unexpectedly so." The man in white said.

"He called you, your majesty."

"He did, didn't he." The man in white said, looking to Michael. "He can be a smidge over dramatic with his formalities." He said with a smile. "I am Myrddin. It's a pleasure to meet you finally, Winston."

"Myrddin?" Winston said, processing this new piece of information. "As in Merlin, the King of Faerie?"

"Oh come now. Myrddin will service our discord just fine. No need for titles and formalities." Myrddin replied jovially.

Winston couldn't balance it all out. This was all becoming too much. Where was his structure? He found himself grasping for focus, for orders, for meaning behind what he was doing, and what needed to happen next. Sweat formed upon his head, an odd feeling in a room that looked like a frozen castle. He felt a hand gently touch his shoulder.

"Calm yourself. You no doubt have questions, and we will do our best to resolve them for you. I too have questions; things I would very much enjoy discussing with you." Myrddin said.

Servers began walking about the tables, setting food down, and filling drinks. The music softened for a moment and then rose to a crescendo. The entire tables populace rose to their feet around Winston. He pulled himself up and looked toward the source of attention.

She stood atop a set of stairs, lovely, powerful, and much like she appeared in the room when she visited Winston while he was healing. The Queen of Winter, Bheur, descended, and took her position at the head of the table. After she sat she motioned for the assembled to also take their seats.

"Looks like we're all here." Winston heard Michael say on the other side of Myrddin.

"Mmmmm.. It would appear that way." Myrddin said in reply.

Winston spoke quietly to the King of wizards and Faerie. "You're right. I do have questions."

"I know, boy. I know."

"But what questions could you possibly have of me? I'm nobody special. I'm an ex-army grunt who works as a security officer for a tech development company in Farmington, Minnesota, and I see a therapist regarding my PTSD. What could you possibly want to know that I could tell you?" Winston asked.

A server placed a plate of food in front of Winston. The aroma of it pulled on his senses, beckoning him to dig in. For the briefest moment Winston had forgotten he had even asked Myrddin a question. That was until the great man's voice came to his ear.

"Your perception of special, and my perception of special, may be vastly different." He said. "As for what I'd like to discuss with you." Myrddin took a drink from his cup. "I want to talk to you about a great many things. Starting with your parents, the Reaper, and the Queen of Winter."

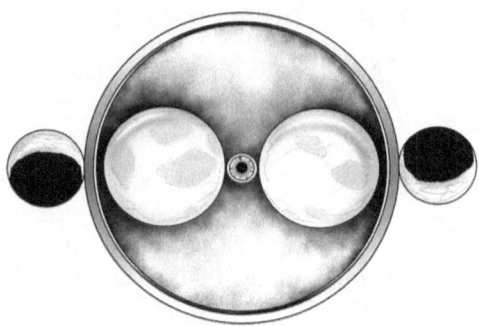

12 – QUESTIONS AND OBFUSCATION

Before

"What were your parent's like?"

"My parents?"

"Yes. Were they kind? Strict? Patient? Severe?"

"Try absent."

"Interesting. How so?"

"They weren't around. I never knew them." Winston said, looking away from her, and focused on the wall. He picked at the seams of his pants. "There isn't any of this in my file?"

The counselor, Ms. White, sat looking at Winston. As she was wont to do. She seemed to think that looking at him would somehow change the answer. It wouldn't, but Winston couldn't fault her for her optimism.

What Winston struggled with most was the utter lack of information she seemed to have about him, or his life. Perhaps he was giving the military a bit too much credit, but he thought for a certainty that a VA assigned PTSD counselor would have been briefed on these basic facts about his life.

"What is your earliest memory?" Asked Ms. White.

The question pulled at Winston's mind. He hadn't thought about his childhood in quite some time. In fact, the thought that he was ever a child was an almost amusing concept. Was he ever really a child? It was a challenging effort, to live every day with the memories of lives lost either in front of you, or because of you, and still hold on to the glow of childhood.

"I don't really remember my childhood." Winston finally said.

"Hmm.. Interesting."

"What?"

"I didn't ask about your childhood."

"Yes you did." Winston insists.

Ms. White smiled. Her hand actively recording more notes. Winston had never known anyone who could listen well and record notes like the councilor did. She didn't miss a beat, or detail. Though he felt she still would have benefited from doing more research into his life prior to their first meeting.

"How do you not know some of these things?" Winston asked.

"What things, Winston?"

"These things. The stuff about me, my childhood, my history. I would think for sure that you'd have been briefed on me prior to our sessions starting."

"Would that have helped you trust me?"

"What does that have to do with anything?"

"Everything." Ms. White said. "This process is pointless if I cannot earn your trust."

"Tell me the truth." Winston said.

"What truth?"

"You want my trust?" Winston asked. "Tell me the truth. Don't try to lead me like a puppy who needs to get outside to do their business." Ms. White began nodding her head, encouraging Winston to continue. "If trust is a goal here, let's be clear." Winston continued. "I didn't ask to be here. They sent me here. The same faceless leaders who sent me to Texas. The same ones who sent me into war. Who got Sam killed. I was ordered to be here as a facet of my honorable discharge. So I'm here." Winston's voice raises and his hands begin flowing through the air as if he were conducting a musical performance. He pauses to take a breath. "You want trust, I'm here. You want my trust? Stop bullshitting me with leading questions and get to the point. You know what you know. I've come to three of these sessions, I have no interest in another if it is going to be more of the same."

Their eyes met, and seemed to suck all other sensory information from the room. "Ok." Ms. White said.

"Ok." Winston said, standing, he reached for his jacket and moved as if to leave.

"You're an orphan," Ms White said, keeping her eyes on a now still Winston. "A product of the system. You successfully avoided jail time in your youth, though you were not void of all trouble, and you sought salvation in the army. Mr. Palmer, your high school social worker prompted you to enlist, and helped you get everything together with the plan for you to attend school after you were done. I know how many kills you have credited to you, and your weapon proficiencies. I've read your CO's log about your performance appraisals, and their comments on your current status. And now we are here."

"Where is that exactly?"

"That will depend upon you." She said. "It could be seen as an end, a beginning, Whatever this proves to be will rest upon the choices you make and the actions you take." Ms. White set her notepad down, and looked keenly at Winston. "Let me ask you a question I absolutely do not have the answer to."

"Go ahead."

"What kind of man do you want to be?"

"I'm a soldier."

"You were. Now you're a civilian. What I'm asking you is if you could be anything, what kind of man would Winston choose to make himself?"

***

Now

Time is the great resource. We have only the time we have, and yet its value is determined through application, rather than simple possession. No matter how we use it, we have no guarantee that we will receive more. Everything requires time from us, and nothing can add time to us. We view time in such abundance that we sort it by weeks, months, and years. We speak of generations, and lifetimes, and what we will do next. Yet the only time we ever know we have is the time we are actively experiencing, and according to scientists, the time our brains are acknowledging has already passed. If this is the case, what time do we even have?

Theories exist that time is a plane we can traverse, bend, and twist about with wibbly wobbly ways. There are even those who view time as some kind of god that tick tocks by, Father Time in cahoots with Death, as they both sit playing chess, waiting for our time to come, and for all we know to come to an end.

Then there are moments where time seems to be all but absent from our experience. We sit captivated and entranced, engaged and invested up to our eyes in a single moment that in and of itself can seem to last forever. There is no exhaustion. No pull on our attention, beckoning us to look away at our phone, or to check a clock. We simply are alive in this scene and remain committed to it as it runs its course.

Winston sat at the banquet feeling exactly this. Moment after moment, and though he knew so much had happened, he had no perception of how much time had passed. In truth he had lost a clear idea of time since waking up on that stone table. Yet here he was thoroughly entranced and unlike on the table where he knew time was passing by without him, here he felt like time no longer mattered. He was enjoying himself far too much.

What started as a formal dinner, naturally evolved into a parade of events. Attendees continued to dance on the main floor. Some participated in displaying feats of strength and skill. Flashes of light and sound flowed about the room, and those at the table ate as if there were nothing amiss. Winston couldn't keep his eyes to himself as the spectacle continued.

"Mind your view." Mhara said.

"Hmm?" Winston replied, not turning to look at her.

"You would be wise to mind who you look upon. Lest you give

the wrong person a reason to pay attention to you." She said, noticing Winston wasn't listening. She pulled on his arm. "Did you hear me, Winston?"

He turned to look at her. His sight flexed as his eyes adjusted to the change in the light. Like moving from looking out over a sunny summer day, to going inside a dim, shadowed room. Who knew an aerial display of winter illusions would shine so bright. "Yes." Winston said. "I'm listening to you."

"What did I say?" Mhara asked.

"You asked how my food was."

"No, you fool. I told you to mind your view."

"Why? What are you talking about?"

"Everyone is here under a certain pretense. Don't let that allow you to think that everyone here is friendly."

"I'm sure they're not." Winston said out of the corner of his mouth as he took another bite of food.

"You can also be certain that given the opportunity they will easily allow you to become part of the spectacle. Faeries are selfish at their core. Deceitful, mischievous, and as keen toward entertainment as they are toward anything of value." Mhara released Winston's arm and leaned close so only he could hear her. "They all know about you in one form or another. Best not to give them an excuse to engage you. Focus on your meal, and keep your eyes to yourself. You should be safe."

"Why are they so interested in me? Because I'm human?" He asked, looking directly at Mhara. Their eyes held each other for a long moment. Her beauty was enough to make him forget about every other sight he'd seen that evening. Yet in her eyes lingered something more than he could properly comprehend. Her lips slowly parted as she let out a breath.

"They're interested in you for the parts of you that aren't."

"What?" Winston asked, shocked. The part of him that isn't what? Isn't human? What is she playing at with this? Her eyes left him, turning back to her own meal.

"Trust me." She finally said. "I know a thing or two about the dangers of allowing others power over you. Keep your skin close, my mother would tell me. I'm telling you, Winston. Heed me on this. Keep your skin close."

The conversation was clearly over, and Winston was troubled. He was tired of guessing games and cryptic messages. He had the weight of his own questions pressing down upon him. The uncertainty of his ever getting home, not the least of them. It rested right next to the questionable correlation between the striking specimen of a woman sitting at the head of the table, the Queen of Winter, and her connection to his former councilor, Ms. White. How long had Faerie been mixed up in his life, and what in all things known did it have to do with his parents?

To his right sat a man of legend, of myth. He claimed to be Merlin, or Myrddin according to him. Was he the man Winston was familiar with? Arthur's Merlin? And like everything else on this adventure, things were threatening his well being, or they were leaving him with half-truths and partial information. Death, his parents, and the Queen of Winter. He listed them like they were already affiliated. Then packed them away for a conversation for later.

This dinner needed to come to an end. The pacification of spectacle no longer lingered warmly upon his senses like a familiar blanket. Instead it itched at him like a dry wool sweater directly upon his skin.

"My Queen!" trumpeted a voice to Winston's right. What was this old man up to now?

Winston looked to Myrddin, who himself was looking to his right. It wasn't him? He looked past the wisps of the old wizard King's beard toward the source of the words.

The caller rose above the seated ones like a vulture sores above its meal. His figure was draped with the skins of animals, and ornamented with their bones. His helm was the skull of a vicious looking beast whose teeth were so long they now rested upon the upper part of the caller's chest. Most troubling was the ever more apparent reality that he was the only attendant in the room that openly carried a weapon.

With a smooth stroke he lifted his axe of bone and stone, a large flowing blade on one face, the other a stumped hammerhead. It swung through the air and came down upon the table with great calamity directly in front of Winston, Myrddin, Mhara, and Michael. The Queen looked on with a stoic expression, saying nothing.

"Forgive the interruption, Queen Bheur." The voice continued. "This charade has continued long enough." The room was quiet and focused on his words. "Summer is in turmoil. Whispers are the staff was stolen. We all know by who. And here you sit, forbidding me my hunt. How long until Jonathan comes for the sword?" The man turned, speaking to the audience. "How long before we suffer as Summer does? Does our Queen care? I beg an answer to this question from you now, mighty Queen. What shall Winter do? Does your realm still matter to you? As you sit here at a feast. Oh and not just any feast." He turned toward Winston, who turned his eyes toward Mhara. "No, not just any

feast. As we are playing host to wizards! King Myrddin himself is here."
The warrior gestured towards the wizard. "And he didn't come alone.
No. We have Jonathan's known accomplice, and the one who set them
free!"

Winston swallowed, and kept his eyes down. Mhara held his arm
gently.

"What do you want?" came the voice of the Queen. Strong,
warm, and sure.

"I want blood!" He yelled. "I want to fight. I do not want to live
in a Winter that waits, but in one that moves upon her enemies."

"You interrupt my feast for this? The tirade of a child?"

"The wizard's rule of Faerie must end. Before we suffer as
Summer does. I will have my blood. Tonight." His voice growled like
low thunder. The attendees stirred. Muttering to themselves and looking
to each other. "My Queen, as your loyal servant, I ask you for this."

"Ask?"

"Give me the one called Winston."

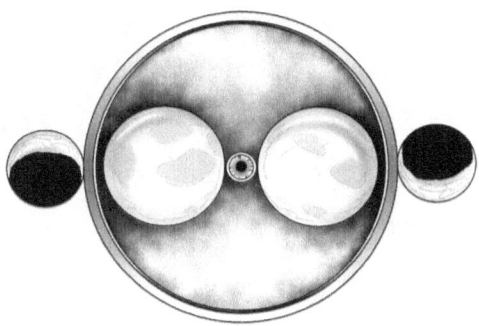

13 – THE HOUND

Cú Roí, the Hound they called him, seethed like a covered pot brought to boil, quiet, calm, yet churning, and building with pressure readying to be overcome by their own selves. He waited, leaning against the far wall. The Hound's eyes glowed in a subtle flame of hunger as they stared down Winston. They reminded Winston of how a dog's eyes might show in the dim light of the evening. The warm orange-green tone was haunting to behold as the room quietly vacated.

The Queen excused all but those affected by the Hound's request. Servants removed the concave table, and chairs as well. Michael, and Mhara stood with Winston against the wall that was behind where they had been sitting. The Hound waited adjacent to them, his breathing heavy, and his chin seemed to reflect slightly in the cool light. Was he drooling?

Myrddin spoke with the Winter Queen at the far end of the

room. Their quiet, yet impassioned conversation was impossible to ignore, and just as impossible to follow. The Hound hadn't expounded further upon his request. For all they knew, he wanted Winston due to harmful intent, as much as he may want to buy him ice cream. Though with the accessory he brought with him to the feast, and placed through the queen's table, this was likely not a moment of peaceful intent.

"What is his angle?" Winston asked no one in particular.

"Whoever knows with the Hound. He's more animal than anything else." Michael said. "He's never cared for wizards. Not since the mandate was instituted, that is. Doubt he paid much attention to us before then."

"Why is that?"

"Before the mandate, he could hunt humans." Mhara added. "In their realm."

The thought sent an involuntary shudder through Winston. He'd looked down the path of death in his life. His reaction wasn't a matter of being scared in that way. There's a difference between facing down gunfire and attacks from enemy combatants, and looking down the predatory gaze of a creature that sees you as what... food?

"What is the mandate you keep mentioning?" Winston asked.

"Ages ago the realm of Faerie regularly spilled over to the realm of men. The legends, lore, and many religions of your world were the product of Faerie's involvement in the lives of men." Michael said. "Not all involvement was beneficial or inspirational. Some were pure terror and torment. The Hound, and his companions, regularly sought the blood of humans. In the wild hunt, the nights of hollow, and other times for their amusement alone."

"How was that allowed?" Winston asked.

"It wasn't allowed, as much as it simply happened." Michael said. "It also was not governed against."

"That's ridiculous."

"Is it?" Mhara asked. Winston gave her a look. "Do you find it ridiculous to harvest the meat of animals for food? Or to hunt for sport?"

"That's not the same." Winston said.

"To these ones, it is." She said. "In the eyes of those like the Hound, humans are but game to run down and acquire."

"As with many things in life, Winston, it comes to a matter of perspective." Michael said. "Humans are not simple animals to be toyed with and harvested, and there were those among them who stood up. Some on their own, and some with the aid of others in Faerie itself. The greatest of these proved to be Arturus of Britannia."

"Arturus?"

"Your people know him best as King Arthur."

"Damn. He was real?"

"Correction. He is real." Michael said. "That is a different tale, however. But yes. Arturus was very real, and though not originally a king, he was a great leader. Many of mankind had stood to ward off the threats from Faerie throughout time, only Arturus organized an actual assault on Faerie itself."

"What happened?" Winston asked.

"Arturus, along with a battalion of his knights infiltrated Annwn, an area of our realm of humans called the Otherworld. They fought their way through Annwn until they stood at the gates of Myrddin and Queen Morgana's castle. Myrddin went out to meet the conquering warriors at his gates. Arturus demanded a parlay with the

King of Faerie, not knowing Myrddin himself was king." Michael paused. "Much like there is a Seelie court of Summer, and the Unseelie of Winter, Faerie is split between the wizard Queen and King. This allows them to make certain choices alone, and other choices must be made together. Arturus was here to stop Faerie from ever interfering with the realm of men again, and this was not a change the King could make alone. Queen Morgana demanded trial by combat in response to Arturus and his men infiltrating Faerie how they did. Myrddin acquiesced to her demands, if she in turn would allow him position of final judgement should they survive her trials. She agreed. The Queen was confident her warriors would destroy Arturus and his remaining men."

"That clearly didn't go her way." Winston said.

Mhara scoffed at that, and a smirk took her face. "Never underestimate Morgana." She said.

"But the mandate. How could that be instituted if they lost?" Winston asked.

"You're making assumptions, boy." Michael said. "Arturus and his men were gathered and set to face a series of champions selected by the queen. They entered the contest numbered in the hundreds. As the blood dried on the field, Arturus lived. He and ten of his knights remained. The contest lasted for days, and if not for Myrddin having placed limitations on Morgana's efforts she'd have seen every soul she could sacrificed to Arturus' ambition until the last of his men had fallen."

"Shit. Only eleven survived out of hundreds?" Winston asked.

"Aye." Michael said. "It was after this that Myrddin instituted the Arthurian Mandate, effectively limiting the ability of those of Faerie to enter the realm of man, and more importantly, limiting their ability to interfere in the lives of men. Myrddin also charged Arturus and his ten surviving knights with protection of the realm of man. To this day they live, and police the activities of those of Faerie in their realm."

"Arthur is still alive? Still?"

"Aye, lives in Britannia still." Michael said. "Forgive me. Britain. He and his knights yet live. This has not stopped Morgana and her minions from continuing their meddling with the lives of man. It has only made their efforts more insidious. The mandate has however had a dramatic effect on the activities of characters such as our friend the Hound over there. It isn't easy for a creature such as the Hound to enter the realm of man undetected. He's had his run-ins with the knights, and now thinks twice before hunting men. All this makes your presence here all the more enticing to him."

"I'll need a weapon." Winston said.

"What?" Mhara exclaimed in surprise. "Surely you do not intent to engage with him."

"What choice will I have? For all I know Merlin is over there plotting my surrender with the Queen of Winter. I'm a soldier. If I'm going to go, I'm going down with a weapon in my hand." Winston stood up, passion flooding his body. He turned to Michael. "I'm about done with all this bullshit as it stands. I didn't ask to be here. Still I helped you escape. I've played along with your plans, and tolerated all the cryptic conversations, and now we're here." Winston turned toward the Hound. "As far as I'm concerned, if there needs to be blood, there will be blood. Let me know what the plan is, give me a weapon and we can do this!"

Across the room the shadowed face of the Hound moved. Was that a smile? His form lifted. The Hound stepped forward, his axe hammer dragging behind him as his long single stride pulled him into the light. The bones of his armor rattled, and he looked directly at Winston.

"The pup has spirit." He growled. "It's been a long moon since I tasted the blood of a tested warrior."

"Keep drooling, Hound." Winston said.

"Step back." Michael said, stepping up next to Winston.

"Do not think you are outside my reach, wizard." The Hound said. He took another step. "Mmmm. What is that?" Closing his eyes, the Hound extended his head, sniffing the air. He moved his head throughout the space in front of him, following the aroma, until he was again facing directly at Winston. An evil smile stretched slowly across his face. "The tales are true then. You are a child touched by Death. The old fool."

Winston involuntarily stepped back. This again. What was he supposed to do with this? Is that really why he was the only one in his unit to remain unharmed? Or was it more than that? What he knew with certainty is he was not dying here. He'd be walking out of here and getting the answers to his questions. Even if that meant getting those answers from Death himself.

"Enough." Every head turned to her. How could a voice so powerful be so calm and warm? With one word she cut the tension and took control back in a room on the edge of mayhem.

"My Queen?" Said the Hound.

"Are you loyal to me, Cú Roí?" She asked the menacing creature, using his true name, with soft comfort and affection. Her words were like a February snowfall in Minnesota. So comforting and beautiful, and yet if you were to fall beneath them their weight could crush you as easily as the cold of winter could take your life. "Are you of winter, or do you stand in obfuscation?"

"Huh?" The Hound said, confused. "My Queen?"

"Am I?" She said. Stopping between them, and turning to the Hound. "I am Queen. Am I yours?"

"Yes, your highness."

"You broke my table." Her tone cold and hard. "You brought a weapon into my home. You interrupted my feast. You threatened guests of Winter. For what?"

"He shouldn't be here." He said, gesturing towards Winston.

"You decide these things now? Are you King?" She didn't wait for his response. "Your actions dishonor Winter. They dishonor me. Regardless of the validity of your contention, my hall, my feast, my home is not the place for your claims to be made."

The Hound lowered his head, stepping back, a low growl escaping his lips. Much like a shamed dog yielding to the judgment of their master, he was subject to his queen and he knew it. Myrddin stood apart from the group, watching the Hound keenly. Who only peeked through his brow toward Winston.

"Forgive me, my Queen." He finally said.

"Return to your place and await me. We will conclude this momentarily."

"What of them?" He asked.

"My guests are not your concern."

The Hound thrust his maw toward Winston. His fierce speed moving the air around them. Winston didn't move. Standing firm as the Hound rushed to within a pixie's wingspan of his face.

"Be wary, pup." The Hound growled in his deep, full voice.

"Not all paths from Winter are safe."

"I'll be seeing you, Hound." Winston said, his eyes locked with the Hound's. "Now go be a good dog, and lay down."

The Hound growled deep and loud, baring his teeth, and then stopped. The change in demeanor was sharp and abrupt. The queen had placed a hand upon him. Not grasping. Not angry. Simply rested her hand upon him.

"Go." She said softly. "Now."

The Hound lowered his eyes, retrieved his weapon, and exited the room without another word. Winston could feel the tension lower in the room, and heard Mhara exhale behind him. He looked toward the queen who was watching the Hound leave.

"Are you who I think you are." Winston asked her.

"I am more than you can comprehend, Winston Bas." Queen Bheur said plainly, not looking at him.

"Please, your Highness." He said. "I'd like one clear answer."

She turned to look at him. Her eyes soft. Her lips hinting at a smile. "You need to trust yourself. Much can be deceiving. Your instincts do you justice." She said. "Such as how you handled the Hound. He is a hunter. Your choice to directly address him was wise. You robbed him of fear. He was held back because of it. Even with me here. He would not have initiated an attack until he sensed fear in you."

"Thank you." Winston said, assuming this would be the best answer she would give him.

"Thank you, Winston." She said.

"For what?"

"For showing me honor." She said. He nodded in understanding. "It's not often I am recognized without my glasses." She said, as she smiled and turned away. "Now come, each of you. Myrddin and I are in agreement. There is work to be done." The Queen looked to Winston. "And answers to be given." She continued walking.

Mhara and Michael followed without question. Winston paused in recognition. He had been right. She was his councilor, his confidant for those many months. A woman who likely knew him better than most was now beckoning him to join her in conference, as the Queen of Winter. He felt a hand on his shoulder.

"Come now, son. We have much to discuss, and precious little time." Myrddin said.

"I can't believe it's her."

"I imagine this revelation is great." The old wizard said assuredly. "I also fear it may only be the beginning."

"What do you mean?" Winston asked, looking up at the king. He was so tall.

"Winston." He began. "You're being here is as much by chance as it isn't."

"That doesn't make sense."

"Listen to me, son." Myrddin said, taking on a serious tone. "In order for a creature of Faerie to open a door as Jonathan did, and go into the realm of man, there needs to be a balance."

"Right. I think Michael mentioned something like that. That's why I'm here and he's there."

"It's more than soul for soul." He continued. "It also is the kind of soul that matters."

"What does that mean?"

"As a part of the mandate we agreed to certain limitations that keep those of Faerie from easily going into the realm of man. And vice

119

versa." Myrddin said. "One of these limitations affects direct infiltration. No one can enter the other realm directly without setting off a kind of alarm. Jonathan needed to go into the realm of men and not be followed. In order to do that he needed another soul, like his, to trade places with him in this realm, to balance the scales."

"And Michael told me that wizards are the offspring of the fey and humans."

"Correct."

"So you're saying…" Winston's head began to spin as the pieces snapped into place. He felt Myrddin's hand more firmly grasp his shoulder.

"Come now, son." Said the wizard King. "We must join the others."

Myrddin began to walk, Winston watch him go. His mind flushed with understanding, and confusion. Questions yelled inside him. Then his inner soldier reinstated himself, and he began to walk, following his King as they headed to speak with the Queen of Winter.

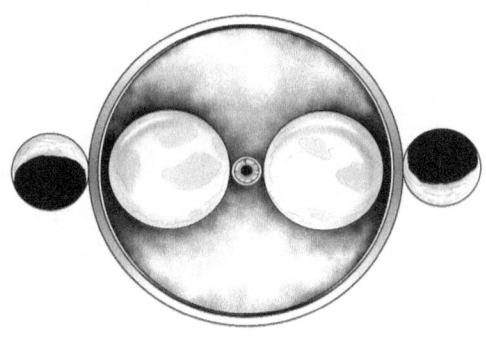

14 – KNOWLEDGE AND GIFTS

"Explain yourselves." Her voice carried the same full, warm, familiar tone that Winston knew, yet in this chamber it rang out with commanding authority. The Queen of Winter looked across the faces of all assembled, her eyes hard and expecting. When her eyes met Winston's there was a soft hint of understanding. She looked back toward Michael. He sat lackadaisical in a chair against the wall, not seeming to feel any stress in the present circumstances. "You ought to be the one to explain I should think." She said to Michael. "You were a prisoner, were you not?"

"Aye. I was." Michael replied casually, picking at the arm of the chair he occupied.

"Quite a fortunate circumstance, I'd say. Your King is here, wizard," Queen Bheur said, motioning at Merlin, "in accord with our laws. Why don't you enlighten me on why you are in Winter, why you have a Selkie with you, and give me a good reason not to imprison you myself."

"John of Nottingham escaped the bonds of Summer, and is in pursuit of Summer's scepter, as well as the Sword of Darkfyre." Michael began.

"This is known to me, wizard."

Winston stirred in his seat. How would she respond to the truth, that they were here to steal the sword? This woman before him, if she could be called a woman, was both the same woman he knew and someone new to him. Would she show the patience and understanding he remembered from his sessions with Ms. White, or would she wield her Queenly power drastically upon them?

"Of course, your majesty." Michael continued. "I was charged to stay close to Jonathan. To watch him, track him, and report back to Myrddin." The Queen looked to the old King, and he nodded in affirmation. "When we became fully aware of what Jonathan was seeking, he and I were already in the custody of Summer. I was not able to reveal my true role. After Jonathan escaped, and Winston here was trapped in his place, my only concern became getting Winston home, and stopping Jonathan by any means."

"Why are you here?" The Queen asked again, placing strong emphasis on her last word.

Michael adjusted himself to a more respectable position in his seat, looking at the Queen squarely. "We came into Winter, to steal the Sword of Darkfyre."

The words rolled out, and his eyes never left hers. The air in the room became consumed by a still chill. Stronger and more defined than the cool crispness that seemed to come with being in Winter.

"Say again, wizard."

"According to the legend Jonathan uncovered, it would take the power of both the scepter and the sword to do what he wants to do." Michael cleared his throat. "In an effort to thwart Jonathan's quest we came here to possess the sword before he could."

"You thought your best course was to steal from me." The Queen said, as a statement rather than a question, her voice hard and sharp.

Winston looked to his left, responding to a quiet crackling sound on the floor. Ice was webbing out and moving toward Michael's chair. He looked up, thinking to warn his friend, who he was surprised to see was sitting comfortably as if no threat existed. As Winston prepared to move he saw Myrddin step forward from where he was standing against the wall across from him.

"If I may." The wizard King's voice came out in an inquisitive flutter, as if he had no perception on the events transpiring. "Pardon. Perhaps we would do best in planning how we can better thwart Jonathan's efforts. Together. Don't you think?"

The crackling stopped near the legs of Michael's chair, and the Queen looked to the aged King. Her demeanor secure, not showing any evidence of the interruption that Merlin's words clearly caused. She stood, looking back to Michael.

"Myrddin is wise, and correct." She began. "Before we continue, I would ask that you acknowledge this, wizard. You are not of Winter, not by lineage or loyalty, and you draw no power here. Though we still remain in Faerie, you will not enjoy the full breadth of your powers here should you try to use them."

"Aye, your majesty speaks truth. I am not." His tone demure

and his skin looked pale with his words.

"Should you return to Winter after these matters are resolved, you will be subject to my judgement, and no effort to draw upon your magic will save you here." She looked to Merlin. "Do we understand each other?"

The Wizard King nodded once.

"Aye." Michael said.

The Queen turned her back to Michael, looking out a cascading wall of windows upon the now dark landscape of Winter. The room remained in a hush. The awkward discomfort moving among them as a dance performer.

"How do we stop him?" Winston asked. She didn't turn, but Winston could swear he saw a smile move across the Queen's face. "From what the Hound said, Jonathan got his hands on the scepter." He continued. "He'll want the sword."

"Aye, he will."

"Michael explained to me, that with both items, Jonathan believes he can retain his abilities, unbound by Faerie. I've been thinking about this, and it cannot be a good plan." Winston said.

"Very astute." Myrddin said.

"What would happen?"

"There are many powers throughout the realms of Faerie and man. We give them many names." Myrddin explained. "Gravity, electricity, magic, they all have their place, and they serve towards the balance of our words. If Jonathan were to be successful, his actions would impact that balance."

"To what end?"

"No one knows for a certainty." Myrddin stepped toward

Winston. "Imagine a balancing scale, weights placed on either side. Now imagine that one side's weights turn to mist in an instant."

"The scale would topple."

"Such could be the fate of our worlds, if Jonathan is successful." Myrddin said solemnly.

"Do we know where he is?" The Queen asked.

"No." Michael said solemnly.

"Michael, you're sure his plan requires the sword?" Winston asked.

"Aye, completely."

"Then we keep it from him."

"It may not be so simple. He has the scepter. That alone gives him great power, especially against Winter."

"This is true." The Winter Queen confirmed.

"Won't the Summer court be after Jonathan?" Winston asked.

"Perhaps." Myrddin said. "They suffered a mighty blow when he took the scepter, as he had help. Also Summer is not in their power. The solstice has passed and Winter reigns, both in your world Winston, and here."

"Ah. Fascinating."

"Is it?" The Queen of Winter asked.

"I never correlated the two in that way." Winston said.

"As Myrddin explained, there is always a balancing of the powers within our realms, and between then."

"Very interesting." Winston mused. "So with Jonathan being in possession of the scepter, and the solstice passing, all of these circumstances leave Summer vulnerable?"

"Yes." Myrddin confirmed. "Vulnerable, and not likely to

expose themselves further by pursuing Jonathan outside of their lands. That isn't to say they are weak. Make no mistake, Summer is volatile and we can be sure Jonathan is no longer within their boundaries."

"Right. They won't further risk themselves by over extending resources. It makes sense to me." Winston said.

"Ever the soldier." Queen Bheur said fondly.

"Where would he go?" Mhara asked.

"That, my dear, is our true dilemma." Myrddin said.

"We may not know where he is, but do we have a way to get word to him?" Winston asked.

"Aye. I may have a way." Michael said.

Each of them turn toward Michael expectantly.

"Alright. Alright. We need to get to the Port of Hollows. There is a correspondent there, and in-between that we've used in the past. I may be able to use them to get word to him."

"Won't he know something is amiss? The last he saw you, you were still in chains, and he didn't do anything to try to help free you. Why would he believe you are contacting him…"

"He'll believe me. Trust me. Jonathan and I have too much between us. He'll not suspect a thing."

"Ok." Myrddin interjected. "Michael, you and Mhara gather the supplies you believe you'll need. I will collect Fionn and his legion and meet you at the Port of Hollows." He turned to the Queen. "Provided, this is pleasing to your majesty."

"It is. But what do we tell Jonathan to convince him to meet with us?"

"We promise him the sword." Winston interjected quickly.

"What?"

"All of Faerie knows we are here. Especially after the Hound's performance at the feast." Winston explained. "You already have real anger you can use, and all of this helps sell the story. He won't be able to resist."

The Queen traded looks with Myrddin. A quiet eternity passed between them. It felt to Winston as if there were a whole other dialogue happening and they were the only two who could hear it.

"Go, and prepare what you will need." The Queen finally said, never looking away from the old Wizards eyes.

Michael, Mhara, and Winston stood to leave, Myrddin's voice called out. "Winston, you stay." They all stopped, looking back. "Winston alone, if you will."

Winston looked to his companions. "It's okay. I'll catch up."

Michael and Mhara's foot falls faded down the corridor outside the Queen's chamber, leaving Winston alone with the Queen of Winter, and the King of Faerie. He found himself keenly aware of just how out of place he was, and how far from home he'd become.

"Sit, Winston." Said the Queen. He complied. "Certainly this is a great deal to process."

"Is this what we're doing now?" Winston interrupted.

"What would that be?"

"A therapy session? Are you Queen Bheur, or Ms. White?"

"Ah. I see." She acknowledged.

"Do you? I mean can you actually?" Winston's voice cracked with emotion. "You're the Queen of fuckin' Winter!"

"Winston." Myrddin said attempting to interject.

"Damnit!" Winston boomed. "How could either of you have any perception of what this is like for me?" He turned to look at

Myrddin. "How could either of you? Hell, you're the King of all of Faerie. You're a goddamned legend!"

"Winston." Myrddin repeated.

"Here's the thing I need you to grasp." Winston took a breath, and continued, emphasizing his words slowly. "I want to go home." He looked at them both hard, and firm, allowing the silence to fill the gaps between them.

"You are." The Queen said smoothly, as if his outburst has no effect on her at all.

"Am I?" He replied indignantly. "The only place I seem to be going is on a wild goose chase after some mad wizard. Because that's my life, right? I'm just a soldier fighting other people's wars." Winston slumped back against his chair, crossing his arms, and turning away from the both of them. He knew he needed to get his anger in check.

"No." She said, finally. "You're not going home." Winston looked at her, fierce and biting back a sharp comment. "You are home." She continued.

You are home. The words hit him heavier than he ever would have wanted them to. After the conversation with Myrddin, and Michael, all the evidence seemed to imply that his being in Faerie might be less of an accident than he had originally been led to believe. Hearing her plainly state the fact held a sharper ring than he was emotionally prepared for. It rang with the kind of truth you associate with statements like the sky is blue, water is wet, and girls will break your heart. You are home. What the hell was he supposed to do with that little nugget?

"You already knew?" she asked him inquisitively.

"I had an idea. Nothing concrete."

"Interesting."

"Winston and I began to touch on these details whilst at the feast." Myrddin added.

"I see."

"Where do we go from here?" Winston asked. "Assuming you're telling the truth, what am I supposed to do now?"

"Wouldn't you like to learn where you are from?" Asked the Queen.

"Do you know?" Winston asked, leaning forward. Moved deeply by unbridled interest, founded in a childhood of questions with few answers.

Bheur looked at Myrddin, who sat patiently, his hands intertwined in front of him. Once again they said nothing, and yet Winston felt as if volumes of information passed between them. Winston watched, and saw what seemed to be the end of their dialogue. Myrddin's head lowered, a soft smile teasing his lips, and he raised his eyes to meet Winston's.

"We cannot say with certainty." The Queen offered.

"What then?" Winston asked.

"You're unique, Winston. Most children of Faerie are known to us. Especially those living outside of Faerie. Young wizards, changelings, and the like. We know who they are, and often watch over them as they grow. Striving to be available should they start to display qualities of Faerie in the realm of man." The Queen stood, and walked to a corner cabinet as she continued to speak. "With you, outside of your parents, it appears only the King and I knew who you were. And only I knew where you are." She retrieved something from the cabinet. "Even with what I know, my knowledge is only partial."

"Why can't you ever give me direct answers?" Winston asked.

The Queen returned to her seat, setting a small object between her and Winston.

"What is this?" He asked.

"It is what answers I can give you."

"Which would be?"

"Direction, Winston."

"From a box?"

"Take it."

He picked it up. "What is it?"

"It was something I was sworn to give to you when the time came. All things considered, I may be delayed, and this time is as good as any other."

"What do I do with it?" He asked.

"You'll need to open it. You're the only one who can."

"Wait? What? What is this exactly?"

"A gift, Winston."

Winston looked down at the small box in his hands. It was tender, intricate, and beautiful. He looked up at the Queen. "Who is it from?"

Their eyes met, she looking deeply into his. Serene and true was her gaze in its comfortable familiarity. Emotions moved within her eyes that Winston was not ever used to seeing from her. As she spoke her, her voice was soft and full.

"It is from your mother."

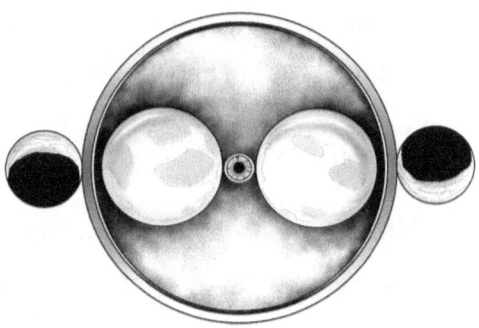

15 – USE THE KNIFE

Winston's skin tightened as if to hug his own body, craving its warmth, in response to the whimsical cold breeze in the courtyard. All of Winter was cold, and he had become accustomed to the brisk bite of the castle's climate. So much so that the breeze he felt while stepping outside into the courtyard beyond the Queen's chamber was affronting and sharp. As much of a contrast that it may be, it was also familiar to him. The wind against his skin drawing up memories of Minnesota winters.

Times playing boot hockey, snowmobiling, and even the one attempt he made of downhill skiing, all replayed in Winston's mind. The torment of a Minnesota snowstorm, and the bitter cold of the bone cutting wind that always seemed to wait patiently for you to get outside with a shovel to clear the drive came to mind. Winston found himself smiling at how pleasant his current environment was in comparison.

"It's practically shorts weather." He laughed to himself.

Walking out toward what appeared to be benches resting around a fountain, Winston couldn't help but appreciate the irony of a fountain installed in the courtyard of the Queen of Winter. Further observation showed him what he could only understand to be flowerpots, and areas where well-manicured bushes would reside in summer. Did summer come to the kingdom of Winter? The Queen didn't seem like one to have unnecessary details included in her personal space.

He seated himself at the far end of the fountain. There was a soft hum in the air from the breeze as it danced through the trees, moving its way through the property. The world around Winston rested in shades of blue and purple, with subtle illuminations courtesy of the fuller than normal moon hanging low in the night sky. The cold of the bench pressed aggressively into Winston as he leaned forward to look at the trinket in his hands.

The small box like object glimmered in his hands. To say it was a box doesn't do it justice, as it didn't seem to open, or even have corners to speak of. It was certainly not a sphere, as it had clearly defined sides. Curving about the corners were intricately carved depictions of vines and foliage. What it was carved of eluded Winston. It didn't appear to be any wood that he was familiar with. More than a carving the object seemed to be cast, as if this were once a box wrapped in real vines that had been cast and molded into what it is now. Winston spun it in his hands, perplexed at what he was supposed to do with his mother's glorified paperweight.

"He keeps sitting there." Came a familiar voice.

"Quiet." Replied its expected companion. "Perhaps he'll die and we can eat him." Winston shook his head. Would these two find him any time he sat still for any period of time while in Faerie? This was certainly not a time where he desired to endure them at all.

"I'm not in the mood, you two." Winston called out, not knowing in which direction Pot and Kettle may be.

"He is never any fun."

"Never fun at all."

"None at all." The voice agreed as two small figures fluttered down in front of Winston.

"Were you sent to watch me?" He asked.

"Watch?" One asked.

"We do not watch. Silly human." Said the other.

Winston could not distinguish between Pot and Kettle, but he was sure these were the two pixies he found himself speaking to. Shaking his head in dismissal, Winston looked down at the object in his hands.

"What's that he has?"

"Can you hear its song? It's of the Lia Fáil."

"Yes, the Lia Fáil. The song is unmistakable."

"What are you two going on about?" Winston asked. One of the pixies reached toward the box shaped object. Winston pulled it away. "Hey now! Keep your hands to yourself."

The pixies retreated into each other, looking on with great interest as Winston held the object.

"The Lia Fáil." They repeated in unison. Their voices taking on a reverence that was awkward coming from these two trouble makers.

"What is the Lia Fáil?" Winston asked.

"Great power." One said. "Not of Winter."

"Mustn't have it here." The other continued.

"Not here. No, not here."

"You two are fools." Winston said, shooing them off with a wave of his hand. "The Queen gave this to me."

The pixies fluttered off. "He doesn't know." He heard one say.

"He never knows anything." The other said.

"We'll leave him to die."

"Yes. It will surely be his end."

"His end, indeed."

"More food for us."

Winston sat alone again, the tumbling breeze around him. What was he supposed to do with this box?

"Those two cannot seem to leave ye be." Came Michaels voice through the chill air.

"No." Winston chuckled as Michael sat near him. "At least this time they didn't go on and on about wanting to eat me."

"Aye. That is a quality change of routine on their part." Michael paused a moment, looking Winston over. "Why ye sitting out here, lad?"

"Queen Bheur, she gave me this." Winston held the box out for Michael to see.

"Oh, my." Michael said.

"Do you know what it is?"

"I have an inkling. What I do know is what it is made from."

"What's that?"

"It's made from the Lia Fáil."

"The pixies said that name too. Do you know what it is?"

"Aye, it's a stone once found on the Hill of Tara, in Ireland. It is the location where they historically crowned the kings of Ireland. They long ago ceased that tradition, but what you hold in your hand was carved from the stone from upon that hill." Michael said.

'How do you know?"

"Can you not sense it? The power the box gives off?"

"No." Winston said, perplexed. "It just feels cold." He scoffed. "Which isn't terribly helpful at the moment. Everything here feels cold."

The expression on Michael's face was one of contemplations, more than of amusement, as he took in Winston's words. Winston looked up and their eyes met. Michael smiled. "Trust me, boy. That thing is powerful. You said the Queen gave it to you, herself?"

"Yeah. After she dismissed everyone from her chamber, and Myrddin and her asked me to stay. She had it tucked away among her things. Said it was from my mother."

"Your mother, eh?"

"Yep, and that's all she said. Nothing else." Winston spun the box in his hands. "She didn't say what it was for, or what to do with it."

"Well ye gotta open it don't ya?"

"Open it?" Winston asked.

"Aye. It is a box after all." Michael said. 'Boxes are like the other fine mysteries of life. They exist for brave men like us to open and explore them."

"You are talking about boxes, aren't you?"

"Aye!" Michael exclaimed with a laugh. "Boxes. And you need to open that one to know why you have it."

"I have no idea how to open this." Winston bit back. "There is no opening on this thing. No latch. No hinges. Hell, I bet I couldn't break it open if I wanted to. Don't ask me how I know that, it's just a hunch."

Michael smiled knowingly. "You'd be right." He said. "Nonetheless it can be opened."

"Then open it." Winston said, extending the box to Michael. Michael reeled back, clearly not desiring to have contact with the box. "What's wrong?" Winston asked.

"Nothing."

"Then why did you react like this cold piece of rock would burn you?"

"I'm a wizard, Winston. That cold piece of rock is an item of power." Michael said calmly. "You may not recognize it, but it is quite powerful, and it was entrusted to the Queen, and meant for you. I would be unwise to unnecessarily touch such a thing. Even with your permission."

"Are you scared of it?"

"Of course I am." Michael said in a tone that questioned why Winston would even feel such a question was needed. "We have no idea how my magic would respond with such an item."

"There's something you're not telling me."

"Aye." Michael agreed. "Ever the perceptive lad."

"What is it?"

"The stone. Not the one you hold, but what it was carved from. It is called by some to be the Stone of Destiny."

"Stone of Destiny?"

"Aye. It was one reason they would crown their kings there. Among other things."

"Other things?" Winston asked. "What, other things?"

"There are always 'other things', Winston. Was before my time however, and I can only relay what I've heard." Michael said. "One thing I've heard is how powerful the stone was, and how remarkably powerful the fragments of that stone remained. Which is why it is startling that you cannot feel the power of the box in your hands."

"The Stone of Destiny." Winston murmured to himself. "What would it do?"

"Not sure. Suppose of the two of us, you'll be finding out." Michael said, extending his hand out to Winston. In it he held a knife. "Take this." He said.

"What am I going to do with that?"

"Open the box." Michael instructed plainly.

"I already told you, there is no openings, no hinges. I can't pry it open with a knife."

"And I heard you. Now are ye going to listen, or keep fussin' to me about what ye clearly do not understand?" Michael asked. Winston looked at him expectantly. "Good." Michael continued. "The box is magic, clearly. It is, and it was constructed by magic. Now magic can differ from wizard to creature, all across the realms of Faerie, but in cases where an item of power contains something for a specific recipient, the rules stay pretty consistent."

"Ok. What are the rules? What do I do."

"You need to use your blood."

"What?"

"Use the knife. Cut your hand and place your blood upon it."

"You sure?"

"It's the magical equivalent of powering on and off your computer to solve a tech problem. Hell, you don't even need magic to use it. In all of nature and life, there is little that can compare to the inert power of blood. It is our life's fluid after all." Michael looked at Winston. "Trust me, this will work. I'll leave you to it."

"Don't want to be here for what happens?" Winston asked as

Michael walked away.

"No, I don't." he called back.

Winston looked at the knife in his hand. It was simple, clean, and the edge shimmered in the cold light of the night. Was he really going to do this? It isn't much crazier than anything else that has happened thus far. Oh, he was not eager to cut himself, especially not on the hand. This was going to suck.

Gripping the knife in his right hand, he placed the box on the area of the bench next to him, and proceeded to run the blade across the palm of his left hand. The metal bit into Winston's flesh with a sharp, hot pain that was strong against the cold air. Holding his hand out, he watched the blood collect in his palm. A soft throbbing grew from around the wound, and the warmth of the blood was a clear, and present sensation upon his skin.

"What the hell are you doing, Winston?" He asked himself. "Shit. Lets get this over with."

He turned in his seat and positioned his left hand directly above the waiting box. The air seemed to stop, and time slowed. He watched the blood flow out of his palm, and down on to the box as he turned his hand over. It splashed, and covered the top of the box in a purplish red hue, brilliant and clear to his sight. Without hesitation Winston completed his action, taking the box in his hand. As his skin touched the stone, light erupted from under his hand. Quickly quelled by the fall of his grasp. He felt it now. At least he thought he did. The power of the box. There was a hum, warmth, and a voice.

"Hello my son."

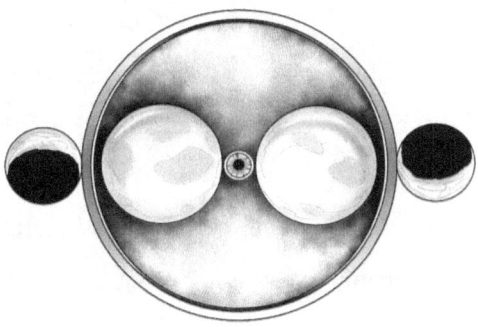

16 – HE DESIRES A FIGHT

Her eyes were beautiful. Not in the traditional, attraction sense, rather in the way the rolling hills, the cliffs of Moher, or the sunset displays its colors across an open autumn sky are beautiful. They seemed to hold all the colors of nature all at once. Cascading from one color to the next like the year moves through the seasons. No pause or hesitation, her eyes simply were, and what they were was captivating.

Winston stared, mouth hanging loose, his eyes seeming to be lost in the middle distance. The box was still warm in his hand. In fact, the air around him felt warmer, pleasant even. Which stood in sharp contrast to the remaining hues of blue and purple that painted the scene. She wasn't blue. No, the woman before him seemed to be standing as a pillar of warmth, and life, in a place devoid of such things.

Tones of red, brown, and gold shone from her hair that rolled down her neck and shoulders in waves and curls. It was pulled back from her face, with various flowers weaved into the braids. Her gown was shades of green and brown, interwoven with accents of purple and blue. She stood about a half a head shorter than Winston, and looked at him with a calm sense of satisfaction.

"Thank goodness you have your father's height." She said with a smile. Her voice comforting and warm. Seeing Winston move as if to speak, she cut him off. "We don't have a great deal of time, my son. This is not how I wanted our paths to meet, yet here we are."

"Why did the Queen of Winter have this box?"

"I gave it to her." She said. "There is more to the tale, of course. More than we can delve into presently. I needed to know a means was in place where we could one day reach each other. A method not easily thwarted by others."

"Why didn't you come to me?" Winston asked. "Why did you abandon me?"

"The circumstances of our lives are not as simple as those questions imply." She said consolingly. "I am of the Tuatha de Danann, and my realm is upon the island you know as Ireland. It is difficult for me to leave the island."

"But you're here now."

"I am." She agreed. "Because you called me. I cannot remain here however. The call of the box only allows for a short period of interaction. There are other areas throughout the world that I can be called to, or even travel to on my own, but they are select and specific in their nature."

"What do you mean?"

"The easiest way to say is they need to be areas of great nature, growth, and containing traits similar to my realm in Ireland." She said, pausing a moment to look at him. "We have little time Winston; do you really only wish to talk about me and where I may or may not have failed you?"

"Heh." He chuckled. "Yes." He said, a bashful tone to his voice. "I've wanted to know you my whole life. I have literally waited my whole life to ask these questions and receive actual answers."

"My dear boy. I am sorry it was necessary for your life to go as it has. It was imperative that you were kept safe." She took his hands in her own, allowing their eyes to connect. "I am Airmid, of Tuatha de Danann, Goddess of magic, healing, and growth. You are my son, Winston."

He could not help himself. Upon hearing the words, upon hearing her again call him "son", tears welled in his eyes, and his breath caught in his lungs. He felt her hands squeeze his. Her skin so warm, like the breath of young fire come to life. There was truth in her eyes as she spoke. A truth that pierced to the core of his soul. He knew this was right. That her words were true. He knew who she was. "Hello, Mother." He whispered.

Airmid wrapped her arms around Winston, as best as any mother smaller than her son could do. He bent to her, needing this embrace, this acceptance. In all the uncertainty of life, in all the loss he had endured, here he was. No longer alone. No longer questioning where he came from. In this moment he knew he had a home. He was home in her arms.

Winston pulled away gently, as he stood tall. Their hands again embraced. Winston paid no mind to the wetness of his face. He just needed to look upon her again. "I wish I had not forgotten you." He said. "If you're a goddess, and reside in Ireland, what does that make me?"

"You are my son."

"Yes. But who was my father? Am I a wizard like Michael? He explained wizards are the offspring of Faerie and humans. Was my father a human?"

"Your father was an impressive man. One of great passion and accomplishment."

"So I am a wizard?" He asked.

"You would know, I would imagine." She said kindly. "Have you accessed your magic."

"Accessed? What do you mean? Do I have to unlock it or something? I've never used magic as far as I know." He said, pausing, and then holding up the now bloody box. "Not until this moment, using this thing. Michael said he could feel the magic before I used it. I felt nothing."

"What is it you really want to know, my son." Airmid asked, softly touching her face. She seemed unfazed by the blood still flowing from Winston's hand.

Winston wasn't sure where to begin. He had so many questions, and yet in the wake of her question his words spilled from his mouth. "I'm stuck in Faerie, and not by choice." He started. "This guy, Jonathan, plans to use the scepter of Summer, and the Sword of Darkfyre to separate himself from Faerie."

"The Sword of Darkfyre?"

"Yes. I think that's what it's called. It's an impressive weapon. Anyways, I've agreed to help stop Jonathan. We have the sword, he has the scepter." Winston looks at his mother. "What I want to know is if I am doing the right thing. Growing up I lived where they sent me. In the

Army I went where they sent me, and did what they ordered me to do. For once I'd like to know that what I am doing has a purpose beyond the desire of those delivering the orders. Does that make any sense?"

"Yes. I think so."

"That's why I asked what this makes me. Am I risking my life yet again for the benefit of the faceless, and the rich, or do I have a dog in this fight? I need to know who and what I am fighting for."

Airmid softly kissed her son on the cheek. "You are a good man, and I am so proud. Your father would be proud as well."

"Would be?"

"Yes. Your father was killed a long time ago, in a battle not dissimilar to this. A battle that would have a direct influence on the scales of balance between Faerie and the realm of man. I am sure he would wish for you to fight." She said. "If Jonathan does what you are saying he hopes to do; he will cause irreparable damage to the realms. We may be separate, but as much as we are, we are also united. What affects Faerie, will affect the realm of man, and vice versa. The separation of the pathways of magic could spell total destruction for us all."

"Total destruction. Damn."

"You asked me what this all makes you. Allow me to amend my reply. Though you are my son, you are so much more. More than I may be able to adequately help you grasp. You are a child of man, and you are a child of Faerie. You are also a child of gods and goddesses, of magic, of kings and queens, of life, and death." She held firm to him, her voice strong. "There is more happening than I can help you fully appreciate, but know this. You must fight. You must. Not for me, or your friends. You must fight for you."

His mother's words hung heavy in the air and Winston took it all in, replaying her words and sounding them down. He needed to fight for him. Not for the country, or an ideal, or for the faceless masses back home. For him. Once again he knew she was right. He knew he would fight.

"What was his name." he heard himself ask without thinking.

"Who?"

"My father. Who was he?"

"When I met him, he went by Pwyll, the lord of Dyfed. He was gentle, whilst strong, and serene while fierce."

"How did he die?"

"He died protecting his lands from invading forces long ago."

"Long ago? How is that possible if he also made me with you?"

A mischievous smile crept across his mother's face. "Magic." She said.

Winston scoffed not knowing what else to say in response to that. He looked up sharply. Her color was fading as if someone were placing a blanket over the light within her. "What is happening?" Hel asked.

"Our time is coming to an end." She said calmly. "For now."

"No. Please." He pleaded. "What can I do to stop this?"

"Nothing, I must go. You can call me again when you leave here." She assured. "Use the box. Or come to Ireland. There will be no limits upon me there."

She reached up, kissing him on his other cheek. He kissed her back.

"Thank you." He said.

"I am proud of you, my son."

Winston opened his eyes to hers and watched as the warm glow faded, leaving him alone again in the garden of ice and snow. He looked down at his hand holding the box. Blood stained the box, and had dripped onto the ground. He pulled his hand off the box to find the wound was healed, leaving barely a scar.

There was a soft fizzing sound, followed by the twinkling light, and Winston watched the blood from the box and ground disappear.

"Cannot have your blood falling into the hands of unscrupulous fiends." Came a commanding baritone voice. Winston turned to see Myrddin walking out to him. "I trust it was a worthwhile conversation."

"Yes, it was. Umm. Were you here the whole time?"

"No, dear boy, no. That conversation was not for any ears but your own." Myrddin said, stepping up to Winston. "When Michael returned inside I waited near the door, watching." He emphasized. "Did you receive answers you were looking for?"

"Some."

"Good. No doubt you'll find yourself with more questions soon enough, and in time I trust we will see you have answers to them all."

"I do have one right now. Am I to call you my King?"

Myrddin guffawed brilliantly, his cheeks taking on a warm pink hue. He looked to Winston, placing his hand on his shoulder in a friendly manner. "No, my boy. There'll be no need for that. Though I do hope in time you may refer to me as your friend."

Winston found himself smiling. "I could get used to that." He said.

"Good!" Myrddin said, patting him once on his shoulder. "Now come. Mhara and Michael have gathered our supplies, and Fionn had returned to us."

"Fionn is back?"

"He is indeed, and itching for a fight."

"A fight? I thought he was with us."

"He is. Thank the stars."

"Then who would he be itching to fight?"

Myrddin looks to Winston with a knowing smile. "You, my boy. He desires to fight you."

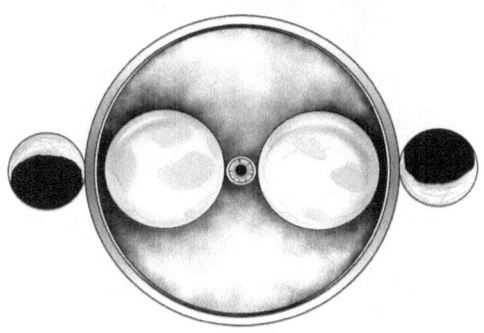

17 – THERE IS BLOOD

"Is this really necessary?" Winston asked, fidgeting with his clothing.

"Aye. Now put them on and stop yer whining."

"Fine. Fine." Winston said. "What I really need to know is how do these clothes all seem to fit?"

Michael gave him an amused look. "Magic." He said unable to hold back a smirk on his face.

"Very funny, but you need a new line. That one has been used already." Winston said, pulling the tunic over his head. "Who are we trying to fool with these outfits? I understood when you had me change at the cottage, so I would blend in better while traveling through Faerie. Why the need for all of us to change?"

"It's all part of the illusion." Michael said. "Everyone at the feast saw us here, in the company of the Queen of Winter. Originally we were heading into Winter to acquire the sword, and our presentation was more inconspicuous. That ruse will no longer serve us, or our ends."

"What are we pretending to be now?"

"You are leaving as my emissaries." The Queen interjected. "When you leave the borders of Winter, they will see you as being of my court, and afford you the appropriate courtesies."

"Where is it we are going?"

"Is he ready?" Boomed a loud voice through the hall. Turning Winston saw Fionn walk in, his armor shimmering, sword on his back, secondary blade at his hip. "Ah." Fionn continued. "It appears I am early. Not to worry, I shall wait."

Winston looked to Mhara, who was helping him with the straps to his own armor. "What is he talking about?" He asked.

"Perhaps it is better if you ask Fionn." She said.

Winston turned to look back at Fionn and was startled to find him within arm's reach, looking at him. A slight smile touched Fionn's face.

"What is it, Fionn?" Winston asked.

"I am looking forward to seeing what you can do, young warrior."

"This armor is all part of our ruse."

"Do not be naïve, boy." Fionn interrupted. "We may seek to sway the mind of onlookers, and yet what of the discerning eye? What of the other warriors? Surely they will quickly identify a boy like you, who has no experience wearing, moving, or fighting in armor." His smile widened.

"Why is that amusing to you?" Winston asked.

"You will need to become acclimated to it. To move in it." He replied. "You will need to fight, and as a warrior, you will feel how the armor moves upon you."

"Myrddin mentioned you were itching for a fight. Is this what he meant?"

"It is." Fionn said, not a hint of playfulness in his voice. "And you will fight me."

"I don't think so, buddy." Winston said, as he tightened his left bracer. "I'll move just fine in this. It's not going to be too different than hoofing a pack through the Afghani hills in 103-degree heat. I'll adapt. We're not fighting."

Something hissed like air escaping from a pressurized door. Winston looked sharply at the sound to find Fionn had drawn his sword from his back. How did he do that so smoothly, and so fast? Winston looked at the sword, and then met Fionn's eyes. Fionn's expression was stern, serious, but not one of malice. They looked upon each other for the full length of a breath.

This couldn't be happening. Did this fanatical warrior really think all that was required to fight was his desire to have it be? No. This was not something Winston was interested in. Not simply because Fionn was an ally, but also because Winston had essentially no experience fighting with these kinds of weapons. On top of that he couldn't remember how long it had been since he was in a real fight. No, Fionn wasn't getting his way this time. Even if Winston was adequately prepared, he would not easily go into combat against a warrior like Fionn. He was clearly no normal knight.

Winston resolved to tell him "No." yet before sound could escape his lips there was a firm resounding slam of something metal next to him. Winston looked to his side, at the table that had been holding his armor. Resting upon it was a sword, still sheathed. It was simple, yet powerful in its appearance. Its handle was a hand and a half in length, it's pummel sleek and straight. Upon the sword still rested the hand of the person who had no doubt placed it there. Following the hand up through the arm to the shoulder, to the face, Winston met the eyes of the Queen.

"You will fight him, Winston." She said with a calm assertion of authority, and confidence that Winston was left unable to contest further.

Fionn no doubt saw this exchange as he satisfyingly exclaimed "Excellent!" as he turned away, walking toward the open area of the hall. Winston watched him leave, feeling Mhara continue to fasten down his armor. He then turned to the Queen.

"Why are you having me do this?" He asked.

"Fionn is correct." She said plainly. "He is also wiser than even he knows. This may not seem necessary to you at this moment, but I assure you this must happen." The Queen handed Mhara the sword for her to affix it to Winston, then turned back to his gaze. "You told me once that you were a soldier."

"Yes."

"Soldiers are warriors." She looked at him intently. "I say to you, not as a Queen, but as your friend, that you need to embrace all that you are. You need to be a warrior now."

Deep inside Winston something turned, tightening, and he knew she too was correct. He looked to his side at Mhara. "Are we done?"

"All done." She said. "Be careful, Winston."

"I'm not the one who wants to do this."

"Fionn is a warrior of legend. Humans have written songs to celebrate his exploits." Mhara said. "You have never faced anything like him before."

"You make it sound like he may actually hurt me." Winston said. "We're on the same side, he's not going to kill me or anything." His words fell upon her stoic gaze. "Right?" Winston asked Mhara, looking for assurance.

"Be careful." She finally said.

"Yeah. I will." Winston said as he walked toward where Fionn was waiting.

Winston's footfalls were quiet. Softened by the new boots he was wearing, it was like each step was upon a padded floor. Each step felt sure. The boots felt as if they were extensions of his actual feet. He felt as if he could run smoothly up the wall and back with no issue. That is if he wasn't burdened by the weight of the armor he was now wearing.

Fionn had positioned himself in the center of the lowered floor of the hall, where the dancing had taken place earlier, at the feast. His sword held casually in his hand, he watched Winston descend the few stairs from the dining level of the hall. Winston thought of a lion calmly watching people walk by his enclosure at the zoo. Eyes intent. Patiently waiting for his opportunity. Only this lion had no high density glass between him and his potential prey.

There was a detached, cold scraping sound as Winston drew his weapon. While not exactly heavy, he was impressed by the weight of the sword in his hand. Thinking back to knife training, and hand to hand combat, Winston's mind quickly assessed the feel and movement of the weapon. Feeling how the weight of the blade pulled on his muscles, and identifying how the balance of the weapons weight may impact his own physical balance during the fight.

"Before we do this, tell me why." Winston said as he came

within what felt like easy attacking distance from Fionn.

"Do you know who I am?" Fionn replied.

"Sure. You're a great warrior."

Fionn's laugh roared out of his chest in thunderous response. His head thrust back in the process, and Winston thought for a moment Fionn might actually drop his weapon with how strongly he was laughing. This was not the case however as his laughter subsided to a rumble, and he looked upon Winston.

"I didn't know I was so funny." Winston said, a snarky tone to his voice.

"Nor I."

The attack was sudden. Fionn's body moved forward as one, with such speed that all Winston could think to do was awkwardly lift his sword in response, and step away hurriedly. The effort was not without consequence as the impact from Fionn's weapon was enough to cause Winston to stumble back, and fall to one knee.

Fionn calmly stepped in a circular pattern placing him near where he was, not looking, or paying much concern toward Winston in the process.

"I typically prefer a spear, you know." Fionn said as if to no one, looking down toward the sword in his hand. "For the span of many lifetimes I've fought to keep the realm of man safe. There have been songs written about me. Painting me as a giant, a hero, they even say I befriended a leprechaun, and fought a fire breathing man." Fionn chuckled to himself. "Clearly these are not without embellishment, and exaggeration. Consider the fire breathing man?" He scoffed, looking to Winston who was now upon his feet. "That's an utter lie." Fionn said. "It was a dragon."

Before Winston's response could leave his mouth Fionn was upon him again. This time he came in first with a thrust, which Winston was able to deflect to the side. Fionn spun, his blade coming down overhand at Winston. Without thinking, Winston lifted his own blade in response. The collision of the blades was sharp, and sent a vibration of pain and recognition through Winston's hands, and up his arms. His shoulders felt as though they planned to give way. With a grunt Winston pushed up in an effort to create separation between himself and Fionn. At the apex of his effort he felt the air within him rocket out of his body as Fionn's heavy boot slammed into his abdomen.

Winston's vision blurred. He stepped back from Fionn's kick, holding his blade before him, in an approximate effort of defense. The glimmer of Fionn's armor proving to be Winston's saving grace as the warrior came in again for another blow. Winston was able to position his sword well enough to intercept the strike, the impact once again sending him to the floor.

The armor's restriction upon his movements was not all that different than being loaded with gear in the service, yet the frustration of not being able to keep his footing stoked a fire within Winston that he had thought died long ago. Was he going to continue to be this man's pincushion, always on the defense at best? No. He knew he needed to take the offense.

Gathering himself to his feet he watched how Fionn was moving, as he walked himself back to his original position on the floor. Winston lowered himself as best as he could in the armor. Performing a squat of sorts, to get a better feel for his available range of movement.

Fionn was speaking again, to himself or no one; Winston was not sure. What he did know was that he was not interested in listening.

If they were going to fight, there was only one thing to focus on. Fionn was saying something to the effect of "and the forgotten lands are yours" or something along those lines when Winston struck.

The seasoned warrior was not caught off guard, smoothly parrying Winston's efforts. Thrust. Slice. Evade. The calamity of the conflict rang throughout the hall as the two traded efforts, and their weapons conducted their song.

For Winston it felt like a dance, you either lead or follow, yet with each step you feel the rhythm of the music more and more. What was initially a clumsy execution at best, was now flowing out of him as a natural extension of self. His vision calmed, the space around him subtly blurring. The limited details allowed him to focus on the movement of his opponent. Winston watched as Fionn's shoulders would drop, or torso would shift, knowing a strike would follow.

Sweat began running down his brow, and between his shoulder blades. How long had they been going at each other? Winston would move, Fionn would adjust. Fionn would come forward, and Winston would counter. He could hear Fionn's breaths deepen, and felt his own body slowing from the demands of manipulating his weapon. What was once a moderately weighted blade, now felt many times heavier, and far less willing to move as he desired.

There was a flurry of effort from both warriors, and a brief pause. Winston wiped sweat from his brow, feeling the sting of the salty liquid in his eyes. He looked up at Fionn who was smiling. Not any simple smile, no, a toothy, wolfish smile. From behind that smile came a deep roar as Fionn moved forward again.

Winston's eyes still stung from the salty sweat infiltrating his eyelids, and acted upon instinct. Wind moved through the area around him. Metal colliding with metal, as the crescendo of violence peeked. He was lost in this dance of no music, unsure of how long they persisted. In his blindness Winston moved, evaded, and in a desperate feeling of effort he advanced to strike once more.

"Enough!" Boomed the voice of Myrddin.

Winston froze in place, arms extended, his breathing labored and fighting for release. He slowly lowered his weapon, and struggled to remove his gloves to wipe the sweat from his face.

"Hold still. Hold still." Came Mhara's voice. "Let me help."

Winston could feel her pat his face with a soft cloth, wiping the sweat and residue away carefully. In the distance he thought he could hear the other talking.

"What are they saying?" He asked Mhara.

"They're talking about your fight." She said quickly.

Winston chuckled. "Their view was likely better than mine. I'm not sure exactly what happened." He said.

She didn't respond. This grabbed Winston's attention. He placed his hand upon her hand to stop her cleaning, moving it from his face, and looked toward the other.

The Queen of Winter, and Myrddin stood on the dining level, Michael close by, the three were no longer speaking, but looking at Winston nonetheless. Fionn stood to the side, sword still in hand, and a huge smile upon his face. He breathed in deep, full breaths. Winston looked closer at him and thought he saw hints of red on his armor, and face. *Was that blood? Was he cut?* He didn't remember getting cut.

Winston thrust himself up, looking over himself. He couldn't focus. Patches of black, like a smoky haze floated in his vision. He growled in frustration.

"Winston. Winston, what is it?" Mhara asked.

"Am I cut?" He asked. "I don't feel cut. I've been cut before, and I don't feel it."

"Cut?" She repeated, sounding confused.

"Yes. There is blood. I saw it. Saw it on Fionn's face and armor. Surely he cut me." He paused in frustration. "Do you see a wound? My eyes won't focus. Must have gotten my adrenaline up too high. I have dark smoky patches in my vision." He turned toward her. "Mhara, look. Help me!"

"Come here." She said softly, and led him to the stairs. "Sit down."

He sat, expecting her to examine him, or look him over at least. A moment or two passed and there was nothing. She didn't touch him, or give any indication that she was examining him for injury at all. Winston's vision began to clear. The dark patches feeling more far off and faded.

"Are you just going to stand there and stare?" He said. "Someone get this armor off of me!"

"There is nothing wrong with you." Came Myrddin's calm, sure voice.

"I saw the blood." Winston contested.

"Yes." Myrddin agreed. "We all saw the blood."

"Well then…"

"Fionn will be fine." Myrddin said.

"What? Of course he's fine. What are you saying?"

"Winston, my boy. Have you ever fought like that before?"

"With a sword? No."

"No, not with a sword. Have you ever fought with that level of intensity and focus?"

Winston paused, he did recall a few other times, but before he could speak Myrddin continued.

"Do you remember your vision being affected?"

He had, at least once. "Yes, I think so. When my adrenaline goes up I get dark areas in my vision. Why?"

"Those aren't in your vision." Myrddin said plainly, gesturing for Fionn to come over to them.

As Fionn walked forward the dark patches in Winston's vision moved, spun and churned in response to him. At one point a patch that was at about waist level with Fionn, but to his side started to move, and Winston watched as Fionn deliberately passed his hand through it. The dark patch moved again, like heavy, dense smoke. He looked up at Fionn's amused, still smiling face.

"I.. I don't understand." Winston said. "What the hell happened."

"As you fought a trail of black smoke began following your movements, and when you stopped moving, it simply rested."

"It did what?"

"Indeed. A most curious thing. Come." Myrddin insisted. "We should prepare to leave. We can discuss this more later." He looked again to Fionn. "You should tend your wounds. We don't need your blood on the air as we travel."

Winston didn't know what to say. He just stared, looking periodically between them.

"Fionn." Myrddin said. "When you are ready, take them and go. I will rendezvous with you at the Port of Hollows."

"As you say, good King."

"Michael, are you sure about this?" Myrddin asked.

"Aye. We get to the Port of Hollows, I can contact Jonathan. We'll set a trap that he'll never see coming."

"Myrddin?" Called Queen Bheur.

"Yes, your majesty?"

"Did you prepare what I asked?"

"I did." Myrddin said assuredly. "The pieces fall ever more in place."

Winston couldn't hear the rest of what was said between the two as Mhara drew him away, and together they loaded their mounts in silence, the whole time he was replaying the fight in his mind, even replaying the events of the last few days. Getting trapped in Faerie. Being challenged by the Hound. Being told he was touched by Death. Meeting his mother, who professed to be a goddess. Then being coerced into sparring with one of the greatest warriors to ever live, only to learn that black smoke was trailing after him as he fought, and he may have injured an ally. What was happening to him? What is he? The more he thought about it he wondered if he would ever get home.

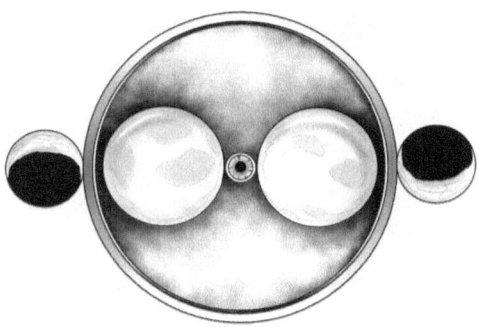

18 – THE LANDS BETWEEN

They really did smell better once you got them out on the road. The heavy, thick aroma of these beasts in the stables was enough to peel paint off walls. A fact that made Winston appreciate all the more that they were kept in stables of unornamented stone and wood.

When he had first seen these creatures it was from quite a distance. He was down a hill, beyond some trees, and the Queen of Winter, and her men were silhouetted in the light of the evening. What is more, he was hidden inside one of Michael's reality skewing veils. Needless to say that brief sighting did nothing to prepare him for the full impression these creatures leave.

Queen Bheur said the beast was named Alban, and was one of her personal favorites. She even went so far as to have her own grooms prepare the beast for him by securing his mount, and affixing his supply packs. Her care and consideration felt like those of a true friend, and her consideration of him seemed unique. Though Winston had very little to compare it to, he could only attribute it to their time in session together.

Alban was a large creature, covered from snout to tail in thick, rich fur of black, rust, and indigo. He made Winston think of a bear, that is if a bear were as tall as a Clydesdale, with the sure footing of a large jungle cat. How they ever thought to domesticate these creatures evaded him. Nonetheless the ride was sure, and remarkably smooth. For a creature so large Winston was sure the mount would sway with each step far more than it had proven to. Instead he was left impressed by the steady ride upon the back of such a powerful beast.

They rode in an almost single file line. Michael in front, Fionn in the rear, with Mhara and Winston between them. Mhara's mount had a secondary creature tied behind it carrying extra supplies, as well as supporting their cover story of delivering items from the Queen to her outpost in the Port of Hollows.

Having all agreed to ride for as long as possible before setting down for camp, Winston had all but lost track of time. What he was certain of was that this was his second sunrise he'd seen since leaving the palace before dawn the day prior. He wasn't sure how the others were holding up, but he knew he would welcome a rest as soon as it was available.

"How do you like riding your mathean?" Asked Fionn. He was riding next to Winston. Had he rode up just to talk with him? Winston had long suspected he was a talkative character, but was this really necessary? "You seem comfortable." He continued.

Winston looked about, Fionn's words making more sense as he realized he had drawn back towards him. Mhara, and Michael were a fair way ahead of them on the road.

"I love riding matheans." Fionn continued as if not noticing

Winston's efforts to collect himself. He looked over to Winston, a wicked smile on his face. "You should try running them."

"Running?"

"Yes. It is like riding upon the front of a storm." Fionn's eyes burned in appreciation. "So much power."

"I'll take your word for it." Winston said.

Fionn laughed. His tone one of appreciation as much as amusement.

"Do you know if we've been making good time?" Winston asked.

"We have. We should leave the kingdom of Winter by night fall. It will be as good a time as any to camp for the night."

"Will we have much further to go to reach the Port?"

"No. Soon we will be at the Plains, and we will be able to move more quickly." Fionn said, trying to refrain from smiling as fully as Winston thought he appeared to want to.

Winston looked at the warrior, considering the fresh pink line on his cheek, as well as the one he knew was on Fionn's left arm. Though he was not fully sure of how he accomplished it. Nor was he the one who initiated the fight itself. Still he felt burdened by a sense of remorse over having wounded this man. His ally. Perhaps someone he'd consider a friend.

"No." Fionn said. His sharp inflection startling Winston.

"What?"

"No, you are not going to apologize to me."

"I'm not."

"You were. I could... feel it." Fionn looked to Winston. "You did as you ought to, as we must in such situations."

"Still…"

"No. You will not." Fionn interrupted, taking a resolving breath. "Hear me, young pup. Hear me now. There are many questions whose answers I cannot provide. I am not a complex man. I am a warrior, I fight. It is what I know. You fought well. More than well. And with what we are setting out to do, you will need to fight again." Fionn adjusted himself in his mount before continuing. "You need not feel remorse for wounding me. These are marks of affection compared to what I've endured. No, instead you need to feel; you need to know, that you did well. For what I believe was the first time in a long time you let go of the man you have allowed yourself to believe you have to be, and embraced the man you are. You stopped being who others have left you feeling you are expected to be, and you were the man you are! This, you must not let go of. Must not forget. Especially with what is to come."

They rode for a short time, not saying a word between them. Winston processed the truth of Fionn's words. He knew Fionn was correct. Even with the frustration of the moment, the sweat burning his eyes, Winston could not think of the last time he felt so free and so fully himself than when he was engaged with Fionn. He felt complete. Reconciling this truth, he resolved himself to do exactly as Fionn instructed. Feeling a sense of relief and warmth from the decision. "I will do as you say." Winston finally said. "Thank you."

Fionn reached out one of his large hands, his arm easily reaching over to Winston's shoulder. The two of them pulling back on the reigns of their mounts. "Winston, my friend, it is I who should thank you. Sharing that moment. Having your trust, and being a part of that moment is an honor only a warrior will understand." Fionn paused, looking at Winston waiting as if to see the recognition in his eyes.

Winston gave a slight nod, and Fionn reciprocated. "Thank you" He said.

"Oy! Are you two about done?" Michael yelled back from further up the road.

Fionn and Winston shared a smile, and urged their mounts forward to rejoin Michael and Mhara. The group continued on riding in silence towards the edge of winter.

While in Winter it was common to see patches of ground here and there, along with areas of ice, and a general covering of snow throughout. Winston assumed the patches of snow would become less and less prevalent as they reached the border, and eventually dissipate completely. He was wrong. Instead a distinct line could be seen the change of the characteristics of the landscape. Almost as if a giant had reached down with an edging knife and scraped back the snow to stop at the end of winter's domain.

Winston couldn't hold back his amusement at the sight. His soft chuckle quickly escalated into manic laughter, and drew the attention of the group.

"What is so amusing?" Michael asked.

Winston, striving to regain control of himself, couldn't answer, and instead gestured toward the ground. They all looked to see the defined line of where winter ends and the new lands began. The juxtaposition of the cold icy landscape, next to rich green grass was not lost on the rest of them. Michael loosed a snort of acknowledgement, and Mhara a soft "Hmm."

"It is a sight not oft seen." Said Fionn. "Do control your amusement though. We know not who may be listening."

Winston forced his mouth closed and composed himself, taking short, controlled breaths. "I'm sorry." He said.

"It is alright. We are all tired, and that is an amusing sight." Fionn said. "I know from experience that nothing like this exists in the realm of men."

Michael steered his mathean in a circle as he surveyed the area. His posture was alert.

"What is it?" Fionn asked.

"Before we move too far from Winter, we should camp for the night." Michael said.

Fionn seemed to grasp his meaning without further discussion, while Mhara seemed unphased.

"I'm all for a rest, but why does it matter how far from Winter we are?" Winston asked.

"While in Winter we enjoy the protection of the Queen." Michael said, and gestured at the ground. "Yet as you've observed, we have now left Winter."

"Ok. So what?" Winston said. "We knew we'd be out of Winter eventually. We need to in order to meet Myrddin at the Port of Hollows."

"These are the Autumnlands." Fionn interjected. "The lands between Summer and Winter. The Port of Hollows is at the far edge of these lands, and to get there we must traverse the Autumnlands via the plains. It is better to rest here, as there will be no camping on the plains."

"You guys ever heard of doing a mission brief?" Winston asked. "Ya know, where you fill in the whole team on all mission pertinent information before engaging in the mission?"

Fionn's face conveyed nothing, and Michael just smirked.

"Aye. We didn't want to be overwhelming you though, boy." Michael said. "There is a lot about Faerie you do not know, after all."

"How about we cover it in steps then? Starting with what to expect as we cross the Autumnlands."

Michael looked to Fionn. "Ye wanna tell him?"

"These are predatory lands, Winston." Mhara said assertively. "We don't camp on the Plains because there is no cover. We may as well lay down and let the cursed things consume us."

"She's right." Confirmed Fionn. "Camping here is wise. We still have tree cover, and we're out of the snow. Tomorrow we'll be in the Plains, and we'll need to see just how swift the matheans can be."

"What exactly are we going to be trying to outrun?"

"There are many predators in the Autumnlands." Mhara said. "The most dangerous on the Plains is the iolains."

"Aye. Think of an eagle that's always angry, flies as quiet as an owl, and is the size of midsize SUV, with the wingspan of a city bus." Michael added.

Mhara and Fionn looked at Michael perplexed.

"What is this SUV?" Fionn asked.

Michael's face looked amused. "My apologies. That was for Winston's benefit. SUV's are a modern human vehicle."

"Ahh." Fionn said. "It will be grand to ever visit the realm of man again."

A hush fell over the group, each of them contemplating the information shared. Their individual mounts chuffing and sniffing the ground and each other.

"Sounds like we should get some rest then." Winston said, interrupting their silence.

Fionn selected a location a little further into the Autumnlands for them to make camp. He tied up his mathean and went out on foot to scout and hunt fresh game. The rest of the group unloaded their packs, and Michael set up a veil.

It wasn't long until Fionn returned with three small furry creatures he'd killed. Winston thought they resembled fat foxes. Fionn saw his look and returned it with a questioning look of his own. Winston smiled and nodded assurance to him. He would happily eat what he caught. It couldn't be worse than eating roots while in the army on weekend survival exercises.

As they cooked at ate their meal the world around them darkened. The sun fell beyond the horizon, and the soft familiar golden hue of Michael's veil showed the circular edge of their camp.

"What do we look like?" He asked Michael.

"What's that?"

"If someone was to pass by us, what would we look like to them?"

"Ah, a large stone and bushes next to a divot in the ground. Essentially nothing of interest."

"Can they hear us when we talk?"

"Sort of." Michael said. "They can see the mathean, which look like a wild pack looming. When we talk, our voices sound like their grunts and growls, or birds chirping. Still, we shouldn't make too much noise. Not many creatures are as noisy as people are."

Winston reclined on his pack feeling satisfied with Michael's explanation, and seeing the logic in being quiet. As he leaned back he felt a hard shaft thrust into his back. He shot up quickly.

"Ye alright, boy?"

"Yeah. I'm good." Winston said. "Trying to get comfortable. Think I put my pack on a stick or something. No biggie." Michael went back to his meal, and fussing with the fire. Winston turned over slightly, trying to figure out what it was that jammed into his back. He lifted his pack to brush underneath it. The ground was clear. Laying his pack back down he felt the object again, only this time it was larger, and it was inside his pack.

He looked about the group, not sure he wanted an audience. The Queen had seen to his mount being packed. Winston doubted anyone knew what was inside the pack if it was something she had placed there. Seemed to Winston that everyone else was occupied. Fionn was reclined, having quickly completed his meal, and deciding sleep was a good plan. Winston wasn't surprised by this. Fionn had eaten an entire one of those plump fox-like creatures all on his own. Mhara was also reclining as well, her outer jacket off, and draped over her head to cover her eyes from the light of the fire.

Turning over again, Winston looked through his pack, there were three pouches and his extra blanket roll. He found the box from his mother in one pouch, extra clothes, and some food supplies in another. As he shifted things around to get settled in, he felt it again, it was inside the second blanket roll. He hadn't taken it out since he was warm enough in his armor, near the fire. Carefully he unrolled the end carefully until he saw it, not wanting to draw undue attention to himself. Winston's heart pounded.

Light from the camp's fire shimmered off the round surface. There were subtle grooved details circling out from a center point. Needing to know if he was right he pushed the fabric of the blanket up more until it revealed the leather wrapped grip that was connected to the pummel of what he was sure was a sword.

"She wanted you to have it."

Mhara's voice nearly drove Winston to his feet. He clenched his teeth together to keep from yelling out, and quickly covered the sword handle with the blanket. "I'm.. I'm not sure what you mean. You shouldn't startle people like that, Mhara."

She lowered herself in front of him, giving him a contemptuous look.

"What is it?" called Michael.

Winston looked at Mhara, conveying that this was her fault.

"Nothing." She said to Michael with a forced giggle. "I'm just picking on our young adventurer over here."

Michael gave an appreciative chuckle in return.

"Careful he doesn't darken our whole campsite in response." Fionn chimed from his relaxed position. "Doubt the Queen can see things clearly within her hall yet because of him." He continued, finishing with a restrained laugh.

"Ha. Ha. Thanks guys." Winston said to the group. "Can I try to get some sleep now please." He said, focusing on Mhara.

"Aye. Both of you rest up." Said Michael. "Tomorrow is going to be a big day. You'll need to be alert for it."

"Alright." Mhara said in acquiescence. Yet before she rose she looked to Winston, whispering. "It's what you think it is. Keep it close."

"But why?" He asked.

"Queen Bheur says you'll know when to use it." Mhara said with a shrug. "She wanted me to tell you that you are meant to have it, and you should not relinquish it ever."

Winston felt like a hammer hit him square in the chest. He

looked directly into Mhara's eyes. "Thanks." He said, not completely sure why.

"Of course." She said, standing. "Sleep well, Winston."

As he laid back, and welcomed sleep to overtake him, he allowed his mind to wander. He took in the sounds around them. Working out from the crackling fire, to the breathing of his companions, and the chuffing snorts of the matheans. He heard the wind moving through the trees, and the scurrying of tiny feet through the underbrush. As the full weight of his exhaustion pulled heavy on his eyelids Winston listened to the far off thrumming sound of churning air, of thrusting wings. Wings the size of a city bus.

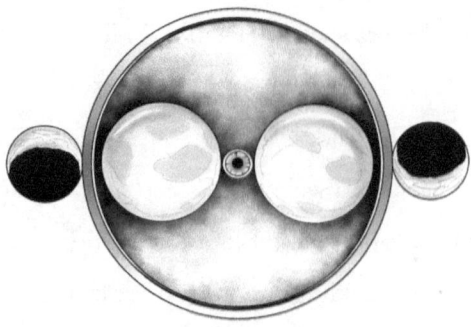

19 – CAUGHT IN THE CROSSFIRE

Before

Clatter of gunfire filled the air, bombarding Winston's ears like a manic percussion band. Sporadic, affronting, and aggressive, while not maintaining any semblance of rhythm. He and Sam were pinned down behind what looked like an overturned late 1990's Toyota. The rest of their unit was nearby, and equally pinned down in their own locations of cover.

The ambush hit them hard as their caravan was heading out of a populated area. An RPG hit the second vehicle in the caravan from the side. The explosion flipped the vehicle and killed two men in the process. Winston, Sam, and their lieutenant were able to escape.

Meanwhile the lead vehicle's front wheels fell into a pit trap in the road, pinning it in place.

"Martins!" Winston yelled from his position. "Martins, are you clear?"

"Clear!" the call came back.

Winston checked his gun, and ammunition supply, as he scooted over near Sam. The lieutenant was leaning against the trunk of the overturned sedan, Sam dressing his wounds. When Winston arrived he performed a cursory check of Sam's gear.

"You good, Sam?"

"I'm good." Sam replied, not turning around.

"The lieutenant?" Winston asked, eliciting a soft groan from the lieutenant.

"Concussion, and shrapnel gash on his side." Sam said. "We need to get clear, man. He doesn't have long."

"Stay with him. I'm going to go over to Martins. See how he is." Winston hands Sam two clips. "I got these from the Humvee. I've got three. Give me some cover."

Sam moved with Winston to the edge of the sedan. They made eye contact, Sam gave him a nod, and Winston was off. Keeping his head down he raced forward hearing gunfire filling the air, and bullets ricocheted off the environment around him. With a slide he came in next to Martins, Sanchez, and Jackson as they took cover behind their Humvee.

"Good to see you boys." Winston said with a smile

"Hey Sergeant." Replied a happy young man, a wide smile stretching his face.

"Smile later, Sanchez." Winston said. "Status?"

"Four shooters, spread out." Martins reported. "Second story, ten o' clock. Rooftop, one o'clock. The others, at ground level. They're on the move."

"Weapons?"

"Locked and loaded." Sanchez said. Still holding on to his smile. "What are our orders?"

"Lieutenant is injured, and we need to get out of here." Winston said. "We need to take out these shooters before that can happen. We get a radio out?"

"Yes sir." Called Jackson. "Operation command says bravo team is close. They could be here in twenty five."

"Shit. I gotta get back to Sam." Winston said. "You boys watch your six, conserve ammo and keep cover."

Winston moved to head back to Sam behind the overturned sedan. They needed to get the Lieutenant up and moved away from here for extraction. Before moving he looked back, thinking he would say one more thing to the boys. A word of encouragement? A joke? Perhaps one last jab at Sanchez and his need to incessantly smile? He would never know. As he turned his head he heard gunfire begin again, joined by the familiar ping of bullets on metal and shattering glass.

Winston looked toward the sedan and could see it was taking fire. "I'm going for the Lieutenant." He called out loudly to no one in particular.

"Copy that, sir." Jackson said.

He felt a hand on his chest. It was Sanchez, still smiling.

"This is some shit, isn't it?" Sanchez said. "All this to transfer some water."

"Yeah." Winston said. He couldn't fathom how Sanchez maintained his level of energy like he did. Always positive. Always finding the funny in the moment.

"Get the Lieutenant, Winston. We'll cover you." Or at least that is what Winston believed Sanchez meant to say. He got to the "We'll" as the rear of his head exploded. Sanchez's body collapsed to the ground.

Winston's breath came out in a growl, then a roar, then a bellow of defiance. His eyesight blurred as he engaged his weapon. Standing, he turned toward the buildings beyond the shells of derelict vehicles, training his weapon, and opened fire. Methodically he moved toward the sedan. He continued to roar his battle cry of challenge as he fired.

Jackson and Martins, now returning fire of their own, created an opening for Winston to move more decisively toward Sam and the Lieutenant. He lowered his M4 and pivoted to run to the sedan. The scene blurred in his sight. Dark areas of smoke now coming from unseen fires, further limited Winston's clear vision of the area. He moved onward. Bullets flew through the air. There was yelling. Chaos. Step by step he pushed forward, his focus only on getting to the Lieutenant and Sam. He never saw the man step out from the protection of the buildings. He didn't see the man position an RPG launcher on his shoulder, aiming it toward him and the sedan. He saw the explosion as the rocket propelled grenade collided with the underbelly of the late 90's Toyota. It ripped open the weathered materials, mixing its destructive fire with the remaining fuel in the car. The power of the explosion doubled, the impact on the air knocked Winston to the ground.

Dark smoke encompassed Winston. He waved it from his face as he pulled himself to his feet. Fire, and the smell of burning oil and rubber, was in the air. Two figures lay near Winston. The explosion of the sedan having thrown them forward, the Lieutenant and Sam now lay bleeding before him.

The Lieutenant's already existing wounds were now compounded, and his body was quickly losing blood. Sam lay near the

Lieutenant. His position in relation to the Lieutenant, implied that he had been in the process of trying to move the Lieutenant, when the car was hit. Winston reaching them, checked the Lieutenant for a pulse.

"He's gone." Said Sam, with noticeable effort.

"Talk to me buddy!" Winston said, shifting over to help Sam. "How are you feeling?"

"Like I could use a drink of water." Sam said, his chuckle giving way to coughing, propelling blood from his mouth.

"Come on." Winston said as he bent down to his friend. He pulled Sam's arm up and over his neck, positioning himself to lift him up. "We need to move."

More bullets rang out, spaced out, and deliberate between bursts. Winston's eyes searched the area for the shooters. The dark smoke had dissipated. His eyes found the man who had shot the car, now lying dead in the street. Reaching Jackson, and Martins, Winston was relieved to see they were alive, though both showing signs of injury.

"Sit rep?"

"Martins took a shot in the arm. I've got shrapnel in my leg." Jackson said. "Extraction is coming. Team Bravo is five minutes out."

"The Lieutenant?" Asked Martins.

Winston lowered Sam to the ground, leaning him against the Humvee tire. "Negative." He said.

Sam coughed as bullets continued to affront their current location. "Winston. Win…" Sam choked out.

"I'm here, man." Winston said, settling in next to his friend.

Sam was bleeding out from wounds in his abdomen and legs. His eyes were wide and unfocused as he looked up toward Winston, not ever seeming to actually see him. Sam's voice was panicked, hopeful, and fleeting.

"I've got you, Sam. I've got... Hang in there buddy." Winston assured, as he looked for help. Another unit was moving in from the west. "We're getting out of here."

Gunfire came again, sounding from a new direction. Jackson signaled to Winston it was Bravo working their way in from the east. Winston felt a gentle tug on his arm.

"Win?" Sam said. Sounding like he wasn't sure he was there.

"Yeah man. I'm here."

"It was worth something, right?" Same asked, coughing. "Did it have value?"

Winston's stomach fell, and panic danced with pain inside his mind. They had been on a recon and support mission, bringing clean water to friendlies. Now they were ambushed and trapped, his squad, while escorting the Lieutenant back to base. They were trapped and they needed out. More than that, he needed to save his friend. He needed to get him home.

"You know it, brother. It was damn near special." He said, forcing a smile in his voice.

"I told you we'd be something." Sam forced out. "I told you we'd be special."

"You sure did, man. You sure did!" Winston said, clinging to his friend, his brother.

Sam's body fell still, the shuddering need for life and air that it had once fought for, now gone. Winston clung to him as Bravo team arrived. He didn't hear them as they spoke to him, checking on his own condition. Even as they took Sam away, Winston clung to him. He clung to his life, his friendship.

When Winston was next aware, he was waking up in medical, back on base. In a panic, he shot up in his bed, to look around. His eyes quickly found what he was looking for. Pulling the IV from his arm, he swiftly moved over to stand next to Sam. He was dead.

"Sergeant? Sergeant, you shouldn't be up." Said a voice behind him.

Winston turned to behold a female medic moving towards him quickly. Her companion followed behind her, waving their hands around as if they were trying to fan away a bad smell.

"What is in the air? Do you see that?" The companion said.

The female medic didn't reply, instead moved to Winston and escorted him back to bed.

"It's like there is smoke in the air." Continued the companion.

Now

The thundering cacophony of their party galloping across the plains, accompanied by the physical sensation of the beast beneath him, and the feeling of the air moving around him proved unlike anything he'd experienced previously. Winston did what anyone would do. He held on for his life.

Fionn initiated their run, racing up from the rear, and thus pulling each of their mounts into stride with his own. Winston couldn't decide if he should be annoyed or impressed. Regardless of Fionn's possibly manipulative motivations, one could not argue with the results. They all knew they needed to traverse the plains quickly, and ideally without incident. It appeared they were doing just that.

Even moving at a casual pace, Winston was impressed by the smoothness of the ride atop a mathean. On a horse, a rider does well to raise themselves from the saddle when at full gallop, both for their benefit, as well as for the horse's. Fionn had told Winston and Mhara, as they prepared for the day's trek across the plain, that this was not the case with matheans. As before, he was correct.

As they raced through the high grass of the Autumnlands, Winston couldn't help but look around. The span of the plain was wide, vast, and rich in color. The group had explained to Winston that the iolains were a great danger. He smiled to himself realizing Tolkien may have had something right. Giant eagles. He thought to himself with a smile.

With visions of soaring above the clouds on the back of a glorious eagle filling his mind, it was not surprising that it took Winston a moment to realize he was in fact flying through the air. His mathean having stopped abruptly, launching him from his mount.

The ground hit hard as Winston tried to move with his fall, tumbling and coming to a stop. Heat, and the smell of burning grass filled his nostrils. Looking about he saw his companions dismounting. They were encircled in flames.

Mhara was at his side, ready to assist him, but he assured her he was alright. "This isn't normal, is it?" Winston asked.

"No."

"To arms!" bellowed Fionn as he pulled a spear from his mount.

Winston turned to collect his own weapons as large dark figures stepped through the flames. Three of them stepped in, one from each side, and one from the rear.

"Bollocks." Michael cursed. "I don't suppose ye fancy goat

hides do ye, Fionn?"

"A hide is a hide, my wizard friend. I could use some new skins."

Low snarling came from all three creatures, though they did not move. They stood, looking coldly at the group.

"What do we do?" Winston asked.

Overhead the thrum came to his ears. Low, steady, and full, Winston was not sure where, or what it was. He felt Mhara step closer to him, her sword in hand. She was looking at the sky. Winston followed her gaze up and beheld massive wings unfurling and blocking the sun as a massive creature landed just outside the fire. Winston watched as it descended, and thought for sure he saw someone upon the creatures back.

"Did you see that?" Mhara asked. She must have seen it too.

"Who is that?" Winston called out. "Michael! There was someone upon its back."

"Aye."

"Was that an iolain?"

"Aye."

"People ride them?"

Michael gave Winston a look, one that clearly indicated he needed to save his questions for after this was resolved.

Fionn stepped back, close enough for Winston to hear him. "Do you remember our fight?"

"Yes, of course."

"If you can call the smoke now, it would be good." Fionn gave him a look. "If not. Aim for the backs of the knees." Fionn said, with a wink.

Winston felt frustration rise within him. He had no idea where the smoke came from, or how to use it. Just as he was about to reply there was a spinning of the air and the section of the ring of fire in front of their group opened, like the sliding of tall flaming curtains.

Slowly a figure stepped through the opening, behind which stood the large and imposing figure of the iolian. As the figure stepped into view, beyond the width of the fire, the wall closed. The figure was hooded in a dark grey cloak, and of average height. Winston noticed a shift in how Michael was standing, as the figure reached for their hood. As the hood was pulled back Winston could see it was a man, with flowing blonde hair.

His breath caught in his chest, and Winston had to place his hand upon Mhara's shoulder.

"What is it?" She asked. But he did not reply.

The figure looked to him and the recognition was clear. Winston knew those eyes, he'd seen that face, though the hair was much worse for wear at the time. Their eyes had connected as he watched this same man close the door from inside the hallway, locking Winston in a stone tower. Winston fumbled for his sword.

"Do you know him?" Mhara asked.

"He surely does." Replied the man, as he removed a radiant scepter from within his cloak.

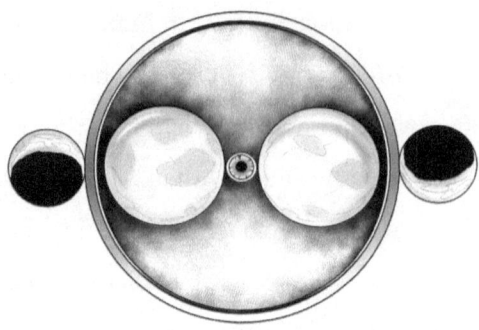

20 – MY LIEGE

Charging a rogue wizard, particularly one in possession of an item of untold power, whilst you yourself are presently unarmed, was not Winston's best plan. He hit the ground, and found himself longing for the forgiving impact of the ocean, after he jumped off the cliff with Michael. Unfortunately, in this situation, the thick grass of the Autumnlands only offered minor comfort.

"Stay back, lad!" Michael yelled as Winston pulled himself to his feet.

Fionn and Mhara had weapons drawn, each positioned as best as they could to address the three massive Billy goat creatures that flanked the three of them.

"Clearly an impulsive boy." Jonathan said. "I see he got you free, Michael."

"Congratulations, yer eyes work." Michael quipped. "What do ye want, Jonathan?"

"I came to talk to you, old friend. To offer you… an option."

"That right?" Michael sneared. "Ye gonna hand over the scepter, before ye destroy the realm as we know it?"

"No." Jonathan said. "I am offering you a final opportunity to join me. To be free of these shackles forever." The scepter in his hand beginning to emit a glowing mist.

Slowly Winston stepped further and further backwards, the voices of Michael and Jonathan grew more indistinct, and his back now pressed against his mathean. Alban snorted, and shifted in response to Winston's contact. Winston found he could relate to the beast's uneasiness. The reality of the situation was creating a stress thick enough to taste in the air.

Winston looked to Mhara, whose eyes were already upon him. When their eyes met he registered a faint smile of assurance, and a nod from her. Winston felt the warmth of her confidence within him. The feeling proved short lived. Winston reached for his sword only to find the scabbard empty. Where was his sword? It must have slipped out when he flew from his mount, or when Jonathan hit him with whatever power he had used that sent him tumbling back.

"We need to act." Fionn snarled from behind him. "This will not be our final stand."

A deep thrum moved through the air, and Winston turned toward Michael. He had pulled out some kind of weapon. It looked like a magic wand and a night stick had a baby. At its end it had a loop that Michael was holding onto as he spun the smooth tapered stick in the air. Rivulets of power emanated out from Michael, and encircled their group.

Winston saw Mhara move, sheath her sword, and go for her

saddle. Turning to look once more for his own weapon, the world went white, and blue crackles of power moved through the air before his eyes. The edge of a blow of magic dissipated out around Winston, not touching him. He looked to Michael to see he had deflected Jonathan's efforts, and it had dropped Michael to his knees.

Winston needed his weapon. He looked about, locating it near Michael, partially covered by the tall grass. He moved to retrieve his sword and was shook in place by the impact of power reverberating through the shield around them as it absorbed the concussive blows of all three of the massive goats at once. Winston stumbled, and once again found himself next to Alban, his mathean. Shadows moved above him, drawing his attention. Winston looked up to see the large goat-like creature before him was slowly raising both of his massive arms in preparation to slam down again on the shield. Winston braced himself for the coming thrum of power.

"Now!" Yelled Michael.

Winston looked toward his friend, and instead saw Mhara, holding a crossbow and unloosed her shaft toward Jonathan. The arrow pierced clean through his forearm, causing him to release his hold on the scepter. In that same moment a final ripple went through the air, a blur passed behind the large goat-like creature whose arms were raised, and dark fluid spurted out from behind its legs. The creature howled an unmistaken cry of pain, and Winston saw Fionn look at him and smile in response to his own handy work.

How fast could he move? There wasn't time to dwell on such thoughts. Winston turned to look behind him, wanting to see where the other goats were. Flashes of power, like iridescent lightning, fluttered and hit the ground all around. As Winston turned, he placed his hand on his mount, out of what was becoming his habit, and was confronted by something cold, and hard.

Having had forgotten it was there in all the excitement, Winston reached up to release the fastenings. In doing so he allowed himself a moment to visually take in the action around him. Fionn had successfully eliminated one goat creature on his own, however the other two were on to his game, and were not proving such easy prey. Mhara was firing arrows as best she could from a defensible position, as Michael and Jonathan squared off in a battle of magic versus magic that would put most Fourth of July celebrations to shame.

"Winston. Move!" Mhara yelled.

He jumped back, pulling his prize with him, freeing it from the bedroll on his mount, and hit the dirt hard as a massive fist came across and collided with Alban, sending the mathean off its feet. The beast growled, and Winston felt a burning rage grow within himself. He breathed deeply as he perceived the world around him begin to blur.

"Are you alright?" Mhara asked.

"I'm fine." Winston said, getting to his feet. Sword still in his grasp, Winston turned his attention to the goat-like creature that had struck his mathean. The creature had turned to look at him, and Winston could feel the recognition as their eyes fully met. "Let's go." Winston said, as much to himself as to the creature, and removed the sword from its scabbard.

The creature roared as the metal began to emerge from its protective casing. Light shimmered in all directions as the blade swung out in Winston's grasp. At first he took it for the light of the fires around them reflecting off the newly exposed metal of the blade. Then he saw the eyes of the creature focus on the blade, as it took an involuntary step back. Winston looked to his weapon to find the blade of the sword consumed by a hungry blue flame. He took the hilt in both hands, turned back toward the creature, and smiled.

Before Winston could fully comprehend the movement the creature was upon him. Moving to evade, he sidestepped the attack. Seeing an opening, Winston lunged his own attack, the blade catching flesh and searing through it with ease. The creature howled. Winston turned, preparing another blow only to find the goat on the ground, not moving. It's body cut open from neck to hip, it's entrails spilling out onto the amber grass.

Winston looked down at the sword of Darkfyre. How had it cut so smoothly? He didn't feel a pull, or snag at any point in the swing. The lack of tension in his swing had left him believing his contact was limited with the Billy Goat. Instead the sword had sliced through the side of that creature with uninterrupted ease.

The third goat-like creature roared in protest at the fall of its brother. Its hide was speckled with arrow shafts, and it bled heavily from one leg. Readying himself for more conflict, Winston looked up to meet the creature. As soon as his eyes met the creatures eyes, it went still. The Billy goat's head slid from its shoulders, the body collapsing to the ground, and revealed a very bloody Fionn standing behind the corpse holding his sword.

"Enough, Jonathan!" Michael yelled.

The crazed wizard looked at the four of them. Eyes afire with determined passion as he looked to Winston. Recognition filled Jonathan's lustful eyes when he saw the Sword of Darkfyre. "No. It is not." He said eventually to nobody in particular.

The ground shook, and a terrible wind came down, churning

around them, pulling the wall of flames up and up into the sky. Winston covered his eyes from the heat, and debris. Hollow laughter came to his ears, along with the heavy pulse of wings.

"No!" Winston yelled. "Do not let him get away."

Winston moved as if to get to Jonathan, and was interrupted as something large collided with his chest. The impact was sudden, and fully pushed Winston to the ground. The weight of what hit him, falling upon him, and pressing the air instantly from his lungs.

In moments the air around them cleared, the fire was gone, and so was Jonathan. Michael lay atop Winston, unconscious, with blood streaming from his head.

"Michael? Are you with me?" He asked.

Michael only groaned in response to being moved. Fionn pulled his limp body up and positioned him on his mount. With Michael draped over his saddle, Fionn used rope to tie him down firmly against the beast.

"We must go." Fionn said, not looking at anyone in particular. "Prepare yourselves to ride."

Winston watched from his saddle atop Alban, as Fionn tied both the supply mathean, and Michael's mathean to his own. The sword of Darkfyre now tucked in his bedroll, and secured. His own sword retrieved from the grass. Fionn looked back at Mhara and Winston, giving them each a short nod, and kicked his beast forward. With that they were on the move again, the wind whipping around them, and the thunderous calamity of their mounts footfalls filling the air.

There was a sense of relief in being back on the move. Winston's eyes kept looking to the sky. Sure they were moving, but what happened back there in the plains? What would compel Jonathan to do that? Winston didn't hear their whole conversation, but he heard enough. Jonathan wanted to recruit Michael. He wanted Michael to join him. Clearly Michael said no, didn't he? He put up the shield. Winston remembered seeing him spinning that shaft, is that how he put up the shield. In all the chaos Winston didn't feel like he could be sure.

The presence of a shield simply raises other questions. Such as why didn't Michael put one of those in place in conjunction with his veil at the campsites? That sure would have helped keep them from being ambushed. Yet Michael never even mentioned an ability to do a shield. In fact, beyond throwing around some power, all Winston had ever witnessed him do was visual illusions. Right? Winston couldn't be sure. He didn't even know exactly how magic works. Let alone not being with Michael all the time to know his actions. For all he knew Michael could be an amazingly powerful wizard. An amazingly powerful wizard, who was knocked unconscious, and now lay tied like a freshly killed deer to his mathean's mount.

They rode onward, Winston trusting Alban to stay with the group. He barely held to the reigns. After the blow Alban took, he imagined the beast needed to let loose some steam. Winston watched Alban's muscles move beneath him, the creatures fur churning from the air as they relentlessly pushed their way forward. Though the blow seemed violent and brutal, Alban showed no worse for wear, as he stayed on pace with Fionn and his mount.

The failing sun was overtaken by the hills of the horizon, and the cool lighting of night slowly moved to cover the land. Winston continued to watch the skies for any sign of threat, not fully registering where they were until he heard the splash of water below Alban's feet. He pulled his eyes away from the smoldering sky to behold the cold blue scene of bustling port town. It looked like something pulled straight out of a Tolkein novel.

The streets were wide enough for carriages to comfortably travel by, and around each other, yet not uniformed like modern roads. The edges of the roads were capped by walkways of varying width. Their traversable area subject to the area left after the roads and buildings were in place. Regarding the buildings, they looked almost casually placed; like a giant pulled them from its play set, and positioned them nonchalantly across the land. Some were well spaced, while others were built atop each other.

Winston was struck by how… human everything looked. Families walked the streets, going into shops, and talking to vendors. The pedestrians wore hats and jackets, waved hello to each other, and if it wasn't for their inhuman skin tones, and different facial structure, Winston could have been convinced he was home. Granted it would be a home a century or so before he was born, but he'd be back in his realm nonetheless.

"What is that smell?" Winston asked.

"Is it bad?"

"No. Not at all. It smells delicious."

"Goose." Fionn said.

"What do you mean, goose?"

"It's goose." Fionn said.

"You have geese here?"

"Ha! No. We trade with humans for them, and they are delicious."

"There are humans here?"

"Of course there are. This is the Port of Hollows isn't it?"

Winston felt confused by the statement. How was he to take this information? To be told they were in a place where humans were able to travel freely, to buy, sell, and trade. Well that certainly meant this place should be a way for him to get home.

"It's not that simple." Michael chimed in. As if he could read Winston's thoughts. "There are rules for who can come and go between realms, and along with that there are regulations on where those people can come from and go to."

"So you need a fairy passport?"

"Aye. Essentially."

"How do I get one?"

"You'll not be getting one." Michael said sharply. "Ye have to earn them, and we've not time for that. Now come, the Inn is ahead."

They rode toward what seemed like the easterly edge of town, toward an inn that looked as much a fortress, as it did an establishment of hospitality. Outside the building stood a group of large, stout figures. Nearing them Winston could recognize their armor as being very similar to Fionn's, if not a tad less ornate.

"Ho, brothers!" Fionn called out, raising his hand warmly toward the group.

"HO!" came the choral reply, as the full called out in trumpeting unison, raising hands in welcome.

They dismounted, Fionn quickly joined the group to talk, as Michael arranged care for their matheans with the young looking grooms keeper at the inn. They were informed that all the arrangements for themselves, and their mounts had already been arranged. Carrying their things in with them, Winston, Mhara, and Michael joined Fionn and the group of warriors.

"He's inside." Said a tall, young looking warrior.

"Right then, cheers." Michael said with a kind smile, and continued inside.

Winston moved to follow Mhara and Michael, and was stopped when one of the other warriors placed a hand on his chest.

"Is this him, M' lord?" He asked Fionn, who was looking on with a feeling of pride to his eyes.

"True as the sun does shine, that's him." Fionn said.

"Shouldn't he be taller?" Asked another voice.

"He's plenty tall, ya big oaf."

"Our apologies for Rif's thoughtlessness, my Liege." The first warrior said, with a respectful bow.

Murmurs came from others in the group, expressing the support of the apology. Winston heard it again. My Liege. Who did these men think he was, and what story had Fionn spun for them. Before he could think on it further Fionn stepped forward through the group, his hand on the shoulder of an embarrassed young man, whose helm had been removed. They stood before him a moment, Winston unsure if Fionn expected him to say something or not. Winston looked to him for some sort of direction, and Fionn replied with a subtle, dismissive shake of his head. He then gave the young warrior a firm shake at his shoulder.

"Go on, then." Fionn said.

"Ah... Forgive me, my Liege." The young warrior stumbled. "I, ah, I meant no disrespect ye see, and.."

"It's alright." Winston said.

Fionn smile widely and stepped forward. "Men." He said. "This is Winston. Winston, these are the Fianna. My trusted, and sworn warriors."

"It's good to meet you all."

"There are more, many more, but these are here for you." Fionn said. "My other warriors are fulfilling other tasks assigned to them. These five here will be at your disposal should you ever need them."

"Fionn, I.."

"No." Fionn interrupted, and stepping close to Winston he lowered his voice. "They know their roles to play, and a time is coming where you will need them. Hmm?" Fionn said, giving Winston a fierce confident stare.

A moment, noticeable and long passed between them. Neither man saying a word.

"Thank you." Winston finally said. "My friend."

"It is nothing!" Fionn said, his voice becoming light and jovial. "Let us continue inside. Myrddin awaits."

Winston allowed the seasoned warrior to guide him inside. The Inn was cozy and warm. Lights of flame filled the space, and welcoming smells of food and ale filled his senses. Michael was speaking with Myrddin, as Mhara waited near. Myrddin looked up from the conversation as if otherworldly aware of Winston entering the room.

"Winston, my boy." Myrddin said. "Come. Come."

Setting his burden down, Winston took a seat near Myrddin, and Michael.

"Michael informed me about your trouble on the road. Are you alright?" Myrddin asked.

"I am, sir."

"You must tell me if seeing Michael tied down to his saddle is as amusing a sight, as I imagine."

Mhara let out a snicker from her seat, and Michael looked less than amused.

"Almost too natural." Winston said, causing a rich guffaw from the room.

"I already explained." Michael said in an effort of protest.

"Oh calm yourself, Michael." Myrddin said. "Can you not appreciate a bit of levity in the face of such certain trial?"

"Well, of course, but.."

"Then sit with me, and Winston, for we have little time."

"What is it, Sir? Do you know where Jonathan went?"

"Not precisely." Myrddin said. "We do have a method we believe will help us find out, if you're willing to help."

"Of course. Just tell me what you need me to do."

Myrddin paused, looking to the collected group, person by person. Slowly he pulled a wrapped cloth from his pocket, and placed it on the table. Then he looked to Winston.

"What is it?" Winston asked.

"To stop Jonathan we must move on multiple fronts. Fionn, and his men will accompany me to Summer, to meet with its Queen. Whilst you join Michael, and Mhara."

"That's not too different than how things have been going so far." Winston interjected thoughtlessly. "What do you want me to do?"

Myrddin unfolded the cloth exposing an amulet of a leaf, intertwined with braided vinery. Its color was that of a greenish brass. Myrddin took it up in one hand and presented it to Winston.

"I want you to go home."

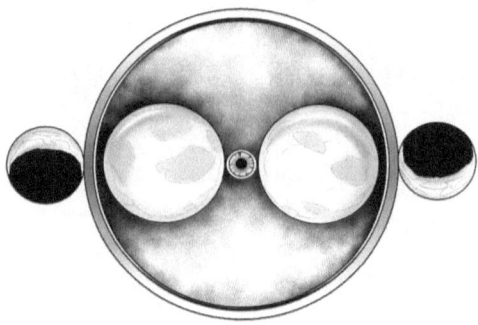

21 – SEE WHERE YOU WANT TO BE

The night was long, and sleep was an elusive prize. Winston lay in the bed provided for him, holding tightly to the amulet from Myrddin. Somehow this item had the ability to allow Winston to travel with Michael and Mhara, between realms. Winston gripped it in his hands as he replayed the brief conversation Myrddin and he had shared when he gave it to Winston.

"You want me to do what?" Winston asked.

"Why, to go home, my boy." Myrddin had repeated in a tone as to suggest the notion should not prove to be the least bit surprising. Winston didn't reply, and Murdinn took that opportunity to continue. "Jonathan is not actively in Faerie. He was here. We felt him return shortly before he ambushed you. Sadly, that knowledge didn't tell us where he would be. Thus why we were unable to intervene."

"And now he's left again?"

"Yes, he has."

"Do you know, to where?"

"No." Myrddin said solemnly "It doesn't work like that. Different areas of Faerie connect to different areas of your realm, and those connections change throughout the year. Moreover, where they open up is also influenced by the one traversing the realms."

"What good will it do to send us back if we do not know where he is?"

"We have, what you could call an investigator, you could contact him. He lives in your realm, and his job is to guard the ways between the realm of man, and Faerie." Myrddin looked at Winston squarely. "Jonathan may be a clever devil, but he is not so clever to move completely in secret."

"So this, investigator, knows where he is?"

"If anyone does, he would. He oversees the North American continent, and if Jonathan transferred over from Faerie to Minnesota, Gawain would know of it."

"Gawain?" Michael asked. His voice cutting into the conversation in a sharp, concerned tone.

"The one and only." Myrddin said.

"Bloody hell! Why don't we ask Arthur for help while we're at it?" Michael exclaimed. "Or perhaps the great King is too long in his castle to care much for the lives of men, or Faerie."

"Take care what you say, wizard." Myrddin said, his voice one of command and control. "You know little of what you speak."

"The Ten are an arcane institution that has failed in their mission." Michael said. "You of all people know this." He continued, pointing at Myrddin and standing as if to command them both. "No matter their efforts, Morgana's minions continue to make their way into the realm of men, even costing members of the Ten their lives. All things considered, one could think that Morgana was."

"Enough!" Myrddin interrupted, standing to meet Michael eye to eye. "Do not use my condemnable wife's name again, lest you mean to undermine our efforts this day." Myrddin looked about the now silent room, then down at Winston. He handed the amulet to him. "Take this, Winston, and keep it close. It is yours now. Tomorrow we will discuss how you use it, and what it can do for you. For now, it seems we have talked enough. We should get some rest. All of us." Commanded the wizard King, while shooting a look toward Michael.

Winston took the amulet in his hand. It was warm, and not simply in temperature. It felt as if it was emitting its own heat. He gripped it tightly in his hand, and stood. He gave Myrddin a respectful nod and looked to Michael, who was looking at him.

"Aye. Sorry, lad." Michael said.

Winston gave Michael a nod. "Good night, everyone." He said to the room as he departed.

"Come." Said Fionn. "I'll show you where you can rest."

By all the stars, Winston tried to rest. He tried to sleep, and not think about the odd tension between Michael and Myrddin. Why did this Gawain character upset Michael so much? Were the Ten the knights of Arthur that had survived the invasion of Annwn, and the trials of Morgana, with Arthur himself at their lead? Winston felt sure that they had to be. Yet when Michael first told him about the Ten at the feast he didn't seem to hold near as much animosity regarding them, or their existence. Where did that come from? Surely Michael could see they needed all the help they could get to stop Jonathan. Especially after Jonathan's ambush of them in the Autumnlands.

Still, Winston knew he could do little about that now. He needed to trust Myrddin, and try to sleep. He did. He tried. Yet hours had passed, and it was no longer a matter of trying to sleep, as that effort was now compounded by the struggle to ignore the sounds of activity outside the door to his small room. As the world outside came to life, Winston yet pursued sleep, and was now challenged to ignore the tantalizing smell of freshly baked bread, and cooked sausages, whose aromas had now infiltrated his bedchamber.

Winston turned to sit up at the same time that the door to his room smoothly swung open. He looked up to see a thick armed, bear of a man standing in the doorway.

"Ho, Winston. You are awake? Good." Fionn said in a manner far too alive for this time of day. "Come. We have food, and Myrddin awaits you."

Just as smoothly as he filled the doorway, Fionn was gone. In his wake he left the door open. No doubt to allow the light in from outside, and thus ensure Winston would not easily fall back to sleep. Little did Fionn know how impossible it was for Winston to get any sleep at all that night.

Winston fastened his britches, and put on his boots. New clothes were waiting for him to wear. These were of a different cut, like modern day versions of medieval garments. More blending in was needed Winston supposed. The Port of Hollows had humans there after all.

After putting on his tunic he fixed his bed, smiling to himself as he tucked down the corners of the bed coverings. It felt good. It was an old habit, but it had been a while since he had made a bed. He remembered an old CO that would remind him every day that the quality of how Winston's day would go could be directly tied back to how he started his day. One of the things that anyone could do to ensure a strong start to their day, and also start it by successfully accomplishing something, was to make their bed. Winston found himself feeling more confident than he had when originally confronted with this day as he turned from the bed to step out and face the morning.

In the main room Winston found plates of fresh rolls, sausages, fruit, and butter. As his senses awakened with the full recognition of this feast before him it became as if there were no one else in the world. Winston sat quickly and began to eat.

An unrecognized span of time had passed when Winston finally sat back from his meal, leaned against the wall behind him, and saw that everyone was either standing or sitting in the room, all eyes directed at him.

"Did ye get enough, boy?" Michael asks.

Winston sat up, stiffening slightly, concerned he may have eaten so much that the others may end up going without. He opened his mouth to speak but was interrupted.

"We already ate." Myrddin said from his spot directly across from Winston. "It is good you had your fill. Was it to your liking then?"

"Yes." Winston said quickly. "It was delicious."

"Ah, good. Mrs. Muffet will be pleased to hear so." Myrddin said, standing. "Now we must be off. Come."

The whole group turned to follow Myrddin out of the Inn. Winston followed, stuffing a couple sausages into two rolls and stashing them in his bag as he exited the building. Outside the air was fresh, like after a fall rain. Myrddin was giving directions to Fionn that Winston couldn't fully hear beyond picking up something about "Winter."

Fionn signaled to his men, who quickly mounted and were ready to move. Winston saw one of the men was riding Alban. A pang of possessiveness came over him, and he found himself jogging up to the beast. Alban turned, snorting, and nuzzled into Winston. He ran his fingers through his fur, hoping badly that he would see Alban again. Winston looked up to the rider. It was the same young warrior who had spoken to him the night before.

"I'll see to it he stays safe, my liege."

Winston smiled, pet Alban again on the snout. "Thank you." He said. As much to the young warrior, as to Alban.

Fionn and his warriors were gone before Winston could fully process their leaving. A part of him wished he was going with them, for they were certainly headed for a fight. Still, a part of him knew that was not where he was meant to be. He also didn't know how well he would do with Fionn's men referring to him as their liege the whole time. He still had no answer to where that habit came from, or what justified their doing it. Yet another mystery to add to the list he supposed.

"Magnificent creatures aren't they?" Asked Myrddin, now standing next to Winston. "For beasts of the land, it is almost as if they run with the wind itself." He looked down at Winston. "Like a winter storm, one could say." He smiled. "Do you have the amulet?"

Winston retrieved the warm metal trinket and held it out to Myrddin.

"No, no, you mustn't give it to anyone." The Wizard King said. "It is yours, and yours alone the moment you took it from my hand."

Winston looked down at the amulet in his own hand. "I don't know what to do with it. Is it supposed to be this warm?"

"It recognizes your power, Winston."

"My power?" Winston asked.

"Surely you've deduced that truth?" Myrddin said.

"I've learned it best never to assume." Winston said. "So all hints, and coy responses aside, I've resolved to wait for someone to give me clear information before drawing any conclusions."

"You must learn to trust your instincts, dear boy. Or at the very least to trust the verifiable evidence around you."

Winston didn't say a word. Instead he looked at the ancient wizard. Looked at him with eyes of cold, sure resolve, as he waited for a clear reply. Myrddin stood a bit taller, his chin dropping toward his chest like the burden of the responsibility now fully weighed down upon his shoulders. He exhaled through his nose, and looked to Winston.

"You have met your mother?" Myrddin asked.

"I did." Winston agreed.

"Do you believe she, as she claimed to be, the goddess Airmid, to truly be your mother?"

Winston searched within himself, his feelings, and found himself with zero doubt on the matter. He knew as surely as the day is bright that she was his mother. "Yes." He said plainly.

"Very good." Myrddin said, his voice almost sounding relieved. "Do you recall what that means when one has a parent of the Fae?"

"Michael explained to me before, that the children of humans and Faerie can become wizards."

"This is true, though not the whole truth."

"What is the whole truth?" an insistent edge to Winston's

question.

"Patience, son. I am telling you." Myrddin assured Winston. "Children whose parentage is of humans and Faerie are unique, and many know them to be wizards. They are also known to be changelings, demigods, and many other kinds of beings long found throughout the lore of man. Some can go most of their lives, even all of their lives, and never know what they truly are. While children between humans and Faeries are not forbidden, they are not as equally received among the kin of their parents as a true blood child would be."

"How do I know what I am?" The question came from Winston's lips as quickly as a breath, and with just as little thought. The moment he said it he knew it had been a question he had been long needing the answer to. He left the question hanging in the air, not saying anything further. His eyes locked on those of the great wizard king.

"That is something we will learn together. I cannot tell you."

Frustration surged in Winston. "What good is it then? Hm? More vague answers, and open ended questions. This is bullshit!"

"Calm yourself, son." Myrddin said firmly.

A wave of power passed over Winston, catching his breath, and he felt the frustration wash away like water flowing from the shore. It was there, but it had receded back into the sea.

"You must be the one to connect to your power." Myrddin continued. "For this reason, you could not simply be told of your parentage, or of your connection to Faerie. Your mother knew this, and that is why she left the box, carved from the stone of fate, with the Winter Queen. Inside you, Winston, there is great power, power that only you can truly harness and release."

"Am I going to become a monster, or…" Winston's voice

cracked. His insecurities and fear of the uncertainty of it all welled within him.

"Anything is possible, son. You will be who you have always been." Myrddin assured Winston. "I am confident you will accomplish this, and to start you upon this journey I gave you the amulet."

Winston opened his hand. It still held the warm metal trinket. It was no bigger than a fifty-cent piece, and far heavier than seemed appropriate.

"The amulet will allow you, anything in your possession, and anyone touching you; passage between realms, yet as with most uses of magic there is always a cost."

"How do I use it?"

"What do you discern from its appearance?"

"It's a leaf wrapped in braided vinery. Does it require blood like the box did?"

"No. That level of sacrifice is not needed." Myrddin assured. "What do you see?"

What do you see? It all felt like more misdirection to Winston. Nonetheless he looked again at the amulet. He felt its warmth. It felt alive to him, as if the warmth wasn't simply its state of being but the result of the heat the amulet itself was emitting. As he looked at the leaf, the vines, taking in the intricate detailing, he found himself having to look over it again, and again, as the details seemed to shift and change. No. It didn't change. The amulet moved. "It's alive." He said quietly to himself.

"In a manner of speaking, yes." Myrddin confirmed. "Do you recall where you were the night Jonathan traded places with you?"

"Yes. I was at work."

"Very good. I need you to firmly picture that place in your mind."

As Winston pictured the sterile hallways of the secure sublevels of Boltex Electronics, the vines on the amulet began to more than shift, they grew in length, reaching out and wrapping themselves around Winston's hand.

"Excellent, son. Excellent!" Myrddin said. He looked to Mhara and Michael who had been standing a short way off. "Come. Come. Are you prepared?"

"Aye. We're ready." Replied Michael. He and Mhara were also wearing different clothing. Winston recognizing that their new outfits were meant to help them blend better in the realm of man.

"Hey! Is this normal?" Winston asked. The vines had now braided, and woven their way around his hand and forearm, creating a kind of bracer.

Myrddin moved to stand directly in front of Winston. He extended to him a leather pack. Winston took it, and was caught off guard by its weight. The wizard had handled it with such ease that the reality of its weight was unexpected. Winston felt a hands resting on each of his shoulders, but it was not Myrddin. Mhara was standing to his left, and Michael to his right, their hands on the corresponding shoulders.

"The amulet will use your will, your life's force, to send you where you choose to be." Myrddin was saying. It was hard for Winston to hear him as a tempest had begun moving around them, churning the ground, and buffeting them all with strong winds. "See where you want to be, son. Picture it full, and true within your mind. Know that you can be there, that you are already there, and it will be so." Myrddin took a step away from Winston.

"How will we find your investigator?" Winston yelled to the wizard.

"Not to worry." He called back. "Gawain will find you."

If the old wizard said anything further Winston did not hear it. He felt Michael's grip increase on his shoulder, and Mhara stepped closer to him, her other hand taking his arm. Dust, dirt, and a rainbow of colors spun around them in a vortex of power, and as quickly as it rose, it dissipated.

Now they stood in darkness, no wind, no other sounds at all outside of their breathing. Winston rubbed his eyes, and moved his pack to his shoulder. As his eyes focused he could make out a red blinking light in the distance.

"Where are we." Mhara asked.

Winston didn't answer right away. Instead he listened. He heard it, the familiar hum of the controlled ventilation system, and the faint ticking of the clock at the end of the hall.

"We need to be moving." Michael said.

"Wait." Winston said. "Would magic have disrupted the electrical systems around us when we arrived?"

"It's been known to happen. Some magic works very similarly to electric and magnetic fields in your realm."

"That works to our advantage."

"How so?" Mhara asked.

"If I'm right, we are on one of the sublevels to the building I work in. All the lights are off because our arrival blew them out." Winston explained. "This is good, and potentially bad."

"Bad?"

"Yeah. It means the security system is down, and cameras are out, so they have no idea we're here."

"How is that bad?" Mhara asked.

"It means security is currently on their way down here to evaluate the situation. Stay with me."

Winston lead them down the hallway to a small utility stairwell. They went up what felt like far too many stairs until they reached a larger platform level. Winston had them wait by an exterior emergency door, while he went through another to retrieve his "shit" he had told them. He returned in a moment holding a backpack.

"What is that?" Michael asked.

Winston reached in and pulled out a collection of metallic, chiming objects. "My keys." Winston said, dangling them in front of Michael's face. "I have no idea how long I've been gone, but I'm hoping my car is still sitting out there in the parking lot."

"Where are we going to go?"

"I have no idea, but we can't stay here. It's a secure building and technically we are trespassing." Winston moved over near the door and peeked through the small reinforced glass window. He let out a short exclamation. "There she is." He turned to his companions. "You two ready? When I open this door we gotta run. An alarm will sound and they will know exactly where we are."

"Aye."

"I am ready."

At that, they exited the building, and stepped out into the crisp night air of a Minnesota winter. The alarm's shrill cry of warning pierced the air as soon as Winston pressed down on the door's handle. They ran. Winston's heart pounded as he sprinted toward his car. Michael and

Mhara had little problem keeping up with him.

His hands fumbled with the keys as he eagerly tried to unlock the door to his vehicle. This slight delay was punctuated by every light in the facility's parking lot illuminating. Before Winston's eyes could fully adjust to the bright lights they were in the car. Michael in back, and Mhara in the passenger side of the front seat. The car started to their mutual relief, and Winston pushed hard on the accelerator, sending them speeding toward the side exit of the lot.

Security personnel began exiting the building, some even heading for vehicles of their own. The exit before them had its arm down, blocking their escape. Winston veered off to the right of the exit, mounting the curb, and drove across the snow-covered landscaping to avoid driving through the gate arm.

In minutes they were a pair of red dots among a sea of red dots, all weathering the joys of winter traffic in Minnesota. As they breathed their relief, they hadn't noticed in the chaos the figure among the trees. A figure in a flowing robe, eyes luminescing in the dark of night, keenly watching their departure. Nor did they detect its pursuit, as it did so not in a car, but from above, with wings of nightmarish legend.

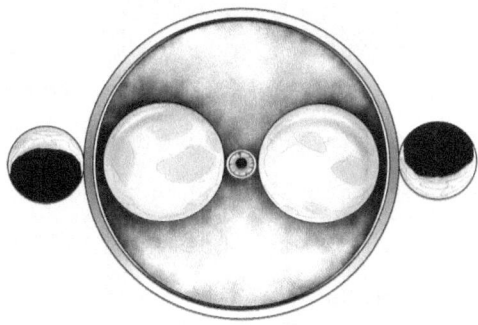

22 – SOMEWHERE BRIGHT

The rays of the rising sun pulled at Winston's eyelids like an eager child. Before he opened them, he could already feel the old familiar soreness in his neck and back, his mouth was dry, and teeth in need of washing. He realized he had not suffered these sensations all the while in Faerie. It also occurred to Winston that it had been quite some time since he slept in his car.

Fingers softly tugged at his right hand. He opened his eyes slightly and turned his head to see that Mhara was holding his hand. A helpless smile pulled at his lips. She was still asleep, likely not aware of the gentle affection. He could hear her breathing, and determined quickly that he could listen to that for hours without complaint. It was a surprising, and pleasant realization. One that was rudely interrupted by the harsh, deep snarl of a snore emanating from the back seat of the car.

At that Winston softly laughed to himself. There was something comforting about this moment.

Without removing his hand, Winston started the vehicle, fastened his safety belt, and began to move toward the freeway. They had pulled over at a rest stop to sleep, though he wasn't exactly sure where they were. Somewhere near Hastings he supposed. They had driven as far and as fast as they could to get away, and now he knew they needed food, and his car needed fuel.

As he approached the exit from the parking lot to the on ramp, a tall man in a long coat waved to him from the shadowed side of the road. Winston thought to drive on but then worried it may cause unneeded attention. The man seemed to want to ask him a question. Winston slowed down, looking about as he did for signs of concern, or at least signs of which vehicle may belong to this guy. He rolled his window down.

"Morning, friend." Said the man.

"Morning." Winston replied, his voice a whisper. "My friends are sleeping, so I don't want to be loud."

"Yes. Yes." Replied the man, lowering his own voice. His eyes were pale, slate blue, and his long black hair moved rebelliously with the wind in front of his face. "I apologize to bother; would you be able to tell me how far Saint Paul is from here? We're from out of town and aren't really sure."

Winston wasn't sure how to respond. One thing he knew is Saint Paul was listed regularly on almost every sign along the roads where you were headed toward the capital. This guy's question, along with his look was making Winston uneasy. "Sorry, man. We drove all night and are just getting our bearings ourselves. Should be a map in the rest stop though."

"Ah. Thank you. I'll take a look." The mysterious man said. "You all headed somewhere fun?"

"We're on an adventure." Winston said without thinking, flashing a warm smile. He didn't want to tell his man where they were going. He also didn't know where they were going, only that they needed to find Jonathan. "We gotta get on the road. Take care."

Winston heard the man say "Of course, you too." As he drove away and rolled up his window. As the car reached the road he looked to Mhara who was still sleeping. The sign on the road indicated he had merged onto highway 61 north.

"We need to get somewhere bright." Michael said firmly from the back seat.

"What?" Winston said, repressing a jump a fright. "Good morning to you too."

"I didn't mean to startle you."

"Its fine. What are you saying now?"

"We need to get somewhere bright."

"Umm…" Winston gestured at the rising sun, his action stirring Mhara. "The sun is rising presently."

"Aye, that I can see. I'm saying we need to find somewhere bright for when the sun's gone down."

"Why? I thought we had to find Jonathan."

"We do, and we will." Michael assured him.

"What's got you all worked up this morning?"

"That man you spoke with?" Michael said.

"What about him."

"He's not a man. He's of Faerie." The wizard said assuredly.

"What's more, he's a hunter, and they are strongest in darkness."

"That's great." Winston said, noting an unconscious increase in acceleration.

"Calm yourself, Winston." Michael said, placing a hand on Winston's shoulder. "They are weakest during the day, and weakened by any prominent light source. Their kind are akin to your legends of vampires and the like. Though I doubt garlic, or religious symbolism mean much to them."

"How am I supposed to respond to that? Should I panic because it's a vampire-like creature of Faerie? Or should I be relieved because vampires don't actually exist?"

"It's not for me to tell you how to feel." Michael said.

"Of course not."

"Vampires do exist however."

"Well, shit." Winston exclaimed. "This day is getting better and better."

"What is the matter?" Mhara asked, now fully alert due to their vibrant interchange.

"Mr. Wizard back there says we just came across a hunter, and we need to get to an area of strong light sources."

"What?"

"Exactly my thoughts." Winston said.

"Did he touch you?" Mhara asked.

"What? No. He never even approached the car. What the hell is going on?"

"If a hunter is here he is here for a reason." Mhara said urgently. "Why didn't you kill him?" She asked, directing her question by glaring at Michael.

"Oi, don't look at me like that, young miss." Michael said

defensively. "What was I to do? Smite him down right there in the clear morning sun? Bloody hell. For all we know he wasn't sure who he was talking to, or who we all were. Even if he did know who each of us were, we have no idea how many companions he has with him."

"But it was definitely a he?"

"Yes." Winston assured. "You two need to start speaking in full thoughts."

"Winston, hunters are the assassins of Faerie. He would only be here if he was assigned to be here. Likely he was waiting for us to arrive, and has been tracking us since we fled in your car." Mhara said, her voice flush with urgency. "Our only solace is that males often travel alone."

"Unless he is with his mother." Michael added.

"His mother?" Winston asked.

"Precisely." Mhara said. "Mothers will keep their brood close for as long as they can, never leaving on the hunt without them."

"Their brood? As in kids, and mate?"

"No. It's their offspring alone." Michael said. "They kill their mates."

"Wonderful. Well here's hoping he is flying solo." Winston said.

"You know they fly?" Mhara asked in surprise.

"They what? No. That was just a figure of speech. Are you serious? They fly?"

"Aye. Only at night." Michael said. "They move fast, and can cross long distances easily, but they can only fly or engage many of their powerful skills in the night. Which is good for us at the moment."

"Agreed." Winston said. "We should get some solid distance between us and him."

"Where can we go?" Mhara asked.

"We're going to Minneapolis. It's the biggest city in Minnesota, and there are always lights on somewhere. I just hope all this running around doesn't keep that investigator from being able to find us."

"Heh." Michael scoffed. "He'll find us fine. Bloody knights. Forgive me, but he'll find us fine."

Winston opted not to press, and instead focused back on the road. They chattered on aimlessly as he drove, sharing observations of the world around them, and not saying anything of noticeable value. The open, tree lined horizon became more and more occupied as the buildings grew in both size and density the closer Winston brought them to the city.

The familiar sights of the downtown skyline, and the entitled behavior of local drivers all felt welcomingly satisfying to him. It occurred to Winston that a part of him had given way to believing he would never return from Faerie. Even with there not being anything or anyone he would be returning to in particular, he now found himself almost gleeful to be back.

They stopped for food, opting for a drive thru and eating in the car. Mhara clearly didn't care for the overly processed food, while Michael released sounds of near ecstasy as he ate his double patty heart attack sandwich. Mhara said she had been to the realm of man before, but she'd never been this far inland, or eaten such food. Through his laughter over her response to the food, Winston promised they would eat better going forward.

The sun hung fully in the midday sky. Its bright light strongly juxtaposed with the cold, sharp winter air. They sought refuge from the season, and the car, within the warmth of a local mall rotunda. Michael was enjoying a chair massage, while Mhara feasted on a nacho cheese pretzel. Winston didn't have the heart to tell her the pretzel was no better than their drive thru food. Instead he enjoyed the sight of someone genuinely enjoying the experience for the first time, and loving it.

"Greetings, Night wielder." Said a voice that rang out crisp and true, cutting through the noise of the crowd, while not seeming to touch any ears but Winston's alone. "How many are with you?"

"Two others." Winston replied aloud, not thinking how it may appear.

"Who are you talking to?" Mhara asked, her face took on a look of recognition as soon as the words left her lips. "Where is he?"

"I take it then, the wizard is with you?" the voice asked.

"Yes. Him, and the woman next to me."

"Gather them, and meet me on the parking ramp's upper most level."

"Ok. Then what?"

"Move swiftly." Instructed the mysterious voice. "There are others. If they are not with you, I can only assume they are here for you."

Winston's eyes shot about the large open space. "Get Michael." He said to Mhara, while gathering his own things. "How many are there?" He asked the voice. "How do I know you are not with them?" There was no response.

"What's happening?" Michael asked when he and Mhara returned.

"I heard a voice, it said we are not alone, there are an untold number of persons trailing us. We are to meet this mystery person on the upper level to the parking ramp. Let's go!"

The three of them weaved through the crowd, up the escalators, and out of the upper level of a department store to the skywalk connected to the ramp. Once within the ramp there were still two more floors above them. They ran. Moving up the flights of stairs and pressing out through the double doors to the open upper level of the ramp.

Winston could hear foot falls behind them. Boots. He motioned for Michael and Mhara to move to the side and positioned himself to draw the sword.

The doors they had just exited flew open, and a body clad in a dark flowing coat soared through them. As the body hit the ground Winston could see the head was no longer attached. Made all the clearer as it rolled away from the body. It was the hunter from the rest stop. To his side, Winston felt Michael tense, and widen his stance. Winston focused back on the doors in time to see a large figure step through.

The man was tall, with brown, golden hair that flowed messily about his face and neck. His face presented a beard of a slightly darker shade. Though his clothing were of the modern, common garb, he was unmistakably a man out of time. Not least of which thanks to the sword he held in his right hand. The man's eyes were steady, and keen as they inspected what was no doubt his handy work. Satisfied the dark clothed hunter was dead, he turned toward Winston.

"Greetings." He said in a familiar and warm tone. "I mean you no harm. Are you Winston?"

"I am."

"I am Gawain, of the third sector, knight of the Ten." He said with a courteous bow. "As per Merlin's request, I am here to offer you my aid."

"Myrddin, you mean to say." Michael interjected.

Remembering the contentious conversation between Michael and Myrddin, Winston tried to calm Michael but couldn't steal his attention away from the knight.

"Myrddin, yes. My sincerest apologies." The knight said with a knowing smile. "Shall we be on our way? That is. Unless you three would fancy to fight twelve more of these things."

"Twelve?" Mhara said in a panic.

"Ah, bullocks."

"What is it?" Winston asked.

"If there are twelve, then this makes him thirteen."

"And?"

"That's a brood, boy." Michael said. "The mother's coming."

23 – CHILD OF DAMNATION

Winston cringed as the car's oil pan scraped against the pavement when they erupted from the parking ramp. Each of his passengers held tightly to their Jesus bars as he took the turn, and directed them away from the mall.

"Think you can go any faster?" Michael asked sarcastically from the back. Winston didn't reply. He figured Michael was still butt hurt over relinquishing the shotgun position to the knight. "Jokes aside," Michael said, "Is she following us."

"I am not able to say for certain." Gawain volunteered after a moment. "I can tell they are there, but we are moving too fast for me to pin them down."

Winston's eyes met Michael's in the rearview mirror. "Why can't you do tricks like that?" He jabbed at the clearly annoyed wizard.

"He uses a different kind of magic than I do." Michael said seriously.

"Really? Are you being serious?"

"Aye. His is of Annwn, the Otherworld."

"What does that have to do with anything?" Winston asked.

"My magic is developed, and drawn from my genetic lineage. His is…"

"Take care for what you are about to say, wizard." Gawain interjected.

"… It is a gift. A tool given by Myrddin himself to aid the knights." Michael concluded, leaning back and looking out the side window. Gawain seemed pleased with that statement, as he sat looking forward.

Winston took another turn bringing them to a straightaway with empty lots and construction on either side of the road. Gawain had said they would be best to take this fight away from the populated area of the mall, should they not be able to avoid it. It was now looking like avoiding it would be out of the question.

"Why are we slowing down?" Mhara asked.

"She found us." Winston said, pointing straight ahead.

In the distance stood a slim, dark figure, that looked all too human except for the massive bat like wings protruding out from her back, and the dark, smoky mist that seemed to flow smoothly off of her. Landing, and walking up next to her were her brood. Some had wings, most didn't.

Tapping into his ingrained military training, Winston looked for paths of escape. He saw a small group of dark figures walking toward the rear of the car. He looked to the sides, nothing. Forward and backward were their only options. Just as the weight of moment crept up his spine he felt a hand squeeze his shoulder.

"Listen to me now." Gawain said. "We will get through this. I need you to do exactly as I say. Will you do this?"

"Alright."

"Wait!" Michael interjected.

"Now is not the time for debate, wizard." Gawain said, looking back at Winston. "Will you do as I say?" He asked Winston again.

"I will."

"Run her down."

Winston paused, looking at Gawain, who tilted his head forward and raising his eyebrows in assured expectation. Without further discussion Winston pressed his foot down on the accelerator. They began to rocket forward, directly toward the mother and her hoard. Winston heard the screams from the creatures that were nearing the rear of his car as they sped away.

"Wizard." Gawain said.

"Yes. Knight."

"Prepare yourself for battle."

"That looks like more than twelve!" Winston yelled.

"Just drive. Faster!" Gawain said, placing is hand on Winston's knee, pressing down to promote him to accelerate.

"That does look like more than twelve." Mhara said.

"Aye, it certainly does."

"What is your focus, wizard?"

"Fire and illusions."

The knight didn't reply. Instead he nodded in approval and turned forward with a smile. The distance between the hoard and them reduced, second by second. They were so close Winston thought he could make out the look on the mother's face. She was... smiling.

"Do not stop!" Gawain yelled.

Winston pressed pedal as far against the floor as he could. The engine of the car purred. Gawain gave way to a battle cry that shook the small vehicle. Michael, and Mhara quickly joined his cry. The pressure of their speed sent vibrations through the car, up the steering column, and into Winston's arms. He was unsure his car would survive this, let alone if they would survive. His vision started to blur. His ears rang from the screaming in the car, realizing in that moment he was yelling too. Thirty feet. Twenty feet. Ten. Five… She was definitely smiling.

The impact came in an instant. The momentums shift pressing Winston hard against his belt. The world went dark as he spun. He heard the crunch of plastic and metal as the car flipped, and the grind of metal on pavement as it slid down the road. Opening his eyes there was a dark haze all around. Smoke? Was the car on fire?

"Winston!" Mhara yelled from his left. He looked toward her voice. How was she outside of the car? Winston thought to ask just as she ripped the door open. "Come on. You need to get out." She said.

More screaming, and the sun was so bright. Winston got to his feet, resting his hand on the edge of the vehicle. The dark smoke trailed out of the car, and around him. In the distance he saw Michael and Gawain fighting the hoard. Flashes of power extended from Michael, sending shadowy figures flying away from him. Gawain wielded a sword of a beauty, and used it like a man dancing with his longtime lover. He would move, and it was as if the sword knew where it needed to be next without him telling it. They were holding their own but something told him he needed his weapons before the hoard was too much for the two.

As he moved to the rear of the car to retrieve his weapons from the trunk of the car it moved. From beneath the car came a guttural growl as the car spun slowly. In a burst the car launched upwards, front over end, and landed next to Winston on its side. The trunk broke open from the impact, and he could see his sword and armor on the ground.

The growl was clearer now, and Winston turned back to see the mother slowly raising herself from the ground. With the car out of the way he could see that the impact had drug her for quite a distance as her blood and flesh left a trail across the pavement.

Winston grabbed his gear, sliding his leather body armor on without the mail, and strapped on his sword belt. As he completed fastening the belt he looked up and saw the mother, she was looking at him. He reached to draw his sword but she was upon him in a fury.

Her hand to his throat she dragged him across the grass boulevard and sidewalk until his back was against the tall chain link fence. With a strong, aggressive inhale, she took his scent.

"Mmmmmmm... You will be truly delicious." Mother said calmly.

"What do you want with me?" Winston asked.

"I am to retrieve what you possess. You are of little consequence." She said, looking almost disappointed in the statement. Her eyes were black with pale irises, and stood out in the contrast of her pale skin. Winston could see the veins in her cheeks and down her neck. "They do not know what you are, do they?" She asked. "It is sad the Knight, and your Selkie bitch will not survive to help you."

At that, a knife was against Mother's throat, and Mhara had a grip on her hair. "Call me a bitch again." Mhara hissed.

Mother twisted to lash out at Mhara, suffering a light cut on her neck in the process. Mhara evaded, moving quickly and bravely, retaining her possession of the blade. She must not have seen the trunk open when the car flipped.

Winston drew the sword of Darkfyre, it erupted into flames. The bright blue radiance of the sword stole Mother's attention, and she turned again to him.

"Give it to me, child of damnation." She called.

Winston anticipated her movement, calling upon the lessons learned from watching, and talking to Fionn. Mother approached with her superhuman speed, at least Winston knew in his mind that she was. His eyes perceived her as if in slow motion, moving at a half speed attack towards him. He prepared himself, and as she reached for him Winston pivoted to his left side, swept confidently, and his sword connected, cutting her down the length of her body.

She howled in pain, and disbelief, as she clenched at her side, trying to keep her body from expelling her entrails. Winston looked to Mhara, who nodded that she was ok. Taking an assertive stance, he focused again on Mother. In her panic she released her hold on her abdomen, and reached to strike at Winston. He avoided her wing's claw, and thrust his sword upwards directly into Mother's neck. There was a snapping pop that accompanied the penetrating impact. Watching, he saw her realize the truth, and saw the widening of her eyes, Winston yelled. A deep, guttural cry of defiance and strength. As he release his cry of victory the flames of the sword surged. Encompassing her head, and burning it from her body.

He stepped back and watched her deceptively heavy body collapse to the ground. Winston then looked toward Michael and Gawain to see some of the smaller, younger creatures fall dead at their feet for seemingly no reason. The remaining mature creatures, who all had wings, looked toward Winston, released a cry of anger, and flew away.

Michael tried to take them down as they fled by slinging more magical fire toward them, but they were too fast, and he was unable to connect in his attempts. Gawain turned to offer a welcoming smile as Winston and Mhara joined them.

"Everyone alright." Winston asks. "Will they be back?"

"They should not return, and not simply because you killed their mother." Gawain said. "I have their scent, as it were. I know they are here. I will find them and take care of them."

"Speaking of finding things. Do you know where Jonathan is?" Winston asks. "That is why we were sent here after all."

"I know." Gawain said. "Though I do not know where he is specifically."

"Great." Michael said dismissively.

"What did the Mother say to you?" Mhara asked.

"She said she was sent to take the sword from me."

"So clearly Jonathan, or someone working with him, knows we are here."

"We don't know that." Michael said.

"No. She's right." Winston said. "It is the logical answer." He looked down at the sword, faint flames of blue danced up its blade toward the hilt. "She also called me 'child of damnation' and seemed regretful that she was going to have to kill and eat me."

"She called you what?" asked Mhara.

"Child of damnation." Winston repeated. "She also said she didn't think 'they' knew what I was. Whatever the hell that is supposed to mean."

Michael stepped forward to speak but was interrupted by

Gawain.

"You need to go to a place of power." The knight said. "There are places in the realm of man that more closely connected with the world of Faerie. You need to get to one."

"What? Wait… Why?" Winston asked.

"The words she spoke are not without purpose. And though Mother is dead, this fight is long from over. You must heed my words."

"Ok, for the sake of argument, let's say I go there." Winston said. "How am I to do this?" He asks, gesturing at his car. "My car is ruined and I have no idea where a good place of power is."

"Wait here." Gawain said. Without explanation or assurance, he walked away.

The sky began to darken as the setting sun grew closer toward the horizon. Winston could tell Michael had had about enough with waiting for the knight to return. They had gathered their belongings from the car, and opted to fully equip themselves in case any of those creatures returned. Winston too was finding himself restless, and contemplating how well their LARP uniforms would be received on public transportation. Wouldn't be the craziest lightrail story anyone had heard.

There was a rumble in the distance, and at the end of the road from where they had come turned a large white pickup truck. Gawain parked it near them and got out, tossing the keys to Winston. It was a late 90's model, Ford half-ton two door pickup with a short bed. There was minor rust around the wheel wells, and a dent in the tailgate, but Winston figured this would work out fine.

"Here you go." Gawain said triumphantly. "Now get in and get scarce."

"Where would you recommend we go?" Winston asked. "We don't know where Jonathan is, and I have no idea where a good place of power is."

"I marked it on the map inside. It is a place called Minnehaha Falls."

"Yes. I am familiar with it. Is it really a place of power?"

"It is, and I have a feeling a good place of power for you specifically."

"For me?"

"Get going. I have to get to work tracking down our friends that got away."

"Won't you need a car?" Asked Mhara.

"I'll be just fine." Gawain said with a smile. "Til our roads meet again." The knight said in farewell.

The three of them piled into the cab of the truck, Mhara squeezed between the men, with Winston driving. As they pulled away he gave Gawain a wave and a nod of thanks. Gawain waved back, and stood watching them leave. A short distance into their drive a shimmer of light caught Winston's eye in the rear view mirror and he looked to see light begin to arise from the ground, wrap itself around Gawain in a whimsical braid, and as it passed up over his body the areas where it touched him disappeared. Within a matter of seconds Gawain had vanished.

"Did you guys see that?" Winston asked his companions. Neither had any idea what he was referring to, and he let it go hoping that someday he would get to meet Gawain again, and learn some of what that man knew.

Minnehaha Falls was not far from the mall, and they were there and parked in under 30 minutes. They walked toward the falls themselves, taking the long stone staircase down to the lower field, and walking up to the falls along the path by the bridge.

"Winston." Mhara called to him.

He was distracted, and caught up with the sounds, the movement of the rushing water, and the life of the park. Winston had loved the falls since childhood. Many a summer day was spent riding his bicycle down here, and through the trails. The majesty of the space was ever present, though unexplained. Now it was all the more clear, especially knowing now that it was a place of power.

He looked to Mhara and she was pointing at his pocket. Winston looked down at himself to find an unexpected sight. His pocket was glowing. Reaching into his pocket, he removed the box the Queen gave him that allowed him to speak to his mother while in Winter. The glow off the box radiated like the sun itself was above them, illuminating everything in sight.

Remembering how it worked before, Winston reached for his knife. As he drew it out the light from the box faded. Unsure of what was wrong, he raised the blade toward his palm.

"That will not be necessary this time, my son." She said, from before him. Her hand stopping his from placing the blade against his skin.

He could feel her, smell her, she was there. Was she really there? "Mother?"

"My dearest boy, has it already been so long that you would forget me?"

"No. No." Winston stammered. "I was just."

"I know. You expected things to perform as they had before."

"I did."

"You must remember, you are not in Faerie, as you were before. Things do not work the same here." She assured him. "We are in the realm of man. I am here."

"How did you know to come? Did you know where I was?"

"Yes, and no. I knew you were in our realm the moment you entered, but did not know your location until you were here, in this place, with the box." She paused, looking at him in his armor, recognizing the sword. "Have you used it?"

Winston wasn't sure how to answer. He looked down at the box in his hands.

"Not the box, my son. The sword."

"Ah, yes. I have used it. Why?"

"What happened when you used it?"

"I've used it twice, and both times it surged with fire and seemed to know me. If that makes sense. It felt familiar, and comfortable in my hands."

"Good. Very good."

Winston felt perplexed, and looking to Michael and Mhara, they didn't seem to know any more than he did. "Why do you say it is good, mother?"

"Because, my son." She said, taking his hands in hers. "It is proper for a son to be comfortable with the sword of his father."

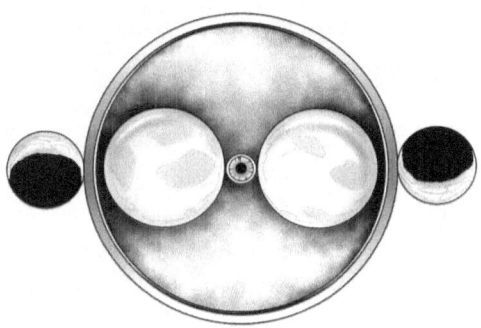

24 – BLESSING OF SUMMER

The rocks moved beneath their feet as Winston, and his mother walked. Michael and Mhara stayed back, nearer to the presently frozen waterfall for which the park took its name. The air was crisp, and the crackle of the wintery ground chirped at them with each step.

"It's been so long since I've been here." Winston said. "I remember loving to come here as a child."

Airmid smiled as soft, warm smile of acknowledgement. "You were a joy to watch."

"You watched me?"

"Of course I did." His mother said. "There were very necessary reasons why things went the way they did. Why I gave you up. That doesn't mean I stopped caring, or that I didn't want to know you were doing well."

"Why didn't you say anything?"

"There were forces; there still are forces, which will not be pleased with you being who you are. Especially when it is known who your father is. These ones may seek to kill you purely based on that, and they surely would have done so if they knew who you were while you were still young."

"People seem to know. Michael, and Myrddin for example, they seem to know who my father was." Winston said, looking toward his mother. "Would you be willing to tell me about him? I have nothing. No name. History. I don't even know if he was a good man."

"Your father was a strong man. Wise. To some he was good. While to others he was known in a different light. He was good to me, though I didn't fully know who he was when we initially met." Airmid chuckled at the memory, eyes shimmering as she remembered something fondly for the first time. "When I first met him, it could be said that he was not himself."

"How so?"

"He had taken on the appearance of a lowly princess' son, Pwyll, and was in our realm adventuring around like an aimless sightseer. I couldn't resist engaging him. Just as I came to learn that I could not resist loving him."

"Who was he?"

"He was no princess' son." She continued. "No. Far more." Airmid paused, her hand brushing across the tips of the leafless branches of a nearby bush. "He was a King. One of the great Kings of Faerie. And now you carry his sword."

Winston stopped walking, his eyes lost in the middle distance as he looked down at the path they were following. She had said this twice now, 'his father's sword', but Winston didn't understand. It was as if there was a block in his mind that would not allow him to fully comprehend the truth of her words. He reached, and withdrew the sword. As before, dark, rich, indigo flames surged, and rippled up the blade as he held the weapon in front of himself. The flames licked at the air like they were affixed to needy mouths, eager for sustenance. In all of its vibrancy and spectacle, the flame gave off no heat, and the light of the flames seemed to only faintly reflect off of anything around them.

"Can you feel it?" His mother asked.

"Feel what?"

"You said the blade acted as if it knew you. Can you feel it? Can you feel the blade?"

Winston paused, focusing on the flickering blade, the weight of it in his hands, and… there it was. It wasn't as a voice speaking to him, more so it was an awareness, a consciousness that responded to his thoughts, his will. Voices were growing closer, pedestrians were coming from the distance beyond the turn in the path. Winston's mother moved to stand between him and the voices, facing him. It seemed to Winston that she was trying to block the oncoming park visitors, from being able to see the sword. Winston thought to himself that he wished the flames were gone so he could simply rest the sword at his side and no one would notice.

"Winston." His mother called in a harsh clipped tone.

Without further thought he slipped the sword down next to his leg. Moments later a small group of young people walked past laughing and interacting with each other. They seemed to not pay any mind to Winston, or his mother. Winston wondered if she were doing something to veil them from sight of the flickering flames, until the last boy in the group looked Winston directly in the eyes, and nodded

227

acknowledgement as they passed.

They watched the group of young people continue on their way, waiting until they were a fair way away before moving at all. Winston felt his mother touch his arm, and he turned to her.

"You are truly impressive." She said.

"That was a close one, right? Good thing they were too caught up with each other to notice us fully."

"What was there to notice?"

"Us, I mean, the sword." Winston said, raising the weapon up between them. Only there was no sword. It only showed in faint glimpses between the licks of the now transparent flames.

Winston turned the blade in his hand. He could see through to the other side as if nothing were there. It wasn't the flames being transparent. The flames were making the whole sword transparent, down to the hilt.

There it was again, the feeling of acknowledgement from the weapon communicating with his mind. He envisioned the blade as it was before, and watched as the flames transformed back to their dark indigo hue. Winston snickered. He couldn't help it. This was exciting, like something from a book or a video game. Next he willed for the flames to cease, and they did. Exposing to him for the first time the intricately carved blade of his father's sword. He ran his fingers down the center of the length of the blade, looking at the carved runes. "Do you know what it says, mother?"

"Long is the day and long is the night, and long is the waiting of Arawn." She said, barely looking at the blade.

"Arawn?"

"Your father. King Arawn, of Annwn, ruler of the Otherworld

228

realm of Faerie." Airmid said, reverence in her voice. "He was killed by Arthur when he invaded Faerie on his crusade to protect the realm of man from the threat of those of the otherworld."

"He was killed by the legendary King Arthur?"

"The same, though how that child became a legend is still beyond me."

"I've heard he still lives."

"Your father?"

"No. Arthur." Winston said. "I've met one of his knights of the Ten, also." He paused, a thought connecting. "Was it from the Ten, or Arthur, that you were trying to hide me from?"

"In part."

"Wait." Winston interrupted, his mind churning as pieces connected. "If my father was killed by Arthur, then he would have died over 1500 years ago." His mother said nothing. "How is that possible?"

"You're assuming that your gestation timeline would follow the same prescribed length as those of men."

"Well. Yeah!" Winston said, exasperated.

His mother chuckled, placing her hand to his cheek. "Winston." She said, beckoning him to look her in the eyes. "Your father was a High King of Faerie, and I am called a Goddess. You are unlike anything born to this realm in a millennia or more. My choice to have you, with your father was already in place, and would not be ceased, even when I heard of his death. What I could do was delay your birth to a point in time where I felt you would be safe."

"So you chose to postpone my birth for 1500 years?"

"I suppose that would be one way to frame the situation."

"What am I?" Winston said, slipping the sword back into its

sheath. "Why? Why didn't you come to me sooner?"

"No matter what reasoning I give you, it will all sound like the rationalizations, and excuses of a defensive parent." She said, stepping closer to him. "I did what I did to protect you. Because I love you. Perhaps it would have been better if I had come to you when you were younger. Even then my access to you was limited by where we were. My domain is not here in Minnesota, nor could I come to you in Afghanistan, and Iraq. Yet I am here now, and you need to be ready for what comes."

"What is coming, mother? Tell me. Someone needs to tell me." Winston demanded, frustration rising in his tone. "From the moment I was dropped into this shit, no one has given me straight answers. Only hints, and vague clues. Hell, I am not even sure who I can trust in all this. Can I trust them? Myrddin? The Winter Queen?"

"Me?" Airmid interjected.

"No. No, I know I can trust you. In the garden of Winter I could feel you were telling me the truth, that you are my mother. That is why I'm saying this to you while we are alone. You may be the only person I know I can trust."

"You can trust yourself." She said, placing her hand upon his chest. "Trust the sword. Trust your instincts." She paused. "I have someone else I know you can trust, at least in this, in stopping Jonathan. Come with me." She led him down the path, and off toward the bank of the stream. "Use the sword. Make this area warm so the water runs freely."

Winston drew the weapon again, holding it before him. The flames were calm, and subtle upon the blade. He thought about what his mother was requesting. Use the blade to melt the frozen waters of the stream. Winston felt perplexed because he had never felt the blade give off much heat. Airmid moved to stand just behind his left shoulder, as if preparing herself for what was to come. He focused on the blade, and not knowing what to specifically tell it to do, Winston instead imagined what he would like to see happen.

The flames leapt from the blade and swirled around them, moving in and through the trees, dirt, ice, and snow. Winston didn't feel the heat from the flames himself, but he could see his mother respond to it. The air and plant life around him warmed from the flame's influence. The dark, rich indigo flames worked their magic, and soon they stood before a flowing stream of fresh water. The flames of the sword receded, and Winston replaced the sword within its sheath.

Airmid moved from behind him, kneeling before the stream. She reached out and slowly lowered her hand until it rested atop the water. Winston watched on, and thought he could see the water of the stream becoming still. It was then that he heard the clambering of foot falls approaching, he turned quickly, preparing himself to draw the sword again.

"Whoa, fella. It's only us." Called Michael as he and Mhara approached. "We saw the light display and worried you were in danger."

"Are you ok?" Asked Mhara, stepping closer to Winston.

"Yeah. Everything is fine. My mother asked me to warm the stream is all."

"Warm the stream? Why?"

"Aye, that seems like a lost effort in this climate." Michael agreed.

"She did so to summon me." Came a melodic, rich voice from behind Winston.

The three turned toward Airmid, and the mysterious new guest. It was a woman, or at least she looked like a woman. She was tall, athletically slender, with fine golden hair that seemed to glow all on its own. She wore a long gown, with intricate embroidery, and jeweled accents. Winston looked back to her face, he saw her eyes watching him, and it was then he noticed what appeared to be a crown of small leaves upon her head.

"Is this one your son, Airmid?" Asked the regal lady.

"He is, your Highness. This is Winston." She said, gesturing toward her son. "Winston, please welcome May, the Queen of Summer."

"Aw, fuck." Muttered Michael.

Winston turned, hearing his friend's curse. Their eyes met and Michael shrugged as if nothing was said. Turning back to the Queen, he bowed slightly. "It is an honor to meet you, your highness. My mother says you may be able to help us in our efforts to stop Jonathan."

The Summer Queen seemed to stiffen slightly at the statement, and Winston noticed she briefly looked passed him to gaze upon Michael, who had stepped a fair distance away from the group. Returning her eyes to Winston she said. "I believe I may be of some aid, to you, in this effort. Though we must speak quickly as my time here is limited."

"Do you know where Jonathan is?"

"Where he is, is not your concern. You have what he desires, and to obtain it he will come to you." She said referring to the sword of Darkfyre. Did everyone know Wiston was now in possession of the sword?

Winston found his hand resting upon the hilt of the sword.

"Alright. He'll come to me. I'm good with that. I've had about enough of all this running around in circles. He has the scepter; how do I stop him?"

"The scepter is a great weapon, and so long as he wields it the scepter will allow Jonathan more access to the power of Faerie, than ever before."

"You mean the power of Summer."

"True. As his lineage is drawn from the court of Summer, he is able to draw strongly upon the power of the scepter."

"And the sword, it's of Winter?" Mhara asked.

"Yes, sweet child." Queen May said, addressing Mhara directly. "It is more accurately of Anwnn, which is within the province of Winter. To best utilize the power of the sword, Jonathan will likely need an ally from Winter to wield it." She said, he eyes moving briefly to look upon the still distant Michael. "You can eliminate this option from the field, Winston."

"Tell me how."

"The reason Jonathan knew he could claim the weapons is because they were unbound. You can forge the connection with the sword anew. You are of the house of Arawn, high King of Anwnn. Bring the sword to his former seat of power in the Otherworld, and you can bond to it fully, just as your father had previously." May stepped close to Winston, as if to speak to him alone. "You must mind your steps, young prince. You, of all of us, stand the best chance in thwarting Jonathan's efforts. This is known. Others will be coming for you." She reached out, placing her hand upon his heart. "The blessing of Summer goes with you, Winston. May we meet again in better times."

Winston opened his eyes, unsure when he had closed them, and found only his mother before him. The Summer Queen had vanished. He turned to look at Mhara, who appeared in awe of what just happened. Winston then looked and found Michael a fair distance from them, a look of relief upon his face.

"I too, must go." Airmid said from behind Winston.

"Mom?" Winston turned, going to her. He embraced her in his arms. "Thank you, mother. Thank you."

"You must stop Jonathan, my son." She whispered to him. "Take care with whom you trust. If you have need of me, come to me. I will be waiting."

Winston pulled back, looking into the eyes of the mother he never knew, feeling as though he'd never known a life without her. "Thank you. I will do as you say."

"I believe in you, and I love you, my son." She said as a soft tears fell from her wet eyes.

"I love you, mom." Winston said, wrapping his arms around her again. One last time. As he pulled away from her the empty smell of the cold winter night came in on him, and he saw she was gone.

"Winston?" Michael said. "I think I know who Queen May was speaking of. Who Jonathan recruited from Winter to wield the sword."

"Who?" Winston said, his voice hard.

"While you spoke with your mother, I received word from Myrddin. The Hound had laid siege upon people of Winter."

"The Hound? Where was the Winter Queen?"

"Not there apparently. The Hound went on a rampage in search of you."

"Can we get ahold of Myrddin again?"

"I believe we can, but we will need a few things."

"Then we will do that in the morning. For now, we find food, and a place to rest." Winston said, walking back toward their vehicle. Before ascending the stairs he turned back to Michael, and Mhara who followed. "I can trust you two, right?" He asked. Mhara looked abashed, ashamed that she would be posed with such a question. While Michael smirked.

"Aye, of course ye can. Daft boy. We've been with you this whole times haven't we?" Michael said, clapping him on the shoulder as he walked passed Winston and began climbing the steep stone stairs.

Winston looked at Mhara. "Look, I'm sorry. I need to ask."

"No." Mhara said. "I understand." She took his hands in hers. "I heard what the Summer Queen, and your mother said. You are right to ask."

"I want to believe I can trust you."

"There is a lot about me you don't know, Winston." She said. "Though I want to say I will not betray you, anything is possible." His hands tightened around hers as she tried to pull hers away. Mhara looked up toward Michael, who was now more than twenty yards up the stairs, then looked back at Winston. "I am here, with you. I care for you. Yet, you need to be wise in this."

"What are you trying to say?" he asked.

Mhara moved towards the stairs, as she passed she leaned in and kissed Winston lightly on the cheek. It was warm, kind, and distracting. "Until this is over." She said softly, her lips almost touching his ear. "Do not trust anyone."

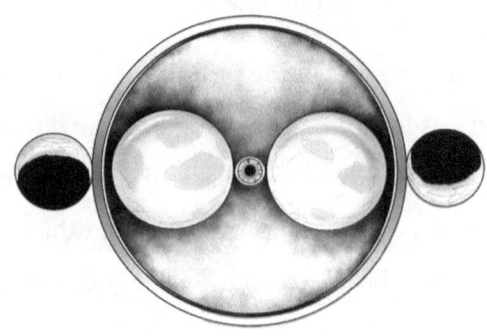

25 – WELCOME TO MINNESOTA

Before

"What happened here?"

"I... I... I don't know."

"There are five of you here, watching, and none of you knows what happened?"

"Joseph and Winston were fighting." Said one boy.

"They were not fighting."

"Shut up, Bobby. They were too."

"No. Joseph was being a bully."

"Shut up, Bobby!"

"That's enough." Interjected the camp counselor. "Bobby, what did you see happen?"

"Bobby wasn't here, Ms. Flowers."

"That is quite enough. I'm talking to Bobby. You had your turn." Said Ms. Flowers. "If you have more to add, once I've finished talking to Bobby, you'll have another opportunity. For now, have a seat on the bench." She gestured toward the entrance to the boathouse, then turned back to Bobby. "You said you saw Joseph being a bully?"

"Yes, Ms. Flowers." Bobby said. "Joseph, Tanner, and Grayson were out on the dock with Winston. Joseph started picking on Winston, calling him names, stuff like that."

"Where were you?"

"On the beach, looking for shells." Bobby admitted, knowing he wasn't supposed to be near the lake either. "Am I going to be in trouble?"

"No, Bobby. Please continue telling me what happened."

"Grayson tried to stop Joseph, but Tanner told him to stay out of it. I heard Joseph threaten to throw Winston into the water. We all know Winston can't swim, but he didn't seem scared. He just told Joseph to leave him alone and sat there at the edge of the dock. That was when Joseph grabbed him and tried to shove him off. They were wrestling. Winston used the railing to keep from getting shoved in. When Joseph started punching Winston, Grayson ran yelling for you or Mr. Tombs. There was smoke coming from the dock, like it was on fire underneath them. Tanner ran off, and I heard Winston yell. They were both on their feet, shoving and pulling on each other. I saw them both go over the side of the dock, and that is when I went to find you."

"Was that all you saw?"

"Yes."

"You didn't see how Joseph found his way atop the roof of the boat house?"

"No. I just thought he was trying to hide knowing he would be in trouble. I mean, I'd hide if I had drowned someone."

"Thank you, Bobby." Ms. Flowers said. "Go to your cabin and get ready for dinner. All will be well." Ms. Flowers said. Bobby went on his way, and she turned to the other boys, waiting on the bench. "Tanner, Grayson, you two go to your cabin and get ready for dinner. No lollygagging." She called out to them. The boys were on their feet and running before she finished her instructions.

With the boys on their way, Ms. Flowers headed to the back of the boathouse to join Mr. Tombs and the camp nurse. Both boys were laying down. Winston was laid out on the dock, under the sun, still wet from the lake water. Joseph was inside the boathouse, his left arm wrapped with a splint, and an ice pack on his head. Both boys appeared to be unconscious. As she entered Mr. Tombs looked to her, a welcoming smile finding his lips. The camp nurse was examining Joseph's legs, a subtle blue illumination coming from where his hands rested on Joseph's legs.

"Will they be alright." She asked Mr. Tombs.

"Thankfully." Mr. Tombs said solemnly. "Merl says Joseph here has a couple broken bones, and a concussion. Suffered a heavy blow, followed by a rough landing. Clearly he had no idea what to expect." He said with a hint of amused pride in his voice.

"And how is our... how is Winston?"

"He is better than expected. Clearly, he is strong. Takes after his mother." He said with a smirk.

"He didn't learn that trick from his mother." Ms. Flowers said, a sharp edge to her voice. "We have to do something. He could have hurt Joseph more severely."

"You're correct. Wiston should learn to swim."

She slapped Mr. Tombs on the upper arm. "You know full well that isn't what I mean. He could have killed him."

"He also did. Before sending him to the roof, he took power from him. Likely in reflex to stay alive." He said, looking toward the floor, and then out at Winston laying in the sun. "He is powerful, Air. More powerful than me perhaps. At least more than I was."

"We have to do something."

"What can we do? We are limited in how much we can do, and I am not much more than an observer at this point. What can we do for him?

"I do not know." She admitted. "This is all too much. I am not sure how we will explain this to the parents, let alone what we can do to help keep Winston safe."

"Perhaps I can be of assistance." The camp nurse offered.

"What do you suggest?" Mr. Tombs asked.

"Installing a block."

"A block? Those are dangerous."

"Leaving him unrestrained is dangerous."

"Yes, but if we let Merl install a block in Winston, may never realize who he is." She said, pausing. "He may never learn who we are."

"Not just Winston." Nurse Merl, said. "We place a block on each of the boys, making them forget this event ever took place." he looked to Ms. Flowers. "There are provisions we can put in place regarding Winston."

Ms. Flowers looked to Mr. Tombs, eyes pleading for his decisiveness, his decree. He saw it in her eyes, and he knew he had to be the one to choose.

"Do it, Merl." Mr. Tombs said. "You have my trust. See that it is done." Tombs turned to Ms. Flowers. "Stay with them. I will go see to dinner with the other campers, and keep others away from this. I'll send the other boys back here before they eat. Will you be alright?"

"I believe I will."

"Stay with Winston." He said, and lightly kissed her forehead before leaving.

Ms. Flowers turned to find nurse Merl looking at her. "I should be able to mend Joseph's wounds enough to pass this off as a freak canoeing accident. The boys will believe the accident was too stressful to remember in detail, and Winston will be oblivious to his actions."

"And his abilities, will they continue to spontaneously manifest?"

"He is thirteen, and in the bloom of youth, it is hard to say. I will do my best to defer the power within him, muting it so it will not have spontaneous dominion over him, while not being completely outside of his grasp." He explained. "Does that sound acceptable?"

"What other choice do we have? Do I have? We need to keep him safe."

"Then let us begin before the sun sets, shall we?"

Ms. Flowers moved over to kneel near Winston. His unconscious body lay prone on the dock, his skin flush and pale from his fight to breath. She gently ran her fingers through his hair, feeling deeply thankful he was alive. An unknown amount of time passed until she was joined by the nurse. The passing of the sun the only indicator of the time passed.

He positioned himself near Winston's head, placing a hand on each side of Winston's head. "Please place his hands upon his chest, and use your body weight to help hold him secure." She did as requested. "Good. We are ready. Yes?" He looked to her.

"Yes." She confirmed, and then looked up to meet his eyes full and true. Softly they spoke to him, all of her emotions waiting behind her words. "Thank you, Merlin."

Now

The parking lot at Como Zoo was all but vacant as Winston pulled in and parked their truck, near the main entrance. Michael had fallen asleep en route, after explaining how environmental factors play a role in how the realm of man connects with Faerie. The fact that all of Minnesota was experiencing the season of winter, would certainly put them in a better position to find their way to the kingdom of Winter smoothly. Yet, if they could find something that was truly of the lands of ice and snow, then they would be more likely to easily traverse into the heart of Winter. Michael had explained that animals, and environments of those animals, are good conduits.

Winston recalled the updated polar bear exhibit at Como Zoo, drove them to the free, mainly outdoors venue, with minimal concern for the increasingly cold weather outside. Michael wasn't completely confident it would work, but agreed that if the bear had been there long, and considered the space to truly be his home, it would be their best bet.

"Michael. Wake up." Winston said, while nudging Michael's shoulder.

"Aye, I'm up. I'm up."

"Here, put this on." Winston instructed, handing Michael a long wool shawl.

"Where did you find this?"

"Stopped by a thrift store while you were sleeping. Thought it may be good to wear something to better hide our weapons, since this is a family environment."

"You humans and your unwillingness to expose your children to the realities of life."

"Just put it on, Michael. I'm not sure how much longer the zoo is open and we need to move."

The three of them exited the white pickup truck. They each donned some manner of shawl. The long draped fabric adding both warmth to their bodies, and concealment of their weapons and light armor. The few families in attendance paid little attention to the three of them as they moved through the walkways of the exhibits to get to where the polar bear was located. Due to the season the bear had been moved inside, and his exterior pool drained.

"Will this work?" Winston asked as they reached the exterior area of the exhibit. He was hoping it would as it would be better to do what they needed to with as few observers as possible.

"Aye, I believe it will. Though I am not certain this is truly our wisest move. We were tasked with finding Jonathan." Michael reminded Winston.

"I know, and you heard what Queen May said. He needs the sword, and he knows we have it. That I have it." Winston emphasized. "He will come to me."

"True as that is, do you truly think returning to Winter is the wise move?" The wind blew through the park, and Michael pulled his shawl tighter about himself. "Bollocks, it's bloody cold. I thought Winter was bad."

"Welcome to Minnesota." Winston said with a rueful chuckle. "As for sticking to the plan, that is clearly no longer an option. Jonathan is ahead of us on this somehow. For Merlin to contact you with news of Queen Bheur, and the attacks on Winter by the Hound, he has clearly been pulled off track of his own plans, in order to aid the Queen." Winston took a breath, seeming to resolve himself to his next words. "As badly as I wanted to return home, and as relieved as I am to be here, here is not where the fight is. This is not where we win this war. We need to return to Faerie, to Winter, and we need to regroup and be ready for Jonathan. With us all being separated, I am afraid that it plays right into his plans."

"Aye. I hope you're right, lad."

"We should go if we are going to go." Mhara said. "We are completely alone in this moment. Do you remember how to use the leaf?"

"I do." Winston said, as he removed his glove, and retrieved the ornate leaf shaped amulet from his bag. Winston held it in front of him, and he could feel the vines begin to move against his skin. "Are you both ready?" He asked, as he slung his bag back over his shoulder. Michael and Mhara were already to either side of him, their hands placed on his shoulders. Winston focused his will, and closed his eyes. He worked to picture the Palace of Winter in his mind's eye, and to see himself there, to know he was there. The vines moved from the amulet, encircling his hand and wrist, yet there was no wind, no churning of the world around them as there was before. Frustration welled up in Winston and as he was about to apologize for his failure he felt Michael's hand tighten upon his shoulder.

"Fine job, boy!" Michael exclaimed.

Winston opened his eyes to find that the glass wall to the polar bear enclosure had opened like a curtain upon a one way mirror. "This isn't how it worked before." Winston observed aloud.

"Too right, lad. Only we aren't traveling like we did before." Michael said.

"What does that mean?"

"When Myrddin first had us leave from Faerie, we were attempting to connect to a place from within your mind. Whereas now we are traversing two places connected between realms. No call for a wind storm when a door will do. Come on." Michael said, as he moved to step through the door, Mhara direction behind them.

The world beyond the portal was a refreshing crisp, and a noticeable contrast to the bone chilling cold of the winter winds of Minnesota. Winston followed them through the portal.

"Ye have to close the door behind ye, boy." Michael said.

Feeling silly that he hadn't thought of this, Winston turned toward the opening between realms, and was confronted with a heavy blow to the head. He hit the snow covered ground, and rolled to see they were surrounded by a handful of vicious looking creatures.

"Ye alright, lad?" Michael called.

"I'm fine." Winston said, getting to his feet.

"Good." Came a low familiar growl. "I'd hate for this to end too quickly."

Winston moved to see the Hound walking up toward them. Instinctively Winston moved his hand toward his weapon. Michael made a halting gesture, and when Winston looked at him, he nodded toward the still open portal. Winston understood. They needed to retreat.

One of the monsters moved on Mhara. As smooth as the rolling tide she drew her weapon and removed the arm of the offending beast. Capitalizing upon her momentum she spun and cut clean through the lower jaw of another.

"Move!" Michael yelled, and they did. The three of them racing back through the portal. "Close it, Winston!" He yelled and released a wave of fire towards the creatures pursuing them.

Winston gripped the amulet in his hand as he ran, feeling his feet hit the pavement he immediately began willing the portal to close. Drawing his sword with his other hand he looked toward the portal. Michael and Mhara were there with him, and the portal had closed, cutting one pursuing creature in half as it did. Greenish blue fluid splattered the glass, wall, and floor around where the portal had been, and continued to leak out of the upper half of the now dead creature. Next to the dead creature, sniffing at its corpse, were two others. They were large, sleek beasts, looking like a cross between a pharaoh hound, and a sort of ape. One snorted, an almost disgusted and displeased sound towards the dead creature. In response the other lifted its head to look at the fleeing trio.

"What are those things?" Winston asked.

"Coin-Sìth." Mhara hissed.

"Are they bad?"

"They aren't good. We need to open another portal. The Hound knows we're here." Michael said. "If he is connected with Jonathan, as it seems he is, he may have the ability to follow us. Meaning we need to not be here when he comes through his own portal."

"What do we do about them?" Winston asked referring to the creatures who had begun slowly pursuing them, and wagging their long tails.

"They look like pups. Mharah and I can hold them off while you focus on getting us an exit out of here." Michael drew his sword. "Move!" He yelled.

The three of them turned and ran, a sharp bark came through the air, and they heard the Coin-Sith in pursuit. Winston looked at their options, assuming any of these enclosures would work, which would get them to a relatively safe area of Faerie? He didn't like the bison as an option, or the African animals. Directly ahead of them was the seal island exhibit and something in Winston's gut said this could work.

"Here!" Winston yelled. "We're doing this here."

"We need to dispatch of our pursuers first, and preferably before they bark three times."

"Three times?"

"Aye." Michael agreed. "It's part of their magic. If they bark a third time, even as young as they appear to be, we will be as good as dead."

The two sleek creatures came around the corner, their hackles raised, and teeth bared. In unison they released a second bark, the volume and force of which collided with Winston's chest like he was front row at a rock show. His breath and clarity of sight faltered. Mhara loosed a battle cry, and Winston saw Michael conjuring power with his hands. The beasts attacked.

"Be ready, Winston!" Michael called out, as he swung his arms and released another wave of fire like energy, this one more focused than the first. It hit the larger of the two Cu-Sith, knocking it away from the fight.

Mhara moved like water, rushing in, striking, then moving away.

The beast she confronted limped now, with two injured limbs, and a third that hung limply at its flank. Nonetheless its jaws were a danger as it lunged for Mhara. She evaded, and Winston watched as she brought her blade around and up, slicing smoothly through the neck of the creature, removing its head. The same greenish blue fluid Winston had seen before spewed out of the wound and released a slight hiss as it made contact with the cement.

Winston pulled his attention away and focused on the amulet. He knew not where this exhibit would connect with Faerie, he only reasoned he must due to it being one of the oldest exhibits of the zoo. It surely had been allowed ample time to gather energy from visitors, and the familiarity of the animals within. Not having a destination to picture, and knowing now he was simply opening a door, rather than creating transportation, Winston focused his will. Within his mind, he saw the door, and commanded the realms to open to him. They did.

"It's open!" He yelled, turning to look toward Mhara, and Michael. They were running towards him, the larger beast enraged and charging.

"Go through! Go through, now!" Michael was yelling.

Mhara grabbed Winston as he saw the remaining Cu-Sith collide with Michael's shield. The energy of the collision thrust them all through the portal. As soon as Winston was sure they were all through he closed the portal, not needing to be told again. The head of the pursuing Cu-Sith came through and was decapitated by the closing portal. It was only then that Winston realized they were airborne and falling.

"Ah, Shite!" Michael exclaimed.

They hit the water, followed shortly by the head of the Cu-Sith, Winston saw it sink past him as he urged his body to the surface of the water. The weight of his armor and weapons pulled on Winston making it difficult for him to swim. Reaching the surface he took a deep breath and sunk quickly below the waves again.

Loosening his belt only enough to remove the armor, Winston sacrificed them to the sea, while retaining his bag, sword, and most of his clothing. The army had trained him to swim in full gear, he could do this. He kicked hard, propelling himself toward the surface of the water. As his face felt air, he gulped for breath, and began treading water. Winston wiped sea water from his eyes and as they came to focus he could see Mhara, and Michael had done much the same as he had. His clear sense of hearing returned last.

"Bloody shite it is." Michael was asserting. "Seal island. Pshh. We're fucked."

"Calm down and think."

"I'm allowed to be angry. Damn fool. Wielding power he doesn't understand."

"Are you two okay?" Winston asked. Michael turned, as if only now realizing Winston was there. "I'm sorry about this. I had no idea we'd end up here." Winston said.

"It is alright, Winston." Mhara said. "We will get out of this."

"I suppose we gotta start swimming."

"Swimming?" Michael asked sharply. "What, pray tell, do ye plan to swim to?"

Winston felt caught off guard by his question. Wouldn't they swim to land, it had to be nearby? Winston turned in the water and looked out at the far horizon that surrounded them. Miles and miles of water, without a shadow of land in sight. Winston was reminded of one of the reasons he never joined the Navy, and in his memories he was called back to a time in his youth, at a lake, where a boy nearly died. Winston was lost in that thought, his companions debating their next move, and none of them paid any heed to the shadow moving beneath them.

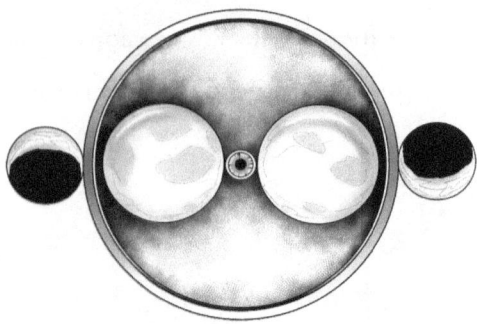

26 – DANGEROUS WATERS

"Did you feel that?" Winston asked.

"Calm down, boy. And keep yer head above water."

"There has to be something we can do other than tread water. You're a wizard, can't you use magic or something?"

"It isn't that easy, boy. I can't make something from nothing."

"Magic would be unwise." Mhara warned.

"Unwise? Magic is what we have."

"No. If Michael uses magic it will attract predators to us quicker than blood in the water."

Winston looked to Michael, who seemed to have the same realization as he. There was already blood in the water. In that same moment the surface of the water not far from them broke from bubbles hitting the surface. Following the bubbles came a clean, white, oddly shaped object. It bobbed a moment, turned in the water, and slowly sunk. As it turned; Winston could make out the sockets, and contours for what they were. It was the skull of the Cu-Sith, and it had been stripped clean. Winston looked back to Michael. "We need to do something." he said.

"Aye." Michael agreed, and disappeared under the water. A short moment later he returned. "That should get us started."

"Where did you go?"

"To get this." Michael said, holding up the skull of the Cu-Sith. "I can use this, reshape it into a boat of sorts for us."

"You can make a boat from that one skull?" Winston asked incredulously. In answer the water around them surged up in bubbles of various sizes. Winston could feel the water was warm, and from within the bubbles, steam released, as they broke upon the surface. Along with the bubbles came various kinds of debre, no doubt released from the sea floor.

"Alright. Ye two kids hold tight." Michael called out as his right arm lifted from the sea, the dark, thick wand in hand. He thrust it down into the water before him.

"Wait!" Mhara cried out but it was to the moment. The water began to churn, spinning like a whirlpool, pulling all the risen debre toward a center most focal point. The various items mixed and pulled apart, making new pieces to a new puzzle. Bone, wood, plants, and the bodies of other sea life mixed together, and all they could do was watch.

The churning sea calmed, and Winston found himself looking at something that looked like a cross between a giant curved dinner plate, and a liferaft. Michael was already hoisting himself up and into the craft. It looked large enough for ten people, and maintained a surprising buoyancy as Michael climbed out of the water, and into his creation.

Mhara swam towards the raft reluctantly, and Winston followed.

"What were you thinking?" Mhara demanded once in the boat. "Do you have any idea what you've done?"

"Aye, I got us a wee bit safer than we were floating in the water."

"You used your magic, Michael!"

"Aye. I did." Defensive anger filled his voice. "And it's better I did."

"Better?"

"Better." Michael asserted. "There was already blood in the water, as it were. Hell. you saw the skull. It'd been picked clean. How long do ye really really think it would have taken for them to turn to us?"

"Do we have a way to move?" Winston interjected. The other two turning towards him, anger still flush upon their faces. "I appreciate being out of the water, but do we have a way to move? Because I see no sail, no rutter, nor paddles."

Michael looked around as if noticing for the first time that he had not accounted for travel when working his spell. "Bullocks. Yer right." He acknowledged with a chuckle. "We're gonna need to come up with something, I suppose."

"What do we do? Harness some dolphins or something?" Winston asked.

"That's a bit too many Disney movies for you." Michael quipped. "But by the looks of things, you'll be learning more of how Faerie truly works presently. He said, pointing out towards the water.

Below the surface of the sea Winston could make out shadows smoothly making their way towards them. The water at the surface showing subtle signs of disturbance as the shadows passed below. There were no fins breaking the surface, or other menessing tells. What Wiston was sure of as they grew closer was that whatever was creating these shadows was huge.

"What are they?"

"Dangerous." Mhara said and slowly moved away from the edge of their boat. "Tell me you have a plan, Michael." Michael only smirked, and removed his outer garment. "You got us into this."

"Me?" Michael asked defensively. "I was not the one that opened a portal and jumped through without knowing where we were jumping into. That would be dear Winston over there."

"It was you who used magic." She asserted. "Now we are being hunted."

"They were attracted to the magic?" Winston asked.

"Not just them, but yes." Mhara confirmed. "We need to find a way to be away from here."

The boat rocked as one the of sea creatures brushed against it. Winston placed both his hands against the bottom of the craft to steady himself. Michael was moving toward the other end of the boat from where he was as the boat was jeered again, this time more upwards, as if the creatures were trying to overturn their boat.

Mhara looked to Michael, a growl in her throat. "What do we need?"

"Materials." Michael said plainly. "Used what I stirred up from the seafloor to meld together and create this raft. I would need more materials to do more."

"Why not just use part of the raft? Surely it is large enough to spare materials."

"Aye, it is, Mhara. But it is what it is. If I take from it, it will cease being what it is."

"You mean…"

"The boat will collapse back into its originally separate pieces, Winston."

"Alright then. We get more materials." Winston declared as he rose to his knees, and looked over the edge of the boat.

"What are ye playing at, boy?"

"I'm going to get us what we need."

"Winston, no!" Mhara exclaimed.

"I've had about enough of feeling like with everything we do, there was more that could have been done, or waiting for someone else to supply an option. No. We need materials, and the sea is offering them to us."

"That is far too dangerous."

"Aye, they are as big as our boat, and could pull you in." Michael agreed. "How exactly do ye plan to overcome them?"

Without a word, or even a look, Winston drew the sword of Darkfyre. He held it out to his side, and like the igniting of gas, the blade roared to life with rich blue flames dancing around it. Winston remained still, watching the shadows as they passed beneath the surface of the sea. They came close, almost touching them again, only to quickly move away. They varied their speed, using their velocity to make waves to rock the boat. Still, Winston waited. Like all those nights on watch, perched in a tree, he quietly waited, knowing he would see his moment to act.

"He's not listening." Winston heard Mhara say. She was correct. He had become completely focused on the task at hand. He slowly released the air from his lungs as he watched the large shadowy body work its way towards their boat. In his peripheral he noticed a darkening of the world around him, like a heavy smoke had moved in on them. He wanted to look to confirm, but he dared not remove his eyes from his target. The shadow grew closer, and closer. It would not be pulling away this time, Winston could feel it like a man can feel the rain coming, and smell it in the air. As the creature grew closer Winston prepared himself. He prepared for the impact with the boat, with the uncertainty of his plan, and most importantly with what he needed to do next.

As the head of the creature made contact with the boat Winston moved, thrusting the sword down hard into the top of the creature's head. A sound like a muffled roar released from the sea beneath them. Winston could feel as the beast thought to exercise its strength, and take the sword, and perhaps Winston down into the depths of the sea. Before this reality could come to be Winston released the second wave of his plan. With a surge of his will he focused on what he wanted the sword to do, and in a hiss the water around the sword began to steam and boil. The boat itself resonated the heat from the water and Michael moved in surprise. As soon as it happened, it dissipated. The beast rested still in the sea, its body bobbing up closer to the water's surface.

"They're leaving." Mhara said.

"Grand fine work, boy." Michael praised as he moved closer to Winston. "Bloody hell, they're larger than I expected." He said taking in the size of the now dead predator. "Why toy with us like that? They could've easily toppled the boat if they're all that size."

"We need to act quickly." Mhara said, moving to counterbalance the boat. "Get what you need, and let us be under way." She insisted.

Michael and Winston went to work. Michael's face took on an expression of determined focus, not seeming to want to respond to

Mhara's insistence. Winston for his part couldn't grasp why she was not more pleased with their success. Nonetheless they worked. Michael had Winston keep the blade in the creature's head, and hold it in place as he removed strips of skin, and a fin. They pulled the wet, bloody pieces on to the boat, and at Michael's assurance, Winston removed the blade and released the carcass to float away.

Michael placed the harvested pieces of the creature in what looked like a purposeful way, and pulled from his coat the same wand type object he had used before. Winston couldn't make out what he said as he mumbled to himself, and could only watch as Michael moved through the ritual. At its culmination Michael again thrust his wand towards the arranged pieces and in the torrent they seemed to come apart and rearrange themselves into a mast and sail.

A soft breeze rose and filled the triangle shaped sail pushing the boat forward. Michael moved to the rear of the boat, taking up an elongated oar. He positioned himself, and lowered the oar into the water. Placing the shaft of the oar between two ridges on the edge of the boat, he was able to pivot the oar left or right, and in turn steer the vessel.

"Which way do we go?" Winston asked.

"Our best bet is to use the wind to move us as far and fast as we can."

"Aye, I was thinking the same thing."

"Is that normal?" Winston asked.

"What?"

"There. Do you see those? Are they dolphins?" In the distance they saw what looked like dolphins jumping out of the water, and swimming sporadically across the surface of the water. "They look like they're headed our way."

"We have to move faster!" Mhara exclaimed. "Michael, there has to be some way you can make us go faster."

"Afraid not lass." She looked at Michael incredulously. "It isn't in my wheelhouse, as it were." Michael explained. "What has you so spooked?"

Mhara didn't answer. In the distance the corpse of the skinned water beast they used for the sail and rudder floated. Winston watched the dolphin like creatures move past it on their way toward them. As the dolphin like creatures grew closer Winston could see they were pinkish in color, and had dots across their body. Their bodies appeared longer, with two dorsal fins on their backs. The power and grace they moved with captured Winston's attention, and he found himself lost in their majesty when the water beyond them exploded upward, engulfing the carcass.

The dolphin-like creatures scattered and vanished beneath the waves. The boat rocked as the residual ripples in the water from the event reached them. Winston looked to Michael who seemed as lost as Winston felt.

"What was that?"

"I do not know, boy." Michael said. "Not my area of expertise." He said with a look toward Mhara.

The water settled and a massive shadow moved under the water towards them. The sea around them went uncomfortably still. Winston instinctively reached for his weapon, and was stopped by Mhara's hand upon his wrist. She wasn't looking at him. Winston looked beyond her to see multiple grooves appearing in the water coming towards them. As they reached the boat there was only a small rocking as the tentacles moved along the rim of the vessel, up and over its edges, entangling it in its grasp.

"What do we do?"

"Nothing."

"Nothing? You cannot be serious."

"We. Do. Nothing."

At those words another vessel rose from the water adjacent to their own. Within it were a small squad of warriors. Winston looked at them and had no doubt these were soldiers, not simply in position, but also in mentality. There were about a dozen of them, all fully armed and armored. As easily as he could recognize them as soldiers, Winston could make out their commanding officer. He was a full chested, powerful looking individual. His beard flowed down in smooth waves to his chest. Ornamented with shells and coral, his hair and beard were that unique color seen when reddish blond hair fades to white. He held a spear that had a hooked blade to the end of it, and his armor was subtle but ornate.

Winston watched the commanding officer converse with one of his men, as their ship moved closer to their boat. The tentacles had stopped entwining them, yet remained in full grasp of their boat. The approaching ship was small, and adequate, and yet shined gloriously in comparison to the feeble boat they were in. Its deck was many feet above the level of where Winston was. A fact emphasized when, as the boats almost touched, Winston watched the commanding officer jump from the deck of his ship, down into their little boat. He landed securely, using his hand to balance his footing, as his legs bent to absorb the impact. He stood, and looked upon the three of them with cold, distant eyes the color of fall leaves. Michael didn't move, and Winston found this to be an example he would be wise to follow. This individual was a phenom before them in his size, stature, and physique. As he looked over the three of them he softly evaluated the scene before him, and Winston could see the wheels of reason working behind this man's eyes. That was until those eyes fell upon Mhara. In that moment the scene changed completely. Winston had no idea why until he processed what he had heard Mhara say.

"Hello father."

27 – FOR THE SEAS

Their descent into the sea was smooth and aggressive, like butter melting atop a hot skillet. As the warriors vessel lowered into the sea the water around them churned and bubbled as it pressed against an invisible barrier around them. Winston felt the pressure of anxiety raise within him as the water enclosed them and their whole world went a shade of greenish blue. It was the anxiety of the now, and the long past. Winston found himself reflecting on the last time he swam below water on purpose. Sure, he had drills while in the army, but those were all part of the training. Part of the job. It wasn't since his childhood that he had last swam recreationally. Swam on purpose. Though that wasn't much of a swim, now that he thought of it.

"Ye alright, boy?"

"I'm as right as I can be, all things considered." Winston said.

"Looked like something was bothering ye." Michael clarified.

"Yeah. I'll be fine."

A kaleidoscope of colors began to sparkle within the waters around them. Sea life swam about, and the glitter of light refracted off the seafloor. Winston had never seen anything quite like it. He identified that light was emanating from the vessel's base, allowing them to see all that was around them. Beyond the limits of the light, large shadowy figures moved. One of them having what looked to be the impressive tentacles that had entangled their small boat.

"It is best not to stare." Michael said softly.

"I'm not staring. It just looks like a…"

"Aye. It's a Kraken. I believe is what your people call them."

"Is it?"

"More or less." Michael confirmed. "There is one specific species that can be found between realms, however here we have all variations of sea monster." Winston looked at Michael, uncertainty in his eyes. "You asked, lad."

Rising from the sand, rocks, and coral of the seafloor came rugged structures of stone and an iridescent glass-like material. The warriors navigated their vessel toward the structures. Winston could make out no visible entrance, and as the vessel came to rest upon an open platform he began to worry they would need to swim from where they were to wherever they were needing to be. Surely the pressure of the sea at this depth alone would make that impossible. Before he could give voice to his concerns the water around the now still vessel began to lap against the transparent barrier around them. Winston had all but forgotten that it was there. He watched as the water level around them lowered, and he was able to see that a dome shaped enclosure had sealed the space within the platform, and the water had been displaced, allowing them to exit into a relatively dry, open space.

Winston's ears popped as the pressure of the vessel adjusted to match that of the platform. It was a sudden and harsh adjustment, almost as if someone had hit him on the side of his head. He gathered himself and looked toward Mhara, who was standing near the warrior she had identified as her father. She had clearly responded to Winston, but was held in place by her father who stoically faced forward, unmoved by the circumstances. Winston smiled to Mhara, knowing she was only doing what she must. The warriors around them shifted, ushering he and Michael off the vessel, Mhara exited as well, following with her father.

As a group they walked from the platform into the closest structure. Doors before them slid aside to reveal an open, grand corridor with walls reflecting the full spectrum of colors, and trim of gold and silver. The group moved further into the corridor, the walls narrowing to that of a wide hallway. Winston heard the doors seal closed behind them, the unmistakable sound of air pressure being balanced, along with the sound of a locking mechanism being put in place. He didn't turn around to confirm his observations. Instead, choosing to keenly watch ahead as they continued forward. The passage was long, with doors spaced here and there along the walls. They had walked some distance before coming to a stop.

"Wizard." Called a deep voice. Michael and Winston turned to find a huge warrior standing behind them, presenting to Michael a pair of iron shackles. "Put these on." He instructed. Michael reluctantly complied. After the manacles were secure, the warrior stepped around them, opening a nearby door. "Inside." The large warrior commanded. "Both of you." He added, turning to Winston. Winston and Michael entered the room.

"Bullocks." Michael muttered as the doors were locked behind them.

"What do you think is happening?"

"Specifically? I do not know." Michael admitted. "What I do know is that we are now locked in a small room, and I am once again bound, and unable to use magic."

"They didn't take our weapons."

"I doubt they are much concerned with what the two of us could do against their army." Michael said, gritting his teeth. "This would be a great time for you to remember your magic."

The statement caught Winston like an unexpected slap to the face. "My magic." He asked. "Who said I have any magic."

"Save it, boy." Michael snapped. "I've been here. I've watched all that has happened. From how quickly ye recovered from yer fall off the cliff, to the way Queen Bheur treated ye, hell, how Myrddin treats ye. I was there when ye visited yer mother. There's no chance ye have that much connection to Faerie without ye having access to some kind of magic."

Winston scoffed. "I hope you like being disappointed."

"Bloody hell, I watched ye fight Fionn! With mine own eyes I saw the smoke come out of ye, the world bend around ye. I watched as a boy drew blood from the greatest warrior who has yet lived." Michael's eyes seethed with contempt. Turning away from Winston, he released a low growl.

"Michael. I'm sorry." Winston started to say.

"No, boy." Michael interrupted. "Yer fine. How could ye know any different? We will simply sit here and wait for our fate."

"Do you think Mhara is well?"

"Aye. She is with her father." Michael said. "Even if she wasn't alright, there is not much we can do for her presently."

Finding himself resolved to the truth of Michael's words, Winston leaned back against the wall, and slid to the floor. Michael reclined as best he could on a chaise hear the window. The room held other seating options that Winston could have utilized, however he choose to remain seated on the floor.

They had no idea what they were waiting for. No idea what was going to happen next. And Winston had no idea where Mhara was, and if she was alright. Michael was right. All they knew was that they were now locked in a small room, a situation all to reminiscent for Michael of his previous circumstances, Winston surmised. He thought about pounding on the door, and demanding answers. That idea quickly lost traction as Winston recalled how other unfamiliar elements of Faerie had responded to his presence. How would these people respond? Were they the kind to resent the presence of a human in Faerie? Is it really wise to test this out with a person who consistently walks around in arms and armour? Winston became increasingly certain that he was in no hurry to find out.

The two of them sat in their respective silence, time passing by with the soft sounds of the sea around them. The window displaying the curious glances of various sea life as they would pass by. Some of the creatures held a familiar appearance to them for Winston, while others challenged the limits of his imagination. They were all bathed in the greenish blue tones of the sea, with a hint of the soft golden light from their room occasionally reflecting off the creatures who braved swimming close to the window. Winston was entranced by the scene and lost all sense of time. Making it a double start when his ears perceived the door to the room being assertively thrust open, while simultaneously the sea life in the window suddenly dispersed.

"On your feet!" Boomed the man as he entered the room. "On. Your. Feet!" He repeated, emphasizing each word succinctly. This wasn't the same warrior who had left them in this room, and he was followed by other warriors, all of them wearing more ornate armor, with rich blue capes draped over their shoulders.

Winston got to his feet, looking to Michael who looked less pleased now than he had previously. Firm hands pressed Winston's shoulder and back, involuntarily moving him toward the door. Winston kept his footing and began walking, not taking his eyes off Michael. Within a few strides they were once again walking side by side.

"What is it?" Winston asked. Michael didn't respond, and they continued down the hallway, and around a corner. "Michael." Winston tried again. "Talk to me man."

"Quiet boy." Michael said. "Stay quiet, and pay attention." Winston looked up to find the lead warrior had stopped. His body tensed as he reigned himself in, and came a dog's hair from walking directly into the back of the warrior in front of him. Perhaps having sensed this circumstance, the lead warrior turned. His eyes looked past his fellow warrior, and fell directly upon Winston. Their eyes met in that way of deep recognition that you only feel when you look upon someone, eye to eye. Winston broke the connection, and the lead warrior turned forward without a word, or gesture.

They began moving again, and this time Winston paid attention. Their group moved out to the center of a circular platform. Round the platform Winston counted ten pillars. When they reached the center of the platform, the lead signaled for them to stop again, and Winston watched as he moved toward a single, smaller pillar that came to about waist level. The lead warrior confidently placed his palm down upon the top of the small pillar. Light radiated from the space between the warriors hand and the surface of the small pillar, and as he focused on this, Winston became aware that the platform had begun moving upward like a giant cargo elevator. The lift was surprisingly smooth, with no jarring, vibrations, or any pulley system visually in sight. Reaching its destination, the platform smoothly rested in placed, leaving Winston thinking that had he not been paying keen attention to his surroundings, he may not have noticed they were moving at all.

Waiting in front of them was a short flight of stairs, and what looked to be an ornate platform. As they stepped upon the platform, Winston recognized that it was not simply an ornate platform, rather they had entered the throne room. The throne itself sat before them, trimmed in gold and silver, its back and arms resembling Staghorn coral in how it reached up and out, and to the sides. Their escort pointed toward a spot on the floor, indicating they needed to wait. Michael and Winston took their spot, and their warrior escorts moved to line the room. A low rumble flowed into the room, and Winston turned his attention toward the sound only to find a full statured man stepping up to the throne.

"For the seas. Hail to the King." Rang out the unified voices of the warriors that lined the room. Their voices booming. Winston could see more than those who had originally escorted them were now in the room. He recognized within the crowd the faces of the warriors of the group that had captured them on the surface. Passing his eyes over the swelling group Winston saw Mhara, and her father in attendance as well.

Winston thought he saw her eyes move to him, but his attention was pulled away as a deep thrum ripped through the room. He turned to see the full statured man now seated on the throne.

Winston's knees buckled beneath him as one of the warrior guards pushed at them with the butt of his spear. He caught himself with his hand upon the floor. "Kneel." snarled the guard. Winston looked to Michael who was also kneeling, though Winston was not able to tell if it was voluntary or not. Hearing a shuffling to his side Winston turned to see the guard move away, having been waved back by the King.

"Rise, and identify yourself." Said the King.

Winston moved to rise, hearing Michael address the King. "Your Majesty, my thanks…"

"Quiet your slick tongue, wizard." Interrupted the King. "Each soul here knows who you are. Fugitive. Vagabond. Thief."

"Your Majesty, if I may."

"You may not. Unless that which you may be inclined to do is surmised of you remaining silent, and contemplating the blessing of my graciousness to allow you breathe the air of my kingdom, then by all means, contemplate. In silence." The King looked decisively at Winston. "You. Speak."

Winston took an instinctive posture, slightly spreading his feel to shoulder width, straightening his back, and looking directly ahead. Breathing in he felt his lungs fill, and as he exhaled, Winston heard himself begin to recount all the events that had transpired. How he ended up in Faerie, meeting Queen Bheur, their original plan to steal the sword of Darkfyre. The audience seemed to churn as he worked through the various events, the actions of the Hound, and Jonathan ambushing them in the Autumnlands. The King listened stoically, almost impassive towards the details of Winston's tale. He didn't tell the King about his mother, however, when he reached the point in the tale that lead to where they were now Winston drew the sword of Darkfyre from its scabbard and displayed it for the King. This garnered a reaction, the King leaned forward intently.

"Why do you have that sword, boy?" The King asked.

"Queen Bheur, of Winter entrusted it to me. We were tasked with tracking down Jonathan in my realm, and she felt I would benefit from it being available to me. We had yet to locate Jonathan, however the sword has been of great use."

"Do you know what it is?"

"It is the sword of Darkfyre. Your Majesty."

"It is the sword of Arawn, the fallen King of Annwn. My friend. Why do you have it?"

"Queen Bheur."

"Yes. Yes. I know she gave it to you. You had already stated such. What I want to know is why she would give the sword to a person such as you."

Winston knew why, didn't he? It was as his mother, and Queen May had told him. Arawn was his father, and some could say that by right the sword was his. An inheritance of throne and kingdom, or at least of this weapon. A pang of truth stung in Winston's mind as he recalled that Michael didn't know all of this. He had stepped away while they spoke. Surely that was due to remaining animosity between he and the Queen of Summer. She had imprisoned he and Jonathan originally, and hadn't seemed pleased in seeing Michael at the falls. Still, there was a reason she whispered, a reason she was wary. Wasn't there? There wasn't time to continue based on half truths, and implied lies. Winston saw Michael in his peripheral, but didn't look at him. Instead he fixed his gaze upon the King and spoke.

"Recently I met with Queen May."

"The Summer Queen?"

"Yes. Your Majesty." Winston said. "She explained to me that Jonathan's efforts to obtain and control the scepter and the sword only held merit because neither weapon was presently bonded. Queen May instructed me to get the sword to Annwn that it may be bound, and out of Jonathan's grasp."

"You have yet to answer my key question, boy. Why you?"

"Because I am the son of Arawn, and I, more than any other, can successfully bind the sword to me." Winston's voice seemed to echo in the quiet chamber. He completed his statement, and upon recognizing the utter lack of sound in the room, he looked around. Winston's eyes met Michael's, and found them hollow. Was it from shock? A feeling of betrayal? Michael looked at him, unmoving, and not displaying any feeling that Winston could decipher.

The King stood abruptly, stepping to the edge of his platform. Winston met his gaze, as did the rest of the room. "You claim to be the son of Arawn, heir to Annwn, and you make this claim whilst boldly holding the sword of Darkfyre." The King restated matter of factly. Winston moved to affirm his reassessment, but was cut off by the King continuing. "Atalantia, heed my words now. Arawn was as friend and brother to me. His son would be as a son and nephew to me. Never foe. Should it be true that this boy, Winston, is in fact the one true heir to the kingdom of Annwn, then he and his companions will go free. Free, and with the full support of our people. Is this known?"

"For the seas. Hail to the King!" Roared all in attendance, save Michael, and Winston himself. Winston then notices the King looking upon him expectantly. Was he waiting for a show? Or perhaps some grand display to prove Winston's story true? Sure the blade shown forth its flame, but the blade burned blue for the Queen of Winter before him, and there was no sign of lineage. Winston looked back upon the King, lost for what to do or say next.

"Your Majesty, what would you have me do?" Winston asked.

"We shall need to prove you for who you claim to be."

"I'm uncertain of how I am able to do this for you."

The King stepped down from his platform, signalling for a servant to bring him a drink. Which he readily took up, and consumed in one go before giving the empty gablet back to the servant. "Proving who you are, or are not, is not all that difficult a process here in Faerie." The King said, stepping up to Winston. "We will only need a few items. Your hair, the sword, your blood, and we will need to go to Annwn."

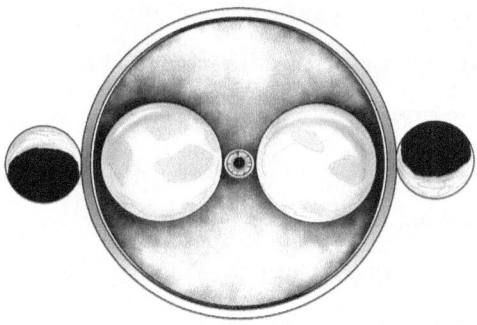

28 – THE FOUNTAIN OF ANNWN

If Winston could say anything at all, it was that the King of Atalantia traveled in style. They were allowed a modest meal before departing for Annwn. Winston had no perception of how far they would need to travel to get there, yet it seemed to take no time at all for preparations to be completed. He had sat down to eat and instantaneously heard the call for departure. Reasoning that they couldn't possibly leave without him, Winston finished his meal before rising to depart. Once he was finished two guards whisked him down a winding corridor, through a series of doors, and upon a vessel which hummed in the expected tone of a machine ready to do it's work.

Winston found himself pondering the value of vehicles. Surely a working, clean car, is a valuable vehicle no matter the make and model. Yet should one go abruptly from a compact commuter car they've had ample time to acclimate with, to finding themselves riding in a deluxe luxury SUV, the argument of a vehicle's value takes on a whole new depth of consideration. This same argument would have a place between the ship they originally took from the surface, down to speak to the King, and the King now had them upon for their trip to Annwn. Gone was the platform style boat, with the transparent dome enclosure. This ship felt like something out of a Hollywood space opera, complete with vibrantly lit control panels, comfortable seating, and superior ability to navigate the churning waters of sea.

As they traversed the sea, various makes and models of sea creature spun and swam along with them. Winston quickly lost count at the expansive appearances of the sea life. Still he remained entranced by the spectacle of the scenery around them as they continued on, and before he knew it the water around their vessel began to lighten as they moved closer to the surface. Light refracted and radiated through the viewport, and then quickly balanced out as the water fell away and the ship came to rest upon the waves.

The King and his guard were pleasant enough for the trip. Michael was released from the iron manacles, yet was confined to one of the small quarters of the vessel. Winston however was permitted to move freely about the ship, and with their vessel now being above water, he moved to the outer viewing deck. His feet thunk'd heavily as he climbed up the steep staircase that led to the viewing deck. The door to the deck opened smoothly, the air was a sweet comfort as it caressed his skin, and he stepped out into the sun. Winston's eyes took a moment to fully adjust to the brightness of the open sea. As they came into focus he could see a figure standing, leaning against the deck railing.

"Not quite what you expected, is it?" Mhara asked, not turning around.

Winston was surprised to find Mhara here, away from her

father. He stepped next to her, taking hold of the rail. "Which part?" Winston asked. "This trip? The ship? Or are we talking about you?"

"I suppose we're talking about all of it." She said, not looking away from the sea. "I miss it, you know. If I'm away from it too long. I cannot remember the last time I had been away from the sea, as long as I was, while with you." Mhara's tone was plain, sincere, and there was something raw within the sound of her words. "Missing it isn't really the right way to express the feeling. You wouldn't say you 'miss' air, if you go too long without breathing. Truly you wouldn't say much, you'd be too busy suffocating." She gave way to a soft chuckle at the morbid humor of her observation, and continued. "Suffocating is a good word for it though. When I am away from the sea too long, I suffocate, and you'd think I would surely notice when I am in such a state. Yet I did not." She said, pausing. Perhaps it was for effect, or to collect her own thoughts, either way the pause was accented by a breeze passing between them, chill and sharp.

"I'm not sure I follow what you are trying to tell me, Mhara." Winston said.

"Perhaps I do not know what I am meaning to tell you, beyond this fact." She stood full, and looked directly upon Winston. The breeze increased, as if the wind were there to compliment her impassioned words. "The sea is my home, Winston. I am a Selkie, and only in the sea do I truly breathe. Yet there I was, a world away from home, traveling on some wild adventure, with you. For you. All the while not realizing I was suffocating. Not feeling how much I needed to breath until you accidentally dropped us into the middle of the sea. I was oblivious to it. Winston, don't you see what I am saying?" Mhara said, her voice full and rich with emotion. "I was suffocating, effectively dying, and yet as long as I was with you, on this foolish quest, I never felt the pain. I never fought to breathe. I didn't know what I was missing, because I was with you." She stopped. Tears rimmed her eyes, and she looked way from Winston.

The weight of her words hit him like a wave upon the shore. Again, and again, each time eroding away a bit more of his limited understanding and exposing for his soul the truth of her words. She was dying? Suffocating? Is this why her father was keeping her so close. Ensuring that she was well, and not quick to run off with Winston again? Surely he had to be a contributing factor. Regardless, Winston knew he had no perception of her truth, nor any of this she just shared. If what Mhara said was true, and Winston had less than no doubt to trust her, she was quite literally on her way to dying for his benefit, and for what? What the hell would cause her to make such a choice for someone she initially did not know anything about? "Why?" Winston asked, not wishing the word to come out, but quickly wishing it'd return to him.

Mhara looked at him, and scoffed. "Perhaps someday, you'll help inform me." She said. Mhara turned to leave.

"Wait, Mhara. I'm sorry." Winston said. "I didn't mean to ask you 'why', it just came out." She had stopped, yet her features were unchanging. "Thank you." Winston said. "In another life I was a soldier. In that life we knew we would or could be called to lay down our lives for our fellow soldiers. Our brothers. I always trusted that those in my unit would do that for me, and that I would do that for them." He breathed, controlling the emotions of his memory. "Then came the moment where we all found out who was telling the truth and who were liars. It was horrific, and as the dust settled all but one member of our unit was either injured or dead. So as you stand here and tell me that you, for some undisclosed reason, may have almost lost your life either directly or indirectly because me, I'm left at a loss of what to say, or how to take it."

"It is alright, Winston." She said. "Now you know."

"Now I know." He repeated.

"Winston?" She called out as he moved to look away and let her leave.

"Yeah?"

"Was it you?" Mhara asked. "Were you the one who lived?"

Winston paused. Silent. Knowing saying the truth out loud never got any easier. "Yes." He confirmed. "It was me."

"Thank you, Winston."

"What? Why? Thank you for what?" He asked.

"For showing me your truth." She said, and walked away, and headed below.

Winston watches her leave, and turns to look out over the water, giving her space to go. Cliffs are clearly visible now, and Winston can approximate where they are headed for port. He should have said something more to her. He should have understood what she was saying. Had any ever in his life ever said as much to him as Mhara did in that moment? Certainly not. He needed to find her, to tell her he was a fool. To tell her he understood. The door open behind Winston, and he turns, excited at her return. "Mhara, forgive me. I…"

"My daughter is a forgiving soul. More forgiving than I am." The fierce looking man said. Mhara's father looked at Winston, a calm surety in his eyes, as if all the answers were already his, and only the questions remain to be asked. "I wanted to see you for myself." He

275

continued. "Do you hold her coat? Is that why she is loyal to you?"

"Her coat? Sir, I do not understand what you mean."

"Do not play coy with me, boy. I will know the truth."

"With all due respect, sir, I have no idea what you are talking about." Winston said. "Mhara and I are friends, only just having met. If not for her, I would be dead."

Mhara's father stepped to Winston, bringing them close enough to feel each other's breath. Mhara's father's eyes glowed with flecks of gold, and he gave off a sense of power that Winston recognized as the presence of a seasoned warrior. The kind of presence you respect without question. "Very well." He said to Winston, meeting his eyes fully. "Steady seas, son of Arawn."

"Lord Muir." Called a voice from behind them.

"Speak."

"The King calls for you, my Lord."

"I will be there presently." Lord Muir said, as he nodded once to Winston and turned toward the door below. Winston watched him go, taking in his confident gate, posture, and the complete fullness that he held himself. Mhara's father, Lord Muir, was someone Winston felt he could easily admire, and someone who's bad side Winston would be pleased to never meet.

The sky was overcast, and wrought with shadows as they pulled into port and exited the ship. The thick clouds rolled heavily overhead, and the soft growl of thunder echoed in the distance. Their party moved from the water, up hill, and toward a small farm that looked to have been blackened by fire sometime in its infancy. Standing near where it appeared a gate once resided was a slender figure, of medium height, holding a short sithe in its left hand.

"Identify yourselves, or by the Goddess, I will see you parted from your lives."

"Beg pardon, Epona. We did not intend to call at such an odd hour, unannounced." The King said.

"Llyr? Is that you?"

"Yes, dear Epona. It is I. My people and I are departing for Annwn."

"This is no time to revisit old wounds, Llyr."

"There will be no revisiting. Only a verifying of what is to come." The Kind said, looking sidelong toward Winston. Turning back to the old woman, he smiled. "Pray tell, do you have steeds in your stable of which we could employ to aid in our travels?"

"This is my Winter home, Llyr, you know this. I do not keep horses here."

"My apologies, dear Epona."

"No apologies needed. I do have something that could be of aid. I've been tending them for Queen Bleur. They were recently used. Should be refreshed enough to get you where you're going." The old woman took her scythe, extended it in front of her, and using the blade she carved three symbols into the dirt. Winston could hear her mumbling something to herself as she enclosed the three symbols within a circle. She then drove the butt of the scythe into the dirt, resting the head of the tool upon her upper chest and shoulder. Closing her eyes Epona rubbed her hands together, and kept repeating her low, indiscernible words to herself. The symbols within the circle began to glow a soft green. Epona continued her mumbling chant, and used the butt of the scythe to break the circle. The soft green light left the symbols, spilling out through the opening in the circle, dispersing and quickly becoming invisible to Winston's sight.

They all stood there in silence for a moment, looking at each other, the King, and the old woman. Winston knew in his core that she had done something, but he didn't know what, or why they were still standing around waiting. Thunder rumbled in the distance again, only it seemed to roll on longer than reasonable. Listening more closely Winston heard through the sound of thunder to discern a familiar sound of heavy paws attacking the ground. Winston did nothing to hold back the smile that filled his face as a pack of matheans raced over the crest of the hill.

Within moments their party was infiltrated by the huge, nuzzling beasts. Their familiar smell filled Winston's nostrils, engulfing him with a surprising familiarity and comfort. As the beasts moved among their group they bumped into each other, jostling everyone about. Winston felt a snout push into his back once, twice, three times, and thought little of it. Animals will do such things when vying for attention. He thought surely it was nothing to be concerned about until the beast bit down on his belt and pulled him away from the group.

"Hey!" Winston called out, as he struggled to keep his footing. The beast's strength more than enough to overtake Winston's footing. The creature released him, as he tumbled to the ground. "What the hell?" Winston asked. His only reply was the sound of Mhara laughing, as she pet the offending beast.

"Don't blame him. Winston has had to deal with a lot in the short time you've been apart."

"Short time?" Winston repeated, looking up at Mhara. The mathean nuzzled his snout down against Winston's jaw. "Alban?" Winston asked, the beast chuffing in approval, and pressing into him more enthusiastically. "My goodness! Alban. Hey buddy!" Winston returned the beast's affection

"Thank you, dear Epona." King Llyr said. "It is good to have seen you, old friend. We must be going."

"Smooth seas, Llyr. Do be careful." She said. "The roads to Annwn are not what they once were."

They mounted their beasts, with Winston and Michael climbing atop Alban. A final nod of farewell was shared between the King and Epona, and they departed. The beast moved with the same sure footing Winston had grown accustomed to when they passed through the Autumnlands. The ride to Annwn was without incident. The only abnormality Winston noted was the gradual reduction in life the closer they came to castle Annwn. First the trees withered to bushes, from bushes to grass, with any sign of animal life lessening with each phase. When they reached the castle itself, all that surrounded it was dirt and stone. The sky itself became darker and darker as they traversed the land. All of this did very little for the morale of the group.

A small group of the Kings warriors were instructed to remain with the matheans, while the rest of them headed inside.

"Clearly, no one is caring for this place." Michael commented as they entered the castle.

"Hard to do that when those who would be here are all dead or dispersed." King Llyr said "After Arawn's fall, those servants who remained, had to flee for their own safety. The quest to capture power and glory, is not a sin exclusive to the realm of man."

"You're sure what we need is here?" Winston asked.

"Yes."

The King led Michael, Mhara, and Winston confidently through what felt like a maze to Winston. A couple dozen of the King's men moving with them. Among the warriors was Mhara's father, Lord Muir. Two more turns, and the corridor opened up to an ornate room, lined with stone pillars, and deep wood accents throughout. King Llyr led the group to a fountain along the back wall. A stone platform rested at an angle in the middle of the fountain, and a large mirror was adjacent to the fountain on either side. As they stepped closer to the fountain Winston could see an outline on the stone platform of an indentation in the shape of a sword.

"Do I place the sword there?" Winston asked.

"You can, however for what we are here to verify, we will only need the waters of the fountain, and you." King Llyr said. He pulled a dagger from his belt. "Hold still, and give me your hand." He instructed. As Winston extended his hand to the King, the King used his knife to cut a small bit of Winston's hair off from near his neckline, and placed it in the palm of Winston's hand. The King then lightly cut Winston's palm, and holding Winston's hand in place he allowed the blood to rise and pool around the hair in his hand. "Now wash your hands in the fountain." The King instructed.

"That won't be necessary." Called a gravelly voice from behind them. The Hound sat on the throne of Annwn, his large axe hammer resting against his leg. While his other leg draped over the arm of the throne. The Hound clapped twice, and the perimeter of the room filled with all manner of creature. Many brandishing weapons, or at least fangs.

"What is the meaning of this?" demanded King Llyr.

"The meaning?" mused the Hound. "In part it is for the sword." He said. "Mainly it is for the sport of it. It's been too long since my tongue was satiated by the blood of humans. I'm sure it won't hurt to include a wizard, and some fish warriors too."

"The only blood you'll be tasting tonight will be your own. Now remove yourself from that throne. You have no right to defile it with your presence."

While the King and the Hound spoke, Winston had lowered his hands into the water of the fountain, and washed away the hair and blood. When he removed his hand the cut was healed. Looking at the water, he could see the residual blood churn in the water, dispersing to nothing. He waited. Nothing happened.

"Enough." The Hound bellowed, standing from the throne. "I tire of this. You have no power here fish king. Let us test the strength of your fight." He said, picking up his axe hammer. The enemies lining the room positioned themselves for battle, their various levels of armor shifting, and rubbing as they adjusted their stance.

King Llyr and his warriors took a trained formation around Winston, Michael, and Mhara. Lord Muir handed a short sword to his daughter. Michael took up a stance Winston recognized as one he employs to help channel his magic. Winston himself took position next to Mhara, and drew the sword of Darkfyre. A low growl came from the Hound in an "I'll be having that sort of way" upon seeing the sword. Winston affixed the Hound with a "you can try" gaze.

One of the creatures from the perimeter moved first. Weapons collided. The Hound roared. Winston prepared himself to fight, while behind him the fountain began to boil.

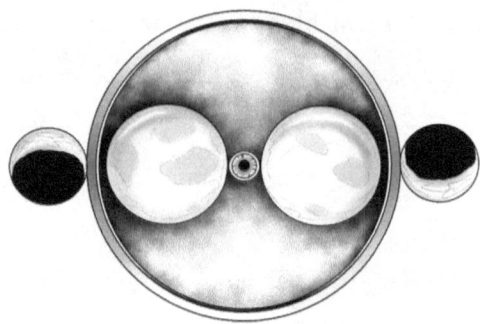

29 – EYES OF A LIGHTER TONE

Blood ran slick down the pillars, and along the floor of the throne room. Weapons collided against each other, and against armor. Bodies speckled the floor, as friend and foe alike fell to the other. Grunts, and growls could be heard of the cacophony of conflict, yet to Winston's surprise, no one was yelling.

The Hound's companions were the same creatures that had attacked them as they raced away from the parking ramp in Minneapolis. Their svelte bodies, pale skin, and fanged teeth were impossible to mistake. Winston watched as they moved to claw and gnash their teeth at King Llyr's warriors. Within the Hound's group were a couple truly nasty creatures, which looked much more monster than human. They used weapons, and seemed to possess strength that rendered the use of weapons a superficial novelty. Winston found himself able to observe all of these details through the advent of being kept within a tight circle of warriors. They moved as if their only task was to keep him safe. Winston found it oddly frustrating behavior.

Bursts of fire and light strobed within the room each time Michael loosed another volley of magic at their assailants. The vampire-like creatures would hiss, and howl as the bursts of fire seared through their clothing, and flesh. A few of them were quiet deaths as the fire's influence on their bodies resulted in them exploding, and releasing visceral gore over the space close to them. Winston did not expect their blood to be the light purple-ish color it was.

An armored body soared through the air, hitting both Mhara and Michael. The impact sent them both to the floor. The limp carcass pinned Mhara beneath its weight. Michael steadies himself on one arm, and attempts to get to his feet. The Hound steps forward and kicks Michael solidly in the head, causing him to drop limply to the floor.

"Find the King." The Hound commanded his remaining creatures. "He seems to have slipped away. Dispose of him while I enjoy my prize." The Hounds eyes looked at Winston with a fierce hunger, and malice within them. The remaining creatures left the room leaving the Hound and Winston alone in a room full of bodies. "I'm going to enjoy this, pup." He growled. "When I'm finished with you I'll possess the sword, and a full belly." His smile caused Winston's belly to churn with a mix of disgust and hatred.

"You talk too fucking much." Winston said, not taking his eyes from the Hound. The sword of Darkfyre danced with blue fire that rolled out from the blade like it was immersed in a dance of passion with a life long lover.

The room shifted in color, sliding into a shade of green. The fountain churned audibly as the bubbles of the boiling water pressed up, and over the edge of the fountain wall. The reddish water glowed in ominous contrast to the green lighting of the room, at times looking black, and in other times it was a hyper-radiant reddish tone. Foolishly, Winston had allowed the sight to distract him, and the Hound was ready.

The impact of the Hound hitting Winston head on, sent him flying back against the wall. The Hound had thrust into him with his shoulder, shoving Winston back a distance. He was clearly toying with Winston, as the Hound could have came in with a killing blow. One that Winston may not have responded to correctly due to his distraction. The shoulder thrust, combined with the impact to the wall, had evicted all the air from Winston's lungs leaving him gasping for air as he pulled himself together.

Behind him, Winston heard the Hound pacing, and dragging his axe hammer across the stone floor. "What seems to be the issue here, pup. Is your lil' Queen not here to save you? Is that it? You stood so tall, so mighty, in the hall of Winter. What are you now? A pathetic creature that cannot make to stand."

Winston rose to his knees, trying to use the edge of the fountain for leverage, his feet slipping on the wet stone. The Hound chuckled and waited, pacing behind him. Winston rose back to his knees, and reached forward to use a pillar for leverage this time. Only the stone was smooth and cold to the touch, completely lacking any feeling of texture or naturalness. Looking up, he saw his hand resting upon the mirror. Thinking little of it, Winston used both hands upon the mirror to guide himself to his feet. He looked forward into his own eyes. Resolving his mind to what must be done. In the mirror Winston saw a shadow move, and he gripped the hilt of his sword. His ears heard the Hound stop behind him, and to his left, like he was taking an expected stance waiting for Winston to turn around. Yet the shadow in the mirror was directly behind him, and as he watched the shadow stepped forward. Stepping through Winston like a ghost until only the ghost's image filled the mirror.

"Too afraid to turn around?" The Hound asked. But Winston didn't reply or move.

The mysterious figure in the mirror wore a dark cloak, tattered in places along the edges, yet clearly a rich fabric of quality. As the ghost's image filled the mirror, its features became more discernible. It was a man, gaunt, tall, and regal looking. His skin was very pale, hair dark, face almost skull-like in his thinness. Winston was thinking to himself that this stranger could be anyone, and as he allowing those thoughts to infiltrate his mind, his eyes were meeting those of the ghost. The connection felt like the mental recognition of crawling into your own bed while in a dark room. The eyes of the ghost were not simply eyes, they were Winston's eyes. Same shape. Same feel. Only these eyes were of a lighter tone.

"Hello Son." The ghost said. "Welcome home." Winston's breath caught in his chest. "It is all alright, my son." The ghost continued. "Though you should truly move."

Winston registered the words through his exceeding perception of shock just in time to recognize the Hound was heading straight toward him, axe hammer raised at the ready. As if in instinct Winston rolled to the side. The Hound, too caught in his momentum, surpassed Winston's position, and tumbled into the fountain. His massive body collided with the angled stone pillar in the fountain, and it broke beneath his impact.

The sword of Darkfyre danced hungrily within its flames. The

Hound howled in pain as the boiling water of the fountain seared his flesh. As he raised himself up from the water, Winston swung down upon him with the sword, ripping open his armor, and cutting deep into the flesh of his torso. The Hound reared back in shock. He patted the wound in disbelief, finding it cut diagonally across his torso, and included a wickedly deep gouge across his cheek, and forehead. Perhaps in panic, or perhaps in surprising wisdom, the Hound exited the fountain, ran out of the throne room, and soon after he vacated the castle itself. Winston heard his howl fade into the distance as he fled.

Shadows moved in his peripheral. Looking to his side, Winston saw the cloaked figure of the ghost in the mirror; it's posture and stance reflecting that of his own. When Winston took a step, the ghost did also. He moved his hand, and the ghosts cloak moved also. He looked up to make eye contact with the ghost and at the distance the features of the ghost were nondescript, but Winston could feel their eyes meet. He didn't have time for this.

Winston bent and pulled the fallen warrior from atop Mhara. She had blood pooling at her side. He moved to search her body for a wound. Footsteps clattered into the throne room, and Winston pivoted on his knee, raising his sword to the ready. King Llyr, and Lord Muir entered the room.

"Easy, son. Easy." Called the King. "It is I, and Lord Muir. The remaining vile creatures fled with the Hound."

"Mhara!" Lord Muir exclaimed as he moved to his daughter's side. "What happened? Where is she hurt?" He asked.

"I was looking for the wound when you two came racing in. She had been knocked down, and one of your warriors fell on her." Winston said. They worked together, carefully moving her to allow them to check their respective sides of Mhara's body. "I don't see a stab wound of any kind. The blood could have been from the fallen warrior."

"I believe you are correct." Lord Muir said. "All I can detect is Mhara suffered a hard blow to her head. Until she wakes, we will not know of any other injuries."

"He's still breathing!" King Llyr said.

Winston looked to see the King positioning Michael against the wall of the fountain. Blood covered the wizard's face, and though he was breathing, he was not yet conscious. The familiar thunder of galloping matheans echoed down the hall from the outer courtyard.

"We have company." Winston said.

"Stay here. I will go." Lord Muir said.

After a moment Winston heard voices at various levels of excitement carrying through the corridor. He strained to listen, trying to discern if they were voices he knew, or if the conversation happening outside was cause for the rest of them to move to somewhere safer.

"So much blood."

"Yes, blood. Like preparation for a feast."

"If we are to feast, does that mean we get to eat him now?"

"Yes, eat him indeed."

Winston couldn't hold in the smirk as he recognized the voices of Pot and Kettle. "I did not expect to ever enjoy hearing your bantering voices." He said.

"Bantering?"

"Bantering."

"We do not banter. We speak with great dignity and class."

"Dignity and class, you messy child."

"What are you two doing here?" Winston asked.

"They are here on my command." She said, her voice as warm and clear as the first time Winston remembered hearing it. Queen Bheur stepped beyond the threshold and the pillars, into the throne room. "Quite a mess you have here, Winston. Though I am admittedly relieved to see the blood is not yours."

"But how…" Winston began.

"As soon as we became aware that your efforts to return to Winter were interfered with, I tasked Pot and Kettle to locate you, and report your whereabouts to me immediately." The Queen said. "When Epona called the matheans to your aid they knew where you were. From there it was not difficult to discern where you were going. Especially with Llyr as your guide."

"Greetings, Queen Bheur." King Llyr said with a bow. "You know this young man?"

"I do."

"Is he who he claims to be."

The Queen looked at Winston. Her eyes thoughtful, almost maternal in their warmth. She didn't look at the King. "He is more than even he knows." She said. "Do you need anything, Winston."

"He needs to congratulate himself." Merlin's said, his voice booming off the stone around them. The legendary wizard king stepped into the room with the grace and vigar of a young man. Excitement and purpose guided his step. "If all reports are to be believed, you've been enjoying great success in the face of substantial opposition, young Winston."

"You're here too?"

"Of course I am, dear boy. Do you think the rest of us went to sitting on our laurels as while you traversed realms, fought a Mother and her hoard, and pieced together the mystery of all that Jonathan is up to? Certainly not."

"You're clearly well informed." Winston said. Myrddin looked ready to speak again, yet Winston continued. "A person could think you've been awfully well informed this whole time. Knowing far more than you're sharing."

"Winston…"

"I don't want to hear your rationale about why this was the best way, the only way, or any other way. I've known for some time that there was more to this story then what everyone was telling me. Still I went along. I had no choice. It was my only way home. Now I'm not even sure that was true."

"What are you saying?" Queen Bheur asked. "What are you planning to do?"

"You mean, will I continue in this fight?" Winston's voice was unapologetically sharp, and his eyes burned as he looked at the Queen. She nodded. "I'll see this to the end. When it's done, I expect clearer explanations. I expect answers." He looked to Myrddin. "Are we clear?"

"Certainly. Yes."

"My friends are bleeding, and hurt."

"We can see to their wounds." Queen Bheur said.

"Good." Winston said, looking out of the corner of his eye seeing the ghost in the mirror looking back at him.

"What is it Winston?" Myrddin asked.

"I need a moment." Winston said, lifting his eyes to meet those of the Queen. "Alone."

The Queen of Winter nodded once and took command of the room. "Gather them. King Llyr help me get them out to the courtyard.

We will tend their wounds."

"My daughter." Lord Muir said. "Her wounds evade me, and I am unable to wake her."

"Peace, strong knight. You carry her out, and we will see to her needs."

Winston watched King Llyr, gather up Michael from near the fountain. Myrddin stood near the King, looking down at the water of the fountain. The King leaned toward Myrddin, whispering. "The water boiled."

"Of course it did." Myrddin said matter of factly. "Get him outside." He instructed, and walked out with Llyr, and Michael, helping to support Michael as they moved.

The Queen's guard came in and removed bodies from the floor. Enemy and ally alike. Winston watched each one go. Not noticing that the Queen had taken position next to him.

"I have an idea of what you plan to do." She said. "We will be right outside if you need."

"I'll be fine." Winston interrupted. "This is no different than any other time. It's me, with a truck load of questions, and the task to find the answers all on my own."

"I am proud of you, Winston."

"Heh. Thanks, I guess. You still think I can be the Winston I choose to be, or am I stuck as the Winston the world expects me to be?"

"Anything is possible." She said warmly.

"I'm asking what you think."

"I think you already are." Queen Bheur said, softly squeezing his arm as she stepped away from him, and exited the room.

Winston waited a moment, listening, needing to be sure he was the only soul remaining. The floor, pillars, and walls all reflected the truth of what happened here. Different shades of blood were splattered about like a toddler was set free in a room with buckets of paint. Winston turned toward the mirror, initially thinking to see how he himself looked, and yet all he beheld was the ghost. In subtle ways the ghosts actions, and posture still mimicked Winston's own. Though when he spoke, the ghost's mouth did not move. "Are you my father? Arawn?" Winston asked. "And before you answer." He interjected. "Let's be clear on one thing. I have no interest in word games, riddles, or any other Faerie bullshit that seems to keep people from giving me a straight answer." The ghost nodded once.

"Arawn is indeed your father."

"I said I didn't want riddles."

"This is no riddle." The ghost assured him. "You are the son of Arawn, heir to Annwn." The ghost paused. "I am what is left of Arawn."

"What do you mean, what is left? I was told Arawn was killed."

"I was indeed defeated by Arturus and his knights when they breached our realm, and plunged into the otherworld on their way to Winter. He did not destroy me, however. Our worlds are layered, intertwined, and though he and his men defeated me in my capacity as King of Annwn, I continued on in my other roles."

"Other roles." Winston repeated, not as a question, but as an acknowledging statement. He looked at the image of the man who would have been his father, the dark, flowing cloak, his gaunt face. "Are you Death?" He asked.

"I've been called Death. In Annwn I was called King. Among

some of the clans of men I was heralded as the god of the dead, of war, revenge, and of terror. Though Arturus' defeat of me stripped me of my position within Faerie, I was still bound to my obligations within the realm of man." Arawn paused, looking at Winston he drew back his hood exposing sleek black hair, pale skin, and sharp, lean features. Winston moved closer to the mirror, and so too did Arawn appear to step closer to him.

"I know you." Winston said. "I've seen you before."

"You certainly have, my son." Arawn confirmed. Winston's face exuding an expression of deep questioning. "Bound to the realm of men, I did all I could to help you stay safe, without exposing who you were. I stayed close to you, watched over you. I was there at the camp when you nearly drowned, I was with you in the army, and I was there when Sam died."

"You were Mr. Tombs." Winston said. "Holy Shit! You're Mr. Tombs!"

"Correct, and your mother was…"

"Ms. Flowers?"

"Yes, correct again."

"Holy Shit! How did I not know? Why didn't anyone tell me?" Winston looked intently at the reflection of his father. "Why didn't you tell me?"

"In part to avoid bringing upon you the kind of mayhem you have been enduring recently. The moment word got out that your mother and I had produced a child, any semblance of a chance you may have had at a safe childhood would have been over."

"Speaking of my childhood. How does a guy who was killed 1500 years ago, have sex with my mom prior to his demise, result in me being born when I was?"

"Magic." Arawn said plainly.

"Oh fuck you, that isn't an answer."

"Yet it is, son. Your mother hid you, hid her pregnancy with her magic, and gave birth to you at a time that felt right to her. No doubt that is an idea difficult to fathom, and yet it is no more difficult than acknowledging you are the son of two gods. One of the realms of men, and the other a King of Faerie. It is not so much the time in which you were born, it is the reality that you were born at all, and what this means for us all. Every day, I know that your mother's choice to give birth to you is a great gift. Greatest especially to me."

Winston found himself looking at the floor, the sword of Darkfyre in his hand. When he looked back toward the mirror he saw Arawn, also holding the sword. In the mirror the flickers of blue fire along the sword's blade licked up Arawn's arm, and seemed to brush away his reflection until Winston saw himself standing within the mirror. Behind him stood the ghost of his father. Winston turned to find his father standing tall and powerful behind him in the throne room, his hooded cloak draping off his shoulders, down to the floor in a way that recalled images of smoke and myst. Winston reached for his father, unsure what would happen. He felt the fabric of the cloak against his fingers, followed by the solid resistance of a body beneath them. His father was there, he was real. They embraced each other, Winston with the arm not holding the sword, and Arawn with both arms. Though they lingered there for some time, it felt all too brief as they released their embrace.

"Come with me, son." Arawn said, and led Winston toward the throne. "Do you see the area there?" He asked, pointing towards a thin, oval shaped opening next to the left arm of the throne.

"I see it. Looks like the opening to a scabbard."

"Correct." Arawn said. "There are more answers to give you, son. More for you to learn. For that to be possible, Jonathan must be stopped. I heard you say to Queen Bheur that you would see this through to the end."

"I will."

"Of that, I am certain. Which is why I am showing this to you." Arawn turned to look intently upon his son. "Will you trust me?"

Winston didn't answer right away. "Yes."

"This next step is pivotal to your success, and key to helping you find answers."

"What do I do?"

"Take up the sword. Run it's blade along both forearms, releasing a flow of blood. Without wiping it clean, place the sword in the sheath upon the left arm of the throne, and sit upon the throne, resting both your arms upon the arms of the throne."

"What will this accomplish."

"It will accomplish what you came here for."

Winston looked at his father. Their eyes sharing a moment of agreement. Winston raised the blade and proceeded to do as instructed. The blade ran smoothly across his flesh, releasing a sizzling type sound as it went. The blood flowed enthusiastically from the cuts in his arms. Winston placed the sword within the throne, and sat down. He rested his arms flat against the arms of the throne, and watched as the blood flowed out from his hands, down thin channels in the stone arms of the throne exposing patterns he hadn't seen with his eyes. Winston leaned back, his father standing next to him.

"Breathe, my son, and be ready."

"Be ready for what?"

"To become what you are."

His father's words rang out, and before Winston could respond he found himself enclosed in darkness.

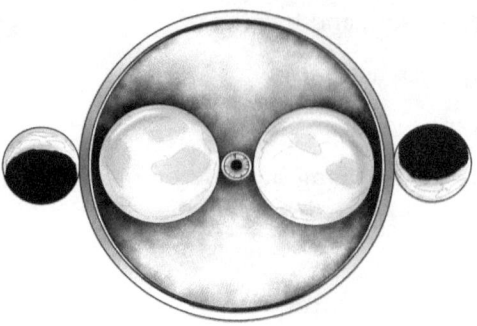

30 – SON OF ARAWN

The winter snows of Minnesota can come on with such overwhelming assertion that the only viewable detail of the environment is the color white. The depth of the world is lost beyond the layers of flaky, frozen precipitation blanketed the world for as far as the eye can see. The combination of snow in the air, and what already upon the surface of the environment, combined to counteract the contours, height, and colors of the trees, houses, and automobiles. Leaving one feeling like they were standing in a very breezy white room. Take away the breeze, the cold, and increase the whiteness by ten fold, and this would be the environment Winston found himself within.

The sudden darkness was a shock to the senses, and it took a noticeable amount of time for his eyes to perceive anything other than the lack of light around him. Now his eyes felt completely in focus, even overwhelmed with receivable data, as he stood in a space that was as white as fresh cotton, and lacking of all seams, shadows, creases, or change in coloration at all. His appearance served as the only contrast within the room. Gone was his armor, tunic, and weapons. Instead he stood in a soft black robe, with black pants of the same linen like fabric. The self inflicted wounds on his forearms were gone, no scars, and no residual blood to be found. Looking to his feet, for as bright as this space was, Winston saw no shadows at all.

"Hello?" Winston called out. "Father? Arawn? Anyone?" His voice came out clean, no echo, and no reverb at all. "Weird." He said aloud as he started walking. Winston could feel the firm resistance of the ground, or floor below his feet. A deeply surreal feeling when all his other senses screamed he was moving within a white expanse and of nothing.

Is this a dream? A hallucination? Is this how it all ends, walking forever in a bright nothingness dream world, while Winston's body bleeds out, alone, in an ancient throne, deep in the world of Faerie, and entire span of reality from everything he had ever known? That would be some bullshit.

A shiver moved up Winston's spine and he stopped moving. Was that the first sign of dangerous blood loss? Winston turned about, his eyes catching an anomaly in the distance. Like a flicker of shadows, it moved subtly in a shifting motion, left to right. He watched as the object grew larger, closer, something. Instinctively Winston began walking toward the anomaly. The shifting shadows became clearer, and took the shape of a body. A human. Winston kept walking, growing closer, the other figure increasing in detail with each step, until Winston stood face to face with himself.

"Well, this is fucking weird." Winston said, looking at himself. This duplicate version of himself, dressed in the same style of linen robe and pants, on his were as white as the space around them. Leaving the duplicate looking like a floating head with two hands, and feet, with soft contours of the fabric folds serving as the faint indication that a full body moved with them. His duplicate looked perplexed at Winston. "I'd never wear that much white."

"Are you ready?" Echoed a deep voice that seemed to come from every direction at once. It wasn't his duplicate speaking. No, that was the voice of his father.

Winston looked around, and saw no one else. He turned his attention back to his duplicate, who was turning his head back towards Winston. Had he been looking around also? Like a reflection in a mirror. "Where are you?" Winston called out. As he did the duplicate lips ·moved also, yet no sound came out.

"I'm here, son." Arawn assured him. "Are you ready."

"Yes." Winston said. Finding himself surprised by the absolute surety in his own voice. As before, his duplicate mouthed the word as he said it, while not making a sound himself. They looked into each other's eyes, or would it be their own eyes, and waited.

"Long is the day. Long is the night. From blood to bone. From speech to sight. Through strength gained. To power removed. The setting sun. The rising moon. Long is the night. Long is the day. As the King lives. So Annwn Reigns." The words repeated around them, like the chanting call of a summoning spell.

Shades of blue danced up his duplicates arm as the words continued around them. Winston looked down to find the duplicate had the sword of Darkfyre. "Long is the day. Long is the night." The duplicate raised the sword, and as if watching this happen to someone else, Winston saw his corresponding arm also rise. "From blood to bone. From speech to sight." The duplicate drew the blade along his forearms just as Winston had. The bright red of his blood shined in contrast to the neutral palette of the space they occupied. "Through strength gains. To power removed." As blood streamed from both of their arms, the duplicate extended his arms toward Winston, right palm down, left palm up. Winston's arms extended similarly, he could feel the duplicate's blood drip down on to his left arm. "The setting sun. The rising moon." Their arms raised and lowered, their hands clasping down near each other's elbows. Light and darkness flickered and sparked out from where their arms met. Smoke from nothing began to stir, and encircle them. "Long is the night. Long is the day." Winston's vision failed and returned to him. One moment he saw himself in white, the next in black. Like his vision was moving back and forth between he and his duplicate. Energy surged through his arms, into his chest. His teeth clenched, his muscles tensed up, hands balled into fists. Opening his eyes, his duplicate was gone, and ever part of him contracted and released as a roar poured from his lungs. Looking down at himself Winston noticed his garments were now grey, and his wounds were gone. "As the King lives. So Annwn Reigns."

"Oi, Winston! Wake up boy!" Michael yelled.
Winston felt Michael slap and shake him in panic. His intuition told him another slap was coming, and he moved instinctively and opened his eyes. "Okay. I'm okay."

"Aye. Of course ye are. How about all the blood you've lost?" Winston looked down at his arms, lifting them, and turning them from side to side. The cuts were gone. The throne told a different story, as it looked like he bled his last drop upon the arms of the throne, and the floor around him. "I'm fine, Michael."

"We heard you scream from the courtyard. Are you certain." Queen Bheur asked.

"I am." Winston assured her. "Where is Mhara?"

"She is outside being seen to. She is awake."

Winston stood, retrieved the sword of Darkfyre from the throne, and moved to the courtyard to find Myrddin with Mhara's father, Lord Muir. "May I see her?" Winston asked.

"Certainly, son." Lord Muir said. "She has asked after you."

Myrddin looked to Winston with concerned eyes as the two men stepped away to allow Winston space with Mhara. She was laying on a hide, upon the cold ground, with a cloak wrapped around her. Winston knelt down next to her. "Are you alright?" Winston asked.

"I have been better, and I am better now that I've seen you. I worried you were hurt."

"Almost. At the moment I am the best I've been in the whole time we've known each other." Winston said. "With the exception of that bath." Mhara smiled, and it cut him. "I have to leave you for a time."

"Winston?"

"I will return to you. I may be imagining things, and if I am I would welcome your correction, but I think there is something between us and I'd like to explore it further." Winston rested his eyes upon hers. "What do you say?"

Mhara reached an arm up, pulling him down to her. Their lips met and it was like all that was life and happiness passed between them. In that moment all that existed was their kiss. There was no dark land of the otherworld, no blood filled throne room, and everything he could ever need rested within the soft warmth of her lips. Their lips parted, and he felt a piece of himself, stay with her that he would never get back, her breath touched his lips and she whispered. "Come back to me."

"I will."

The matheans chuffed, and shuffled at the edge of the courtyard. Winston walked over to them, and found Alban. They shared a wordless goodbye. The beast had been as much a friend to Winston as anyone.

"You look like a man preparing to die." Myrddin said, walking up. "Did you get answers you were looking for?"

"Not all of them." Winston said.

"What is your plan?"

"I'll have to ask you to trust me."

Myrddin seemed to think about this a moment before a look of resolution washed over his face. "Certainly, I trust you, Winston."

Winston walked past the wizard King, draping a heavy cloak over himself that he had retrieved from Alban's saddle pack. He walked beyond the courtyard, the outer courtyard, and ascends a small hill toward a lone pillar like structure silhouetted by the light of the moon. Behind him followed Myrddin, Queen Bheur, and Michael. As Winston approached the pillar he could it was not a pillar created by man, rather an impressive stone standing erect from the dirt of the hill. Upon the stone were runes carved into the rockface.

Winston ran his hand down the stone, his finger searching in the limited light. He found what he was looking for, a slot similar to the area for the sword to be placed upon the throne. Carefully, Winston slid the sword of Darkfyre into the slot. Once the sword was fully inserted the runes upon the face of the stone began to glow in the same blue of the sword's flame.

"What does it say?" Michael asked.

"Winston, are you certain?" Winston looked to Myrddin, wordlessly responding to the wizard's question. "Certainly."

Mist slithered over the landscape, as layers of fog moved in. The moon played peek-a-boo with the clouds, and shadows began to move beyond the viewable distance. Winston could feel Michael aching to have his question answered, and in a different time, and especially if he could read the runes himself, he may have answered. In this moment Winston knew only what he should do. What he needed to do. So Winston didn't turn around, didn't respond, and didn't pay any heed to conversations and murmuring happening around him. Instead, he waited and watched the shadows as they walked directly toward them.

"This is bloody ridiculous." Michael said. "Are we sure he isn't permanently damaged?"

"Quiet, Michael."

"We're standing here doing nothing, and you're telling me to be quiet?"

"Michael!" Myrddin said. "Be quiet. Can you not hear it?"

As if on cue the sound of a large branch snapped, followed by the rustling of an entire grove of trees. The group went quiet, barely moving to breathe. Moonlight refracted off the rigid edge of a massive creature, the light shifting with each step it took toward them. Winston could see it's breath now, as hot steam poured out from its nostrils. Floating behind the mist of its breath were its eyes, glowing a warm amber hue, and growing brighter with each passing moment.

"What soul doth dare disturb my rest?"

"It was I." Winston said, stepping forward to distinguish himself from the group.

"Lo, I know you not." The massive creature rumbled. "Make known the justification of thine decision, or reap the consequences of your ignorance." It said, stepping further into view. Clear now were the layered armor of its scales, it's devastating claws, and its protruding snout with vicious looking teeth.

"Fuck me." murmured Michael.

Winston replied to the Dragon, by removing the sword of Darkfyre and holding it up before him. "I am Winston Bas. Son of Arawn, fallen King of Annwn. I am the current bearer of the sword of Darkfyre, and rightful heir to the throne of Annwn. I am King of these lands, and I call upon you now for your service!"

The dragon adjusted its posture, pulling its head up, and establishing better footing beneath itself. As it evaluated Winston and his words, other shadows moved around and behind it. Three dragons stepped forward to position themselves next to the first. Winston could feel the tension from his companions. He remained steadfast, looking up at the first dragon waiting for a response.

With an assertive low short growl from the first dragon, each of the other dragons extended one of their front claws, and lowered their heads in a bowing motion. The main dragon followed suit, and remained in its bowed position when it asked. "How may we be of service, my King"?

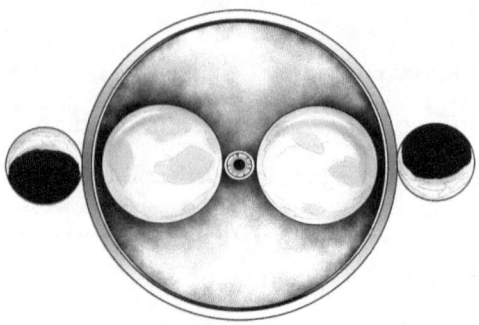

31 - EYES OF HIS ASSAILANT

"Surely this is not your plan!"

"It is." Winston assured. "Michael, do you believe you can do it?"

"Aye. I'll need a moment alone, but I should be able to get word to him."

"Good. Please go do that now." Winston said. "I assume you will not be joining us." He said to Myrddin.

"It would be best that I not be directly involved." The wizard King said.

"Only indirectly."

"Precisely." Myrddin smiled. "Are you certain of your plan?"

"I'm done chasing him, or our tails any longer." Winston said. "We know Jonathan still wants the sword. Michael believes he can arrange a meet. Which Jonathan will no doubt treat as a potential trap, and come prepared to fight. Which is fine by me. Fighting is what I'm good at."

"We can send warriors with you."

"What will you be doing?"

"Preparing for the fallout, dear boy." Myrddin said soberly. "Faerie is a layered, and interwoven place. Balance is the key to all that we do, and all that we are. We've known, Queen Bheur and myself, that to stop Jonathan would be to challenge the balance of our realm. He had positioned himself with the right amount of influence to evoke real change. We strived to handle things subtly, to work to redirect, and restrain. As you know, that didn't work out well for us."

"I'm sure me getting stuck here hasn't helped."

"Oh, Winston, you finding your way to Faerie may prove to be our greatest blessing, and the key to Jonathan's downfall. Certainly he did not expect you to live as long as you had."

"That's comforting."

"I meant no discomfort. It is simply true." Myrddin said.

"Winston?" Queen Bheur said.

"Yes."

"Do you have all that you need?" She asked.

"I believe I do, but there is something you could do for me. You know where we are planning to go."

"Yes, I am aware."

"When we arrive I imagine Jonathan will be waiting for us. I won't have the means to get my full bearings you might say."

"I'm not sure I follow what you are saying, Winston."

"Here." Winston retrieved from his pouch the box the Queen had originally given him. "Please see that this stays safe for me."

The Queen looked down at the object considering. "Where

should I keep it?"

Winston smiled. "Sometimes the safest place is to put items, is back where we found them. That way, they are there, when we need them again." Their eyes met in understanding, and a shared look of assurance.

Michael returned to the group a short time later, looking serious, and walking with intent. "Oi, Winston." he called. "Response came back, and he'll meet us."

"You were able to contact Jonathan?"

"I was able to reach a mutual acquaintance. She will see that Jonathan arrives on time."

"That was almost too easy. We should have done this sooner."

"Doubt it would have worked." Michael said. "Too many unknown variables."

"Would have saved everyone time."

"It would have also lacked all strategic value for Jonathan. Now he has perspective, feels he knows his opponent, and most of all he is confident in his victory." Michael paused, as if to arrange his own thoughts. "Recall when he intercepted us in the Autumnlands. He was careful, manipulative. He didn't know what to expect of you, Mhara, or myself. Now, an offer like this has appeal to him. It holds value."

"What did you offer him exactly?"

"Only what you said, the sword for our ability to walk away uncontested."

"But through a third party."

"Yes. A shared acquaintance. It'll all be fine."

Winston nodded to Michael, and picked up his riding blanket. Outside the outer courtyard the dragons waited. They looked to

Winston like massive winged puppies the way they lay about together. Occasionally stretching, nuzzling, and nipping at each other, they were undeniably charming, while also being unquestionably intimidating. Winston had learned the lead dragon's name was Cael, and she was female. Her fellow dragon's were her children. Winston drew close to her. They were alone on the hill, as Michael wanted as limited of interaction as possible with the dragons. This proved amusing to Winston to see his friend so fearful. Cael shifted, and looked toward Winston as he approached.

"Is it time to depart?" Cael asked.

"Very soon." Winston said, reaching out his hand to touch the snout of one of her young. "Are you comfortable with what I have asked of you?"

"You are King of Annwn. My comfort is secondary to your command."

"No, my friend, it is not." Winston said firmly.

She looked down at him, her amber eyes glowing. "I am comfortable."

"We were unsuccessful in finding the mounts you described. My hope is that if we employ your young, and use rope and blankets, we will be successful."

"Lo, you are a brave King." Cael said with a snort.

"I will collect my companions and we will depart. Yes?"

"Agreed."

The dragons positioned themselves nearer the courtyard as Winston retrieved Michael, and some of King Llyr's warriors. They mounted the three young dragons in pairs, with Winston and a warrior on one, Michael and a warrior on another, and the third carrying two more warriors. Cael's size made mounting her very difficult without proper equipment. She assured Winston that her young would be more than capable of carrying two each.

Winston was immediately thankful that Queen Bheur suggested he apply his riding blanket. He was unsure if any of the others had grabbed theirs, but the sharp pain of the thick scales stabbed into his thighs and buttocks even with the blanket running interference. This was going to be an interesting experience to say the least.

Cael took the lead, extending her magnificent wings, she thrust down, lifting her massive body into the air. As she did, Winston saw Lord Muir, who was fully invested in tending to the matheans, and completely unprepared for the gust of air that ripped across the ground from her wings. The wall of wind hit him like a professional football linebacker, taking him clear off his feet, and throwing him backwards. Winston would have laughed had his dragon not lifted in that exact moment, following Cael into the sky.

They were each positioned at the base of the neck, directly above where the neck connects to the back. Within reaching distance were the areas where the wings connected to the body, and with each thrust of the wings Winston could feel the power exerted ripple through the rest of the beast.

Winston pulled from his pouch the amulet he had received from Myrddin. He ran his thumb over the details of the leaf, not surprised to feel it was warmer than ever. As their group reached a height in the sky, the air around them cooled, and then warmed as they moved out over the sea. Cael had taken an altitude below that of her young, allowing her to keep an eye on everyone. Looking to his right he found Michael clinging to the dragon as they flew, while the other warriors looked as calm as they'd be riding any other creature. Winston held the leaf amulet to his chest and cleared his mind.

He had explained to Cael what he planned to do, and though she didn't seem to fully understand, she said she would trust him. Myrddin however was not so easily convinced. To travel with the amulet it was recommended that whomever Winston was trying to transport be touching him. Where in this circumstance, not only would they not be touching, they'd be flying some undisclosed height above the sea. Winston assured Myrddin that it wouldn't be so different than when we opened a portal for them to go through to return to Faerie. Myrddin cautioned Winston, reminding him that the amulet utilized Winston's life force to operate. Winston reran that conversation through his head as he worked to open a portal in the sky before them.

He knew something must have been happening when he heard the dragon beneath him respond. Then Winston saw it. It looked like a crack widening in the dark, cloudy sky, opening up to a clear, star filled, cloudless sky. Light seared from the edges of the opening. Winston started yelling, unsure how long he could keep it open. "Go! Go! Go!"

Cael roared, and surged forward, followed closely by her young, as they raced through the portal. The air around them changed as they passed through the portal, and Winston's ears popped. He released the portal and felt a stream of warmth run down, from his nose. Wiping at it he found blood on his hand. He used the sleeve of his tunic to clear the rest of it away.

The dragons banked, and circled in. He had done it. In a matter of moments Winson felt the wind off the salty sea pass across him, and saw the cliff sides, and the rolling green hills of what could only be Ireland. The dragons rested down in an open field between two hills.

The six passengers dismounted.

"Thou hast arrived safely." Cael said to Winston.

"We have. Thank you."

"What will ye ask of me?"

"Only that you stay safe for the moment. We have work to do."

Cael gave a sort of nod, released a short snorty growl, and without any further words her and her young took to the air, staying low and close to the hills.

"Let's move." Winston said to Michael as he turned east.

Michael and the warriors followed without hesitation. They walked together in silence for some time, both of them keeping their senses attuned to their surroundings, watching and listening for anything out of the ordinary. The signs showed their journey starting near Puddenhill, and was taking them through homesteads, and farmland. After about a half an hour they crossed N2 Road, and continued east. Another hour or so a heavy treading through the country the six of them crossed the M3 Motorway. When they crossed the R147 Winston signalled for them to halt, and group in.

"Everyone, ears up. We're roughly forty five minutes out from the Hill of Tara, tops. Michael and I are going in directly. You four," he said, signalling to the warriors, "I need you to pair off, and come in at our flanks. Watch for anyone they may have waiting in the wings."

"They, my Liege?" Asked one of the warriors.

"They." Winston confirmed. "There is no way Jonathan is arriving at this conversation alone. Hell, I doubt he is working alone."

"Where're ye grabbin' that from?'

"We already know the Hound with involved. It's not much of a stretch, Michael." Winston said. "Are we clear on the plan?"

The warriors each confirmed their understanding, and Michael gave his "Aye" in affirmative. They moved out. As they traversed the fields, jumped streams, and hopped fences, Winston was continuously impressed with how light and quiet his armor was. Clearly not a man made product. It was completely lacking the weight, restrictions on movement, and the inescapable reality of heat retention. All in all they made quick work of the ground they had to travel, finding themselves at the foot of the Hill of Tara sooner than Winston had mentally prepared for.

They entered the area through the walkway through the cemetery at Saint Patrick's Church. As they passed through the brambles of thick bushes, and mature trees, Winston saw there were lanterns lit atop the hill. They continued on.

The ground of the hill rippled like two giant drops of earth had fallen, and as the ground rippled out they froze in time. The path the center of the hill moving up the outermost ripple, then falling down only to follow the second ripple up, and once more for the canter area of the hill. In the evening light, accented by the lanterns, the shadows of the hill looked ominous and foreboding to Winston. Within the lights stood three objects. One was the battle monument to the rebellion of Meath, which looked like a tall grave headstone. The next was the Lia Fáil at Tara, also called the Stone of Destiny, and it stood in a distinctly curved, pickle like shape. The last of the three was the only one of the objects to move. Jonathan stood, the image of patient confidence, as Winston and Michael approached.

"I was beginning to worry you lost your way." Jonathan said. "This is a fitting place for our meeting. I applaud your choice. Did you know, this was where they would anoint the Kings of Ireland?" He paused to smile. "Most fitting indeed."

"Do you really believe your plan will work?"

"Ha! Believe? Oh, child. I know it will work." Jonathan asserted. "In fact, if there were any chance of actually stopping me, would not, good Merlin, or Queen Bheur have done more to aid in stopping me? Most certainly. But they know, just as Queen May knows, there is no stopping what is coming." Jonathan spun the scepter absentmindedly as he spoke. "To your credit, you were wise enough to heed the advice of dear Michael, there. Coming to your senses on which side of this is best to be on."

Winston looked to Michael, who gave him a reassuring nod. Looking back to Jonathan, Winston said. "I want to hear from you."

"Hear what, pray tell?"

"I want to hear that you agree to our deal. I want assurances."

"As was communicated to me through our… acquaintance, you will turn the sword of Darkfyre over to me, and I will in turn give you your lives. You will be free to do as you like, as I usher in our new world. One where those of Faerie, and the realm of men, coexist together."

"And if it doesn't work?"

"It will work." Jonathan said. "I've been bound by the laws of Faerie, restricted from reaching my full potential, and no matter the cost, I will be free." Jonathan stepped toward them, holding out his hand. "Where is the sword?"

From the shadows of the night around them Winston heard hisses and growls, as ghoulish forms stepped forward into the light of the lanterns, bearing their teeth, and flexing their claws. Winston joined his own sound to the scene by pulling the sword from its sheath, its flame churning about the blade as it slid free.

"This doesn't look like what we agreed to." Winston said.

"This is exactly what you expected, foolish boy." Jonathan said. "Do you truly think you stand to survive this encounter?"

"You say that as if I came here alone."

"Didn't you?"

With those words a searing heat burst upon the back of Winston's hand, and a heavy blow hit him from the side. Winston was knocked to the ground, the sword falling from his grip. He shuffled, trying urgently to retrieve the sword. "Michael!" he yelled. "Help me." Where was the sword? Winston heard the scrape of metal against the rocks of the ground, and then felt a blade to his neck. Not just any blade, but one that burned blue from a flame that gave off no heat, and emitted only subtle light from its vibrant flame. Winston turned slowly to find the eyes of his assailant. As their eyes met, a sobering reality came over Winston.

"Yield, boy." Michael said. The sword aglow in his hand. "There not be anything ye can do now."

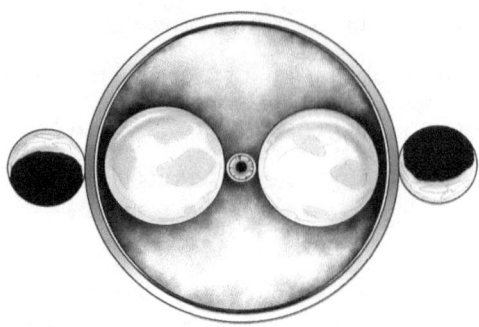

32 – STANDING IN JUDGMENT

The pieces began to fall into place within Winston's mind, like a bad puzzle. He felt his anger rising within him, and it seemed like lanterns were getting dimmer. Or was that a fog moving in. "There wasn't any acquaintance, was there?" he asked Michael.

"Calm yerself now, lad." Michael said, looking about. "There be no need for anymore fightin'."

"Answer me!"

"He is a keen young man, bloody brilliant one might say." Jonathan said. "Oh, tell him the truth, Michael. There was no acquaintance."

"And in the Autumnlands, that was you too." Winston said. It came out more as a statement than a question. "Were you in on this from the beginning?" The anger boiled in Winston's voice. "Were you involved in trapping me here from the beginning!"

Michael held the sword between them. His eyes showed the

314

struggle he was feeling. He swallowed before answering. "Aye. I was who identified who ye were, and that you'd be our best mark to help us complete our mission. Twas' nothing personal, lad."

"What of Mhara?"

"What of her?"

"Is she a part of this? A part of your mission?"

"Yer concerned with whether her affections are genuine." Michael said.

"Now that is truly precious." Chimed Jonathan. "The poor boy fell for the love of a selkie. Careful she doesn't drown ya."

"Tell me. You owe me at least that much."

"No, Winston." Michael said. "Sure, she was our ally, but she was not a willing participant." His hand moved to a rolled hide tied under his cloak. "Hardly needed this tho, especially after yer talk is the bath. Never knew what happened, in full. One thing I was sure of, is that she chose to remain willingly after that. Stayed for you, I suppose."

"I believed we were friends, Michael. I thought I was helping you, that I was making the right choices, but it was all a ruse. Myrddin thought you were his man. I thought you were my friend. Yet, all the while you were his puppet." Winston said, gesturing at Jonathan.

"Oi, I'm no one's puppet."

"Sure you are. If not a puppet, then an instrument."

"And how's that?"

"Because you've just been played." Winston said with an angry smirk. "Now, give me back my sword, you son of a bitch!" He yelled. Like gasoline to a flame, the fierce anger in Winston flared within him, and within the sword in Michael's hand. The flames of the sword engulfed the blade, and bent toward Michael, enclosing around his arm.

Michael panicked, lunged away from the flames, and dropped the weapon.

As Winston retrieved the weapon, he heard the creatures around him snarl and growl. One was coming at him from his left, Winston swung the sword up at an angle, separating the head and left arm from the body of the creature. Turning he found the others had moved in, encircling him. Over a dozen of the creatures stalked in menacingly around Winston. A particularly vile looking one looked to lunge at him, but before Winston could respond, and before the creature could complete its action, a large bolt collided with its head. The arrow hit with such velocity that it came out of the back of the creatures head, shoving him back, and plunging the arrow head into the chest of the creature behind it. The second creature appeared more annoyed than hurt as it removed its fallen companion, and arrow from its chest and roared at Winston.

Battle cries came up from all around them. A sense of relief fell through Winston as he recognized the battle cry to be that of his allies. Winston paused for a moment, tilting his head. That sounded like far more than four warriors. As if in response to his thoughts, Fionn collided with the monsters surrounding Winston. His men followed directly behind him, and engaged the enemy.

Winston took up his sword, planning to join the foray. Only Fionn and his men seemed to be adequately holding the creatures at bay. He turned his eyes beyond the colliding bodies and blood to find Michael and Jonathan standing near the Stone of Destiny. Winston moved toward them, avoiding getting pulled into the battles between the warriors and the monsters. They saw him approaching, and yet stood as casually as a youth enjoying summer on the beaches of Lake Bde Maka

Ska.

"Now to finish our game, pup!" Yelled a voice over the mayhem. Winston knew the voice and froze. "I look forward to tasting your blood this night." The Hound said as he rushed at Winston. His axe hammer high above his head.

Winston watched as he approached, the edges of his vision darkened, and something like smoke began moving in to the space around him. This time he expected it. He welcomed it. The Hound's weapon hummed through the air as it came down, but Winston was already moving. The hammer end of the weapon collided with the earth causing vibrations to flow through the ground, and large chunks of dirt and stone to fly into the sky. The Hound roared, only this wasn't a roar of threat or accomplishment, it was a roar of realization as Winston's sword seared through the back of the Hound's legs.

A flash of light blinded Winston as a stream of power thrust him back, and away from the Hound. Jonathan lowered the scepter, and moved to have a better line of sight on Winston. "Truly a clever boy you are. Michael was right about you." He released another blast of power and it surged through Winston like electric shock. "There was a time, I hoped you may be an ally for us. A partner. Now I see that you were a pawn at best." Jonathan aims the scepter at Winston. "I do thank you for gathering the sword for us. Once you are dead, it will be free for Michael to possess, and we will make short work of your warrior friends. Sadly you will not be here to see it. Goodbye, Winston."

The scene went white, and Winston braced himself for a pain that never came. Was this death? Instantaneous, and numb? No. Winston could still hear the conflict around him. The light in his eyes dissipated, allowing him to see that Jonathan's blast had been displaced by energy shield around him. Though not from him. Standing over him was a strong, beautiful woman, dressed in garments that were as much fashion as they were of nature itself.

"Enough." She commanded. "You will not harm my son further."

Jonathan's eyes went wide realizing who she was. "Airmid?"

"You are not as dense as your actions suggest."

Jonathan released another blast from the scepter. It hit his mother's shield, and though it was dispersed, something told him she would only be able to last for so long. Behind Jonathan, Michael was slowly exiting the scene.

"That snake!" Winston said, knowing Michael was attempting to flee. "Mother? Will you be ok?"

His mother looked at him, a face of charmed amusement. "We are in the heart of my power. He has little chance of overwhelming me."

"I need to stop Michael." He said.

"Do what you must, my son." Airmid said, before lowering her shield and returning a blast of power upon Jonathan. The impact sent him spinning horizontally into the grass.

"I'll kill you, pup. I'll hunt you and sharpen my teeth on your bones." The Hound growled as Winston approached.

"You'll lay there and bleed, you pathetic thing." Winston said as he passed.

"Know this, child of damnation," the Hound howled. Winston stopped walking to listen. "I'll heal, and I'll come for you. I'll also find your selkie bitch. Surely she will be sweet."

Wordlessly Winston pivoted, swung the sword of Darkfyre down toward the Hound. Its blade erupted with flame as it connected with the mad dog. Blood sizzled as the blade cut clean through his neck, separating the Hounds head from his body. Winston watched it roll and come to a stop, before turning to pursue Michael. Satisfied the Hound was dead, he turned and ran after Michael. Winston caught up to Michael near Saint Patrick's Church.

"You going to steal a car and try to drive away?" Winston yelled.

Michael turned, panic and rage pouring out of him. "Fuck you! Yer but a stupid boy. Ye have no perception of what it has been like fer me. Yet you stand here now, in judgment. No. No. I'll not have it. Ye can go fuck yerself before I'll do that."

"You betrayed me, Michael." Winston said calmly. "That is something I cannot allow to go without consequence." Winston knew Michael had more to say. Yet Cael's jaws came down over him before he could utter another word. He watched as the massive dragon raised her head, bit down again on Michael's corpse, and then swallowed him whole. She looked at Winston, an acknowledgment passing between them. He was her King.

The remaining warriors, Fionn, and Airmid were waiting for Winston upon his return to the Stone of Destiny, on the Hill of Tara. Jonathan was on his knees, hands bound in iron, and his limbs tied tightly together. The warriors stood in respect as Winston approached, and Fionn, in his consistent enthusiasm, embraced Winston warmly.

"You are becoming the great warrior, I know you are meant to be." Fionn said.

"Thank you, my friend. I still have much to learn."

"I shall instruct you. Yes?" Fionn said. "I saw you fight the Hound. I saw you embrace the shadows."

Winston knew there was no negotiating this. "Sure. Yes." He

said. "I will train with you." Fionn was visibly excited. "Only we will train wisely." Winston asserted.

"Of course, my Liege." Fionn said, a sly smile upon his face.

"I take it Queen Bheur relayed my message." Winston asked.

"She did." Airmid said. "I helped get Fionn and his additional men here as quickly as I could."

"You were wonderful. Thank you, Mother."

"You know, Winston. Jonathan was correct about one thing."

"What is that?"

"You are a clever boy." Airmid said with a chuckle.

"Speaking of, is he alive?" Winston asked, gesturing at the incapacitated Jonathan.

"He is."

Fionn and his remaining warriors help fasten an unconscious Jonathan to one of the young dragons. Collecting the scepter, Winston climbed upon his dragon. "I'll return." he said to his mother.

"Where will you go now?" She asked.

"There are a few loose ends to address." Winston said. "My first stop is Summer, to talk with Queen May."

"You may need this." She said, handing him the wrapped hide Michael had possessed.

They said their farewells, for as long as they may or may not be, and the dragon's took to the skies with Cael in the lead. Winston smiled as they flew up and out, toward the sea, and the rising sun, knowing he may never fully get used to the rush of riding these beautiful creatures. With each thrust of her wings, Cael lead the way as his dragon carried Winston out of Annwn, and onward towards Summer.

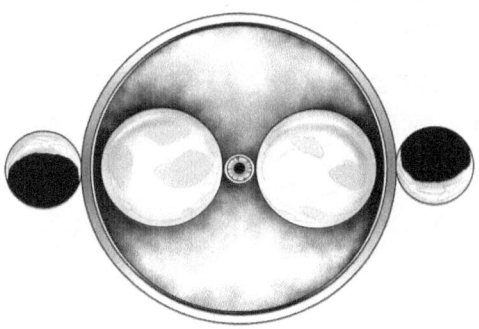

33 – ANYTHING IS POSSIBLE

Cael, and her other young, waited at the edge of Summer, as Winston entered upon his dragon. She was concerned for her young's safety within the borders of Summer. A position that seemed aptly held the further they flew into Summer. Towers protruded above the tree lines, and those stationed within them turned suspiciously as they flew by. As they passed, Winston could make out their large crossbows, though not one went for their weapons.

Winston had directed the young dragon to fly low so they were easily seen, as he hoped this would reduce the misconception that they were a threat. He had begun to think to himself that this was proving to be a brilliant idea, only the closer they came to Summer's castle, the guards in the towers began waving, and calling out to him by name. Clearly someone told Summer they were coming.

A reality proven more true as they came to find Queen May and her guards waiting for them just outside the castle gate. Winston patted the dragon on its thick and sturdy neck, indicating this was where he needed to land. The dragon pulled up its body to an erect position as it hovered down like a massively winged helicopter. Each minor flap of its wings pushed the air below them to assault the guards around Queen May. Curiously she barely seemed affected. Her dress moved, and some of her guards had their feet swept out from under them, yet aside from her hair, and dress, she stood securely. Waiting soundly for them to land.

Winston slid down from the dragon. A maneuver he was becoming quickly comfortable with. Still, he would be keeping the riding blanket. At least until they found, or remade the saddles. He retrieved the scepter, which he'd tied securely three ways as to not lose it while flying. Winston hadn't trusted his grip fully enough to be confident he would make it without incident, let alone the scepter too. With it firmly in hand he looked to Jonathan, who was draped over the neck of the dragon, and both bound to himself, and securely tied to the dragon's neck. He had cut the second rope when he saw Queen May come from around the dragon.

"I see you were able to bond with the sword." Queen May said. "Only the sword bearer could call these magnificent creatures to bare."

"Your guards don't seem to find him too magnificent."

"Our history with dragon riders is not the most positive, true. This does not take away from their power and majesty." She said, sliding a soft hand smoothly down the scales of the dragon. He chuffed in what felt like approval. The Queen smiled up at the dragon.

Winston cut the last rope, eliminating whatever tension or counter balance may have remained that kept Jonathan in place. Jonathan released a sharp yelp, as he plummeted head first from atop the dragon. Winston enjoyed a chuckle watching Jonathan attempt to recover from colliding with the hard ground. "This is yours, Queen May." Winston said, holding out the scepter to her. A guard stepped up and retrieved the weapon. "And THAT is yours too." He said, gesturing at Jonathan.

"Thank you for returning them to me." Queen May said. "I know exactly what I will do with each. Is there anything Summer can do for you, Winston? Or should we be calling you something else?" She asked, a smirk dancing on her lips.

"Winston will do fine, I think. At the moment, I don't know if there is anything you can do for me." He said. "Something tells me that we will see each other again."

"True enough. I will remember your generosity, and repay it fully in time."

"Thank you." he bowed. "I must be going. Thank you for your hospitality."

"Until next time, then."

Winston climbed atop his dragon, tightened down his ropes keeping his blanket in place. "Until next time, Queen May." Without further prompting, the dragon reared up, extended and flapped its wings once, launching them high into the sky. Winston was impressed by the young dragon's speed, and also thought it showed how eager the beast was to part ways with Summer. It was a fractional length of time, when compared to their travel into Summer, that it took for them to leave and be rejoined by Cael and her other young.

Cael elevated herself to fly at eye level to Winston, looking to him in a way that felt like a "Thank you". Winston kindly touched the neck of his dragon and returned Cael's gaze, nodding and smiling at her.

She released a thunderous roar, and plunged ahead, into the clouds, leading them to Winter, and Queen Bheur's castle.

This time, all four dragons remained together as they took Winston into Winter, landing at the edge of the garden outside the castle. Winston dismounted and walked toward the entrance into Queen Bheur's private study. Outlines of bodies moved beyond the cloudy colored glass, the details to vague for Winston to identify who was inside. Resolved to enter, he moved for the door. It opened before he reached it, and a smiling Myrddin ushered him inside.

"It is good to see you, Winston." The old wizard said as he closed the door. They were alone in the room. Myrddin turned to look at Winston. "What is it? What is wrong?"

"Michael." Winston choked out. The weight of the reality of Michael's betrayal and death affecting him more than he had expected.

"Ah. Yes. Yes. Your mother got word to Queen Bheur, not long after you departed Ireland." Myrddin took a breath. "Michael. He lived a dangerous life. Too often walking the edge of civility, and anarchy, madness, and brilliance. Traits that made him an invaluable ally, and sadly, a questionable friend." He placed his hand upon Winston's shoulder. "I am sorry you were put in that position. No doubt it was difficult when it came time to stop him."

"It was easier than I expected."

"Was it?"

"Yeah." Winston chuckled. "Cael ate him before I could do anything myself. It is almost like she knows my thoughts, like they all do."

"Hmmm… A most insightful observation."

"Winston! I'm very pleased you're here." Queen Bhuer said,

returning to the room. "Have you come to see Mhara?"

"Is she here?"

"Why yes. I convinced her father it was better for them to rest here, rather than trying to make it back to Atalantia. Thought surely you knew they were here."

"I had intended to find her." Winston admitted. "Before that, I wanted to ask you what a selkie is. I'd heard that term applied to her a few times, but I have not been able to figure out what it means."

"It is what she is, Winston." Queen Bheur said.

"Selkie are a kind of merpeople." Myrddin added. "They live in the sea, and in many ways rule it within Faerie."

"She can change, can't she? Into a seal."

"How did you learn that?"

"Michael had this." Winston pulled the hide from his bag. "It was retrieved after our battle at the Hill of Tara. I think it's Mhara's."

"That very well could be the case. Would go a long way to explain why she stayed with him, and this escapade, for as long as she did."

"Michael alluded to something like that, what does that mean?"

"The hide your holding is her skin, her coat, and whoever possesses it holds power over her." Myrddin explained. "Essentially, as long as you carry it, she will abide almost any command you give."

"That is terrible!"

"It certainly can prove to be. Making it all the better that Michael no longer has it."

"I need to see Mhara! I need to return this to her!" Winston exclaimed.

"Alright, Winston. I will take you to her. First, I need you to calm down."

"What do you mean? I am calm."

Queen Bheur tilted her head, and looked at him through her eyebrows. A look he'd seen sent his way a few too many times, over deep rimmed glasses, while in her office. She motioned for him to follow her, and she began leading them from the room. "Answer me this, Winston Bas." she smiled almost knowingly. "A long time ago I asked you if you could be any kind of Winston, what kind would you be. Have you found your answer?"

"I've been thinking about that, actually." Winston motioned at his attire. "This seems to be working out alright."

"So you will reign as King of Annwn?"

"Heh. Anything is possible." Winston said, not needing to see her face to know the look she was giving him. "I still have many questions. Questions I need answered."

"I know you do, Winston. As your friend, I will do all I can to help you answer those questions." Unexpectedly the Queen hugged Winston. Perhaps more unexpectedly, he hugged her back. "Mhara is inside." She said, indicating the room to her left. "Thank you, Winston."

"Thank you… Councilor."

Queen Bheur playfully shoved him as she continued walking down the hall, leaving Winston alone standing outside Mhara's door. Taking a deep breath, he knocked on the door. Voices sounded from within the room, more voices than Mhara's own. The door was released, and opened slightly. As Winston entered he heard them.

"Knocking. Knocking."

"Foolish human with all the knocking. How do you expect her to heal with you knocking?"

"Foolish humans; knocking. Always so dramatic."

"Let's knock him about. Can we?"

"Now, now, play nice, Kettle." Mhara said from her bed. "Ignore them, Winston. They claim Queen Bheur tasked them with caring for me."

"That could be. The Queen had them tend to me before."

"She did? When?"

"Before the feast, while I was healing. Remember?" She nodded to Winston, not wanting to interrupt his story. "Yeah. Well, they helped me get dressed."

"Most uncooperative; humans." Pot offered.

"All legs, and no arms he was." Kettle confirmed.

"I'm sure that was an interesting process." Mhara said.

"It wasn't my most awkward." He said, as he sat upon the edge of her bed. Their eyes met and the distractions of the world were gone to him. All that existed was her, and those deep, enveloping eyes. "Hi."

"Hi, Winston. Are you ok?" She asked.

He tried to shake himself loose. "Um. Yes. Yeah, I'm good. I, brought you something."

"You did?" She watched him set the seal skin on her bed. "Oh." Mhara said, looking up at Winston. A look of apology in her eyes.

"I retrieved it from Michael's possessions after he died, and Queen Bheur and Myrddin explained to me what it is." He paused. "It sounds like something important for you, and I thought you should have it back." Winston smiled at her. "I also understand better now why you were with us that whole time. You had no choice."

Mhara looked to the skin. "It wasn't the only reason, Winston."

"But as long as Michael had it, you had no choice."

"We always have a choice." She said sharply. "You know this. I could have fought, I could have done a great many things, so long as I was comfortable with the consequences. I chose to stay."

"And look where that got you." Winston offered playfully. "Full pixie care package at club Winter."

They laughed together a moment, before Mhara took Winston's hand in hers. She placed his hand upon the seal skin, and he looked to her questioningly. "I want you to hold on to it."

"Wait. Why."

"Keep it safe for me." She smiled. "I trust you to keep it safe, Winston." Tenderly she reached her other hand up, pulling him at the shoulder, guiding him toward her. She wrapped her arms around Winston, pressing her lips to his. They kissed and held each other long enough for the lighting in the room to change. As they lay next to each other, Mhara running her fingers softly along Winston's features, and lips, she asked. "What will you do next?

"I'm not sure." He admitted. "There are many things I still don't understand. About me, you, this place, and how I fit into it all." He intertwined his fingers in hers. "I supposed I could walk through one door at a time, and see where they lead me."

"Sounds like an adventurous plan. Think it will work out well?"

"Anything is possible."

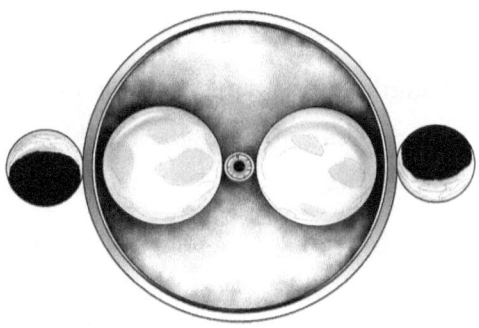

EPILOGUE – SAYING GOODBYE

The golden kingdom of Summer seemed to shine vibrantly even in the soft light of the midnight moon. It's occupants had all turned in for the night. A contrast to the evening revelries of Winter. Perhaps that was why he was still awake. Too many nights with Michael Scot, more aptly, Michael of the Scots. The Winter to his Summer.

The wizard known as Jonathan Knottingham sat confined in chains within a dank cell, in an empty tower, in the middle of the kingdom Summer. Once again a prisoner. Once again separated from his power.

He was so close. His goal was within his reach. He could taste it, smell it, feel it, and then it was all ripped away from him by that foolish boy, Winston. How dare he interfere? Jonathan howled like a wounded animal as he slammed his manicalled hands against the floor. The chains whipping about, creating an ear ringing clatter. Exhausted from his tantrum Jonathan collapsed back against the damp, cool stonewall.

Time had begun to evade him again. All the light into his cell was reflected light, leaving him no concept of night and day. His meals were sporadic, eliminating his ability to track time that way. He had even stopped seeing others altogether. As if they knew when he would fall asleep, and deliver his meals while he slumbered. He'd been through this before, only before he had Michael. Michael was strong. Jonathan attributed it to his Scottish blood.

Michael would tell stories, sing songs, anything to keep them from losing themselves in the monotony of imprisonment. That was in Winter. If one wanted to find true cruelty, they had to look no further than Summer. Or so Michael would tell it. Regardless, Jonathan would give anything to be back there, chained up with his friend again.

That time was gone.

Something inside Jonathan broke with that acknowledgement. He didn't even know if his friend was alive. He only knew he was here, trapped, and alone. He pulled his knees to his chest, crossing his arms over them, and began to weep.

"How many problems would be fixed if only tears were the solution."

"What are you doing here?" Jonathan asked, wiping his eyes.

"I came to thank you for your wonderful work."

Jonathan scoffed, the irritation and disdain clear. "I failed."

"Did you?"

"Of course I did. Or did you forget the plan?"

"Certainly not. It was my plan after all."

"Then you can tell by the look of me that my efforts were unsuccessful."

"Unsuccessful by your standards, perhaps. Yet for my aims, you accomplished exactly what I needed you to."

"By losing the scepter and getting locked up again? You have skewed goals, to be sure. Though, if I had been alive as long as you have, maybe I'd understand."

"You brought me the boy. He is the tool we truly needed. Not your coveted scepter and sword."

"The boy? Surely you don't mean Winston?"

"Precisely."

"You are daft. There is little that foolish child can do to benefit anyone. With the scepter I would…"

"You would do little to nothing." The man interjected. "Certainly the scepter is an item of great power, as is the sword, but there are factors in play that you will never have the capacity to understand. Why do you think I told you of the boy? Why did I set you free, and arrange for your exchange? Do you really think it was because I believed in your fruitless cause? Certainly not."

"You played me?"

"Like a celebration fiddle. Our realm needs the realm of man, just as they need us. We are symbiotic, united, and for as layered and fragile as Faerie is, there is only so much I can directly do. I needed a… "

"A tool? A pawn? You self-righteous prick. I've had enough of you." Jonathan got to his feet, moving as close to the opening of his cell as he could. "You tell me this, you tell me now. Where is Michael?"

"Dead."

"He's what?" Jonathan couldn't believe it. "No, this must be a mistake. Surely he is not dead."

"He is dead. Eaten by Cael, the matriarch Night Dragon."

"I'll kill her! I'll kill her like we did her kin." Jonathan pulled on his chains, straining to get as close to his visitor as possible. "Let me out. You said you got what you wanted. We were successful. Let me out."

"I am afraid I cannot. Summer would grow suspicious, and suspicions have their way of making their way to Morgana. I cannot suffer her involvement just yet. I'm afraid you'll need to stay here."

"Think this through. I can stay hidden. Subtle. Give me the means to come and go on my own. No one will know. It will be even better than before. Come on. Come on!" The visitor turned to leave, shaking their head. "Fine. Leave. I'm sure Queen May can get ahold of Morgana, and I'm sure one of them would have an interest in my story." Jonathan's words echoed like they were amplified within an empty cathedral. The visitor stopped walking.

"I suppose, I am here for two reasons. To thank you, and to say, I am sorry."

"You're sorry? Heh. Of course you are. Good. Now let me out."

"Goodbye, Jonathan." The robed man said, extending his arm. Within it he held an ornate white staff. Light formed like a spinning ball of flame at the end.

"Merlin. No!" Jonathan began to yell, his voice cut down by the white flame as it ripped through him. His lifeless body slammed against the back wall of his cell, collapsing to the floor.

Myrddin returned his staff below his cloak, taking no time to assess what he had done. He turned toward the exit, and vanished into nothing.

THE HOUND
CÚ ROÍ
"The Hound of the Field."

THOR

LOOK FOR HIM
IN BOOK TWO OF
THE LORE OF MAN

ABOUT THE AUTHOR

Anthony lives in Minnesota with his wife, Tracie, their two cats, Nomi and Brodie, and their dog Saoirse. He has worked as a professional illustrator and storyteller since 2001, applying his passion for stories within the fields of commercial illustration, comic books, and graphic novels. His favorite authors include Robert Ludlum, Jim Butcher, Patrick Rothfuss, Brandon Sanderson, and Neil Gaiman. For Anthony there are few things that compare to the privilege of connecting with others, especially in a way that adds value to their life. Being able to create connections through his craft has been one of the great gifts of his life. It is with that hope in mind that this story is shared with you. May you enjoy this story as much as Anthony has enjoyed bringing the world of Lore of Man to you.

AUGUST RITES

BOOK TWO OF THE LORE OF MAN

COMING SOON